Praise for Barbara Metzger
and her enchanting romance novels

"Romantic and funny!"   —Mary Balogh

"Funny and touching . . . delicious, delightful!"
                                         —Edith Layton

"Metzger's gift for re-creating the flavor and ambience
of the period shines here, and the antics of her dirty-
dish villains, near-villains, and starry-eyed lovers are
certain to entertain."   —*Publishers Weekly*

"The complexities of both story and character contrib-
ute much to [this book's] richness. Like life, this book
is much more exciting when the layers are peeled back
and savored."   —*Affaire de Coeur*

"Delightful [and] fun."   —Under the Covers

"A true tour de force. . . . Only an author with Metzger's deft skill could successfully mix a Regency tale
of death, ruined reputations, and scandal with humor
for a fine and ultimately satisfying broth."
                                 —The Best Reviews

"Queen of the Regency romp. [Metzger] brings the
Regency era vividly to life with deft humor, sparkling
dialogue, and witty descriptions."
                            —Romance Reviews Today

"Metzger has penned another winning Regency tale.
Filled with her hallmark humor, distinctive wit, and
entertaining style, this is one romance that will not
fail to enchant."   —*Booklist* (starred review)

SIGNET

REGENCY ROMANCE
COMING IN SEPTEMBER 2005

Lady Dearing's Masquerade
by Elena Greene
After kissing a stranger at a masquerade, widow Lady
Dearing's name is blemished. Since that soiree, Sir
Fairhill has searched for his masked beauty. Soon, their
passion will create a scandal—or love.

0-451-21478-1

Dedication
by Janet Mullany
Broken-hearted years ago by Adam Ashworth, Fabienne
Argonac Craigmont finds solace in the works of a
British novelist. But when Fabienne begins a corre-
spondence with her idol, she could never image he's
really her long lost love.

0-451-21636-9

The Convenient Bride
by Teresa McCarthy
Lady Briana has adored Lord Clayton since she was
sixteen. And although he must marry within three
weeks of lose his fortune, Briana knows he will break
her heart—but that does nothing to lessen her desire.

0-451-21637-7

Available wherever books are sold or at
penguin.com

Lady Whilton's Wedding
and
An Enchanted Affair

Barbara Metzger

A SIGNET BOOK

SIGNET
Published by New American Library, a division of
Penguin Group (USA) Inc., 375 Hudson Street,
New York, New York 10014, USA
Penguin Group (Canada), 90 Eglinton Avenue East, Suite 700, Toronto,
Ontario M4P 2Y3, Canada (a division of Pearson Penguin Canada Inc.)
Penguin Books Ltd., 80 Strand, London WC2R 0RL, England
Penguin Ireland, 25 St. Stephen's Green, Dublin 2,
Ireland (a division of Penguin Books Ltd.)
Penguin Group (Australia), 250 Camberwell Road, Camberwell, Victoria 3124,
Australia (a division of Pearson Australia Group Pty. Ltd.)
Penguin Books India Pvt. Ltd., 11 Community Centre, Panchsheel Park,
New Delhi - 110 017, India
Penguin Group (NZ), cnr Airborne and Rosedale Roads, Albany,
Auckland 1310, New Zealand (a division of Pearson New Zealand Ltd.)
Penguin Books (South Africa) (Pty.) Ltd., 24 Sturdee Avenue,
Rosebank, Johannesburg 2196, South Africa

Penguin Books Ltd., Registered Offices:
80 Strand, London WC2R 0RL, England

Published by Signet, an imprint of New American Library, a division of Penguin Group (USA) Inc. *Lady Whilton's Wedding* and *An Enchanted Affair* were previously published by Fawcett Crest, a division of Ballantine Books.

First Signet Printing, August 2005
10 9 8 7 6 5 4 3 2 1

Lady Whilton's Wedding copyright © Barbara Metzger, 1995
An Enchanted Affair copyright © Barbara Metzger, 1996
All rights reserved

 REGISTERED TRADEMARK—MARCA REGISTRADA

Printed in the United States of America

Lady Whilton's
Wedding

to Ramona the Donor
and all the other givers of this world

Chapter One

It was an arranged marriage. Unlike most such marriages of convenience, this one was arranged by the bride-to-be herself. Miss Daphne Whilton of Woodhill Manor, Hampshire, left the crowded lawn of her birthday party and approached Lord Graydon Howell, heir to the Earl of Hollister, where he stood apart from the other guests under a shading elm tree. She kicked him on the shin to get his attention and said, "All of the other boys are toads. You'll have to marry me, Gray."

Lord Graydon rubbed his leg and looked back toward the others. The boys were tearing around, trying to lift the girls' skirts. The girls were shrieking or giggling or crying for their mamas, who were inside taking tea with Lady Whilton. At least Daffy never carried on like that. And she could bait her own hook. He nodded. "I s'pose," he said, and they shook hands to seal the contract.

Their parents were delighted to join two ancient lineages and fortunes so pleasantly. Their children would be out of the reach of fortune hunters and adventurers and misalliances. Besides, the couples were lifelong friends and neighbors. The Hollisters preferred the politics and parties of London to the rural pleasures of their Hampshire seat, whereas the Whiltons chose to spend their days close to the land on their Woodhill barony, but the two families spent summers and the Christmas holidays in nearest and most welcome proximity. Their offspring had played together since they were in leading strings. Each being an only child in the house, and the only children of nobility in the region, they were natural playmates.

Since he was the elder by three years, and a boy besides, with the run of the neighborhood, young Lord Graydon ran tame at Woodhill Manor. He often stayed there overnight when his parents accepted a house party invitation elsewhere, rather than remaining in solitary, servant-surrounded splendor at Howell Hall. It was Graydon who taught Daphne to ride, albeit not in a style conducive to her mother's mental ease, had Lady Whilton known. And 'twas the handsome lad who taught Lady Whilton's curly-haired blond cherub to climb trees, catch fish, and carry the hunting bag without complaining. Miss Whilton, on the other hand, caused her young Lancelot to learn how to repair dolls, how to sit through countless imaginary teas, and, most important, how to be gentle with small, fragile things.

Daphne thought the sun rose and set with Graydon's company; Graydon supposed he liked Daphne better than his spaniel, who sometimes didn't come when he called. Daffy always did.

If not made in Heaven or Almack's sacred precincts, the proposed marriage still gladdened the hearts of the readers of both *Debrett's Peerage* and purple-covered romance novels, and the couples' fond parents. No announcement was made, of course, due to the tender ages of the pair, nor papers drawn, since neither father wanted to force his child's hand if preferences changed with time. No formal notice would be taken, the earl and the baron decided, for ten years, until Miss Whilton turned eighteen and had a London Season. But the understanding was accepted, acknowledged, and toasted with champagne. And watered wine for the children.

Succeeding years did bring changes, as time usually does. First, the death of Daphne's aunt Lillian brought her two new boys to dote upon, the little brothers she never had. Torrence and Eldart were just five and six when their mother took her own life, rather than suffer their father's profligate ways. At twelve Daphne was too young to understand the servants' gossip about Spanish whores, French pox, and Greek love, but she knew they didn't mean Uncle Albert was well traveled. Her father's brother was a mean-spirited, angry-tempered man who kicked dogs, shouted at children, and had hair growing out of his ears and nose. Daphne didn't blame Aunt Lillian a bit, despite the scandal. She vowed to be even kinder to the quiet, timid little boys her father fetched home from London, rather than leave to Albert's untender mercies. So she passed on Graydon's teachings while he was away at school, the riding and fishing, skating and sledding. Her letters to him were full of her cousins' achievements, how Dart could climb Gray's favorite elm tree, how Torry loved the rope swing Gray had built for her.

If Graydon felt the merest twinge of jealousy when he read his old playmate's letters, it was more for her carefree days than for the affection she was showering on her little cousins. Why, Daffy spent a scant few hours a day with her governess, then some minutes practicing her scales and perfecting her needlework, while Graydon was hard at work at his studies and his sports. He hardly had time to learn the ways of the world, which, for a teenaged boy, meant women, wine, and wagering. Those happened, in fact, to be the vices Daphne believed Uncle Albert indulged in, and which she therefore, for her cousins' sakes, deplored.

Uncle Albert couldn't have cared less about the opinion of his brother's girl-child. He could hardly remember the chit's name. Nor was he jealous of her attention to his sons either, no more than Graydon. Albert was only glad someone had relieved him of the burden of the brats' upkeep. For certain he was not about to offer his brother any recompense for taking in the motherless boys.

Then Daphne's father died in a hunting accident and Uncle Albert became baron. He got so castaway, celebrating his succession to the title and estates, that he missed the funeral altogether, to no one's regret.

Graydon stood by Daphne's side during the service, while his parents supported her mother. He didn't complain when Daffy's tears made his neckcloth go limp, although it was the first creditable Waterfall he'd managed to tie, nor that she wadded up his monogrammed handkerchief and stuffed it in her pocket. She was his to comfort and protect, especially now that she had no father. She was his even if, at fifteen, she was as graceful as a broomstick, with a figure to match. His father nodded approvingly.

Graydon returned to his books and burgeoning manhood. Daphne washed and ironed his handkerchief and slept with it under her pillow. With foresight, Graydon's parents stayed on in Hampshire to assist Lady Whilton. Despite having more funds at his disposal than he ever hoped or dreamed of, Uncle Albert would have tossed all of his relatives, his own sons included, out on their ears and sold off the property to finance his gambling, if not for the entail. Even then he would have emptied the coffers and beggared the estate, except for the power and influence of Lord Hollister, who was watching out for his friend's widow's interest. The earl threatened to take Albert to court if he mishandled Dart's inheritance; he threatened to see him blackballed from every club and gaming den in London if he misused the widow or the children.

Lady Whilton could have taken her handsome jointure and her well-dowered daughter and set up a comfortable household of her own, but she stayed on at Woodhill Manor for the sake of the boys and the tenants. The new Lord Whilton stayed away for the most part, except when he came to see what monies he could bleed from the Manor acres, what costly repairs he could refuse to make, which servant he could dismiss to save the price of his wages. But Lady Whilton stood firm, the bailiff and her loyal butler beside her. Daphne was always nearby, too, which only served to infuriate her raddled uncle further, since he believed the earl would have kept his long nose out of Whilton business if the chit weren't to be Lord John Hollister's future daughter-in-law.

"And a good thing you made a cradle-match, too," Uncle Albert sniped at his ungainly young niece whose unruly curls refused to stay in ribbons or braids, whose skirts were muddied from playing with the barn cat, and whose face tended to break out in spots. "For you'd never snabble such an eligible *parti* as Hollister's whelp on your own, no matter how large your dowry."

Daphne stuck her tongue out at him from behind her mother's back. If Graydon were here, she told herself, he'd call the old mawworm out. But Graydon wasn't there. He was at university, practicing profligacy, or in London being introduced to his parents' world, which amounted to the same thing. Veering between the *ton*'s debs and the demi-mondaines, he might have agreed with Uncle Albert's assessment of the betrothal, if he thought of it at all. Marriage and the future and Hampshire seemed an eternity away.

Barely a year later, Graydon's mother contracted an inflammation of the lungs at a boating party and passed on between the ball at Devonshire House and one of Catalani's solo performances. Her last comment was that she'd be sorry to miss the fireworks at Vauxhall.

Distraught, Lord Hollister could not bear being alone at Howell Hall in the country with so much extra time on his hands, since even the local assemblies and card parties were denied his mourning state. The earl leased the Hall to an India-trade nabob and returned to his life in London, throwing himself deeper into politics and errands for the Foreign Office. He did maintain a warm correspondence with Lady Whilton, and he did make sure Albert knew he kept his interest there. Lord

Hollister's presence in London kept in check Albert's greed, if not his gambling and affinity for low company.

Daphne and Graydon met occasionally when his father sent him to Hampshire to confer with the Hall's steward. He came between university terms and house parties and walking tours and hunts in Scotland. They still roamed the countryside together, Daphne sopping up the tales of his experiences, expurgated, of course, like a thirsty seedling. And like a tender flower, she turned to his warmth as to the sun. Like the sun, he smiled down, accepting her worship as his due.

He taught her to shoot and to use a bow and arrow, and to retrieve his practice cricket shots. He also instructed her in what ladies of fashion were wearing and reading and thinking. In turn Daphne taught him not to laugh at a girl's first attempts to bat her eyelashes or flutter her fan. His knuckles were raw from that lesson, but he learned, the same as she learned the latest dance steps. They were the best of friends. She still thought he was Romeo and Adonis and the hero of every one of Maria Edgeworth's novels combined; he thought she was all right, for a dab of a chick.

Then the little boy cousins went away to school, Daphne and her mother agreeing they required more than petticoat governance. After all, Eldart was going to be baron one day, and not that far off either, if the wages of sin took their usual toll. Dart needed a broader education and a stable male influence to offset his father's reprehensible example.

Lady Whilton also felt that her daughter should get a shade of town bronze before being thrust into the London whirl next year. Daphne was too much the hoyden still, with her open, countrified ways, to find acceptance among the *haute monde*. She was too innocent and trusting to survive there, besides. So Lady Whilton took a house in Brighton for the boys' summer vacation, where Lord Hollister happened to be in attendance on the prince.

Daphne adored the sea bathing in the morning with her cousins, then visiting the shops and the tearooms in the afternoons with the crowds of young people her own age. There were picnics and dancing parties and amateur theatrics, just for those too young to take part in the doings among Prinny's crowd. Daphne didn't even mind being left alone evenings with her books and the fashion magazines while her mother went about to the concerts and fetes and banquets at the Regent's onion-domed pleasure palace, escorted by Lord Hollister. Daphne played at jackstraws and speculation with the boys. Then she played piquet with her mother's cousin Harriet, an impoverished, opinionated spinster who was thrilled to act as companion to Lady Whilton and occasional chaperone to Daphne, especially since Dart and Torry had a tutor of their own. Not even schoolboys were exempt from Cousin Harriet's dislike of the male species. In Lady Whilton's eyes, this made Harriet the perfect chaperone for Daphne on those afternoons when the baroness was preparing for the night's festivities ahead or resting after an early morning return from the previous evening's entertainment. Lord Hollister was insisting she deserved such gaiety, after being buried in the country so long. Cleo Whilton was finding that she agreed with him.

Daphne thrived. She grew an inch and gained a few pounds—some even in the right places—and her complexion cleared, to her mother's relief. She made friends, and her bow to royalty, and she even made her way through the snakepit of petty jealousies among adolescent females. She didn't need to compete with the other well-born daughters for the lordlings' regard; she had Gray. Her calm and composure won her approval among the hostesses, and her unthreatening friendliness made her a favorite among the boys, when Cousin Harriet let them approach at all. If Daphne wasn't quite blossoming, she was at least a bud ready to be unfurled. In London, for Graydon Howell.

Chapter Two

*H*air up, hems down. Remember your governess's etiquette lessons, forget the stablehands' vocabularies. Curtsy at the drop of a title, but never run, laugh out loud, or dance with the same man more than twice, even if he is your almost-betrothed.

Daphne's head would have been spinning, if not for her early forays into society at Brighton. Lady Whilton congratulated herself that her daughter had done so well: She was well behaved, well informed, well dressed, and well endowed. Welcome to London, Miss Whilton.

Daphne was presented at the Queen's drawing room, then at a ball in her honor at Howell House, where she and her mother were staying, at the earl's insistence. They couldn't very well take up residence with Uncle Albert, not when he'd turned Whilton House into a sinkhole of depravity no respectable member of the *ton* would enter. Besides, he hadn't invited them. The earl had, citing the absurd expense of renting a suitable location for the

Season, and the acres of empty rooms at his Grosvenor Square mansion. It would do his heart good, he said, to see the ballroom in use again, to hear the sounds of music and laughter. And there could be no hint of impropriety attached, not with the earl's widowed sister and the baroness's misanthropic spinster cousin in residence, and his son not. Graydon had bachelor quarters at the Albany, but he was there to lead Daphne out for the first dance at her come-out ball.

"I can see I'm going to have to look to my laurels," he told her as they took the lead spot for the cotillion.

Daphne was too lost in her own dreamworld to pay attention. Here she was, eighteen and finally Out, in the arms of the most attractive man in the ballroom, and he was her own dear Graydon. Soon their betrothal would be formally announced, then the wedding, and her life would be started at last. She floated on a cloud of joy, *his* hand in hers, *his* spicy cologne scenting the air, *his* flowers in her hair, *his* locket at her neck. His. Life was so intoxicating, she had no need for champagne.

"I say, success gone to your head already, that you don't even listen to another compliment?"

She looked up at him, into teasing brown eyes she knew so well. "Oh, I'm sorry, Gray. I was woolgathering, I suppose, just thinking how happy I am right now. The room looks so lovely, and everyone has been so kind. What were you saying?"

"I was trying to pour the butter-boat over your head, brat, by telling you what a success you'll be by morning. You'll have every beau in town at your feet by week's end, unless I miss my guess. They'll be writing poems to your eyebrows or your elbows, or whatever poppycock is in fashion this sennight. Just see that your head doesn't get turned by all the praise."

"Gammon," she said with a laugh, flashing her dimples at him. Trust Gray to try to make her feel comfortable when all eyes in the room were on them, as if she cared what anyone else thought of her. He'd already complimented her with a wide grin before the family supper earlier. His father had said she was almost as pretty as her mother at that age, high praise indeed, but Gray had whispered, "Fustian, no one can hold a candle to my Daffy."

It wasn't just Spanish coin he was handing her either, Graydon reflected. His little tagalong chum had improved no end. She almost reached his shoulder now, for one thing, especially if you counted the blond curls piled high on top of her head. They were threaded through with blue ribbons that matched her eyes, and the white roses he'd sent, on his aunt's advice. Daphne was dressed all in white, of course, but with a gauzy overskirt embroidered with tiny blue flowers that made her seem a fairy sprite. That fall of lace at the neckline was a clever touch, too—Lady Whilton's fine hand, no doubt—adding a hint of mystery where he knew very well there wasn't much of a secret, or anything else. Still, she was the comeliest deb of this season, he thought with pride, but perhaps too comely. Those dimples were deuced appealing.

Gray frowned over Daphne's head at the young bucks on the sidelines who were ogling his partner as if she were a tempting morsel. "You're no lobster patty," he fumed out loud, causing her to miss a step.

She giggled. "If that's a sample of the handsome compliments I can expect to receive, you needn't worry my head will swell."

"Not what I meant at all, brat, and you know it. I just don't like the way those chaps are looking at you, like cats about to pounce. Stop showing those dimples, blast it!"

She laughed the harder. Dear, dear Gray.

"I'm serious, Daffy, you have to be careful. You'll be all the crack, a regular Toast. Add a dowry rich enough to set the poorest makebait up on Easy Street, and they'll be after you like flies on honey. And those whose dibs are already in tune are looking for a pretty, well-born chit to be mother to their sons. Deuce take it, you're the daughter of a baron, with an earl sponsoring you."

"Do you think that's enough to make people forget about Uncle Albert?"

The current baron had arrived that evening at Howell House, uninvited. Luckily he came before most of the invited guests, for he stood in the entryway ranting that Daphne was way too young and gauche to be presented, much less engaged. She wasn't betrothed, not formally, but Uncle Albert never asked, too concerned with losing the interest on her dowry. He was also too castaway to put up much of a fuss when Graydon and two footmen bundled him into a hackney and sent him home before he could ruin Daphne's big night.

Remembering how the man stank of stale whiskey and staler linen, Graydon brightened. "Right, no one would want that dirty dish in the family. I cannot imagine how he and your father came from the same parents."

"Neither could Papa. He used to call him Awful

Albie, you know, and wondered if Grandmother had played her husband false."

"Nice talk, Daffy. Don't let the old tabbies hear you or they'll label you fast. You'll never get vouchers to Almack's."

"Sally Jersey already promised them. So did Princess Lieven, I'll have you know."

"Lud, when you show up at the Marriage Mart, every basket-scrambler in Town will be sniffing at your skirts."

"If you're so worried about other men paying their addresses," Daphne told him in what she thought was a reasonable tone, instead of the breathless yearning she really felt, "why don't we announce the betrothal tonight?"

Graydon had to reach up to loosen a neckcloth that was suddenly too tight. "Tonight? No, no, there's no reason to rush the blast—ah, blessed thing. I only meant you shouldn't go putting on airs like every other belle who makes a splash."

Daphne looked away and bit her lip. Graydon misinterpreted her disappointment. "I'm not saying you will, Daff, just that it'll be hard to resist all the lures cast your way. But then that's what this Season is for, isn't it? To give you time to meet other chaps, to know your own mind."

To know her own mind? She'd known what she wanted since she was six! She wasn't about to change it now. But that was just like Gray to be so fair and considerate. Of course, the thought of her falling top over tail for another man was too silly to mention, so she just danced on happily.

Graydon wondered at her silence and the knowing smile that softly curled at the edges of her mouth. Deuce take it, when had little Daphne

14

turned into such a charmer? And why, for heaven's sake? He looked around to see if anyone else noticed that beguiling grin. "Everyone who's anyone is here tonight," he said, caught between pride and chagrin.

"Everyone who matters to me was here for dinner."

Since they'd dined *en famille*, Graydon's chest swelled and he relaxed. She was still his sweet little Daffy. This first dance together should put his mark on her for anyone unaware of the understanding between them. A few words here and there should refresh a few other memories, so he really didn't have to worry about the hordes of admirers waiting next to Lady Whilton hoping to sign Daphne's dance card. He couldn't have another set with her until the end of the evening, he knew, but would have to do his duty by every wallflower in the room, under his aunt's gimlet stare. He kissed Daphne's hand when he left, purposely lingering over her fingers so everyone noticed, and said, "Enjoy yourself, brat, but don't forget about me."

Forget about him? Forget to breathe, more like. Smiling, Daphne fingered the gold locket he'd given her. She was the luckiest girl alive! Graydon was the kindest, most handsome man in the world— and he was jealous!

Daphne was the success Graydon had predicted. Word of their almost-betrothal was circulated all over, but that simply made her more appealing to the bucks who liked a challenge, or the Tulips who liked to worship at some goddess's shrine without paying the ultimate sacrifice, marriage. She was a safe flirtation, and she was delighted to play this new game.

There were Venetian breakfasts and balloon ascensions, rides to Richmond and ridottos. Sightseeing and being seen in Hyde Park at the fashionable hour. Musicales, masquerades, and military parades. Morning calls, afternoon at-homes, three balls a night. Sometimes Graydon escorted the ladies; more often Lord Hollister did when the entertainments were too tame for his son. Daphne understood: Gray was letting her spread her wings. She was soaring.

Then came the night at the opera when she looked across the vast concert hall to see him, her almost-fiancé, Graydon Howell, in a private box with a lady no lady would recognize. Thud. Her plummeting spirits fell so hard, she was surprised the sound didn't drown out the tenor.

"Ignore it," Cousin Harriet hissed in her ear. "It's the way of the world."

"Not my world," Daphne protested.

"Of course not, you ninny. It's a man's world, and they're all alike." Cousin Harriet had never married, and had never met the man who could make her regret that fact. She pointed out Lord Oglethorpe with his hands all over Lady Armbruster, while Lady Oglethorpe was being ogled by Sir Gervase Ashton. Lord Armbruster, across the aisle, had his arm across some demirep's shoulder, and on and on.

But not Gray. Those old court-cards, that reckless here-and-thereian, but not her idol, her Lochinvar, her best friend.

Her knight's shining armor took a severe dent when Graydon nibbled on the woman's ear, and a bad case of tarnish when one of Daphne's new "friends" was quick to inform her at the first intermission that Lord Howell's "friend" was an actress from Drury Lane. It seemed that friendship meant something different here in London.

"Mama, I have the headache. May we go home early?"

"That was not well done of you," the Earl of Hollister lectured his son the next morning, having called at the Albany for the express purpose of ruining Gray's day, since Lord John's own pleasant evening had been cut short with weeping and recriminations. Four women—Daphne, her mother, that man-hating cousin, and his own sister Sondra, b'gad—could get up a deal of caterwauling.

Graydon didn't require anything else to make him miserable; his aching head already took its toll. After dinner with Fancine at the Pulteney, and dessert, to put it nicely, at her place, Gray had gone on to White's. Everyone there had wanted to know if his deliberate insult to Miss Whilton meant the understanding was off. Was the fair lady fair game? He might be able to whistle her fortune down the wind, but other chaps weren't so fortunate. That's when he'd heard his Daffy had left the Opera House near tears. Bets were running high against the odds of his winning the Toast's hand. He had to cover the wagers, of course—his pride demanded no less—and drink to each entry in the betting book. Then he had to stay and drink to show he wasn't really worried. Then he had a few more brandies at home, because he *was* really worried. He wasn't concerned Daffy'd take up with one of those fops who followed her around, but he was deuced sorry he'd hurt her feelings.

His head was pounding and his position was indefensible, yet he answered his father's sermon with: "Dash it, Daphne knows I'm not a monk."

"She's a sweet young thing, still new to the social rounds. It's her innocence that makes her so appealing, and at the same time so vulnerable. Who knows what she thinks? You could have shown a little discretion, however."

"Blister it, I have enough trouble keeping track of my own social calendar. Am I supposed to memorize hers, too?"

The earl studied his fingertips. "Perhaps it might be a good idea to move the wedding forward, to relieve her worries."

"The wedding? We're not even formally engaged! I'm not ready for leg shackles yet. By Jupiter, I've barely reached my majority. Most chaps wait till they're thirty or so to set up their nurseries."

"If you're having second thoughts about Miss Whilton, you'd do better to bring them out now, when she can make another choice. I'd hate to see it, naturally."

Graydon dragged his fingers through his already tousled hair. "Lud, that's not it. I know my duty to the name and all. You've told me often enough that there are no other Howells to succeed me, and Daffy's just what I'd want in a wife, if I wanted a wife now. Daffy's a right 'un. She'll understand. After all, she sat next to that Fanshaw fop all night and I'm not complaining."

"But she didn't sit in his lap. And Fanshaw's a viscount. He'd never go beyond the line."

"And I would, you think?"

"I think you could break her heart."

"Gammon, Daffy's too downy for that. She knows it's all in fun."

"Fun? Seeing my promised husband making a cake of himself over a . . . a lightskirt in front of half the *ton*? No, I do not consider that fun, Lord Howell."

"Cut line, Daffy, we aren't even engaged yet, and it's just your pride that's hurt. I said I'm sorry, and I swear I won't embarrass you that way again."

"You won't embarrass me by taking your fancy piece out in public, or you won't take her out at all?" she wanted to know. "There is a big difference, my lord."

They were dancing at Almack's, not the most propitious place for such a conversation, but Daphne hadn't been home the afternoon after the opera, not to Graydon, at any rate, and then he'd gone out of town to a mill planned ages ago. Almack's was his first opportunity to smooth the waters, and her stormy look told him he'd better paddle hard and fast. His apology hadn't worked, though. Daphne wanted her pound of flesh, too.

"You're asking me if I'll give up my, ah, outside interests before we're even betrothed?"

"I'm asking if you intend to be faithful to your vows or not, Graydon Ambrose Hastings Howell, and you very well know it."

He missed his step, causing the next couple in line to fumble. "The devil! We haven't taken any vows, Daffy!"

"We've been pledged for ages, haven't we?"

"That's different. After we're married, of course . . ."

"Oh, then I can take lovers now?"

He stopped dancing altogether, earning them frowns and mutters from the rest of the set. Gray pulled his partner to the side. "Don't be a widgeon. It's altogether different."

Daphne stood her ground. "Why? If you don't consider yourself promised, why should I?"

"It's different, that's why. Promised or not, you are supposed to stay pure and chaste for me—for your husband. It's the man who needs the experience."

Daphne stamped her foot, oblivious to the stares from those around them. "The deuce it is! Do you think I want a man like Uncle Albert? Is he experienced enough?"

Now Graydon was starting to lose his temper, too. "Blast it, are you comparing me to that old reprobate?"

"Why not? Everyone's been quick to keep me informed about your drinking and your reckless wagers and the low company you're keeping. What's so different there?"

He wanted to shake her, and would have, if not for Lady Drummond-Burrell's throat-clearing. "I am not like your uncle Albert," he ground out. "And you're making a mountain out of a molehill, brat. It's not like I'm even keeping a mistress or anything, just having a little fling here and there. It means nothing, Daffy."

"Obviously it's my feelings that mean nothing to you! You can't even give me your word!"

"After we're married, I swear!"

"After? If you loved me, you'd never look at another woman, before, during, or after!"

The music had stopped. Now everyone was staring at them, still on the sidelines of the dance area.

He tried to tug her farther out of the way, but she dug her feet in. He couldn't very well pick her up and toss her over his shoulder the way he used to. Instead he turned his back, trying to shield them from prying eyes. "What the devil does love have to do with anything, Daffy?"

"If you don't know that, Graydon Howell, then I don't want to know you!" she shouted. So much for a bit of circumspection. When he was sure they had every eye in the place on them, Daphne ripped the locket off her neck, threw it to the floor, and stamped on it twice for good measure. "That's what you've done to our understanding, you dastard!"

Now there was nothing for it but for Graydon to grab her arm and pull her after him, willy-nilly, into the refreshment room. He shoved a glass of punch into her hands. "For heaven's sake, Daffy, calm down. You're making a scene."

"I'll make more than a scene if you don't unhand me, sirrah. And stop calling me Daffy. I'm not that little girl who used to follow you around, happy just to be in your shadow. I'm a woman now, even if you haven't noticed, with a woman's feelings."

"Then act like one and drink your punch instead of looking daggers at me for everyone to see. And what am I supposed to call you? Miss Whilton? After wiping your nose for you a hundred times? Listen, things will look different in the morning. We'll go for a ride, talk this out."

"We have nothing more to say. Good evening, Lord Howell."

She made to leave him, but he grabbed her arm again and spun her around. "Dash it, Daffy, don't make this any worse. You can't stir up a bumble-broth at Almack's."

"Why not? Why can't I complain about my fiancé's lack of fidelity here, of all places? After all, everyone does it, they tell me. The best people, the highest sticklers, every one of them seems to cheat on their husbands and wives, if you listen to enough gossip. Why, even Sally Jersey is said to be having an affair with—"

He clamped his hand over her mouth, so she kicked him in the shin. Then she poured the contents of her punch glass over his head. "I don't care if they never let me back in this dreadful place, and I don't care if I never see you again either. I wouldn't marry you, Graydon Howell, if you were the last man on earth."

Chapter Three

As far as public notices went, Daphne's went far indeed. And fast. By morning, everyone in London knew that her informal betrothal was infamously ended. What Rumor didn't spread, the gossip columns did. Daphne couldn't have put her nose outside even if she wanted to, even if it weren't all red from weeping. What she wanted was to get out of this wicked city of shattered illusions, out of his father's house of painful reminders. She wanted to go home to the country. The air was cleaner, the people were more honest, and one didn't have to work so hard at having a good time. Besides, after that outré outburst, she might be invited to another London party in a year or two, if she was lucky.

Lady Whilton and Cousin Harriet were even now making travel arrangements and overseeing the packing, when they weren't trading recriminations over the incident. Lady Whilton blamed her cousin for Daphne's intractability; Cousin Harriet blamed Mama for raising her daughter with blinders on.

While her relations bickered, Daphne took care of some housecleaning. A bundle of letters, a box of fairings, a monogrammed handkerchief, and a recently pressed white rose all joined the broken locket in the dustbin. With them went the last of her childhood.

So many years, so many dreams. So very, very stupid. Gray didn't love her and never had, except in an offhand, brotherly fashion. He was used to her, perhaps even fond of her, but he never loved her. He was prepared to do his duty by his family name and social standing eventually, that was all. He'd be comfortable married to his childhood pal. Daphne'd be miserable, even more miserable than she was now, if that were possible. She shredded those letters into bits so small, they could have been grains of rice, at a wedding that never took place.

Lady Whilton had a few broken dreams of her own, but she set them aside for her daughter's sake and took up the loose threads of her country life again. She was a mother first, she told herself as she visited tenant farms instead of the theatre, and sat in on church-lady committees instead of literary salons. She could catch up on her resting, reading, and needlework, fiend seize them all—and that wretched, wretched boy.

Cousin Harriet felt vindicated. She'd always said the only thing between a man's ears was a hatrack, that what they used for brains was between their legs. She'd just been proved right again, damn them all, especially that Howell fellow for making such a mingle-mangle of the whole thing. Harriet never wanted little Daphne to fall into a decline, and she never wanted her to dwindle into an old maid. Men did have their places, after all—in bed making children, and at the bank making money. If there was a way to do without them, Harriet certainly hadn't found it, loving her cousin's child and living on her cousin's largesse. That wasn't what she wanted for Daphne. Neither was a lying, cheating, womanizing, silver-tongued devil of a handsome man for a husband.

The lying, cheating, etc., non-husband-to-be was still in London, but not for long. He was a laughingstock among his friends, and a great deal poorer after paying off those exorbitant wagers at White's on his chances of turning Daphne up sweet. Sweet? She'd rather suck a lemon than read one of his letters, it seemed. They were all returned unopened. He paid up; the betrothal was off.

Graydon should have felt like a free man. He didn't. He shouldn't feel guilty for doing what every other man in London did, engaged, married, or otherwise. But he did. Damn and blast! He wasn't ready for parson's mousetrap, but he wasn't prepared to be the target for every matchmaking mama in town either. Two young ladies had already tripped outside his rooms, and one fell off her horse in front of him at the park. Peagooses all. If he wasn't ready to wed Daffy, he surely wasn't going to drop the handkerchief to some conniving miss who had designs on his fortune and title, and who couldn't ride. Why would a man marry someone he couldn't trust? A tiny voice that sounded remarkably like Daphne's echoed in his conscience: Why would a woman?

Deuce take it, the worst thing was, he couldn't even confide his confusion to his best friend. If she wouldn't answer his letters, she sure as Hades wasn't going to welcome him at Woodhill Manor. If the impossible brat weren't so damn honest and open . . . he wouldn't like her half so well.

Maybe it was for the best. Maybe she'd find a man worthy of the adoration he'd accepted as his due for all those years. Maybe she'd find a man to love her to distraction, like those heroes in the novels she was always reading. And maybe Gray would tear the dastard's heart out. With his teeth.

Did he love her? She was just Daffy, his fishing companion. She wasn't the most beautiful chit in the world, though not far behind, nor the most even-tempered or seductive. She wasn't even the brightest female of his acquaintance or the most talented. Then why did he feel that a vital part of him had gone missing, an arm or something? If he'd just taken her for granted, always there, always ready for anything, then why was he lost without a road map for his life? What was he going to do if he wasn't going to marry Daphne Whilton? The endless rounds of parties and sporting events didn't hold much appeal, nor did women who put a price tag on their charms. Daffy'd been his for the asking.

"You're asking me for advice? Now?" His father was no help. "How did I ever raise such a fool? You had what every man wants: the love of an honest woman who's an heiress to boot. And you toss it away for a bit of slap and tickle. Faugh! I wash my hands of you, you gudgeon. Besides, if you weren't my own son, I'd call you out. The gel's like a daughter to me and you insulted her, made it hard for her to show her face in town, dash it."

As upset as Lord Hollister was for Daphne's sake, he was more irate for his own loss. "And that means her mother won't put a foot out of Hampshire either, blast you. Deuced comfortable woman, Cleo Whilton."

Graydon put his glass down and sat up. "Meaning . . . ?"

"Meaning nothing yet, you cawker. And likely nothing ever, thanks to you. How can I go courting a woman whose daughter hates the sight of my son?"

Courting? His father and Daphne's mother? Now that he thought of it, they were perfect together. Lady Whilton had thrown herself into the earl's busy political schedule with pleasure, and she was the first woman the earl had squired about since the death of Graydon's mother.

"For all I know," his father was going on, "they hold me to blame for your sins. That Cousin Harriet's got us both tarred with the same brush anyway. Slammed the door in my face when they left. My own door, too." The earl stared morosely into his brandy glass.

Lud, now he had to feel guilty for blighting his father's chance for happiness, too, Gray thought, as he downed his own drink. The governor needed a hostess and social partner, and deserved a warm companion as much as anyone. There was no one Gray would rather see in his mother's place than Lady Whilton. She was already one of the family. Or had been. His father was right: She'd never take up with Gray or his family now.

"Deuced shame, too," the earl mumbled. "One of the finest females a fellow is like to come across."

"Lady Whilton?"

"Her, too. But I meant little Daphne. Sweetest gel *you'll* ever find. Too bad she thought you were some kind of god, a regular hero. The silly twit."

There was nothing for it but for Graydon to leave town. No, the country. If he was gone, perhaps Lady Whilton and the earl could get together without upsetting Daffy, who'd never had a selfish bone in her body. She wouldn't curse his father if he wasn't around to embarrass them all. So he'd leave. To hell with the empty London life, and to hell with the succession and his father's dreams of a government career for him. Graydon emptied his purse and bought himself a commission. She wanted a hero, he'd damned well be a hero.

Graydon was right, the older couple did manage to settle their differences eventually, without his presence as a source of conflict. They shared his letters from the Peninsula, glowed with pride when his name was mentioned in the dispatches, and worried together over rumored battles. What they didn't do was plan his homecoming.

Daphne never asked about him or showed any interest in his posted valor. Her mother was careful never to mention his name, in return for Daphne's agreeing to reenter society. Since it was either that or see her mother mope around the house all day, Daphne attended a few local assemblies. The men she danced with were mostly old friends like Squire Pomeroy's son Miles, too delighted Howell was out of her life and out of the country to ask awkward questions. The new young curate, a visiting scholar, someone's nephew down from university, were all pleasant partners, undemanding and unexciting.

Lady Whilton got her to Brighton for the summer by pleading her cousins needed the holiday. Torrence had had the measles that spring at school and was still recuperating. Eldart was growing so fast that, at thirteen, he was almost as tall as Daphne. Lady Whilton insisted she couldn't manage them on her own, when Daphne tried to stay behind in Hampshire, and the boys added their persuasive voices. No one was more fun at the beach than Daphne, no one could ride better than their favorite cousin. How could she refuse? They were turning into fine lads, with no remnants of that nervous timidity they'd shown at first. Any father would have been proud, except Uncle Albert, who ignored his sons' existence altogether. Daphne believed this was a mixed blessing, for the rakehell's influence could only have been for the worse, but his cold disregard had to hurt the boys' feelings. Daphne had to supply what sense of security and family feeling she could, even if it meant going to Brighton.

There were some stares and titters at first, until Lady Minton ran off with her head groom. Daphne's broken troth was old hat, after all, and the scandalmongers had other bones to gnaw. Besides, Daphne spent the majority of her time with her cousins, letting her mother accept Lord Hollister's invitations with a clear conscience.

Daphne held out against London in the fall, but her mother was so disappointed and restless, she surrendered by the spring Season. She refused to stay at Howell House, though, no matter what arguments were brought to bear. If the expense of renting a house was too dear, they needn't go at all. If her mother was insecure without a male's presence, let them take their trusted butler, Ohlman. Daphne would not stay at *his* house under any conditions, even if he was on another continent. It wouldn't be proper, she said; it would lead to more gossip. It would hurt.

They took a small house in Half Moon Street, Mama, Cousin Harriet, Daphne, and Ohlman. It was nicely furnished, large enough for modest entertainments, and had its own stable mews, so Daphne could keep her own horses in Town and ride in the park mornings before the rest of society was out of bed. She found most of her pleasure there on horseback, or playing three-handed whist with Ohlman and Cousin Harriet when Mama was out with the earl, rather than at the grand balls and extravagant displays of wealth and social standing.

Miss Whilton was still popular at the parties she did attend, but not as outgoing as before. Now she had to look at each dance partner for ulterior motives. Was Lord This only interested in her fortune? Was Lord That only interested in seduction? Cousin Harriet's warnings stuck in her mind, that men were deceivers ever. Or was that Shakespeare? No matter, trust betrayed is a trust not easily bestowed again. She danced, she flirted, and she kept her distance from all the eligible men who would have paid her court. Daphne's gaiety became so forced, her mother reluctantly permitted her to return to the country she preferred over town life, to Lady Whilton's bemusement. Ruralizing was all well and good, but hadn't they had enough of that for all those years?

Lady Whilton had commitments that would keep her in Town, however, a dinner she was throwing for Lord Hollister's party members, a reception for one of the foreign delegations she was helping him plan.

So Daphne went home, along with Cousin Harriet and Ohlman, and Mama gave up the little house and moved in with the earl and his widowed sister. Why pay rent for one person when she was at Howell House most days anyway, conferring with his chef and housekeeper?

Lady Whilton begged Daphne to accompany her—and the earl—to a round of house parties that July and August, but Daphne didn't want to leave the boys with servants when they were home on vacation. Besides, it was time Dart learned about the land he would inherit someday—and in the not too distant future, either, if the rumors of Uncle Albert's continued dissipation were true.

In the fall there was the harvest and repairs to some of the tenant farms. Daphne had to stay in Hampshire to make sure Uncle Albert didn't come and divert the monies. And there was the Sunday school class she volunteered to teach. The roads were in disrepair from the fall rains, and the boys would be home soon for the holidays, anyway. Daphne stayed in the country; Mama stayed in London, or wherever Lord Hollister went. At least someone's courtship proceeded apace, to the point that Lord Hollister stayed with them over Christmas, and came to ask Daphne's permission to wed her mother in the spring.

"I know it's not the regular thing to do, asking a young chit like you, but your mother couldn't be happy if we were to cause you any discomfort.

There'll be family gatherings, you know, and the wedding itself, where you'll have to see my son. He is selling out after that last injury, finally. I begged him to, the succession, don't you know, and I can't lie to you and say I'm sorry he's coming home, because he's my son, for all his faults, and I've missed him."

"Of course you have, and I'd never want you to—"

"But he has his own rooms, so you won't have to see him night and day when you come stay with us in Grosvenor Square. I mean to say, you'll always have a home with us where you can be comfortable, even if I have to banish the nodcock to the Jamaican properties."

"No, no, that won't be necessary, my lord. We're adults. I'm sure we can rub along well enough." Daphne tried to swallow her panic, lest she let her own fears stand in the way of her mother's happiness. He did keep separate rooms, and he did have a different circle of acquaintances. And she hardly went to London anymore. She'd go less, after the wedding. "We were always friends," she said with more enthusiasm than she felt. "We should find no difficulty as relatives by marriage. It's been nearly two years, after all." She could have said how many days, hours, and minutes, but didn't.

Lord Hollister was smiling, relieved. "I knew you were a reasonable chit. Told your mother you were too sweet to hold a grudge so long."

Nineteen months, eight days, and seventeen hours since she'd seen the dastard. Nineteen awful months of hating him and missing him and worrying to death over his horrifying heroics. Daphne vowed to stay in the country until she put down roots like a turnip, rather than batten on the newlyweds—or have to worry about confronting Gray at every social gathering. She supposed it would get easier in time, except for the occasions when she had to look across the theatre at him every night, wondering if the woman in his box was a new bird of paradise or a prospective bride. No, Daphne rather thought she'd prefer to set up housekeeping somewhere with Cousin Harriet and raise pug dogs and roses. She hated pug dogs. And roses made her sneeze.

Chapter Four

*J*ust when you think things cannot get any worse, they usually do. Lady Whilton decided to hold the wedding in the country. Not only would Daphne have to come face-to-face with Graydon at the ceremony, she'd have to entertain him at her own home! Howell Hall next door was still under lease to Mr. Foggarty of the India trade, so the earl and his family would stay at Woodhill.

"Don't you think they should put up at the inn?" Daphne tried. "It's bad luck for a bridegroom to see the bride before the wedding, and all that."

"Rubbish," Lady Whilton replied. "That's just for the day of the wedding, and I'll be so busy dressing and such, I won't get a chance to visit with John, anyway. Besides, can you really imagine the Earl of Hollister putting up at the Golden Crown?"

No, but she could well visualize his son there, drinking with the local farmers and flirting with the barmaids. And good riddance to him, too.

"But a tiny chapel wedding, Mama? Wouldn't you

rather have a lavish gala in London, with all of Lord Hollister's grand connections? Perhaps the prince might even come."

"He'd most definitely come, which is why John and I decided we'd rather have a quiet, private ceremony instead of some absurd public spectacle. That's for the young people. We're too old for all that folderol, and we've each been through it once, anyway. Now we want a simple country wedding, with only those closest to us."

Too close. Daphne was getting desperate. "Then why not one of those lovely little churches in Richmond? Or you could even hold the ceremony at the earl's house in Grosvenor Square."

"What, and have everyone thinking there was some hugger-mugger we were trying to hide? Never. There will be talk enough as is. Let it come after the fact, I say, after a perfectly respectable wedding in the church where I've worshiped for half my life. You have to admit our own St. Ethelred's is quaint and dear, especially when it's filled with flowers. Besides, your father lies in the graveyard there. I'd like to think of him at the wedding. He never wanted me to stay a widow, you know. I think he'd be pleased I'm marrying his friend John."

"Yes, Mama, I'm sure he'd rest easy knowing you were so well and happily circumstanced. But . . . but what about Graydon?"

Mama willfully misinterpreted. "Oh, he's pleased as punch, too. He wrote back immediately after his father sent the news. The dear boy wants to know if he should call me Mother when he gets back. What do you think?"

Daphne thought the dear boy should drown on his way home from Portugal.

Her mother was going on. "And that's another reason not to plan a complicated affair: We're not entirely sure when dear Graydon will arrive, or how well his leg will have healed. His father does want him to stand up as best man. You'll be my attendant, of course."

Of course, so she'd only have to stand next to him for the wedding, the rehearsal, the receiving line, the breakfast after. Good grief! If her mother weren't so much in alt, Daphne'd accuse her and the earl of planning this whole thing just to throw the two of them together. No one got married just to see their children made miserable, though, not even Lady Whilton. "How delightful, Mama. I'd be thrilled." She'd rather be boiled in oil.

Lady Whilton might want a small, simple wedding, but she had to have her bride clothes made by her favorite London modiste and the refreshments ordered from Gunter's.

Daphne refused to accompany her again, this time citing the need to ready Woodhill Manor for the occasion. Under Uncle Albert's decree, no funds had been spent on the house for ages, other than standard upkeep. Now Lady Whilton would use her own substantial income to refurbish the parlor and a few of the guest rooms. Someone had to remain behind to oversee the workers, Daphne claimed, and it could not be Cousin Harriet, who'd have them all tossing down their paintbrushes and hammers in a day and a half. Besides, someone should turn out the closets, inspect the linen, and inventory the china if they were having company. And someone should not have to face her former sweetheart's homecoming.

Daphne decided it would be better to meet here, perhaps with just the family as witnesses, rather than under the eager eyes of the upper ten thousand. She could be mature about this, she told herself, nod graciously, welcome him home, inquire for his health. And Gray could be trusted to be dutifully polite back, she supposed. After almost two years, he couldn't still be angry over her public humiliation of him. Just because she blamed herself for sending him into army-exile, endangering his very life, was no reason to believe he outright hated her. He never cared that much anyway, so why would he feel awkward now?

She practiced upstairs to match his supposed *savoir faire*, to get it right without trembling. Welcome home, Lord Howell? Major? Graydon? Rats, she couldn't even think what to call him, other than a word Torry had his mouth washed out with soap for using. Perhaps she should try calling him brother, Daphne thought, half-humorously, half-hysterically. Lud, those were going to be a difficult few days.

She mightn't go to London to welcome the prodigal son, but Daphne heard all about him. Mama's letters were full of how handsome he looked in his uniform, how well received he was in his hero's homecoming. No party was a success without his presence, Mama reported, and his company was sought for six events a day. Women were throwing themselves at him, Lady Whilton added in her crossed lines. He caught a few, too, Daphne read in the society columns she swore never to look at. The gossip pages enumerated every woman the newest Nonpareil sat out with—his leg being not entirely healed—and who shared his box at the opera. A dashing young widow seemed to be in the forefront of the pack for the Hollister heir stakes.

Daphne recalled Lady Bowles well from her time in London, although Seline was a woman with no time for lady friends. She spent her days striking attitudes as the lunar goddess her name denoted, wearing silvery gray gowns that looked spectacular next to her pale skin and ebony hair. At night she donned spangled gauze as the other moon deity, Diana the Huntress. She'd once commented in Daphne's hearing that a rich old husband was the best kind.

Daphne supposed even the Moon Goddess, as Seline was termed in the clubs and scandal sheets—where her name was mentioned with shocking frequency—could make an exception for a rich young man if he was the most eligible bachelor in town. Perhaps his injury was bad enough that Seline could envision herself becoming an even wealthier young widow. Or maybe Gray's practiced charm could melt the harpy's mercenary heart, and her dampened muslins could rouse his ardor. Maybe they'd fall madly, passionately in love and fly off to Gretna Green to sanctify their vows. Before Mama's wedding. And maybe pigs would fly.

Ah, well, Daphne thought, it was only for a few days. She'd survive seeing him, the same way she'd survived the last twenty-three months, twenty-one days, and seven hours of not seeing him. Miserably.

* * *

A few days, she could manage, but weeks? Miserable did not begin to describe how her mama's next letter made Daphne feel. They were all returning to Hampshire shortly, Lady Whilton wrote. Graydon's doctors thought he'd recover better in the country, away from all the hustle and bustle of his busy social life. He was staying at the Grosvenor Square mansion, having given up his third-floor bachelor quarters on account of his injury. Lady Whilton was able to report that it was no wonder the leg was still bothersome. Dear Graydon was seldom in his bed before dawn, if at all.

She and the earl, therefore, had suggested Graydon accompany them to Hampshire next week for the first reading of the banns. The wedding could take place three weeks hence, if Daphne thought all the arrangements could be made in time.

Well, no, she didn't think she could book passage to the Antipodes so soon.

The first meeting did not go so badly, for a hanging. In the first flurry of welcoming Lady Whilton home, greeting the earl and his sister, Cousin Harriet grumbling as footmen and maids scurried about with baggage, no one heard the beating of Daphne's heart. Ohlman the butler was taking wraps and asking for preferences of refreshment as he escorted the company into the parlor, and Mama wanted to know if the invitations had arrived from the printer, whether the boys would need new suits of clothes again, which flowers they could expect to be in bloom. Daphne answered her mother's chatter, then busied herself pouring the tea.

The blasted man couldn't take wine, like his father, from the decanter Ohlman was pouring. No, he had to stand next to Daphne, waiting for his cup of tea. And she, like a ninny, fixed it just the way he always preferred, without asking. His mouth quirked in a smile, but he did not comment on her blushes.

His first words, in fact, eased her mind somewhat. "You must be wishing me at Jericho. I offered to put up at the inn, but your mother wouldn't hear of it. I can make some excuse to leave until the wedding if you want, if you'll be too uncomfortable."

Daphne had to face him now, had to look right up into his warm brown eyes. He was even more handsome than she remembered, more muscular, too. The cane he carried added distinction, with the limp barely noticeable. She wondered if Mama had made up the whole faradiddle about his needing to recuperate, to explain his presence here, but why would he want to come so early? Gray wouldn't have left the gay life of London just to cut up her peace. He was doing a fine job of it, though, waiting for her answer, gazing straight through her eyes to her very soul. She wanted to tell him, yes, put up at an inn, on the moon preferably, and stop tearing her life apart, but she couldn't.

She handed over his tea and said, "The inn? No, of course not. The sheets aren't even aired properly."

"After Portugal, any sheets at all are a luxury. Truly, I wouldn't mind if you'd rather," he offered nobly, still standing as though poised to leave.

"Nonsense, unless *you'd* rather," she countered.

He shook his head quickly and finally sat down.

"Not at all. And the notion of more traveling about doesn't appeal either. Thank you."

"For what? You've always been welcome here. That is, Mama's always treated you like part of the family. I've prepared your usual room, unless you'd rather one on the ground level." Daphne wasn't sure it was polite to refer to his injury, but she didn't want him maiming himself for life on the stairs. She had enough on her conscience. "I could make the switch in an instant."

Graydon seemed relieved at her hospitality, but embarrassed to be reminded of his wound. "That's not necessary at all, but thank you. The leg is almost healed, the sawbones say, so the exercise should be good for it. In fact, I'm looking forward to some long tromps through the countryside," he mentioned, leaving room for her offer to accompany him, as she always had.

If he needed exercise, why hadn't he stayed in London with all its attractions? He could have strolled down Bond Street with the other town beaux, or danced all night at Vauxhall. He'd be bored with the tame rural pastimes within a day. Tromping through the countryside, indeed! Hadn't the papers claimed he'd cut a wide swath through City life since his return? Instead of expressing her doubts and distrust, she replied, "Then you'll enjoy the pleasant weather we're having. The roadside wildflowers are in color, and the formal gardens are beginning to look lovely. Mama won't have to worry about the church being decorated properly."

Daphne couldn't believe this conversation they were having. If anyone had said she'd be discussing spring blooms with Gray Howell, she'd have laughed. The empty phrases made her want to cry, though, all the while she was congratulating herself on how well she was handling an awkward situation. She wasn't berating him for tearing her heart out, nor was she throwing herself on his broad chest in joy that he'd come home safely. Her hands weren't even shaking. Those twenty-three months, etc., had taught her something besides arithmetic, after all.

How kind the years had been to her, Gray was thinking as he stared at Daphne over the rim of his teacup. He'd aged, a century it felt like, with scars and weathered wrinkle lines, but Daphne had ripened. She had been an adorable child and a pretty girl after that awkward stage, but now she was a beautiful woman, poised and elegant. She could have been a duchess sitting at the tea table, in her Nile green silk gown that shimmered with every graceful motion. No demure debutante white for Miss Howell anymore, and no fall of lace at her bosom to hide her lack of assets, either. His old playmate had assets aplenty.

Only her unruly blond curls remained of the hoyden who used to tag at his heels, but now the vibrant gold locks were cropped into a short fashionable do, with a ribbon threaded through to keep the curls off her perfect face. She looked like a wood nymph, innocent and seductive both.

God, she was everything he remembered, and more. And less, for this time she wasn't promised to anyone, himself included. The gentlemen hereabouts must all be dicked in the nob or in their dotage, or dimwits of the tenth degree. Of course, when it came to fools, he'd take every prize. Still, she was going to let him stay at the house. There was hope ... unless she'd just pasted on a polite veneer like all the other stone-cold London Diamonds. Not his Daffy, please.

Chapter Five

𝒯hings weren't going badly, for a disaster. Daphne even managed to find a few bits of silver lining in the cloud that hung over her head. It wasn't pouring rain, for one thing, and no virulent epidemics were ranging the countryside, so Graydon was getting the exercise he wanted—and getting out of Daphne's way. At least she was managing to avoid his company most of the time. With Mama in such a dither over the wedding plans, changing her mind over the guests, the refreshments, and the decorations, it was easy. There was so much to do that Daphne found it simple to make excuses for missing lunch or tea. She took breakfast in her bedroom, the better to consult her lists, she said, and she planned her busy day by watching the front door for his departure. Other times she left by the kitchen door, if he was still around at the front of the house. She often stayed away on her errands and commissions— with a novel, a blanket, and a packed lunch—until late in the afternoon, returning the same back way to avert any chance encounters.

Graydon was keeping busy, too, it seemed, refamiliarizing himself with the neighborhood and conferring with the bailiff at Howell Hall. His father had never taken the same interest in the land, so there was a great deal to be done after Gray's absence. He'd also studied some new farming methods while he was recuperating, and was anxious to implement the latest advances. Or so Daphne gathered from the conversations at the inevitable times when she could not escape her mother's machinations, mostly at dinner and the hours after. No amount of cautious maneuvering could politely excuse her from taking supper with the guests, Lady Whilton insisted. Lord Hollister and his sister would start to think she was avoiding them. How many headaches could she claim?

Instead, Daphne took to inviting company: old Squire Pomeroy when he was well enough to leave his sickbed, and his family, including Squire's married daughter Sally and her husband, and Squire's son Miles, of course; the Hartley sisters and old Admiral Benbow, who was mostly deaf; the vicar who would perform Mama's wedding ceremony, his wife and young curate; even Mr. Foggarty, Lord Hollister's tenant, who, while a bit rough around the satin and lace edges, had wonderful stories of his India days.

The guests reciprocated with invitations of their own, so that meant a few less evenings Daphne had to spend in Graydon's company. She made sure she was never alone with him even then, nor available for private conversation. Daphne thought she'd scream if he tried to get up a flirtation with her,

45

since he'd be missing his London lightskirts. Instead she conferred with Mama about the wedding, or practiced the pianoforte, concentrating fiercely, or she got up whist games with his aunt and Cousin Harriet while Lord Hollister and Mama cooed in the corner. And she was always the first to scurry off to bed, claiming another early morning. At least she was getting a lot of reading done.

No, things were not going too badly at all, Daphne congratulated herself, and almost a whole week had gone by.

Almost a whole week of his visit was gone, without one comfortable tête-à-tête, Graydon fumed. He was as close to recapturing their old friendship as he'd been in Portugal. He'd been hoping for companionship at the very least. Instead she wanted to know if his room was to his liking, if there was a horse up to his weight in the stables, if he preferred macaroons to poppyseed cake with his tea. She was being a blasted hostess, when he wanted his playmate back! The woods were indeed full of wildflowers, and the streams were full of fish. He wanted to share them with her, the way they used to. He wanted to discuss his plans for Howell Hall, to see if she was interested. She was too busy interviewing musicians. He never even managed to get her alone long enough to ask her forgiveness, an apology he'd been carrying around for nigh onto two years.

This wedding nonsense was taking all of Daffy's time, dash it. The poor puss was being run off her feet. Why, she never had an afternoon free to just sit and chat, and she was yawning over her teacup every night right after dinner. Her eyes weren't their usually wondrous clear blue, he noticed, but looked tired, as if she'd been poring over her mother's endless lists too long. As for Lady Whilton, she was practically useless, giggling like a schoolgirl with her first beau. Graydon was delighted to see her so enamored of his father, of course, but couldn't help resenting the absurd juxtaposition of the older woman's giddiness while her daughter drudged to make the perfect wedding.

The situation was deplorable. Graydon vowed to be what assistance he could, to lift some of the burden from Daphne's slender but alluring shoulders. He made a note to ask Foggarty if he'd mind denuding Howell Hall's gardens and forcing houses for the occasion. The older man was pleasant enough, accommodating Graydon's wishes to inspect the house and grounds, even though Foggarty knew it meant the end of his stay in the neighborhood. Gray thought he'd miss the nabob's tales and exotic dinners when Foggarty's lease was up, but of course, the chap had to go if Graydon was going to reclaim his own home. The governor didn't care for the Hall, but Graydon did. He was tired of rented lodgings, army bivouacs. He wanted something permanent, even if it meant dislodging his amiable, well-heeled tenant.

Maybe Foggarty would make an offer on Pomeroy's place. With the old squire ailing, perhaps the Pomeroys would rent a house in Bath. Lud knew Graydon would be happy to see Miles Pomeroy out of the neighborhood, the way he was looking at Daffy. According to Lady Whilton, Pomeroy had been hanging around, biding his time. Miles was older than himself by a few years, and firmly entrenched in the neighborhood, acting as magistrate since his father took ill. From all Graydon heard or remembered, there'd never been a more upright and honest man. Or a duller one.

Miles Pomeroy took his job as magistrate seriously. For that matter, he took life seriously. But crime was no laughing matter, so when he heard of an attempted robbery in his precinct, he was quick to make an investigation. When he realized the victim of the attack was none other than a relation of Miss Whilton's, on the way to Woodhill Manor for the wedding, he hurried to offer his assistance. Thus it was that Miles, hoping to find favor with Miss Whilton, dropped into the midst of an already awkward house party the one person in the world Daphne would less like to have stay at Woodhill Manor than Graydon Howell.

"You're the ninnyhammer who brought Uncle Albert here?" she shrieked at the unfortunate Mr. Pomeroy in the Manor's now-deserted hallway. Ohlman the butler was assisting the foulmouthed and foul-breathed Uncle Albert up the stairs—to the master suite. Mama was having hysterics in the parlor, being comforted by Lord Hollister, of course, while Cousin Harriet was threatening to start packing, swearing she'd not spend one night under the same roof with such a fiend. Meantime Harriet was administering smelling salts to Lord Hollister's sister in the morning room. Daphne neither knew nor cared where Graydon was, but she could only assume he was having a grand laugh at her predicament. "Whyever did you have to bring him here, of all places?" she wailed at poor Miles.

"Well, he is Baron Woodhill. Naturally I assumed ... I mean, this is his home and all."

"His home is a gaming hell in London's slums. That loose screw has only come to make trouble, I know it!"

"But I couldn't have left him at that tumbledown hedge tavern with his valet injured and his carriage missing a wheel."

"Why not? I assure you Uncle Albert is quite at home in the lowest dive. He must have crawled out from under a rock to get here."

"Please, Miss Whilton, you're merely overset at the unexpected arrival of an additional guest. He's your relative, an older gentleman. You must strive for a little respect."

Daphne was striving not to beat her slow-top suitor over the head with an umbrella from the nearby stand.

"You do not understand, Miles. My uncle is not in the least respectable. He'll insult the other guests with his gutter language, or try to cheat them at cards if he doesn't cast up his accounts on their shoes or molest their servants. The old rakehell will ruin Mama's beautiful wedding."

Miles Pomeroy refused to listen to gossip and never read the latest crim. con. stories in the London papers, so he truly did not know the worst of Albert's reputation, only that he preferred city life to the country. "Nonsense," he said now. "You've hardly seen your uncle in years. And what should a young miss like you know about rakehells and loose screws? Nothing, I'm sure, but the tattle-mongers' tripe. Come, he is the head of your family. In fact, I was delighted to be of service to him. Perhaps he'll look more kindly on my request for a private word about a certain matter."

Lud, it needed only that. "Miles, Uncle Albert is

hardly ever sober enough for a rational conversation, and the only family he's head of is the lizard family. He wouldn't recognize his own sons if he passed them on the street, and I do not recognize him as taking my father's place in anything but title." There, that should cure Mr. Pomeroy of his latest notion. Nothing, she feared, would cure him of his pomposity.

He merely patted her hand and said, "Tut, tut. I can see you're still overset."

Daphne jumped on that excuse to see Miles on his way. "Yes, I'm sorry I cannot invite you to stay for supper, but, as you say, we are all at sixes and sevens." She stepped closer to the door, forcing him to head in that direction, too.

"I'll just be off then to pursue my investigation." He reluctantly took up the gloves and hat she handed him. "I'm sure the miscreants are long gone, although Lord Woodhill did think he wounded one of them. I'll call tomorrow to see how you get on, and to report to Lord Woodhill on my findings. Nothing was taken, at any rate."

He most likely didn't have anything the thieves wanted, Daphne thought. Uncle Albert's pockets were perennially to let. She was positive now that her uncle had come, not to disrupt the wedding, which was still two weeks away, but to threaten to do so. Lord Hollister was certain to buy him off, or Mama would. Daphne'd hand over her own pin money to see the miserable muckworm out of the county. For now it was enough to see Miles out the door. She leaned against it when he was gone, her eyes closed. Then someone put a glass of sherry in her hand. Her eyes snapped open.

"Here, you can use this." Graydon was smiling

down at her. "I'm afraid we'll all need some Dutch courage before the night is over. I cannot promise to slay your dragons for you," he added with a nod toward the door, "but at least I won't desert you."

"Miles didn't—" she began, but Ohlman returned down the stairs then, holding on to the banister. For once the implacable butler's composure was shaken. Daphne shoved the glass of wine into her loyal retainer's hand. "You need this more than I do," she said. "Was he in a rant?"

Ohlman drank the wine down in a gulp, said, "Thank you, Miss Daphne," and mopped his brow. "It wasn't so much what he said, as what he threw. I'm too old for all that ducking. I'll make sure to send two of the quickest footmen up with his dinner tray. Then I'll say my prayers that his valet recovers enough to get here tomorrow. If I have to shave the man, I refuse to answer for the consequences." Ohlman straightened up, bowed to Daphne and Lord Howell, and resumed his stately tread to the small butler's pantry where he likely kept a stronger restorative than sherry.

Daphne took one look at Gray's twitching lips and had to clap her hands over her mouth. One tiny giggle escaped before she remembered where she was—and with whom. "It's not funny, Major." She'd decided on Major as being the middle ground of names and titles, not as formal as Lord Howell, not as familiar as Graydon. "I'm afraid that man"— she jerked her head upward—"means to cause trouble."

"Oh, I'm certain of that. We'll just have to make sure he doesn't, won't we?" And he grinned at her, emphasizing the "we." He would have taken her hand, perhaps to kiss it, but Ohlman returned then to announce that dinner was served.

No one ate much of Cook's fine meal except for Graydon, who was delighted with the turn of events. Being partners in adversity was better than not being partners at all.

Chapter Six

If dinner was dismal, the gathering afterward was ghastly. Everyone was on tenterhooks, hoping the tea cart—and an excuse to retire—arrived before Albert. They didn't.

The baron hobbled into the parlor supported by a heavy bone-handled cane, looking more raddled and rheumy-eyed than ever, aged well beyond his years. Lord Hollister's sister gasped when he brushed past her, and held a lace-edged handkerchief to her nose.

"Niminy-piminy female," Albert wheezed, sinking into the most comfortable chair in the room, the one Daphne's mother had just vacated to flee to Lord Hollister's side on the sofa. From his place near the fire, Uncle Albert took out his quizzing glass and surveyed the company, his gaze lingering longest on Daphne. He licked his lips. Lord Hollister's sister drew in another quick breath of air, which in turn drew the most ignoble nobleman's attention.

"What, trying to fix m'interest, are you? Too bad your husband left you as poor as a church mouse, else I'd offer you a tumble, even if you are as shriveled as a prune."

The lady ran from the room, weeping. Her brother, the earl, said, "Here now, Baron, there's no call to be insulting the ladies."

Albert laughed, or wheezed—it was hard to tell which. "Thought I was payin' a compliment. Don't expect the old bat gets many offers these days." Before Lord Hollister could decide on an appropriate response, feeling that planting the decrepit man a facer was beneath his dignity, Albert turned to Graydon. "You, boy. Get me a drink."

"I'll just go see what's keeping the tea tray, shall I?" Lady Whilton hopped up again.

"Sit down, sister. I ain't about to maudle my insides with that catlap. I said I want a drink." He pounded his cane into the floor next to his chair, making the china shepherdesses on the nearby étagère shake, along with Lady Whilton.

Not Cousin Harriet. She headed for the bellpull. "I'll tell Ohlman to bring coffee. That's what you need, you old sot, not any more Blue Ruin."

Albert sneered at her through his looking glass as if she were a cockroach. "What's that Friday-faced old sapphist doing here? Get out, woman. It's my house and I'll drink what I want. Get out, I say."

Harriet stormed to the door. "Don't worry, sirrah, I wouldn't stay under the same roof as you. One of your so-called social diseases might be catching."

"In your dreams, woman, in your dreams."

Cousin Harriet left in a huff as Ohlman entered with the tea cart. Daphne didn't know whether to go after her or stay to comfort her mother, who was sniffling into Lord Hollister's handkerchief. She poured a cup of tea for Mama first.

"Where's my drink, damn it?" Uncle Albert thundered, slamming his cane down again.

Daphne started to ask how he liked his tea, but Graydon, who'd been standing near the mantel, reached for a decanter and poured out a glass. He handed it to the older man, saying, "Here, Baron, some fine brandy. No need to disturb the house." Then he came to stand behind Daphne's chair.

"Why did you give him brandy?" Daphne whispered. "Anyone can see he's had more than enough to drink."

"Yes, but this way he's liable to pass out. Otherwise he'll just get meaner. Trust me, I've seen enough drunks in my day."

Well, she certainly hadn't, so Daphne held her peace while Uncle Albert sloshed down his drink, then rapped the glass on the chair arm for more. To distract him, Daphne said, "Mr. Pomeroy wasn't clear on the details of the robbery. It was a whole band of cutthroats that attacked you and your valet?"

"Aye, a murderous band of road pirates." He turned to growl at Lord Hollister. "And if you blue bloods did your job and took better care of the highways, none of it would have happened, by Jupiter."

No one cared to mention that Albert's blood, what wasn't turned to vinegar, was as blue as anyone's, and as a major landholder, he was equally responsible for seeing to the roads. Daphne just thought to keep him talking until he lost consciousness, as Gray had promised. "I thought Mr. Pomeroy said the attack took place at a low tavern."

"Which I'd never have patronized, missy, if my blasted carriage hadn't lost a wheel to the bloody ruts. So there we were, Terwent and I, stranded at some dingy pub while a grubby urchin went to fetch a blacksmith. Most likely took my coins and left the neighborhood," he muttered, staring at his glass. "Still empty, blister it!"

Graydon poured out another round. Daphne frowned, but he winked at her as he took his position behind her chair with the cup of tea she had prepared for him. "And then?" he prompted. "You and, er, Terwent found yourself at a hedge tavern, you say?"

"Thieves' ken, more like. They must have pegged us for nobs right off."

If the highwaymen figured the two were rich swells, Daphne thought, looking at Uncle Albert's rumpled clothes, spotted linen, and scraggly, unkempt hair, then Terwent must cut quite a dash. He surely wasn't much of a gentleman's gentleman, judging from his master.

Albert was going on: "I had my purse out to pay. Blasted innkeep wanted to see my money before serving the swill he called supper. That's when the band of robbers made their move. Set a big dog on me, they did."

"A dog?" Lady Whilton asked in faint tones. "You were robbed by a dog?"

"No, by George, I foiled their plans. That big ugly hound lunged for my wallet on the table. I was wise to that ploy. Not born yesterday, don't you know. Dog steals a man's purse and runs off, but no one claims the cur, so they get away. Takes a real organized band of felons, I figure. But I stopped 'em dead in their tracks, I did." Albert lifted his glass and toasted his own genius. "I knew which crafty devils had been feeding the beast: an old gaffer who must have been the mastermind, and his two apprentice thieves, one big, the other real small. So when the dog grabbed my lamb chop—"

"A lamb chop? I thought it went for your purse."

"Didn't anyone teach you not to interrupt, gel? Of course, I wasn't going to let any mangy mutt get my blunt. I had that back in my pocket before the landlord could put the dishes down. So the dog grabbed the dinner instead. I demanded my money back, right off, then started laying into that brute of a dog with my cane." He waved the heavy-handled instrument around, in illustration. Graydon hurried to move the oil lamp from the table next to the baron's chair.

"And I was right, for didn't the old codger jump up to defend the flea-hound? So I hit him a good one right across the brain-box. He went down, but then his accomplices waded in, the big one screaming and the little one whining. So I laid into them, too. Left. Right." He waved the cane over his head, left, right, and snagged the lace doily on the back of the chair. It sailed across the room and into the fireplace, where it sizzled into threads in seconds. "Got Terwent a good one, too, sad to say. He should be right as a trivet tomorrow, as soon as the carriage is ready."

"But what about the thieves, Uncle Albert?" Daphne doubted the band of footpads was anything but an innocent party of poor travelers and their hungry dog.

"Got away, of course. Your magistrate didn't show up for hours, either. Couldn't find a trace of 'em, then he tried to say they didn't get away with anything anyway. Surprised the gudgeon can find his way home at night."

Daphne felt she had to defend Miles, perhaps because she could hear Graydon chuckling behind her. How the beast could find anything funny in this situation was beyond her. "Mr. Pomeroy is very conscientious about his position as justice of the peace. He works quite hard at it, as a result of which we have very little crime in the neighborhood."

"Very little of anything else in the neighborhood, either. Deuce take it what you turnips find to do in the country."

Lord Hollister tended to agree with him, but only said, "If you find the rural life so tedious, I wonder why you've left the city at all."

Uncle Albert started wheezing again. Or laughing. No, Daphne thought as the sound went on and on, he was definitely wheezing. She poured him a cup of tea, which he batted out of the way. She sat down again with the cup. She could use it, if he couldn't. When he caught his breath Albert gasped, "The wedding, you gabby. I've come as head of the family to stop the wedding."

Mama cried, "I knew it!" but the earl patted her shoulders.

"Don't be a peagoose, Cleo," he said. "You're of age and need no one's permission. Whilton cannot stop the marriage."

"He cannot even stop a dog from stealing his supper," Graydon murmured into Daphne's ear, which riffled the curls there and tickled. She shifted farther away in the seat, fussing with the pastries on the tray.

"But I can point out you're blighting your children's chances of making a good match, I can. You almost ruined it already, raising 'em up like brother and sister. Took all the spice out of it, if you know what I mean. Of course, there's Byron and his sister. . . . Any road, making 'em brother and sister in fact likely makes it illegal for them to marry anyway."

Suddenly Graydon did not find the situation quite as humorous. "Gammon, we're hardly relations. Besides, with enough money, one can get a dispensation for anything." He bit down on the lemon tart in his hand.

"Mama and Lord Hollister must think of their own happiness, Uncle," Daphne put in, ignoring Gray's rebuttal as mere argumentation. "I am thinking of making a match elsewhere, if it is any of your business."

The rest of Graydon's lemon tart fell to the floor.

"What, that prosy stick who hinted he had an interest here? You'd do better with Hollister's cub, gel. He'll be an earl someday, no matter how wild he is now."

"Wild?" Graydon sputtered on the crumbs in his mouth.

"He's a good, reliable, steady man, for your information, Uncle Albert."

Graydon cleared his throat, but both Albert and Lord Hollister exclaimed, "Howell?"

While the major glared at his father, Daphne answered, "No, Miles Pomeroy, of course."

"Faugh, with a husband like that, you'd be taking lovers in a month."

It was Daphne's turn to glare, at her uncle and at the choking sounds behind her.

"No," Uncle Albert was going on, "you'd do a parcel better with Howell." He ogled her from under his bushy eyebrows, looking her up and down—and inside and out, it felt. "Didn't turn out half bad, for a filly from a weak stable. Too bad you're so prim and proper; you'd make some man a cozy armful. As it is, you'd send him"—with a nod toward Graydon—"back to his mistresses afore the cat can scratch her ear. That little protégée of Harry Wilson's as good as she looked?" he asked the younger man. "Or are you saving your shot for that Bowles widow, like a regular mooncalf?" He slapped his thigh at the witticism, and almost knocked himself out of his seat. "She'll be more expensive in the long run, mark me, boy. And if she does get her claws into you for the gold band, that's the last you'll see of her panting to get between your sheets."

Mama gasped, and Lord Hollister said, "I must protest this frightful conversation, Baron."

"Protest all you want, from the other side of the door. You don't like it here, get out. It's my house, remember. Besides, where the boy makes his bed wouldn't matter if you weren't marrying an old biddy like my sister-in-law, Hollister. Man like you ought to be getting himself a young wife who can give him more sons. The one whelp you've got's bound to get his head blown off; did you think of that? Then where'll you be? Even I've got two boys, the heir and a spare."

"Enough, Baron," Graydon said with enough force to rattle the teacups in their saucers. "We've heard enough of your filth. Now, what did you really come here for? You must have known you couldn't stop the wedding, and I doubt you want to give the happy couple your blessings."

Lord Whilton took a piece of crumpled paper out of his pocket and tossed it on the table in front of him. "This is what I want, my brother's widow's signature. It's a waiver of her widow's benefits, is all."

Daphne and Graydon looked at each other. "But Mama's annuity will cease when she remarries, of course."

"Oh, but m'brother had a crackbrained notion of seeing her married again. She's to get twenty thousand pounds."

"Is that true, Mama?"

"Yes, John didn't want me to stay a widow, and he wanted me to be able to marry a man of modest means, if I wished, without having to live in a cottage."

Uncle Albert grunted. "That's so sweet, I could puke. But you ain't marrying a poor man. You're marrying a regular Golden Ball, so you don't need the blunt. I do, and I aim to have it. I'll sit right here, in m'own parlor, until you sign the thing."

"That's outrageous," Lord Hollister fumed as he waved a vinaigrette under his fiancée's nose. "It's blackmail."

"But you can't do a thing about it, can you? Can't throw a chap out of his own house, Earl."

Graydon was clenching his fists as if he wanted to, very much.

"Try it and I'll gather up those two brats of mine you females dote on and I'll sell them to a chimney sweep. Then you'll have no excuse to be here with your noses in my business."

Daphne spoke up, horrified: "They're your own flesh and blood! Besides, they're too big for sweeps. That's how much attention you've paid them, you awful man, not even to know how big they've grown."

"Awful, eh, missy? Then mayhaps you'd rather I sent them to a flash house. Do you know what they pay for clean young boys, gel, do you? It's not a bad idea, now I think on it. The brats disappear, there's no entail. I get rid of you harpies and I can unload this millstone. Not a bad idea at all."

"Why, you despicable—" Daphne felt a firm hand on her shoulder.

"I'm sure Lady Whilton will think about your suggestions, Baron," Graydon said in a reasonable tone, quite at odds with the grim look on his face. "Why don't you retire after your adventurous day and let her and my father discuss things in private?" He opened the door to find the efficient butler waiting on the other side with two footmen for just such a call. "The baron is going to bed, Ohlman. He might need some assistance up the stairs."

Then again, if he fell and broke his scrawny neck, no one would mind.

Chapter Seven

"Oh, why did that dreadful man have to come here now?" Mama wept in Lord Hollister's arms. Daphne hovered nearby with fresh tea, sherry, and the smelling salts, but the earl seemed to be managing. Daphne looked at the tea, then drank the sherry. Graydon nodded approvingly. He was pouring himself a glass of cognac from the new decanter Ohlman had brought, Uncle Albert having taken the other one with him.

Lady Whilton sat up and dabbed at her eyes. "I cannot imagine how he found out so soon, with the banns just being read last Sunday and no notice in the newspapers yet. I made sure none of my particular friends would gossip, not that they travel in the same circles as Albert." She shuddered to think of those noisome circles, one of whose denizens was right this moment upstairs in the bedchamber adjoining hers. She'd make sure Ohlman checked the locks before she put one foot inside her room. Otherwise she'd sleep with Daphne, or Lord Hollister—

and propriety be damned! "Oh, why did he have to find out before the wedding?" she lamented anew.

The earl cleared his throat. "I'm, ah, afraid I told him, my dear. I called on him at Whilton House before we left. The place is like a stable, Cleo. You'd be embarrassed to own it."

"Well, I don't own it, so the wretch can use the Chippendales for kindling for all I care, as long as he stays away from Hampshire and the boys. But, John, why the dev—uh, whyever did you call on Albert in the first place?"

"Yes, Father," Graydon put in. "Why the deuce did you have to give him notice of the nuptials?"

Lord Hollister wasn't pleased to be the recipient of three sets of condemning stares. "My duty, don't you know," he blustered. The stares did not abate one whit. "I didn't want him thinking we were doing anything havey-cavey. He *is* head of your family, Cleo."

Daphne groaned. Here was another misguided male whose sense of honor outweighed his sense. Couldn't they see that Uncle Albert was a headache, not head of anything?

"Furthermore," Lord Hollister continued, "I wanted to discuss the settlements with him."

"What was there to discuss?" Mama asked. "My widow's pension ends, and I get the twenty thousand pounds dear Whilton set aside for me. He was thinking of my happiness."

"Yes, well, so was I. I felt it wouldn't be right to take your first husband's money along to your second. You wouldn't be comfortable."

"I? I'd be perfectly comfortable taking what's mine, and keeping every shilling I could away from that old goat. He'd only gamble it away, or spend it on other evils too depraved to mention. Why, the monies I've spent on his children and his home alone entitle me to my bequest."

"Well then, *I* wouldn't be comfortable. Dash it, Cleo, a man wants to support his own wife. And I told Whilton that."

"You what? You discussed my income with that gallows-bait, without talking to me first?" Lady Whilton was rigid now, not the limp, weepy female who not a minute before was clinging to the earl for support. "How dare you? That money was not yours to dispose of!"

"Now, now, Cleo," the earl tried to soothe, "you know that a wife's assets become her husband's on marriage anyway. And it's not as if you cannot have anything you want. All of my wealth is at your fingertips."

"Yes, for you to dole out in pin money or paid bills. What if I wanted to do something special with my own money?"

"Like what, dearest? Name it and it's yours."

Lady Whilton was not mollified. "Like give it to Daphne, for one thing."

"But Daphne already has a handsome dowry. It's all in trust where Albert cannot touch it."

"But her husband can. He can gamble or invest unwisely; he can even spend it on his mistresses." She fixed a basilisk eye on Graydon, who was trying to fade into the upholstery, wondering how he got dragged into this domestic quarrel.

"Mama, you know I wouldn't marry a man like that," Daphne put in. "If I wouldn't have Gray . . ."

"Oh, for Heaven's sake," that gentleman started, only to be interrupted by Lady Whilton again.

"No, but you might marry Miles Pomeroy, and

the money would be handy so you didn't have to live with Squire and play nursemaid to him all the time, under his wife's high-handed direction. The woman is a shrew," she said of one of her oldest friends.

"Daffy is not going to marry that prig Pomeroy!" Graydon exploded.

To which Daphne shouted back, "I'll marry whomever I please, Graydon Howell. And Miles is not a prig! He is a fine, upstanding man who doesn't consort with fallen women or fast widows."

"He's a pompous windbag, and you know it! Wasn't it you who dared me to put glue on his seat at church?"

"I was seven years old!"

"And he was fifteen going on forty-five!"

"And you were ten, and a hellion even then. Reckless and foolish and—"

"Children!" Lord Hollister shouted, to be heard above the bickering. "You are acting like infants. Daphne, you may marry where you choose, of course, although I had hoped ... At any rate, you have a fine enough dowry that you can pick for yourself, without needing your mama's twenty thousand."

Daphne had her arms crossed over her chest. "Perhaps I'll choose not to marry anyone at all. I cannot see where there's much joy in it for a woman. Perhaps I'd do better to set up housekeeping in a cottage and take care of Dart and Torry, to keep them out of Uncle Albert's way."

"You see?" Lady Whilton cried. "Now she's talking of never getting wed! And without the marriage, she cannot touch the dowry, no matter how fine it is sitting in the bank. You can be sure Albert will never release it to her even when she turns thirty. Thirty!" she wailed. "My precious girl will dwindle into a down-at-heels old spinster because you gave away my twenty thousand!"

"Gammon, she'll be snapped up within a year, if that prig, ah, Pomeroy doesn't come up to scratch. Besides, she'll always have a home with us, you know, and I'll always support her."

Mama wasn't listening. "My baby will end up on the shelf, and I'll never have grandchildren, all because your wretched son broke her heart!"

"Mama, he didn't!" Daphne shrieked in mortification while Graydon had another glass of wine.

"Balderdash!" Lord Hollister exclaimed. "If Daphne wasn't such a stubborn little prude, they'd be married by now and starting their nursery, and my son wouldn't be off trying to get himself killed."

Mama was sobbing hysterically. She paused to howl, "That's right, tell her she's welcome in your home one minute and call her names the next! Why would Daphne want to live with me, her own mother, when you'll be counting out her allowance and inviting disreputable characters like Albert into our house? Cousin Harriet is right: Men have too much power. That's not what I want for my darling girl, and it's not what I want for me! I don't want to live in your stuffy old house either, so you and your rakehell son can have all the orgies you want!"

While Lord Hollister was shouting that he'd never let Albert cross his doorstep, that he'd always loved Daphne like a daughter, Lady Whilton struggled to pry his engagement ring off her finger.

"No, Mama," Daphne cried, and Lord Hollister yelled, "Don't be a fool, Cleo," at her.

"Fool, is it? You're right! I was a fool to be so blind. Daphne saw it years ago. I was a fool to trust a Howell." The ring was so thick with diamonds and emeralds, she couldn't get a good grip on it. "Even your blasted ring is trying to choke me."

She finally got the ring off and threw it at the earl. Then she grabbed Daphne's arm and dragged her from the room, where Lady Whilton collapsed into Ohlman's waiting arms, to be led upstairs.

Graydon handed the earl a glass of wine. "Orgies, Father? What orgies?"

Graydon proceeded to help his father get drunk. There was not much else to do. Not only hadn't Graydon killed any dragons for Daphne, he'd managed to let slime get all over everyone. Blast his reputation! His case was worse than ever.

"Think she'll see things differently in the morning?" his father asked, staring at the ring in his hand.

Why should she? Her daughter hadn't, not in the morning, not two years later. "Strong-minded woman," was all he could offer.

"Aren't they all?" the powerful Earl of Hollister humbly noted, and his son drank to that.

Graydon wished he could offer his father a smidgen of hope. Oh, how he wished it, both for the governor's sake and his. Deuce take it, Daffy'd never forgive him for contributing to the jeopardy to her mother's happiness. Somehow she'd fix all the blame on him, he just knew it. Besides, if the wedding were off, he and his father would have to leave Woodhill. In fact, he wouldn't be surprised if Ohlman scratched on the door any minute to announce that their bags were packed and their carriage was waiting outside. Daffy must have mellowed some after all, or else she was too busy calming her mother to worry about ejecting the rejected, dejected suitors in the parlor.

If they did have to leave, though, Graydon believed he'd never have another chance. He'd be leaving the pigheaded chit at the mercy of that Pomeroy flat. With Uncle Albert making threatening noises, Daphne might think she needed to marry for protection, for her and her mother and those young cousins. She never listened to reason before; he doubted she'd start now. He could only pray her mother wasn't cut from the same bolt.

"Perhaps an apology is in order?" Graydon suggested.

"Even though I still think I was right, if I thought she'd see me, I'd beg her forgiveness. Me, the Earl of Hollister. Can you believe it?"

"Easily. I've seen stranger things in the name of love. And you did insult her pride and her intelligence, don't you know, by negotiating away her portion without a by-your-leave. If I were you, I'd grovel."

"That's if she agrees to see me. I cannot very well barge into the bedroom of a respectable female and demand she hear me out."

Graydon had seen stranger things than that, too. In fact, he'd been considering undertaking such a maneuver soon, if he couldn't have a private talk with Daffy. Now a private talk was the last thing he wanted, if he had to pay for his father's sins as well as his own recently resurrected failings. What he had to do, and do fast before anyone questioned his presence here, was get this hobble with Albert resolved so his father and Lady Whilton could reach an understanding.

Graydon saw nothing for it but to cut a deal. Having recently come from the battlefront, he was a great proponent of negotiation. What they had to do, as he saw it, was get the old sot to hand over Lady Whilton's twenty thousand pounds. The loose screw would do it, Graydon figured, for a like sum from the earl, under the table, of course. In effect his father would be paying his own bride's dowry, but as long as she didn't know it, she'd be satisfied at having got her money and her own way. The governor might have to up the ante some to win assurances from the bastard baron that there would be no future demands or threats on the boys, but he could afford it. Any price was worth it to see the last of that curst rum touch.

"But that's dishonest," the earl protested after Graydon explained his plan. "It's lying to Cleo, and letting her keep her addlepated notions besides. Women's independence and all that rot. I'm not sure I want to live under the cat's paw."

Graydon picked up the engagement ring from the table in front of his father. "Do you want to live alone the rest of your life?"

After seeing her mother put to bed with a dose of laudanum, Daphne didn't know what to do. She wasn't tired, but she didn't want to face the earl—or his son—again this night. She was sure her mama would reconsider her hasty and impassioned decision in the morning. She just had to, Daphne swore, for Lady Whilton and the earl were meant for each other. Daphne didn't dare go offer Lord Hollister her reassurances, however.

Gracious, she couldn't let difficulties between herself and Gray get between the older couple again. But how to convince her mother of that? By convincing Mama that Graydon hadn't broken her heart, not by half. She'd been disappointed in his character, that was all. With all the recent gossip being confirmed and amplified by Uncle Albert— and not denied by Major Howell, Daphne noted— her assessment had been correct: Graydon was a libertine. Her heart wasn't involved one jot in the decision to jilt him, she told herself firmly, rehearsing what she'd tell her mother in the morning. Not one iota.

Miles would make a much better husband. He'd teach her cousins and her future sons about the land and about honor. Yes, she'd do well to accept Miles's steadfast loyalty. For sure Daphne could never go live with Mama and the earl, not after this upset, not if her presence was going to remind them of their children's brangling. She'd pay them visits, of course, when she knew Graydon was elsewhere. Daphne knew she couldn't stay on here in her childhood home, either, not when awful Uncle Albert was liable to pop in. That left Miles, worthy Miles, who was most likely too high-minded to outsmart that low-blow bounder.

Mama had to marry Lord Hollister, if only to protect the boys from Uncle Albert. She and Cousin Harriet were right: Men did have all the power, and they needed every bit of it to keep her cousins from falling into their father's evil clutches. Daphne didn't think Uncle Albert would go through with his threats to see his sons sold into slavery or whatever, but the threats were bad enough.

She'd have to go to him herself, Daphne decided,

and tell him she didn't want the cursed twenty thousand pounds, that she'd convince Mama to sign the paper if he'd just leave them alone. It would be Daphne's decision and her mother's, not Lord Hollister's. That should please Mama, even if losing the money didn't. One couldn't ask for everything.

Chapter Eight

As she walked from her mother's room to hers, Daphne heard noises coming from Papa's—now Uncle Albert's—bedchamber. The mutters and mumbled curses she would have ignored, but the thumps and thuds sounded ominous. If she called for a footman, she'd likely wake the rest of the house, Cousin Harriet and the earl's sister included, so Daphne decided to investigate herself.

She scratched on the door and softly called: "Uncle Albert, it is I, Daphne. Do you need anything?"

What she heard could have been "Get in here." It also could have been "Get out," but she chose the former, cautiously opening the door a crack, prepared to duck flying missiles. When no boots or books came her way, she edged into the room, leaving the door ajar behind her, just in case.

Uncle Albert was lurching about, his cane neglected, as he tried to open the brandy decanter. His hands were shaking so badly, he could not remove the stopper, and his face was empurpled with his rage and frustration. His breath was coming in short, gasping inhales and long, rasping exhales. He did not look well, even for Uncle Albert.

"Uncle, are you ill? Should I send for the doctor?"

"What, some bloody rustic leech? Wouldn't trust one of your quacks," he panted out. "Terwent'll be here in the morning with my potions and stuff. Not that they do much good anymore." He stumbled closer and thrust the bottle at her. "May as well be of some use, now you're here. Open the blasted thing."

Daphne was undecided, until the baron started waving his arms around, saliva dribbling out of the side of his mouth. Maybe Graydon would prove right after all, Daphne thought, and Uncle would collapse, unconscious, once he'd drunk his fill. For sure he was working himself into an apoplexy this way. She pulled the stopper away from the neck of the crystal decanter and looked around for a glass.

"Here, give me that," the baron snarled, grabbing the bottle and lifting it to his mouth. Daphne could hear his every gulp, and watch his bony Adam's apple bob up and down. He finally lowered the decanter and wiped his lips with the back of his coat sleeve, and belched. "Better," he grunted, and indeed his breathing was more even and his coloring more restored to its usual splotchy flush. He clumped over to the bed and threw himself down, still holding a firm grip on the bottle.

"Should I ring for Ohlman to help you undress, Uncle? You'll be more comfortable without your boots on, I'm sure."

"Wouldn't let that bugger touch me. Or my boots. Terwent'll be here in the morning," he repeated, with another long swig from the bottle.

"Then perhaps a blanket?" He was lying on all of his. The last thing Daphne wanted was for the soused baron to take a chill and have to be nursed here at the Manor. She found a quilt over the back of a chair and brought it closer, hesitating.

"What's the matter, gel? I won't bite. Not enough teeth left, heh-heh." And he began that half laugh, half wheeze again, necessitating another hard swallow of brandy.

Daphne tossed the blanket over him and stepped back quickly, hoping that if the baron was going to fall into oblivion, he'd do it soon, before the brandy was gone and he threw another fit. His eyes seemed to be drifting shut, so she backed away cautiously. Unfortunately her foot hit his dropped cane on the floor, and she squealed as she tried to regain her balance.

Albert's eyes snapped open, and he stared at her wildly, trying to recall her identity. He must have figured it out, for he growled, "What are you doing here anyway, gel? Young chits ain't supposed to be in a man's bedchamber. Didn't your ma teach you that? She sure as hell didn't teach you good sense, whistling a fortune down the wind when you tossed Howell out on his ear. No gel of mine'd be given the choice, I can tell you that. At least m'sister-in-law had the brains to hook the big fish, even if she let the minnow get away. Hollister's as rich as Croesus," he rambled on, eyes going unfocused again. "Doesn't need my blunt. Shouldn't get it. Ain't right."

Daphne decided to take the chance on a rational conversation with her uncle now that he was somewhat subdued. She didn't think he'd be any more open to reasonable discourse tomorrow, when he finally awoke. "That's what I came to discuss, Uncle Albert, Mama's twenty thousand. You know it would cost you less in the long run to give it to her now, than if you had to keep paying out her widow's pension if she never remarried."

"What's a female know about finance? You ain't figuring the interest on the twenty thousand, interest I get to keep. And you ain't figuring that my long run is getting shorter every day. I could have one more good ride on all that brass afore I cash in my chips."

"Yes, well, that's actually what I wanted to talk to you about. And to see to your comfort, of course."

"Of course," he mimicked. "You always cared so much for your dear uncle's well-being, you used to run and hide when I came around. Still would, I warrant, if you didn't want something. What is it, gel? Spit it out, I can't stand mealymouthed chits."

Talking so much made him wheeze again. The level in the bottle was getting dangerously low, so Daphne hurried into speech. "You're right: Mama doesn't need the money, and Lord Hollister feels he'd rather support her himself. She only wanted it for me, it seems, so I wouldn't have to worry about marrying for money. I think I can convince Mama I don't need it."

"What, going to have young Howell after all?"

"No, definitely not."

He pounded the bottle down on the bed, spilling a few drops. "What are you using for brains, girl, pigeon droppings? Fellow's rich and handsome. So what if he's a rake? You look the other way a bit like every other female, and in return you can have anything you want, even get to be a countess one day. Who knows but the jackstraw'll come down heavy for your own dear uncle."

"So that's why you think I should wed Graydon, so you can bleed him dry? Well, think again. I won't."

Albert laughed, which turned into a long gasp for air. When he could speak again, after another swallow, he said, "So it's to be that countrified chowderhead, is it? You'll be sorry, mark my words."

Daphne stood firm. "Your opinion is irrelevant, Uncle. If I marry Miles, my dowry will be sufficient, and he'll still see that I want for nothing."

"Nothing except a little rum-diddly-dum," he said with a snicker. "What you ought to do is bed both of 'em. Then you'd see."

"That's a horrid suggestion, Uncle! As if I ever would do, you know, before marriage!"

"I know, all right. It's that prunes-and-prisms Pomeroy that mightn't." He thought this was so funny, he slapped his knee, unfortunately with the bottle. He doubled over, choking again between cackles. The sniggers came less frequent as the wheezes and ragged inhalations took longer. He did rattle, "Try 'em both, you'll take the rake every time."

To which Daphne replied, "Never!"

Albert fell back on the pillows, the bottle tilted up, but he was gasping too hard to swallow. "Famous . . . last . . . words," he managed to whisper, which turned out to be his. Last words, that is.

"But will you leave if Mama signs the paper relinquishing the money?" Daphne persisted.

Uncle Albert had already left.

"Uncle? Baron? Should I send for the doctor?" In her heart Daphne knew the doctor would be too late, by years. She tried to convince herself, though, that the baron had simply passed out finally. But his chest wasn't rising, wasn't falling, no matter how closely she watched. The hairs in his nose weren't fluttering with every breath. There was no breath, period. Daphne tiptoed closer and lifted the bottle away from Albert's hand, to stop it from dripping on the bed. He let her take it. He must be dead.

"God have mercy," Daphne whispered, her hand to her mouth.

Not on this sinner, He wouldn't. Uncle Albert was dead. He was going to stay dead, and he was going to get deader, if possible, soon, unless Daphne did something, but what? It was too late to send for the vicar, not that a few last-ditch prayers could have gotten this heathen into Heaven.

Mama. Daphne'd go ask her mother—no, Mama was fast asleep and liable to stay that way through half of tomorrow, after taking the laudanum tonight. Besides, she'd only go off into hysterics again.

Ohlman would know what had to be done. Their devoted and organized butler was capable of meeting any challenge. He'd send for the vicar, the undertaker, the lawyer—goodness, little Eldart was baron now!—and the heir. Efficient Ohlman would see to notices in the papers, hatchments for over the doors, refreshments for the funeral guests.

Guests. Wedding guests. "Oh no!" Daphne moaned. The wedding would have to be canceled, whether Mama and Lord Hollister became reconciled or not. The Whiltons would be in mourning, and even if they chose not to wear black for the blackguard, they couldn't very well hold a festive celebration in his own house, with him fresh in the grave. A year, they'd have to wait. Six months at the minimum. The wretched marplot had managed to disrupt the wedding after all, for all the good it did him. The cad couldn't even die without making things difficult for his relations.

If they let him. Perhaps it was reaction to the death, or the wine she'd had during the last crisis downstairs, or just all the tension of the past weeks, but Daphne wasn't ready to concede. There just had to be a way to cheat Uncle Albert of this final victory. Heaven knew he'd cheated often enough in life. With a little time and thought, she'd figure a way to queer his game. And Ohlman must be asleep by now anyway. There was no reason to wake the man—he wasn't getting any younger—or to rouse the whole household, which would be inevitable. No, Uncle Albert would still be dead in the morning. Unless Daphne could come up with a plan.

Somewhere in the back of Daphne's mind was the idea that if she could just get rid of Uncle Albert before anyone found out, and just for the two weeks till the wedding, then the marriage could take place. Mama would be happy, Lord Hollister would be named guardian for Dart and Torry, and Uncle Albert wouldn't be laughing at all of them from the depths of hell.

She'd need help, of course. She couldn't ask the servants to take part in anything so improper, though, no matter how loyal and trustworthy they were, not even Ohlman. That wouldn't be honorable. Pretending Uncle Albert was still alive was. At least it was in a good cause.

The name that kept popping into her thoughts, a

name that, indeed, was rarely out of her thoughts, she refused to consider as a co-conspirator. She would *not* go running to Gray to get her out of a scrape the way she used to do when they were children. This was not like being caught in Farmer Melford's orchard with a pinafore full of apples. Graydon was no relative, not much of a real friend except in her memory. She couldn't even trust his loyalty the way she did her butler's. Ohlman didn't share his devotion and his talents among every other family in the county, not for all the years he'd been employed at Woodhill Manor. He never did; he never would.

Graydon was reckless and daring enough for such a hey-go-mad scheme, that was for sure, but Daphne couldn't ask him. She didn't want to be beholden to him, she told herself. She didn't want to involve him in another possible scandalbroth, and she didn't want him to think her attics were to let. Mostly she didn't want to be alone with him, to ask.

His father was much too much the gentleman for such a venture. Besides, the earl would be too busy mending his fences with Mama. Daphne refused to consider that the wedding plans might be terminated anyway, regardless of Uncle Albert's terminal condition. Cousin Harriet was too outspoken for subterfuge, if she hadn't already packed and left. Which left . . . Miles.

Miles was the justice of the peace. He'd have to be involved one way or the other in his official capacity. The question was, could Daphne ask upright Miles to bend the rules for her? Then again, if she did ask, would he agree? He would if he loved her. He'd see that she wasn't looking to hurt anyone or cheat anyone out of anything, just help her mother find happiness. He doted on his own ailing father, after all. Of course, pushing the man's Bath chair wasn't quite the same as stashing a body and sidestepping statutes, but he was bound to understand, Daphne tried to convince herself. And if he didn't . . .

She wasn't about to take Uncle Albert's outrageous advice about taking Miles and Gray to her bed. That was beyond consideration. On the other hand, a comparison, a test of faithfulness, perhaps, was not a bad idea. She had always insisted she wanted a man she could trust, one whose first loyalty was to her and no other. Graydon had already failed the test. He'd ride *ventre à terre* to her rescue, she knew in her heart, grinning the whole way, but she couldn't trust him. Miles was the most trustworthy soul of her acquaintance, but if he wouldn't stand by her, no matter what, then it didn't matter, not a whit. It wasn't as if she were asking him to put love above honor, not precisely. And it wasn't as if there were any grand passion on either side, either. There had to be some strong foundation for a decent marriage, though, and she thought steadfastness was a good place to start.

Through all her cogitations, Daphne had been straightening the room. She picked up Uncle Albert's cane and put it and his portmanteau on the mattress next to him, then she drew the velvet hangings closed around the bed. Anyone looking into the chamber would think the baron was sleeping, not to be disturbed. They'd think he liked fresh air, too, for Daphne opened the windows and banked the fire. For certain it wouldn't do to let the room get overwarm. She blew out the candles, except for her own, and closed the door firmly behind her.

The house was dark and quiet. The only one who appeared to be stirring was Daphne's maid, quietly mending while she waited to put her mistress to bed. Daphne quickly dismissed her, chiding the woman for thinking she couldn't undress herself, and then asked her to spread the word belowstairs that Baron Whilton was ill and possibly contagious. The doctor would be called in the morning if he did not improve. Meantime, Daphne would see to his needs since she was already exposed. Most important, Daphne emphasized, none of the servants should enter his room until the baron rang. Which would be a long, long time.

Chapter Nine

*O*nly one footman remained on duty late at night at Woodhill Manor. It was his office to make sure the candles were all doused, the fires all extinguished, the windows and doors all locked after the last guest retired. He also got the job of aiding Major Howell in helping the earl up to his room. While he assisted Graydon in supporting Lord Hollister's substantial, stuporous body up the stairs, the servant passed on the information that Lord Whilton was ailing.

"Gammon, castaway is more like it."

"No, milord, Miss Daphne told her maid to inform the staff to stay away in case it's the influenza."

"Bosh, the man is just disguised. Worse than the governor here, I'll warrant."

"Begging your pardon, milord, but Miss Daphne did say as how no one is to go into the baron's room but herself." As if anyone wanted to.

"Devil take it, she already has enough on her

shoulders without worrying about some cad in his cups."

The footman nodded his agreement with that assessment, Miss Daphne being a favorite with the staff, Baron Whilton being the bane of their existence. "Mayhaps it's as you say and his lordship is just above himself. Miss Daphne did say as how the doctor wasn't to be called until tomorrow, if then."

"Then he cannot be that sick. Good."

He couldn't be too sick for a visit, Graydon decided after he put the earl into his valet's competent hands. It wasn't all that late by London standards, and if the baron was suffering from his overindulgence, perhaps Graydon could fetch him a restorative or something. If he did require a doctor, the servants would be only too happy to ignore his bell after Daphne's warning, and wake her up instead. She needed her sleep.

The major didn't fear being struck by anything more than a tossed boot. He'd gone through two years of the army without succumbing to any vile diseases; he wasn't going to get one now. And if Awful Albert wasn't really sick, then Graydon could discuss how much blunt was required to see him gone.

It was extortion, pure and simple. And it had to be paid if Gray's father and Lady Whilton were to make a match. They deserved their chance for happiness, and he, Graydon, deserved two more weeks to try to change Daphne's opinion of himself.

He stood outside the baron's room, listening. Lady Whilton's chambers were next door; he could hear snores from there. Daphne slept a few doors down, but that was too tantalizing a thought for this time of night.

There were no sounds from Albert's room, so Graydon rapped softly at the baron's door. When he still heard nothing, he quietly entered, shielding his candle.

No noises came from the bed, but tarnation, it was no wonder if the man took a chill if he liked to sleep in so cold a room.

The bed-curtains were all drawn, but Graydon decided that since he'd come this far, he had better make sure the old man was all right. He could ride for the doctor himself if necessary, and not disturb Daffy at all.

So he pulled the curtains a bit, thinking that if the tosspot had passed out, there'd be no worry over waking him. In the pale circle of his candle's light, he studied the recumbent figure.

"Lord Whilton? Baron?" Yes, he was passed out, sleeping like the dead. That was too bad, for now conversation and negotiations would have to wait for the morrow. Nothing could be resolved between the governor and his bride.

Just to make sure it was the drink and not a disease that had Albert laid so low, Graydon put a hand to the man's forehead to feel for temperature. The baron had none whatsoever. He was as cold as a stone, and Graydon didn't think it was because the windows were open. He brought his candle closer. Bloody hell, the baron was dead. The major had seen enough death in the war to recognize it.

Gray took a minute to consider the implications. "Thunder and turf," he cursed out loud, knowing there was no chance of waking this sleeper. The implications did not please him. Oh, there'd be no question of Lady Whilton getting her money from the estate now, but there'd be no question of holding the wedding now either. And complications, there'd be a blizzard of them: naming a guardian for the boys, the funeral arrangements, the legal rigmarole. No doubt Daphne would take up the reins as she usually did. She adored her cousins and was devoted to her mother, who had no head for details, as charming and delightful as she was.

And Graydon couldn't even help. Since he was no relation, he couldn't stay on, battening on a house of mourning. Which meant he couldn't show Daphne he was not such a frippery fellow as she thought. But maybe he could do something to help. . . .

He could get Albert out of here and back to London, for his valet to find. Considering the time it might take for the valet to get here, then there, then send a message back here, to which a message would have to be sent back there saying to send the baron back here for burial, perhaps they could hold the wedding after all. Especially if Albert weren't found dead on his back here in the house.

Graydon could say that Lord Whilton had a change of heart and realized his sister-in-law was entitled to the money after all. No one would believe it, or that Albert had a heart to change, but the old rip wouldn't be there to refute anything.

There was no big problem with making a run to London, but not in the middle of the night, and not without telling anyone. They'd have the whole county looking for him, and a fine hobble that would be, getting caught with Albert's corpse. No, Graydon decided he'd have to wait for tomorrow night. He'd have all day to make up excuses for the baron's departure and his own, and to figure a way to get the dead man into his carriage. Meantime, he couldn't just leave him here. Poor Daffy'd come in in the morning and find the blighter. Not a pretty sight. The girl had bottom, but she was a delicate female for all that. She shouldn't be exposed to such dire experiences. Besides, she'd raise a ruckus so there'd be no hiding the facts. Graydon had to hide Albert instead.

It wasn't going to be a pleasant job, but Graydon had done worse in the army. He kept telling himself that he was doing this for Daffy, as he wrapped the baron in the quilt on the bed and slung him over one shoulder. Thank goodness Albert was not a big man. The major needed his other hand for the candle, so he had to leave the man's satchel and cane, and his own cane. He'd manage.

Graydon staggered his way down the endless flight of marble steps, praying that last footman had gone about his rounds, then gone to his bed, and wondering if he'd do better to roll the bastard down. Then he could just dump him in some London back alley. The authorities would assume he'd been beaten and robbed at one of his usual low gaming hells—when they managed to identify him, hopefully after the wedding. No, even Gray's larceny knew some limits. He trudged on. At the bottom he propped the shrouded body against the carved newel post at the foot of the stairs, to rest.

"Couldn't even have the grace to cock up his toes on the ground floor," Graydon mused, then took up his burden again. He lurched down the long corridor to the back of the house, bashing his elbows on the narrower walls while Albert's booted feet kept banging into his legs, especially the wounded thigh, which was throbbing at every step. He put the body down again, to mop his brow, but none too gently this time. The dastard's false teeth fell out. Oh, how Daphne had better appreciate what he was doing for her, Graydon swore as he gingerly picked the ivory chompers up in his handkerchief and stuffed them into Awful Albert's coat pocket.

He slung him over his shoulder again and bent down for the candle. The teeth bit into his collarbone. He grunted and proceeded through the kitchen and down another flight of even more narrow, twistier stairs to the wine cellar.

His leg protesting vehemently, Graydon found Albert a nice, cool resting place behind the well-stocked shelves. "You like it cold?" he asked the corpse, his voice echoing in the silence. "Better enjoy it now, old man, because it's hot where you're going."

Graydon wanted to wipe his sweating forehead and his hands, but his handkerchief was irretrievable. Thank goodness it did not have his monogram. He used his coat sleeve.

Albert would keep until tomorrow, but Graydon still had to go back up all the stairs to bring down the man's satchel and his cane. No one would believe he left without them.

By the time the major was finished, his leg almost buckled under him, even when he used his own cane. It was a marvel that no one in the house, upstairs or down, thought burglars had attacked. He collapsed onto his bed.

He needed a hot soak, but that would mean waking too many servants or carrying cans of water himself. Not tonight. Sleep was a long time coming, though, with that continuous ache. His last thought before he finally drifted off was that not even Daphne was worth this.

No one was having a good night. Of course, no one was having quite as bad a time of it as Uncle Albert, but *bad* was a relative term. Jake of the recently named Lamb Chop Thieves was having a lot of problems with his relatives, too.

The baron's wayside-tavern assailants were formerly called Sal's Fleas, Sal being the ugliest dog in the kingdom, and the smartest. The big tan hound would grab a purse, a parasol, or a parcel, anything of value, although her favorite was lunch pails. The bitch could prig fancy laundry off a line before the maids finished pegging the sheets. She could make off with small merchandise if the shop counters weren't too high, and she could drag away a haunch of beef while the butcher was wrapping Jake's measly sausage. Sal was so smart, and so well known to Bow Street, the Watch, and the shopkeepers, that Jake and his nephews had to leave London for a while.

Jake's nephews were so stupid that when Jake dyed the dog's fur to disguise her, Sailor and Handy were the only ones who couldn't recognize the four-legged felon. They were so inept, they couldn't keep a decrepit old man and his prissy valet from battering Jake's skull with a cane.

Now Jake had a bad headache. He also had no money, no place to sleep, and nothing in his belly. Sal was too smart to share the lamb chop. He also had two fools with nothing in their brain boxes. They were city boys who couldn't start a fire in the woods, couldn't snare a rabbit or tickle a trout. Nor could they be trusted out of Jake's sight without getting lost, since Sailor couldn't remember in which direction the sun rose and set, and Handy couldn't figure out why north wasn't up. It always was on the maps Jake tried to show them. Sal had more brains than the two of them combined.

Jake had always wanted a gang of his own. Some youngsters dream of having a fancy carriage, a yacht, a big house. Jake wanted a gang, a band of cutpurses, pickpockets, highwaymen, all under the command of his master thievery. That's why he took in his sister's two half-grown brats when she ran off with that cardsharp, the bailiffs at their heels. He didn't blame her for leaving; it was a step up for the girl. But Jake should have known she'd have taken the brats with her if they'd been worth tuppence. They weren't.

She'd named her sons after their respective fathers: Hey, Sailor, and Hi, Handsome. Sailor was too big and clumsy to be a pickpocket, and Handy was too weak to run fast enough. Sailor couldn't load a pistol correctly, and Handy was too squeamish to handle a knife. They were just as bad at cutting off ladies' reticules as they were at rolling drunks. Thank goodness for Sal, except that Jake resented being dubbed one of her parasites. It was supposed to be his band of rogues, not a blasted dog's. He'd have hated being part of the Lamb Chop Gang, if he knew that's what the denizens of that rural thieves' den were calling him and the boys. But he'd love the lamb chop.

After the old toff made the barkeep send for the magistrate, there was nothing for it but to take to the woods, Sailor and Handy supporting Jake between them. They were lucky to find an abandoned cottage. Hell, Jake was lucky the boys didn't drop him in a stream to drown. They had to lie low for a while, at least till his head cleared from that knock. He sent Sal out to see if she'd bring back a rabbit or something, or a chicken if they were near a farm. If his luck held, she wouldn't eat the whole thing.

While Jake nursed his broken head in the broken shack, he was plotting, as a clever ringleader was supposed to do. The old codger'd been talking of a wedding hereabouts soon, with earls and baronesses. That meant money. Lots of money. Rich guests would be arriving from London, and so would fancy foodstuffs to serve them and gifts for the newlyweds. With all that coming and going, a downy cove ought to be able to turn this setback into a golden opportunity.

Jake's plan was diabolically clever: it had two parts. One was to get his nevvies hired on as temporary help at that Woodhill Manor where the wedding was to take place. Jake still had a copy of those glowing references from Sir Winfred Prustock, that set him back a bundle from Frankie the Forger. Once inside the house, the lads could wait till nightfall and then hand him out any number of forks and spoons, silver teapots and gold plates, whatever they could carry off and fence. The rig almost worked twice in London, but the first time the incompetent gudgeons were dismissed in an hour. The next time they were put to washing windows, outside. They did manage to steal the rags and buckets.

The wedding wasn't for two weeks, from what Jake picked up at that tavern. Those swells wouldn't be desperate for hired help yet. Meantime, Jake was ready with the second part of his masterstroke: they'd take to the high toby. Jake and the Boys,

Highwaymen. It had a ring to it. And watches, stick-pins, purses.

Jake had a bad headache, and a really bad idea.

While Daphne was discovering the dead baron, Jake and his nephews were back on the main road not too far away from Woodhill Manor, lying in wait. Sailor was sleeping in wait, having been lying so long. Jake kicked him. A coach was coming.

Highwaymen usually had horses and guns. That was the accepted *modus operandi*. Jake was doing it the hard way, on foot, with one battered old pistol between the three of them. Sal stayed in the woods hunting rabbits. The dog was too smart to get involved.

While Graydon was struggling to convey the corpse to the wine cellar, a carriage was nearing the narrow part of the road Jake had selected. They could see by the lanterns on its sides that the coach was big and shiny and prosperous-looking. Jake gave the signal, a whistle. Then he whistled again. Finally he shouted, "Now, you dunderheads!"

"Stand and deliver," boomed Sailor from one side of the roadway.

"Or we'll shoot," squeaked Handy from the other, while Jake stood in the center of the road in front of the oncoming vehicle, brandishing his pistol. Jake let his eyes follow the movements of his nevvies. They were right in position, so the driver would think he was surrounded by highwaymen. A regular band of bridle culls, Jake thought proudly, except that Sailor had forgotten to raise his ker-chief over his round, red-haired, baby face, and Handy was waving a tree branch, leaves and all, instead of the short oak limb that was supposed to look like a pistol. The coach kept coming. The driver whipped up his team. The guard on the seat next to him raised his blunderbuss.

Jake fired his pistol to show he meant business, hitting the coach dead on, taking a big chunk out of the polished woodwork. "Good shootin', Uncle Jake," Sailor yelled when the splinters stopped flying. Now the coachmen knew who they were, and knew Jake's gun was empty. They kept coming.

At the last minute Jake panicked and jumped aside, yelling, "Run, boys," as he dove into the woods. The coach didn't hit him, the wheels didn't run over him, the iron-shod hooves didn't come close, and he rolled down a sudden incline so fast that the blunderbuss missed him by a foot.

Then he struck a rock with his head, which wasn't made out of steel any more than were his nerves.

Now they were wanted in a whole nother county, and Jake had a lot worse headache.

Chapter Ten

$\mathcal{T}$here was no rest for the weary, not at Wood-hill Manor, and no avoiding old flames over the kippers and eggs, not for Daphne. She had a hundred things to do this morning, all of them problematical. Having breakfast with Gray was not high on her list of things to worry about. Making sure none of the servants went in to light Uncle Albert's fire or bring him hot water was.

She'd hardly slept all night, hearing noises that couldn't possibly be there. Her exhausted mind was merely playing tricks on her, she told herself. Uncle Albert was *not* coming back to haunt her; he had *not* been walking the manor house corridors and moaning on the stairs because he hadn't received proper burial. It was too soon.

Daphne didn't bother calling for her maid, but scrambled into an easily fastened dimity round gown and pulled a comb through her curls. No amount of primping by her abigail was going to erase the shadows under her eyes or put color back in Daphne's complexion, and there wasn't time.

Before rushing downstairs, Daphne popped her head into Mama's room. The bed-curtains were still drawn; Mama was still asleep. Next she peeked into Uncle Albert's room, after making sure the hallway was empty. The bed-curtains there were still drawn, too; Uncle Albert was still dead.

Then she had to spend time begging Cousin Harriet to stop her packing and come down to breakfast. Daphne told the older woman that the baron was too sick to be a bother to anyone, and Mama needed her support at such a time. Furthermore, Daphne needed her as a chaperone downstairs in the morning room. She shouldn't be alone with the two male guests. Thus appealed to, Cousin Harriet relented. In truth she didn't have anywhere else to go, Lady Whilton and Daphne being her only relatives, so she didn't need that much persuasion to stay. Her niece's wan face most likely would have been enough, after a hasty review of her own bank statements.

While Cousin Harriet changed out of her traveling costume, Daphne raced down the back stairs to the kitchen, scandalizing Cook and the other servants gathered at the table there by asking for a tray for Uncle Albert. No, she'd carry it herself, Daphne insisted, in case his illness was catching. She'd already been exposed. And no, she did not think a doctor should be sent for yet, but perhaps soon.

Cook fixed a tray of dry toast, thin porridge, and weak tea. Daphne decided her uncle would be too ill to eat much. The toast she could crumble into crumbs for the birds outside the open window, and the tea she could pour onto the lawn, but the gruel had to be returned to the kitchen unless she was to eat it herself. How could she think of eating anything, much less that mush, when her nerves were already gnawing at her insides? Besides, she still had to face breakfast with Graydon and his father.

First she scribbled off a note to Miles Pomeroy, begging him to come at his earliest convenience. The footman she handed it to said he'd get it to the stables instantly. A groom would set out within minutes. Daphne could breathe again. If Miles didn't come, didn't help, didn't have a plan ... Oh dear, and she was supposed to make polite conversation?

No one at the table had much to say. Lord Hollister looked as bad as Uncle Albert, and his son looked worse. They must have stayed up half the night imbibing, like typical males trying to drown their sorrows instead of doing anything about them. At least the earl had an excuse for holding his head in his hands; his son never seemed to need an excuse for overindulging. Now Graydon's fine brown eyes were bloodshot, his complexion was pasty, and his usually laughing mouth was drawn down in a grimace. He even took his time standing when she entered the morning room. Good. She hoped he was suffering for his sins, of which he had many. She had made a good decision, Daphne told herself, to choose Miles—for help with Uncle Albert, that is.

As Daphne pushed some eggs around her plate, she wondered how soon she could expect him, and how soon she could expect Uncle Albert to make his presence, and present condition, known now that the sun was up on a lovely spring day. Even with the windows open and the drapes pulled, the room would grow warm.

No one else made a good meal of it either, except for Cousin Harriet, who ate as if this were her last breakfast. If that old buzzard left his sickbed, she might have to leave the manor. Daphne could not reassure her, not under the present circumstances. She just sent Ohlman out to refill the serving platters.

The butler returned with a fresh pot of coffee, since the gentlemen were making inroads there, at least, and a footman bearing a tray with additional portions of steak and kidneys. He also brought Miles Pomeroy, who was a frequent and welcome enough visitor that strict formality needn't be observed.

"I took the liberty, Miss Daphne—" Ohlman began, only to be interrupted by Daphne's scraping her chair back and leaping to her feet.

"Miles! You came even sooner than I hoped! Thank goodness."

Politeness dictated that Graydon and his father also stand up. Lord Hollister didn't bother. He just groaned and whispered, "Don't shout, girl." The major struggled erect, frowning mightily, both for the aggravation to his leg and the effusive greeting Daffy'd given her local swain.

Daphne recalled herself, and the company, and said, "But we can speak later. Won't you join us for breakfast?"

"Only for a moment, Miss Whilton. Shire business, don't you know." He took a seat next to Daphne, Graydon noticed with annoyance, and Ohlman poured him a cup of the fresh coffee while the footman filled his plate. If he ate all that, Graydon thought, the local pillar of virtue would turn into the local pillow of lard. The fellow was already leaning toward a paunch, Gray noted with satisfaction, as he sucked in his own firm abdomen. Besides, if Pomeroy's errand was so urgent, why was he wasting time, his and Daffy's?

"What is this official business, Pomeroy?" he prompted, hoping to get rid of the fellow with a reminder of his duty. It usually worked with those conscientious blokes.

Miles did put down his fork, but only to drink some coffee. "Another attempted robbery, Major," he said after a moment.

"What, did some poor starving mutt swipe a leg of mutton this time?"

"No, no dog was seen, but a band of ruffians did try to hold up Mr. Foggarty's coach last night. We think it might be the same gang"—Jake's heart would have swelled—"for they were just as bumbling and incompetent." He would have cried.

"Did they get away with anything?" Graydon wanted to know, thinking of his own ride tonight.

"No, Foggarty's guard scared them off with his blunderbuss, and the driver kept on moving."

"How awful," Cousin Harriet declared, watching Miles finish the last rasher of bacon, "that a body is not safe on these country byways. What are you doing about it, young man?"

"I've got men out trying to follow the bandits' paths, but they scattered into the woods. They're most likely long gone by now, but I'm trying to gather descriptions for a wanted poster. Strangers aren't all that frequent in the neighborhood. Two of the men wore masks, but the driver can identify the third robber. I want to see if his description matches Lord Whilton's of those footpads at the tavern with the dog."

"You want to see Uncle Albert?" Daphne asked in a faint voice. She had to get him aside first. "That's, ah, too bad. He's ill. You can't—"

"What Miss Whilton means is that you cannot see the baron because he already left," Graydon interrupted.

Daphne dropped her spoon. "He did?"

"Yes, I was about to tell you before Mr. Pomeroy arrived. The baron felt a bit better, but wished to consult his own London physician. Rather than wait here for his valet, he decided to ride to meet him on the road back, saving time. He left before the household was fully awake and entrusted me with his good-byes."

"Dash it, I must have just missed him!" Miles tossed his napkin on the table.

"To ... to London, you say?" Daphne asked. At Graydon's nod, she put her own cloth down and stood. "Will you gentlemen excuse me for just a minute? I, ah, forgot something upstairs."

The men could hear her soft slippers scampering down the hall. Miles frowned. Miss Whilton shouldn't be running in the house that way, although he'd naturally not mention it in front of her relatives. He'd take her aside later. A little whisper in her ear should do it, unless she was rushing to get back to his company. His brow cleared at the thought and he was able to take another helping of shirred eggs. With the baron gone, there was no need for him to rush off in an ill-mannered frenzy.

Daphne tore up the stairs and raced down the

corridor. The last thing she was worried over was being thought a hoyden. None of the servants were about, so she dove into Uncle Albert's room and pulled open the bedhangings. Uncle Albert was gone.

To London? Daphne sank back on the bed where the baron had recently expired, she thought. There wasn't even a crease on the cover. Could she have been wrong, or was it all just a bad dream? Perhaps the oysters she ate last night had gone off. No, he'd been there, gasping and wheezing, then neither wheezing nor gasping. He was dead. She knew it. Could God have wasted a miracle on such a sinner? She didn't think it was likely. But Uncle Albert was gone.

She went back to the breakfast room, a great deal slower. The men stood until she resumed her seat, Graydon scowling. Daphne didn't notice. Miles did and thought the major was going to scold Daphne for her manners. Frippery fellow had no business calling Miss Whilton to account, had no business being here at all, if anyone asked his opinion, which they hadn't. But then, the lady had seemed happy enough to welcome him this morning, even effusive. "Had you wanted to see me over anything particular, my dear?" he asked, preparing to leave.

"What's that? Oh, no, just a detail about the wedding or something." She waved him away, leaving the butler to walk him to the door.

Yes, Miss Whilton's manners were sadly lacking. Of course, Mama could take her in hand.

Graydon felt better, seeing Daphne's absent-minded dismissal of her stalwart suitor. Now, if he could just get rid of everyone else, he might have her to himself for the morning. He suggested his father go up and start trying to make his peace with Lady Whilton. "Now that the baron is gone, there is no problem about that money. She doesn't have to sign anything to get rid of the dirty dish. So go tell her the twenty thousand is as good as hers, for goodness' sake, to do with as she wants."

"I don't know . . ." the earl began.

"What, are you afraid she's going to take the blunt and run off with some stable hand after you're wed? You have to know she's devoted to you. Besides, the money means nothing to you, and means a great deal to her."

"No, I meant I didn't know if she'd see me. I decided last night to swallow my pride, but she won't talk to me. I tried again first thing this morning."

"What, in her bedroom?" gasped Cousin Harriet, who was already irritated that young Howell could so cavalierly dismiss a sum of money she'd never see in her lifetime.

The earl gave her a sour look. "Never fear, her maid wouldn't let me in." He vowed to dismiss the hatchet-faced abigail as soon as he could, and find someplace else for this sharp-tongued cousin to reside. Maybe Cleo would give *her* the blasted twenty thousand pounds so she could set up her own establishment—in Ireland.

Daphne had been ignoring the conversation, but now she explained: "Mama was sleeping. She took laudanum." Then she went back to concentrating on the muffin she was shredding.

"You see? She didn't slam the door in your face. She'll see you soon, I'm sure. And you can turn on the Howell charm so the banns can be called Sunday."

"That vaunted charm didn't work for you, you silver-tongued devil," Harriet sniped as she left the breakfast room to fetch her pug for its morning walk.

Daphne was still not paying attention. She didn't even hear Graydon say he had an urgent task in London, that he might leave later that afternoon, or early the next morning. He'd return in a day or so, if anyone had any errands for him.

"I say, Daffy, I asked if you had any commissions in London for me."

"Commissions? I thought you were resigning yours."

Graydon shook his head at her vagueness. She didn't show a great deal more interest in him than she did in the Pomeroy popinjay. Deuce take the female, she was supposed to be relieved now that Albert was out of her hair. Perversely, she was drifting out the door, her brow furrowed with worry, her linen napkin still clutched in one dainty hand.

The earl left to camp outside his lady's door. Graydon decided not to follow Daphne while she was in this humor. Whatever charm he did possess would be wasted. He went to the stables instead, to notify the grooms he'd be leaving soon, and to see how hard it would be to get Albert into his carriage. The short walk convinced him he'd better go back upstairs and rest his leg before facing that ordeal. He didn't want Daphne to think him a paltry, whiny milksop, so he snuck in the kitchen entrance and requested a hot bath. Then he hobbled up the back stairs. Lud knew he was familiar enough with the route by now.

Daphne went about her business mechanically. She consulted with the housekeeper about the menus, tallied wedding invitation acceptances with the master guest list, and counted the flower tubs in the conservatory, all in a daze.

There was only one answer her reeling mind could come up with, an answer so unlikely that a miracle had better odds. Now, of course, the infuriating officer couldn't be found. Daphne knew Gray had gone out to the stables, she'd seen him head that way, limping badly, the clunch. He must be off on a long ride instead of resting his leg, and then he was leaving for a time. She shook her head.

Ohlman the butler was also shaking his head. He knew what he knew, and what he didn't know, he could find out. That was a butler's job. He knew the baron's hat and gloves were still on a shelf in the cloakroom where he'd put them himself. He knew Lord Whilton's bed hadn't been slept in. Ohlman checked: No carriage had been called out, no horse was missing, no carter had come by that morning. It was a definite puzzlement.

Ohlman wouldn't put it past that scamp Howell to have abducted the baron and spirited him away. Master Graydon had been a naughty little boy, a brash young man, and now a decidedly quixotic gentleman. Ohlman had hoped he was settled down enough for Miss Daphne, but if the handsome devil was still getting up to these mad starts . . .

But what was the point to abducting the baron? The dastard was still head of the family, to Ohlman's continued disgust and dismay. He shook his head and continued his chores.

One of those butler's duties was counting the bottles of champagne in the wine cellar to see if more was needed for the wedding, if there was to be a wedding. Ohlman prayed so, for he dearly loved his mistress, who kept him from having Awful Albert as a master. He'd been here at Woodhill Manor since she came as a bride, and he'd do anything to see her happy, her and Miss Daphne, of course.

And of course he found the baron, satchel and all. So the blackguard really was leaving, without any assistance of Lord Howell's, it seemed. Albert was obviously trying to pilfer some bottles from his brother's stock before he went. He'd even brought a quilt with him to keep the bottles from clinking. He must have got cold, though, taking a spasm or something, for he had the quilt wrapped around his shoulders. The villain never had time to lift one bottle. He never called for a coach because he never made it up the stairs.

But the family believed he'd left. They believed it enough to proceed with the wedding, without Albert's wretched interference. Ohlman knew what he knew, and he knew what had to be done to see his ladies happy. That was a butler's job. The question was if he was strong enough, and if the baron could bend enough. The rotter never bent when he was alive.

An hour later, Ohlman sent two strong footmen down to the wine cellar to move a huge cask of ale into the icehouse. The brew mightn't stay good till the wedding otherwise, he explained. There were bucketfuls to be sampled, to test the quality, so the lads were happy enough to comply. Albert didn't complain either.

Chapter Eleven

$\mathcal{G}$raydon knew his way around Woodhill Manor, thank goodness. Having run tame there forever, and having played innumerable games of hide-and-go-seek with Daffy on rainy days, he knew all of the old place's ins and outs. One of those ins, or outs, used to be a door between the wine cellar and the service drive outside.

After a hot soak and a rest, therefore, Graydon went downstairs to reconnoiter, wandering through the pantry to the indoor entrance to the cellars. He found himself explaining his presence there to Cook, two helpers, and the pot boy, all looking at him curiously.

"Just checking to see if there is any special vintage I can pick up in London for the wedding celebrations. Something they mightn't have, don't you know."

Cook and the others knew Ohlman had spent an hour down there this very morning, checking the stock for the coming occasion. She shrugged and ordered her minions back to work. Cook didn't know what deviltry Master Graydon was up to now; she didn't want to know. She banged a few pots and pans as he lit the candle at the head of the cellar steps.

If he remembered correctly, the stairs to the outside door were along the opposite wall to the one he was on, and halfway back. The doorway was installed so large deliveries or huge barrels didn't have to be carried through the kitchens and wrestled down the narrow stairs. Yes, there it was, bolted from the inside. His luck was in that there was no padlock or key. All he had to do was draw the bolt now, bring his carriage around after dark, load up his burden, and be off.

He decided to bring that burden closer to the door, to save time later. He wouldn't want to keep his horses standing unattended any longer than necessary. Too, his leg would be less troublesome if he did the carrying in shorter segments.

Graydon carefully unlocked the door, in case there was someone about on the other side. Trust Ohlman to have even this exit so well oiled there wasn't the slightest squeak. He could only pray Ohlman wouldn't be around to check the lock today. Next Graydon retraced his steps down the stairs and back to the racks where he'd stashed the baron. Then he retraced his steps again to the racks in the other direction. And back. He ran to the other steps, the ones that led up to the kitchens, to reorient himself. He'd gone straight back last night, then right. No, maybe he'd gone left. Then again, maybe carrying the baron made the distance seem longer. He checked every narrow aisle, behind, under, and alongside every rack.

Unless there was another wine cellar altogether, Awful Albert was altogether missing. And Graydon's leg was throbbing again from tromping around the cold, damp, dirt floors.

He sat himself down on an upturned barrel to think about this new twist.

Jake would have been happy for a barrel or anything else to keep him off the cold, damp, dirt floor of the old cottage. But they'd burned the last stick of furniture in the place yesterday, just to cook a rabbit Sal brought in. Jake had set some snares last evening, but Sailor couldn't find them, and Handy couldn't bring himself to dispatch the trapped game anyway.

His head wrapped in a dirty bandage, Jake started to explain his new plan. The boys liked the old one better, where they'd go get positions at the manor house. They'd have dry beds instead of a pile of straw on the floor, and hot meals instead of the dog's leavings. Jake tried again for the fourth time, which was all right, because he was seeing two of each of them.

They couldn't go up to a nob's house looking like they were living off the land, he told them. No one was going to hire a down-at-heels vagabond to polish the silver. The servants might give them a bowl of soup, looking the way they did, but that was all. That was enough for Sailor and Handy.

"Then what about tomorrow and the next day, you misbegotten moth-brains?"

There were other big houses, weren't there? Sailor and Handy saw nothing wrong with making a living asking for positions but accepting handouts. They didn't even have to do any work that way.

They also couldn't provide for their poor old uncle, who cuffed Sailor along the head. "My way, we won't have to work for a long time neither, not none of us. We'll be on easy street with one quick job."

All they needed before approaching Woodhill Manor for that wedding was a stake. Clean clothes, a wash, a shave for Sailor, a haircut for Handy. Then they could even rent horses to make their getaway, Jake elaborated, forgetting that neither of his nephews had ever been on a horse. They'd never been footmen before, either, he said, brushing off their complaints. They just wouldn't make as fast a getaway, he reassured the boys, knowing that once they'd handed the sacks of booty to him through a window, he didn't care if they escaped or not. He'd be too long gone to know. Blood might be thicker than water, but it sure as hell wasn't as thick as the gold from melted-down candlesticks.

His new plan involved the rusty old saw he'd spotted in the back of the cottage. They'd lop a tree down right at that narrow part of the road, so carriages would have to stop. None of this getting mowed down by a fast-moving coach. When the guard got down to move the obstruction, Jake would aim his pistol at him, while the boys relieved the passengers of their valuables.

The plan was so simple, it had to work, if Sailor and Handy weren't simpler. They couldn't find the narrow part of the road, then they couldn't find an appropriate tree. They finally found a half-dead birch leaning against some others that seemed to fit the bill. If they could just push it hard enough, it might topple far enough into the road that they could drag it the rest of the way or roll it.

While they were preparing, Jake came walking down the road to see what was keeping the bacon-brained idiots. Two carriages had gone by and there'd be another any time now.

"One . . ."

"What the deuce is taking you nodcocks so long?"

"Two . . ."

"It doesn't have to be a big—"

"Push!"

"—tree—eeyee."

The birch tree didn't hit Jake. He jumped out of its way just in time. He did catch his foot on a protruding root, though, twisting the ankle so badly that he fell over, into a growth of stinging nettles that went right through his clothes but didn't manage to cushion his fall enough to keep his head from contacting yet another rock.

The boys dragged Jake back to the cottage, once they found it.

The next coach did come by shortly, but it was no grand equipage, which would have made Jake's regrets less, if he were conscious to appreciate the fact. The carriage, in fact, did not even have a guard or groom. It merely had one dour driver and one prissy passenger, Terwent, the baron's valet.

The driver refused to leave his cattle, smelling a trap. Terwent refused to leave the carriage, scenting hard work. So they sat there arguing long enough for seven gangs of cutthroats to steal the baron's baggage. Luckily a farmer came by in his empty wagon first, anxious to get to the bank to deposit the earnings from his successful sale. He kicked the birch aside as if it were a twig, spat on the ground, flicked the reins over his mules, and patted the heavy purse tucked into his shirt. Poor Jake. He'd have gone after the wrong vehicle anyway.

A dank wine cellar wasn't a great place to rest a wounded leg, but it was a fine place to think of ghosts and ghouls and dead bodies coming to life to haunt their tormentors, if one were of a gothicy turn of mind. Graydon wasn't. Unlike Daphne, he never once considered the metaphysical, miracle or mirage. No, he immediately figured that someone—not one of the servants, who would have caused an uproar at finding a cadaver between the Chablis and the claret—had made off with the baron's corpse. For sure Albert hadn't gone to seek better accommodations on his own.

Graydon knew that plenty of people in the house might have wished to see the baron disappear; in fact, he couldn't think of a single person who would weep at the wastrel's funeral. He could, however, think of only one resident of Woodhill Manor with enough daring and drive to do something about it. He slapped his thigh, then winced. But she was still his Daffy. They hadn't drained the pluck out of her after all, in making her a perfect lady.

Then Graydon thought some more, and was less pleased with the results of his cogitations. She couldn't have done it alone, moved Albert out of here and up one set of stairs or the other, to wherever she had him hidden. She must have had help, but who? Deuce take it, that must have been why she was so eager to see that Pomeroy twit.

How dare she turn to someone else in time of need?

It was Graydon who'd fished her out of Ryder's pond that time before she drowned. (He chose to disremember that it was he who let her tag along on an illicit swimming trip.) And it was he who dragged her off the back of that stallion to safety when the horse took exception to a hare breaking cover. He did not forget that she was on a horse too strong for her to handle—his horse, in fact—because he'd given in to her teasing to let her ride the brute. He'd never forget the lesson, that Daffy had more bottom than brains sometimes, and had to be protected from danger, from distress, and from her own often disastrous impulses. He'd made a mull of things in the past, but he was trying now. It was his job, looking after her. Let Pomeroy watch out for the rest of the county.

Which Pomeroy was doing, Graydon was sure. Miles had left after breakfast without a private parley with Daffy, without even a fond farewell. The conscientious clod was out looking for a pack of sneak thieves, not a hidey-hole for a dead nobleman. He'd been on horseback besides; the baron wasn't riding pillion.

If not Pomeroy, then who had helped Daffy, and why, and what the hell was she planning on doing with Uncle Albert?

"I? What have *I* done with him? What have *you* done with him, rather."

They were alone in the conservatory, except for a gardener shuffling about at the potting table in the corner. This wasn't how Graydon had planned on being alone with Daphne for the first time, but now wasn't the time for what he had in mind anyway.

"What do you mean what have I done with him?" he asked now, watching her clip withered blooms off a rosebush. "You didn't move him?"

She stopped clipping to look over her shoulder to make sure the gardener was out of hearing range. "Move him where?"

"How the devil should I know where! He's not where I put him."

"Aha! I knew you must have had something to do with—" Then his words penetrated. "He's not . . . ?"

"He's not in the wine cellar. Where did you leave him?"

"In his bedchamber, where he wheezed himself to death making nasty remarks." She shuddered.

Graydon wanted to take her in his arms but couldn't, not with the gardener present. Besides, she still seemed as prickly as the rosebush. "Poor puss," was all he said. "I didn't know you knew he was dead when I moved him. I hoped to save you from that, at least."

"Well, thank you, I suppose, although I lost two years off my life when I discovered him gone. What did you intend to do with him anyway?"

"Take him to Whilton House in London for his valet to find. I thought it might take long enough that the wedding could take place before the funeral."

She nodded. "That was my hope, too."

"By leaving him in his bed?"

"Of course not. I'm not that much a peagoose, Major. I simply hadn't figured it out yet. I was waiting to ask Miles—"

"Blast it, Daffy, how could you turn to that pompous jackass when I'm right here?"

She was cutting furiously at the plant now, half-live blossoms as well as the faded ones. "How was I supposed to know you'd help me?"

"You should have known, by Jupiter! I have always pulled your chestnuts from the fire."

"That was ages ago. We're not the same people. I have no reason to trust you the same way now." And plenty of reasons not to, she implied, turning her back to him, attacking a different bush.

That hurt. And he had no answer except his word on it: "You can."

The discussion had grown too personal for Daphne's peace of mind. She wasn't ready for this. Changing the somber mood, she turned back and taunted, "Certainly I can, after you've gone and lost Uncle Albert. Highly trustworthy, sir."

Graydon smiled. "A hit, Daffy, a palpable hit. But I insist he's not lost, just temporarily misplaced. We have to assume Ohlman knows where."

Daphne nodded. "Ohlman knows everything. I'll go ask him before luncheon."

"*We*'ll go ask him. I'm in this, too, sweetheart. I have to prove my reliability, don't I?" He reached out to pick a rose, to tuck in her curls, but she must have guessed his intention, for she swatted his hand away from the bush.

"Don't, we need them for the wedding," she said, as if she hadn't been decapitating the flowers and buds.

"So you think there will be a wedding after all? If so, there must be hope that the Whilton ladies have some forgiveness in them."

"Mama will do what's right for Mama," Daphne

stated firmly. "But yes, I think there will be a wedding in two weeks' time. If we are not all arrested for body-snatching."

Chapter Twelve

$\mathcal{T}$he noontime meal consisted of cold chicken, cold beef, and a cold shoulder from Lady Whilton. She had consented to join the family for luncheon; she had not yet forgiven the earl. She wasn't ready to forgive his toplofty treatment of her, despite his seeming sincerity. He hadn't groveled enough, in her estimation, to ensure there would be no repetition of such despotism in the future. She did thaw a bit when she realized he wasn't just trying to coax her out of the megrims by saying Albert wouldn't bother them anymore.

"You mean the baron has really gone back to London?" she asked the company at large. Cousin Harriet shrugged, but Daphne nodded vigorously.

It was Graydon who replied: "That was my understanding of his destination, ma'am, but perhaps his plans changed. Your estimable butler might have additional information. Have you anything to add, Ohlman?"

Daphne watched as Ohlman straightened from

serving the earl's sister some pigeon pie. She saw that Graydon had none too subtly laid his finger alongside his nose, signaling the butler of his comprehension and connivance.

Ohlman cleared his throat. "Such was my understanding, ma'am, that the, ah, master was feeling poorly. Quite ill, indeed, and in something of a rush to be gone. You might say he was dead set on leaving us."

Daphne hid her face behind a napkin. Graydon winked at her. Ohlman continued: "Of course, I have no way of knowing if he reached his final destination of London as of yet, but I doubt it. However, I can assure you, madam, that he is definitely no longer in the house."

Graydon nodded and Daphne smiled at Ohlman, who continued serving the meal and directing the footmen. The old butler could only wonder if at least and at last these two recalcitrant lovers had reconciled, so in harmony did they seem.

Ohlman found out to the contrary later, to his disappointment, when they met after luncheon in the small butler's pantry to make plans for the evening. Ohlman would see that the servants were all busy close to the house, if Miss Daphne would ensure none of the guests chose to take an evening stroll.

"But I'm coming with you," she declared.

To which Lord Howell replied, "Oh, no, you're not, brat. You are staying inside."

Daphne stamped her foot. "Don't start giving orders, Major. You are not in the army anymore."

"And I've never turned a raw recruit over my

knee, so don't tempt me. You're to keep as far away from the icehouse as possible, for your own good."

"Now you're sounding as patronizing as your father, thinking you know what's best for everyone else. Don't you Howell men ever learn?"

"And don't you Whilton women ever use the brains God gave a duck to see what's in your best interest?"

Ohlman cleared his throat.

Daphne took a deep breath. "Don't be a cake, Gray. You'll need help. You and Ohlman cannot manage Uncle Albert and the horses and the icehouse doors, and keep watch, too."

"I'll have my groom."

"What? You might as well publish Uncle's death in the newspapers!"

"Nonsense, the man knows better than to gossip. Besides, I'll just say I'm carrying a load of bad ale back to London to complain to the shippers. Doing Ohlman here a favor."

"No one will believe such a Banbury tale, the dashing Major Howell playing errand boy."

"Thank you for the 'dashing,' my dear, I think. But they're more liable to believe that than they'll believe you just innocently happened near the icehouse in the middle of the night! Be reasonable, Daff; your reputation will be in shreds."

Daphne knew he was right; the icehouse was nowhere near the gardens. "That's Miss Whilton to you, Major."

"And that bird won't fly, brat, so stubble it. Save your airs for Moral Miles. You can't be a lady and a grave robber both."

"And I can't be a grave robber, if that's what it is, sitting in the parlor with my embroidery."

They all knew she'd be at the icehouse after dark. Graydon should have saved his breath to convince the baron's valet.

Terwent arrived midafternoon, insulted over his treatment at the hands of the bumbling footpads, bovine farmers, and insolent coachmen. Nor did he think the bandage tied around his head, from where it had connected with the baron's flailing cane, did much for his appearance. He was wrong, it did; the wide swath of white cloth hid some of the pinch-faced valet's resemblance to a dyspeptic dachshund.

Terwent refused to believe that his master wasn't at Woodhill Manor. That was the ultimate indignity. He'd had to suffer some rustic quack's ministrations, then a night in a hedge tavern sleeping on unaired, and likely unwashed, sheets, and a morning in a rattling coach going nowhere fast. And he had it all to do again in reverse, to find his missing master.

"No, the baron would not have left without me," Terwent insisted. "He distinctly ordered me to arrive here as soon as possible before he drove off with that bumpkin."

"That bumpkin is Miss Whilton's devoted friend and hopeful suitor," Graydon interjected with a touch of deviltry that brought a charming blush to Daphne's cheeks and a splotch of something else altogether to the valet's pasty complexion. They were in the butler's pantry again, which was becoming more and more crowded. Ohlman had sent for the major when the valet refused to be dislodged, recalling Master Graydon's facile tongue and easy disregard for the truth. Daphne had naturally followed, scenting more intrigue. Graydon was paying her back for snooping.

"Pardon, I'm sure, miss," Terwent stammered. "But, but, I have his lordship's medicines. He'd never go on without them. Or me."

"But he didn't, old chap." Graydon placed his arm across the valet's chicken-narrow shoulders and started herding him toward the front door. "He just tried to get to you sooner, to save you part of a wasted journey."

"But how could I have missed him then?"

"Who knows? We're not precisely sure who took him up. Perhaps they took a back road, or were in a closed carriage."

The valet was confused. He hadn't seen any carriages at all, just the farmer's wagon.

"It's possible he stopped in the village first," Daphne suggested, seeing the indecision in Terwent's beady eyes. "The Golden Crown serves a tolerable punch, I've always heard. The baron did like his, ah, refreshments, you know."

Terwent knew all too well. He was afraid the baron was lying in some field right now, passed out among something unmentionable but common in uncivilized rural areas, something for Terwent to try to remove from his clothing tomorrow. The valet wrinkled his long, thin nose.

"No," Graydon reflected. "I think he went straight to that low tavern where you were accosted and forced to spend the night. He was that worried about your health."

That was pitching it too rum, Graydon realized. The baron's being concerned with anyone else's well-being or comfort was as likely as him traipsing cross-country through the cow chips, or staying at the village inn when he owned the whole of Woodhill Manor.

The valet's eyes narrowed—from beady to slits—as Daphne, Graydon, and Ohlman watched him cogitate. They could almost hear the wheels spin. Terwent didn't know what to think, except that the two nobs and the oldster in the wig were mighty eager to see him gone. There was some huggermugger afoot here, or his name wasn't Versey Terwent, which it wasn't, but he wasn't going to confess his forged references now.

So what game were they playing, and was the baron in on it? Terwent wouldn't put it past the old sot to shab off on him, owing his back salary and all. But Terwent had the luggage. The baron had to know Terwent would sell everything he could, and ditch all those potions and elixirs that were going to keep the dissipated drunkard virile, he thought. No, there was something deuced odd here. He was even more sure when Major Howell tossed him two golden boys, for expenses, until he found the baron.

In general, Terwent was not at all devoted to his employer, just to his salary, when he got it. Meantime, it was not an arduous job, since the baron didn't change his clothes that often, and there was hardly any bathwater to lug around. He paid well when the dibs were in tune, which wasn't often of late, but Terwent always managed to find the odd coin or two in the baron's pockets when the old man was in his cups. Besides, other positions were hard to come by. With the baron as referent, they'd be just about impossible. Then, too, Lord Whilton clearly had one foot in the grave, despite all the nostrums in the kingdom. Terwent would have helped him lift the other foot, if he thought the baron had made the changes in his will the old rip had promised.

Meantime he had to find him. It sure as hell didn't look like this bunch was going to join in the search. What did they care that the baron was wandering around the wilds of Hampshire somewhere, cold, lost, hungry—and holding Terwent's back salary?

No one thought to put a lock on the icehouse door. There was a heavy bolt to keep children out and away from danger, but who would steal ice?

Sailor and Handy, that's who. Of course, they did not know it was an icehouse when they found a low door set into a rock arch near a pool, toward the edge of the woods. They were looking for the traps Jake had set, while he lay back at the cottage, alternately moaning from the pain to his foot, cursing from the sting of the nettles, or unconscious from the new blow to his head. The boys thought he'd be happier if they could find something to eat besides the stale bread and rabbit stew. He'd be happier yet if they could find something worth stealing.

The brothers were astounded to find a door so far from any sign of habitation. Country folk were different, but this was passing strange.

They watched from the woods for a good long while, waiting to see if anyone came or went. No one did, so Sailor pushed Handy out from under the concealing bushes. "Go knock."

"Why me?"

" 'Cause I'm bigger." What he meant was that

he'd box his little brother's ears if Handy didn't do the dirty work.

Handy scampered over to the low wooden door, rapped twice, then scampered back to Sailor's side. "No one home."

So they looked around some more, and listened to birds singing and Sal splashing in the pond. Then they approached the door. Handy kept looking over his shoulder while Sailor took a minute to figure out the latch. The cold breath of air that hit his face had Handy back in the woods before the ghost could say "Boo." Sailor went in, seeming to be swallowed up by the hill of dirt. He came out and beckoned to his brother. "Not even a pat of butter keepin' cold. Nothin' but ice, slabs what must've come from the pond in winter. And this big barrel what smells like ale."

So they took the barrel. Sailor slung it over his back and hunched toward the woods. Handy stole the ice, or as much as he could get into his hat and Sailor's hat.

They returned to the crumpled cottage and packed the ice around the still-sleeping Jake, around his swollen ankle, under his broken head, and on the angry red welts from the nettles. Uncle Jake was going to feel a lot better when he woke up, they were positive. Uncle Jake was going to have pneumonia when he woke up, his clothes sopping wet, his whole body chilled. But that was later.

First the boys were going to sample the ale.

Oh, boy.

Handy keeled right over, right on top of Jake's good ankle, which wasn't going to be so good after this.

Some time later, they sat in the cottage again, shaking their heads over the strange country ways.

"D'you think they do all their dead 'uns this way, like pickles?"

Handy giggled. "An' put their gin in coffins?"

They had found the baron's ivory-topped cane and his satchel that held a clean shirt and fresh cravat, a nightshirt, and a silver flask of Blue Ruin. Uncle Jake needed the cane. He could use the neckcloth to tie up his head, and the nightshirt in strips to bind his ankle. The silver flask he'd sell for food—but he wasn't getting the whiskey.

If Jake were awake, he'd recognize what a valuable commodity they had on their hands. A dead nobleman was worth something to someone, especially to those folks who were keeping him on ice instead of giving him a proper burial. But Jake wasn't awake, and his nephews weren't about to spend the night with a baron in a barrel.

"His spirit's comin' to haunt us already," Handy swore, hearing a nightjar call.

"Our blood'll be sucked dry by morning, you wait'n see." Sailor was already pale, his freckles standing out like ink spots, or blood spatters. "He must be a vampire. That's why he's not in a church graveyard or nothin'."

Handy shivered. "No, I say he comes back as a demon what steals our souls 'cause we stole his barrel. Or else he wanders forever, wailin' 'cause he ain't got a comfortable restin' place, all scrunched up in that keg."

"Think we got to bury him?"

"Not me. I ain't touchin' him. You're bigger."

They decided to take him back, to let whoever put him in the icehouse suffer the consequences.

They'd return him, barrel and all, as soon as the silver flask was empty. Maybe they better wait for Jake to wake up, or for dark.

Chapter Thirteen

"*B*loody hell! Not again!"

They were out by the icehouse after dinner. Lady Whilton wouldn't hear of Graydon setting forth for London after dark, especially with highwaymen in the neighborhood, so she moved dinner forward an hour. The earl had taken his son aside and begged, "Not that you've ever heeded my words, boy, but this isn't the time to be kicking up a lark. I don't know why you think you have to go haring off to the city, but if it's to stir up any more scandalbroth, please wait till after the wedding."

Graydon was able to assure his father that such was not his intention.

"Good, because if Cleo gets wind of your tomcatting, she'll have my hide. Insult to the chit, don't you know, even if you have no intentions there. Staying at the house and all."

"Don't worry, Daphne knows exactly why I'm going to Town, and she approves heartily."

His father smiled knowingly and bobbed his

head. "A surprise for the wedding, eh? That's aces, then."

A kegful of corpse would certainly be a surprise. Getting Albert packed off to London was definitely something for the wedding, so Graydon saw no reason to disabuse the governor of his happy surmises.

"Glad to see you two on better terms," the earl continued. "Make things easier for me with the gel's mother. Speaking of Cleo, could you stop in at Rundell's for me and buy her a trinket? I've got diamonds for the wedding, but might be she'd come out of the boughs a little quicker with a gift. You'll know what kind of gewgaw, something sincere."

Graydon agreed, eager to be on his way before the governor thought of any other errands. He didn't want to be in London when Albert's body was found. But his father wasn't finished: "Wouldn't do yourself any harm to get Daphne some frippery or other either, but that's neither here nor there. You never did take my advice," he complained, still angry that his son and heir had joined the army against his wishes. "You could never do better than the chit."

"I just might listen this time," Graydon said as he saw his father take his place at the whist table with Lady Whilton, Cousin Harriet, and his aunt Sondra. "And you take my advice," he whispered in the earl's ear. "Let her win."

Then Graydon had gone out to the stables to collect his curricle and pair. He gave some excuse not to take his groom after all, for the barrel had to be tied on behind where the servant would have stood. Unless they decanted Uncle Albert and laid him along the floorboards, which was Daphne's suggestion. Buy her some folderol indeed! That chit wouldn't be happy with rubies. Nothing less than his arrest would do!

She was waiting out there with Ohlman when Graydon drove around to the icehouse, blankets and ropes in her hands. She put them down to go to his horses' heads, crooning softly to the well-mannered pair. At least she was a competent co-conspirator, his Daffy. And she looked adorable in some dark-colored cloak, the hood sliding back from her golden curls, like a fairy nymph in an ineffective disguise.

Ohlman was holding a lantern. While he unbolted the icehouse door he reported that the servants were all indoors celebrating the prenuptials with the ale that had been in the barrel, before the baron. They would be too busy in the next two weeks for much belowstairs festivities, the butler had explained to the staff, and no one had argued.

So the baron's pallbearers and hearse were ready. The baron wasn't.

Daphne laughed. There wasn't much else to do, and the look on Gray's handsome face was priceless. Ohlman frowned, relatched the icehouse door, bowed, and made his stately way back toward the house in search of something a bit more sustaining than the ale in the kitchen.

"Thunder and turf." Coming around to the horses' heads, Graydon cursed again. Daphne laughed again, and he had to join in, so absurd was the situation. "Where the devil do you think he's gone to now?" he asked when they stopped chuckling. Neither, of course, had any answer, so the major piled the ropes and stuff onto his curricle. When he lifted the old blankets, he couldn't resist asking: "Care for a picnic by moonlight, sweetheart?"

To which his ever-romantical darling replied: "Don't be a clunch." But he noticed that she did clamber up into his carriage quickly enough for the ride to the stables, rather than walking back to the house by herself. Graydon wanted to tell himself that it was his company she sought. He rather suspected it was Uncle Albert's she was avoiding.

Miles Pomeroy was waiting for Daphne when they returned to the drawing room. He was waiting none too patiently, judging from how he was swatting his gloves against his thigh, Ohlman not having been on duty by the door to relieve him of those articles. The two older ladies were rapt in a hand of piquet, and Lord Hollister had finally got Lady Whilton to grant him a private conversation on the sofa across the room. They were all ignoring Pomeroy's presence, having grown accustomed to his frequent after-dinner visits. Not so Major Howell.

"What, back again, Pomeroy?" Graydon asked as he escorted Daphne to a seat near the fireplace. "Crime wave over for the day?"

Miles looked on the major with equal disfavor, noting the highly polished boots, the intricate cravat, the well-starched shirt collars of the dandified Town rake. "They told me you were leaving for London."

Cousin Harriet raised her eyes from the cards. "Thought you left already on some urgent business. Daphne said she was going to see you out."

"Yes, but one of my horses came up lame. I decided to wait for morning after all."

The major lied with an ease that had Daphne impressed at his ready ingenuity, and horrified at his lack of conscience. The man must make a habit out

129

of prevarication, so readily did rappers fall from his lips. Uttering the slightest falsehood always had Daphne nearly stuttering, as now, when she saw Miles observing her wet slippers and damp hem.

"I, ah, went with him to the stables to, ah, look at the horse, too." Knowing how conscientious Miles was with his own cattle, although they were nowhere near the high-steppers Graydon drove, she added, "The horse seemed to be fine." That at least was the truth.

If he wasn't satisfied with what these two had been doing together for so long, Miles did not get the chance to complain, for Ohlman brought the tea tray in then. Daphne invited Miles to stay, of course; he accepted, of course.

Deuce take it, Graydon thought, didn't the fellow ever eat at his own table? Then again, he looked like he ate two of every meal. Pomeroy would soon look like a turnip if he wasn't careful, besides acting like one. What could Daffy see in the gapeseed?

Daphne saw a comfortable country gentleman who didn't like subterfuge, who disdained pretense, and who wasn't so puffed up with his own conceit that he spent more time with his tailor than with his tenants. With simple sandy hair turning to gray and hazel eyes, he wasn't stunningly handsome like Gray, but he was attractive in a pleasant, friendly way. If he was perhaps more solemn than she could have wished, well, he took his responsibilities seriously, unlike others she could name who almost broke their fathers' hearts by hieing off to war.

Mostly what she saw, as she looked from Miles to Graydon and back again, was that they were glaring at each other like two dogs with one bone. As ridiculous as it seemed, Gray, who could never be happy with just one woman, was jealous. It was ridiculous, and delicious. Let him see what it was like to share someone's affections, she thought with satisfaction, and smiled.

Graydon saw that smile and thought it was for puff-belly Pomeroy. He took his tea, sweetened just the way he liked it, and moved over by his father. Graydon took the opportunity of Lady Whilton's passing cups and plates to whisper that, with the London jaunt off, the governor would have to do his own wooing, without counting on buying the lady's favor.

The earl jerked his head toward where Miles hovered over Daphne and the raspberry tarts. "And you'd better look to your own interests, son."

Graydon did love raspberry tarts, but he didn't think that was what the governor had in mind. Still, he casually strolled back toward Daphne and Pomeroy. The female relations had gone to bed, and the earl and the baroness were resuming their conversation at the other side of the room.

Graydon dragged his chair closer to Daphne's. "What brings you out so late, Pomeroy?" he asked, hinting at the other's ill manners in calling after dark.

"Oh, Miles knows he's always welcome," Daphne chirped, revenge being as sweet as one of Cook's tarts.

But Miles insisted he was here on duty. "Some of us don't get to lounge by the fireside all night," he sniped.

"And some of us earned the right to some peace, at Salamanca," Graydon shot right back.

Daphne intervened. "There are many ways to

serve one's country. But tell us, Miles, are you still looking for those footpads?"

"No. I mean yes, but that blasted—pardon, Miss Daphne—that valet of Lord Whilton's has been pestering me all day. The fellow was at the Golden Crown claiming the baron must have met with foul play, and demanding I make an investigation."

"And you listened to a valet?" the major asked.

"Deuce take it, the man showed me all the baron's pills and potions. He swore the baron couldn't live two days without them."

He couldn't live one day without them, it seemed, but Daphne wasn't going to tell Miles that. Gray was no help, suddenly finding great interest in selecting another pastry. "Did Terwent go back to that hedge tavern where he was staying? Uncle Albert might have returned there looking for him."

"Yes, and he looked all through town and everywhere between. He says no one's seen hide nor hair of the baron. You have to admit they'd recognize him hereabouts."

"And if they didn't, they'd remember him," she agreed. Uncle Albert certainly made an impression.

"Terwent claims no one here could tell him who drove the baron away or who saddled a horse for him. He even suggested the man might never have left the Manor."

"Oh, he left, all right." Graydon wiped a crumb from his breeches.

Daphne said, "You know what Uncle Albert was like. Why would we keep him?"

" 'Was'? What do you mean, 'was'?"

Graydon jumped in. "She means the day you

brought him here. He was castaway and in a snit. We were all of us glad to see him leave." Not as glad as Graydon'd be to see this parsonlike Pomeroy leave.

"Then who took him, and where?" Miles demanded.

"Oh dear." Daphne just couldn't do it. She couldn't weave a story out of whole cloth, not to poor Miles, who never swerved from the truth, no matter how unpalatable. "I think we have to talk."

"Devil take it, Miss Daphne, we are talking."

"No, I mean really talk."

Graydon was frowning and shaking his head. "It's not at all necessary."

But it was, to Daphne. She couldn't lie to the man she was thinking of marrying. "Excuse us a moment please, Miles." She pulled on the major's coat sleeve until he rose with her and walked over to the window alcove. "We have to tell him. He's going to be looking for Uncle Albert anyway. Now he'll help us find him."

"But then what? He'll blast his find from the church steps."

"No, he won't. Miles is loyal and trustworthy and helpful," she insisted.

"Devil a bit, Daffy, if that's what you want, get a dog, for goodness' sake! Don't get porridge-head Pomeroy involved in this."

"Don't call him names, don't call me Daffy, and don't tell me what to do! You haven't been a whole lot of help in this situation, Major Missing-bodies, and Miles is my friend."

"Then go ahead and tell him, and wait for your friend to clap us all in gaol."

While Graydon was still seething, Daphne did

just that; she told Miles about Uncle Albert. She didn't have long to wait.

"You did what?" Miles shouted.

Daphne tried to shush him, looking toward her mother, while Major Howell grinned. Pomeroy's face had gone all red, and his cheeks puffed out. "That's criminal," he screamed, but in a hoarse whisper. "It's against the law!"

"What law?" Graydon wanted to know.

"There must be a hundred statutes about reporting dead bodies! I'd have to check my books. Lud, people'd be burying their grandmothers in the backyard rather than pay funeral costs." He took a deep swallow of tea. "Tarnation, Daphne, Miss Whilton, how the deuce could you think to keep it a secret?"

"Graydon and I thought it was more important to hold the wedding, for our parents' sakes." She nodded again toward the older couple, sitting closer together than they had been.

Miles didn't like that partnership, not the earl and Lady Whilton, but that "Graydon and I." He didn't like to think of his future bride—for so he was wont to think of Daphne—intriguing with that hey-go-mad Howell. "Well, you can't do it," he therefore stated. "As an officer of the law, I insist you declare him legally dead. I can fill out the forms. Then you must see him properly buried."

"That's just the problem, Miles. We can't bury him. We can't even find him."

Miles spilled his tea. Graydon helpfully handed over his own napkin. "Yes, someone stole the corpse on us," he offered. "Likely for ransom."

Pomeroy ignored him and glared at Daphne. "You

see? Do you see what your interfering with the law has done? Lies only lead to more lies, crimes to more crimes." He angrily swiped at the damp patch in his lap. "And you never did say what the baron died of."

Daphne was taken aback. "What, do you think I killed him?"

Now Miles turned his ire on Graydon. "I honestly don't know what to think anymore. That you could be involved in such hugger-mugger ... and an ex-soldier. Everyone knows how cheap they hold life."

"No, everyone knows how precious they consider it, having been so close to death," Graydon responded furiously, restrained from contradicting his own words only by the lack of his sword at his side. "And that old makebait died because his heart finally shriveled up out of meanness."

"No, Gray, he died because he couldn't breathe right. He was wheezing something terrible when I went to see him. I do think I may have killed him after all."

"Don't be a goose, Daffy. You heard how many powders and prescriptions he took. He stuck his spoon in the wall after fifty or sixty years of dissolution. And last night he was as drunk as a—"

"Lord?" Miles put in, from his position in the landed gentry, and from seeing this handsome titled devil rush to Miss Whilton's defense.

Daphne was oblivious to them both. "But he mightn't have died right then if I hadn't argued with him again about the twenty thousand pounds."

Pomeroy's ears perked up. "What twenty thousand pounds?"

"The money Papa set aside for my mother, in

case she married and her widow's annuity ended. Mama's dowry, I suppose. Lord Hollister didn't approve, but Mama wanted the money for me, it seems."

"For you?" That widow's wedding was growing more important to Pomeroy by the minute. The major groaned as he saw the light of greed shine in Pomeroy's eyes. Poor Daphne, and she thought the dastard loved her. At least maybe Pomeroy would be more cooperative about keeping Whilton's death quiet now.

"So what will you do?" Graydon asked, bringing Pomeroy's attention back to the present and away from a town house in London, a racing phaeton, a box at the opera, and a yacht.

"Do? Oh, yes. I'll have to look for the baron, of course, as that Terwent character requested." He tried to make light of his defection. "Can't leave a body littering the countryside, don't you know. I suppose I'll have to look for the extortionists, too, once you get a ransom notice. If I find him, the corpse, I mean, I'll have to make the death public. But if I don't, there's no one else to say if he's dead or alive, right?"

"Ohlman knows," Daphne told him, ever truthful. "But he won't tell anyone."

"Then it's a matter of *habeas corpus*. No body, no, ah, need for a death certificate and all that."

Daphne smiled. "Thank you, Miles; I knew I could count on you to understand."

Graydon almost choked on his tea. Love might be blind, but was Daffy so enamored that she was deaf and dumb besides? He couldn't believe she'd lost all her wits—to this puff-guts.

Then she reached over and patted Pomeroy's hand and put the last raspberry tart on his plate. Hell and damnation!

Chapter Fourteen

Jake woke with a smile on his face. His pants were damp; his youth was coming back. No, he was just wet. He looked up through the holes in the cottage roof and saw stars. It wasn't even raining. He remembered a tree falling on him, or near enough as made no difference, the way he felt. Those nimwit nevvies of his must have dragged him through a streambed before taking him home, if the abandoned shack could be so called. It was a wonder he didn't catch his death from the dowsing, whatever the dunderheads had done to him. Then he sneezed, coughed, shivered, and stopped wondering.

One good thing about the country: when the furniture was gone, you could still find something to burn. Jake hobbled to the stack of kindling he'd made the boys find yesterday, and threw some on the crumbling stone hearth. The fireplace might give off more smoke than heat, but it was something. He hobbled back to his pile of wet blankets to drag them closer to the miserly flames. Damn if both his legs didn't feel broke. One was wrapped in something, the other wasn't, and his cloth-head kin were nowhere in sight. He coughed some more. The smoke was worse than usual.

When his eyes cleared, he spotted a bundle of something in the corner, so he lurched in that direction. His eyes filled with tears of joy—or smoke. The boys had managed to steal something after all. On their own, after years of his lessons and lectures, they'd made a haul. Not a big haul, true, and they might even now be rotting in gaol for their crimes, but they'd done just right: they'd brought the booty to Uncle Jake. They were finally as smart as the dog Sal.

The satchel was of good quality, he could tell even in the dim light. Leather, with brass catches. Someone would pay something for it. Next to it was a silver flask, engraved, but with no initials, thank goodness. It would fetch a handsome penny, too. Too bad it was empty. And too bad he wasn't in London.

The rotten thing about the country was, there was so much of it, with nothing in between. Jake knew he couldn't try fencing this stuff in the local village so close to the crime, even if there was a pawnshop, which he doubted, and the next town was a good five miles away. He couldn't just walk to the corner and hail a hackney, either. In London he'd have traded these items for a heavy wet, a hearty meal, and a bit of jingle that could keep him till the next opportunity. Now all he could do was try to inhale fumes from the flask and keep looking.

Behind the suitcase was a cane, one whose

carved bone handle Jake recognized well. He should. There was a matching indentation in his head. So his gang of geniuses had managed to lift that old bastard's poke. Well, well, well. Jake hoped they bashed his head in while they were doing it, but his confidence in Sailor and Handy was not quite that high.

Either way, that old bugger was a flash cove with a carriage of his own and a valet, so there must be a fortune in the bag. There wasn't. Jake dumped the contents on the floor. No wallet, no jewels, no bank books or important papers. Nothing but linen. His addlepated relatives had robbed a well-heeled toff, and come up with his underwear!

Unless, Jake mused, there had indeed been a roll of soft that the boys had made off with, abandoning him here. He knew that's what *he* would have done. Jake rubbed his sweaty brow, thinking. He thought that he was too cold to sweat. The fire wasn't that hot; he was feverish. If they didn't come back, he was like to die here. Then again, with their level of competence, he was like to die if they did come back, only quicker.

Meanwhile he pawed through the stuff from the satchel. Shirts, hose—and a white flannel night-shirt that was the softest thing he'd touched since that French whore when the dibs were in tune, a long, long time ago. He quickly shed his damp garments and put on the long, flowing gown, marveling at its warmth and clean smell and feel of luxury. He used the cane to limp closer to the fire, almost crying with the pleasure.

That's how the boys found him when they returned from restoring the barrel: a white-robed figure standing in the smoke, moaning and waving the dead man's cane around.

"He's back!" Handy shrieked. "I knew he'd come back to haunt us!" He fainted again, this time missing his uncle.

Sailor didn't, when he keeled over.

"He's back," Ohlman whispered into Graydon's ear as the butler poured his coffee at breakfast the following morning.

"Who, that nincompoop Pomeroy?"

"No, the baron."

Graydon took a quick swallow, burning his tongue. "Well," he said loudly enough for the others present, "it looks like I'll be off for London after all. The horses are fine."

Neither his father nor Lady Whilton was down for breakfast yet, although it was Sunday and the banns were to be read in church today unless Lady Whilton sent word to cancel them. Major Howell's announcement was received with disinterest from his aunt and Cousin Harriet, but Daphne sat up straighter. She looked tired, as though she hadn't slept well for worrying, but pleased now.

"Do you have to leave before church? I know you don't care about not traveling on a Sunday, but Mama would be happier."

"I thought I might wait until dusk again, since it bids to be a clear night." And since he'd rather not be seen with an ale keg instead of a tiger up behind him.

Ohlman cleared his throat. "If I might suggest an earlier departure, my lord. The, ah, barometer is falling. I'm afraid there will be some, ah, deterioration in the, ah, weather."

Agh. Graydon made a face at the butler's none too subtle hints about the baron's condition. He pushed his plate away, having lost all appetite.

Daphne was anxious enough to see him gone now that she understood. "Yes, the sooner you leave, the less traffic there will be. You'll make better time. Unfortunately you'll miss Mr. Pomeroy"—please, Lord—"for he usually takes luncheon with us on Sundays."

"And any other day," Cousin Harriet added, making Graydon smile again. He even took a bite of salmon.

Daphne was impatient with him to finish his breakfast and leave. "Miles will soon be out looking for—"

"His breakfast? I'm surprised the chap isn't here now, or are we not in good odor with him?" Graydon teased, knowing she'd understand how some of them were not in good odor at all. Devil a bit, if he was going to drive the hearse, he may as well get the pleasure of seeing Daffy's dimples one last time. And if he could make Pomeroy appear the glutton, so much the better.

Daphne was starting to give him a setdown when Cousin Harriet pokered up. "What's that? The Whiltons not good enough for a mere country squire?"

"No, no, Cousin, that's not what Major Howell meant to imply. It better not be," she muttered under her breath. If she weren't ages out of the schoolroom, she'd stick her tongue out at him, insufferable man, teasing at a time like this. And picking on poor Miles, who was only trying to do his job. "Miles is just busy these days. There seems to be a rash of crimes."

Cousin Harriet went back to her hearty meal. "That figures, with Awful Albert in the vicinity. Rashes, fluxes, the pox. I wouldn't be surprised if that man brought plagues and locusts to the neighborhood."

Flies, perhaps, Graydon thought. "Yes, well, I had better be going."

They met again at the icehouse for a hasty conference. Daphne felt somewhat like one of Macbeth's witches out in the mist plotting their spells, eye of newt, tongue of bat, potted peer. Graydon had to be on his way before the family left for church and before the sun was much higher in the sky, but they had to rethink their plans.

It was too chancy for Graydon to be smuggling Uncle Albert into the baron's own town house by the light of day, or even after dark if any neighbors were about. The major might have done it sooner, carried the baron home as though he'd found him drunk somewhere. No one would question such a common event in Uncle Albert's life. But not even Gray could get away with such a thing now, and even if he did, no one would believe the baron had died a natural death, finding him in a barrel. Or bent over double. Ohlman was of the opinion that Uncle Albert might not straighten out again for three or four days, if ever. The very last thing they needed was a murder inquiry.

"So what now?" Daphne asked. "It's too bad we can't toss him overboard like a burial at sea. But we cannot just dump him on the side of the road. Miles would have a fit."

"And it matters what Miles thinks?" Graydon wasn't teasing anymore, but Daphne ignored his

143

lowered brow. He had no right to ask such a personal question, and she did not want to think about her answer.

"It matters if Miles finds Uncle Albert under a bush somewhere. Besides, it would be wrong. I mean, hiding him for a while is one thing; never getting him into the family plot is another. Oh, I wish we'd never got into this!"

"What about the wedding, then? I thought you believed your mother's happiness depended on delaying the baron's official demise."

Daphne swallowed her fears. "I did. I do."

Ohlman nodded approvingly and opened the icehouse door.

While Graydon and Ohlman struggled with the cask, his lordship went on: "Besides, you make it sound like we've sunk into a life of crime. You've been listening to Prosy Pomeroy too long, my girl. Buck up, I have a better idea."

Ohlman allowed as how Major Howell's strategy might work. Daphne thought Gray was so brilliant, he should be running the war effort instead of Wellington. She almost threw her arms around him in excitement and relief, but she caught herself before she embarrassed both of them. They were not on such familiar terms, not by half, and she had to keep it that way. He was doing this for his father's benefit, Daphne reminded herself. And he was still an unprincipled libertine. Uncle Albert secured to the back, Gray stole a quick kiss before he climbed into his curricle, proving her point. She wished him a sincere Godspeed anyway.

After the major left, Daphne waited for her mother to come down, feeling that she really had to discuss recent events with Mama. Lady Whilton

144

ought to be informed about Uncle Albert and their plans for him—especially since the plans couldn't be changed now whether she approved or not. Otherwise Daphne was as guilty as Lord Hollister of going behind Mama's back, even if Lady Whilton had been flat on that same back in bed, in her laudanum-induced stupor.

When her mother did not come down, Daphne went up to her mother's room. They were going to be late for church soon, and then she'd have to wait for later to have a private conversation, after Miles had come and gone.

Before she reached Mama's room, she saw Lord Hollister coming out of that selfsame door, in a burgundy velvet robe and slippers. Daphne ducked quickly back to her own room before he spotted her, spotting him. No, she could never make her home with those two. At least Lord Hollister's presence in the family wing resolved one question: the wedding was on, the banns were going to be called, whether Mama was ready or not.

Daphne didn't suppose Mama was ready to discuss her unlamented and uninterred brother-in-law either.

"Ashes to ashes, dust to dust." Ah, Daphne thought, if the vicar only knew . . .

Miles came for lunch after church, as he usually did. Graydon's innuendos taking effect, Daphne started thinking how Miles most often appeared at mealtime. Yes, he was a trifle pouchy near the jowls, but he was fit, not flabby, although he did have to loosen a waistcoat button after a Cook's excellent vol-au-vents.

Miles was just a good trencherman, Daphne told

145

herself, and he was older than Gray. That made it harder to keep trim, she understood, no matter how active the man was. Furthermore, Miles was too busy for the idle exercises of the town bucks, boxing and such. She shook herself to stop making excuses for her country neighbor. Miles was an upstanding man, a conscientious landlord, a suitor to be proud of even if he was no Bond Street beau. And he was understanding, too. He'd better be, because she had to tell him about Uncle Albert so he'd call off the search.

Chapter Fifteen

Sometimes a good meal can make bad news more palatable. Not this time. Daphne's confession that, not only had they recovered Uncle Albert without notifying the local magistrate, but they'd already removed the evidence, did not sit well atop mulligatawny soup, eels in aspic, fricassee of lamb, and custard pudding.

She had no trouble getting Miles alone after the meal, the two older ladies retiring for naps, and Mama and the earl retiring for heaven knew what. Mama was so distracted, she didn't even question her daughter's unchaperoned state. Of course, Daphne was no schoolroom miss, and Miles was too decent to take advantage; everyone knew that. Not even proper Ohlman blinked twice when Daphne suggested a walk in the gardens after nuncheon.

Daphne hated to do it, cut up this good man's peace in such a way, but she saw no alternative. He couldn't be permitted to waste his days searching haystacks for a needle that was safely found. Waiting to tell Miles until after Graydon was long gone seemed even worse, more devious than the act of moving Uncle Albert in the first place. At least she felt more guilty about using Miles in this shady way. It did not bode well for the open, trusting, mutually respectful relationship she craved. Instead it smacked of manipulation, of managing him for her own ends rather than considering his wishes.

Right now Miles was wishing for his usual midday nap. He was also wishing he'd never laid his eyes and his hopes on Miss Daphne Whilton. She was a fetching piece, all right, in peach muslin with trailing ribbons, and her dowry was considerable and her connections were impeccable. Married to a baron's daughter, b'gosh. He never thought to rise so high. And if this proposed wedding came off, he could be the next thing to son-in-law to an earl.

On the other hand, he might be caught up in a horrid scandal, forced to resign his cherished post as magistrate, humiliated before his friends and neighbors. His father would suffer a relapse; his mother would go into a decline. Miles looked at Daphne and saw, not the poised and polished lady who captivated half of London, but the hobbledehoy urchin who used to follow Graydon Howell around, falling into one scrape after another. Now she was dragging him into her mingle-mangles, too.

Miles prized his reputation and his position, especially since he lived in a neighborhood of wealthy aristocrats. Usually the office of justice of the peace went to the richest landlord, the highest title. The Earl of Hollister could have been magistrate for the asking, but he preferred city life and national politics. Daphne's father had in fact held the local laws in his capable hands before Miles's father the squire took over at his death. Thank heavens the recent baron had shown no interest in presiding at shire affairs.

Miles did, and he did the job well. His even-handedness was well known, his diligence was commended by peer and peasant alike. His precinct was almost devoid of crime until this recent spate of chickens missing from yards, hams pilfered from smokehouses—and dead bodies. Now his honor, his impartiality, was severely compromised.

He didn't see the glorious spring day or the budding flowers; he saw his consequence crumbling into dust.

"You have placed me in a deucedly awkward position, Miss Whilton."

"Yes, sir, I realize that, and I truly would not have had there been any choice. I felt that keeping you in the dark was somehow worse."

Sometimes the darkness was a comforting place. "Worse? What could be worse than obstructing justice? Don't you realize that all of you could be clapped in gaol for this ill-advised prank?"

"Prank? I assure you, sir, this was no prank. And I do not believe any crime was committed, whose solution could be obstructed." Daphne was getting annoyed now, that Miles was being so unrelentingly stiff. Uncle Albert wasn't this rigid. She marched back and forth in front of Miles, as if her agitation could make him understand. "We merely removed my uncle's remains to prepare them for burial."

"You purposely hid a dead body, for heaven's sake!" Miles found himself shouting. He could envision his hopeful future with Miss Whilton and her dowry going the way of his reputation, so he tried to moderate his tones and his temper. "That is, you thought you were acting for the best, I'm sure."

Daphne stopped her pacing and sank down on a bench under a lilac bush. "No one was hurt, Miles, and it's done. Give over, do. You are not to blame; you knew nothing about it. And the only one who could possibly care is that weasel Terwent."

Miles was trying to let himself be convinced, he really was. He sat beside her on the bench, thinking. "I suppose a family does have the right to select a mortician. But London?"

"No one does cremations in the country."

He groaned. "And why the deuce did the baron have to be cremated if there was nothing to hide, like a bullet wound or a broken neck? The gossipmongers will surely have a party over that one."

Daphne was well primed. "He was cremated because we were afraid of disease. My uncle was ailing, you know. The doctors were not certain of the cause. Cremation is the safest precaution in these cases."

"Fine, but why are you not telling anyone else, if this is all so aboveboard?"

"Because we don't want the boys to hear about their father's death secondhand," she replied promptly.

"The boys? Your cousins?" Miles was incredulous. "You're the only one who remembers that Albert was their father. I doubt they care one way or the other, if they even recognize him."

"Still, it's only proper they be notified first. Eldart will be baron now. That has to be monumental, and we do not wish him to be besieged by hangers-on until his guardianship is legalized."

Miles took time to wonder about that guardianship. A minor baron with vast resources ... and Daphne his closest relative if one discounted her mother, who'd be in London with the earl. "I suppose that might wash, excusing the delay, that is. When do you propose telling the heir?"

"As soon as the boys get here next week. They've already left school with their tutor, en route home for the wedding, you see, so we decided there was no rush. Cremation cannot be done overnight, you know."

He didn't. He didn't suppose cremating a body would take the two weeks until that wedding either, but somehow suspected it would, with Howell pulling the strings. "That's all well and good to tell the children, but what about Terwent? The fellow is dashed persistent."

"If he calls again, I'll direct him to London. I'm sure Uncle Albert is there by now."

"And when he doesn't find his employer there, he'll go straight to Bow Street. Those chaps aren't going to be nearly as easy to convince as I am."

Miles hadn't been easy at all. Daphne could feel a damp spot on the back of her gown. She turned to pick a stem of lilacs. She took a deep, calming breath of the fragrance. She hoped they'd last until the wedding. "Bow Street will understand that the baron's family did not see the need to consult a servant about the disposition of his body."

"But there wasn't any body," Miles persisted. "How are you going to explain how the baron got to London, Miss Whilton, and how come that jackanapes Howell delivered him to the mortician?"

Gray might be a jackanapes, but Daphne reserved the right to call him that for herself. "Graydon Howell has been a friend of the family forever, sir, and I'll beg you to remember that. If he heard rumors while he was in London on business that the baron had been taken ill somewhere, of course he would lend what assistance he could. As for how and when and where and why, that is no one's business." Daphne was proud. Cousin Harriet couldn't have done better in depressing pretensions. Of course, Miles was correct—he usually was, in his prosy way—there could be embarrassing questions. Gray had given his assurance that he'd take care of everything, so she could only pray he was right. He usually was, too, as in his pointing out that Miles was developing considerable *embonpoint*. Unless her starchy suitor was wearing two sets of clothes, he was gaining weight. "And isn't it time you stopped calling me Miss Whilton, Miles?"

Not when she stuck her nose in the air like a duchess, it wasn't. If Daphne wasn't happy with her suitor at this moment, he wasn't happy with her, either. "It wouldn't be proper," was all he said, as if they hadn't been having the most wildly improper and implausible discussion of his life. "I cannot sign the death certificate, you know, if I have not examined the body."

"Of course not, Miles. I would not ask you to." She ignored his sigh of relief to go on: "All I'm asking is that you not tell anyone that Uncle Albert is dead. You could just say you are investigating, which you are. After all, as you say, you've not seen him since you brought him here, and without proof . . ."

Miles was happy enough to jump on that suggestion. The whole thing was too smoky by half, and the least said, the better. Besides, no rational person would believe the story anyway, disappearing bodies and such. Which reminded him, "That still leaves the question of who removed the baron from the icehouse."

"But they brought him right back. Likely it was some of the servants—we've taken new ones on, you know, for the company—who thought it was a barrel of ale. They returned the barrel as soon as they realized the mistake. It wasn't your dire chicken thieves, Miles."

The chicken made a nice change from rabbit stew. Handy threw in a handful of the herbs and stuff he'd pulled from someone's kitchen garden. He and Sailor and Sal had visited a farmhouse last night after bringing back the body in the barrel. Sal got the chickens, Handy got the vegetables, and Sailor made away with a shovel and pitchfork, the only things he could find lying around.

The boys hadn't spotted anything that looked like a potato or an onion, not even in that farmer's own garden, only some green stuff. In disgust, Handy threw into the cooking pot another handful of leaves and stems from Mrs. Bagshott's herb patch, the ones she grew to keep her cat from getting fur balls.

At least the ensuing digestive upset gave Jake something else to think about besides his aches and pains, and how his nephews had let a dead body get away. The way he lit into Sailor and Handy with that cane would have made Uncle Albert proud, if Jake hadn't been so weak on his feet that every swing sent him reeling into one or another of the stone walls.

"You didn't even look for a wallet or rings or nothing! How could you be so dumb?" *Swish* went the cane through the air, *whap* as it connected with one of the hapless lads, then *thud* as Jake's head hit another wall. "Marks what carry canes like this allus have a watch or a lookin' glass on a chain, or a stickpin in their chokers. They got brass buttons and pockets full of change. Hell, they got gold in their teeth!"

No way were Sailor and Handy going to go back and pick the fillings out of a dead man's mouth, or pocket in this instance. But they still needed a stake. Jake didn't think he could hold the pistol steady enough to hold up another coach. Hell, he didn't think he could lift the pistol, much less aim it, and he didn't trust either of his nincompoop nevvies with it. They'd likely shoot each other. No, with his luck, they'd shoot him.

Instead he sent Handy into the village with the silver flask. He chose Handy because Sailor was too distinctive, being of inordinate size, with flaming red hair and freckles. The runt, contrariwise, was a frail-looking lad with pale silvery hair down to his shoulders and a high-pitched voice. No, not too distinctive at all.

So Handy took the flask and went from back door to back door, asking if anyone knew who owned the thing, because he found it on the road and wanted to return it to its rightful owner. "I juth want to do what'th wight," he lisped. The menfolks looked away, but the women cooed over him and handed him baskets of muffins and paper-wrapped sausages and jugs of cider. Such a nice boy.

Handy was far out of town with two pillow slips filled with booty before any of the housewives realized that while he had their attention in the

154

kitchen, his accomplice was stealing their laundry off the clotheslines. "Good dog, Sal."

Now they had food on the table—or on the floor, since the table had long been consigned to the fire. And they had clean, respectable clothes to wear to look for jobs at that wedding. Of course, they'd both have to find some kind of disguise since the law would be looking for Handy and Sailor and Sal after today, but they'd do it. And they weren't going to hand any loot out the window to Jake neither. Let him do his own stealing for once. The boys meant to snabble what they could at that mansion, then run with it before Jake knew they were done. They were going to Portsmouth and buy passage to America, to start new, decent lives. Sailor was going to be a pirate, and Handsome was going to be a gigolo.

Chapter Sixteen

Terwent the valet heard about the pilfering in the village with the silver flask as decoy. He decided against going to London, and went to Magistrate Pomeroy instead.

Even Miles had to agree that the man made a good case for foul play. The descriptions of the flasks matched, and Terwent swore his master never went anywhere without his "medicinal spirits." Miles could believe that, from his short exposure to the old tosspot.

So what happened? Had that here-and-thereian Howell ditched the body under a hedge for some vagabond to find and strip? Or had the whole tale been a Banbury story for his benefit and they really killed the old coot? Miles was so upset, he couldn't finish his dinner. He left some peas.

Here was a fine rowdydow indeed. Terwent was demanding they form a search party to comb the area for the baron's corpse. The townsfolk were insisting he call up the militia to rid them of the ring of vicious hoodlums. And Miss Whilton was asking him to keep his mouth shut. His worst problem was Miss Whilton.

Any female so lacking in delicacy as to suggest he suborn the law for her was capable of anything: lies, misdemeanors, murder. Her beauty, her bounty, and her blue blood couldn't change the fact that Miss Whilton would be the death of his career as justice of the peace, to say nothing of his peace of mind. And he'd have to marry her, b'gad, if she accepted his proposal! A gentleman couldn't renege on an offer. She was thinking on it, she'd said, begging him so sweetly to be patient. Pomeroy could have bitten his tongue out, to get back his honorable proposition. Deuce take it, he'd waited years for her to grow out of her hoydenish ways, then two more for her to forget that childish attachment to Rake Howell. Patient be damned. Why the devil couldn't he have been a bit more patient?

Daphne, meanwhile, wasn't thinking of Miles at all, his proposal or his predicament. Nor was she any more patient than he was, chewing on her pencil stub as she waited for Graydon to return. No matter what he'd said, she couldn't help worrying over what problems he'd face in London. What if his curricle turned over and Uncle Albert rolled out? There'd be hell to pay, and no mistake. But that was borrowing trouble. Gray would never put his carriage in the ditch. He was the most competent whip she knew, for all his other sins.

Just what had the infuriating man meant by inviting her on a picnic after dark, or blowing her a kiss as he pulled off this morning? Probably nothing. Gray simply couldn't help dallying with any female in the vicinity. And she couldn't help wishing it were otherwise.

Graydon was making quick work of his job in London, anxious to get back to Hampshire and Daphne. He didn't like leaving her alone to face that prig Pomeroy. He didn't like leaving her alone *with* that prig Pomeroy. Hell, he didn't like leaving her alone, period.

He stopped at a grave site at the edge of town and asked the sexton where to go for his special needs, congratulating himself on his cleverness. He couldn't see driving about the city all day asking directions, not with Uncle Albert's barrel in the boot.

Of course, the place he wanted was shut up on Sunday, but Death didn't wait for a weekday; the major saw no reason for himself to wait either. He banged on doors until he found someone who could direct him to the establishment's proprietor, who wasn't best pleased to be dragged from his Sunday dinner. Until he saw the color of Lord Howell's gold.

"And the family isn't in such a rush to get the thing done," Graydon explained, "so you can take your time. I just couldn't leave him lying around, you understand."

Jedediah Biggs didn't understand why the cove couldn't wait for a mortician and a regular funeral wagon, nary a bit. More gold joined the pile. Then Jed Biggs wiped his soot-stained fingers on his pants and said, "Time is all I've got, till you bring me a death certificate. No death certificate, nothing for me to put in my records. No records, and I could be transported for removing evidence of a crime. You could've kilt your old granfer for his gold and no one the wiser, iffen I don't keep records. Hell, he might be the husband of some sweet young thing you've got your eye on, randy-looking buck like you."

Graydon wasn't interested in hearing any more of the man's theories. He supposed the fellow was hinting that enough gold could eliminate the need for any records whatsoever, but the lawyers and such would have to be notified anyway. And he hadn't killed the old shabster. There was nothing to hide except his body for a bit.

So Graydon left to get a death certificate.

"Ain't you forgetting something?" Mr. Biggs jerked his permanently blackened jaw toward the barrel, now in the yard of his brick row house, right on his wife's primroses.

Graydon saw no need to encumber his search around town with such a traveling companion. The pyreman, as he liked to call himself, saw it differently. "There's no magistrate going to give you that piece of paper without seeing the body. You could say it's your aunt Tillie, what's leaving you her silver tea set, or a servant, instead of some bloke you killed in a duel. Magistrate's going to want some proof."

"Bloodthirsty chap, aren't you? I suppose you've seen it all in your days."

"That's neither here nor there. I gots to have that paper. The magistrate might even want to hold an inquest."

Graydon gave the notion some thought. "Interesting how the legal system works. How long do you think an inquest would take?"

Biggs scratched his head. "A day or two for them to send a sawbones out to examine the body to fix the cause of death, then maybe weeks before they hold the hearing, to let you hire a barrister, or leave the country."

Graydon could only suppose he looked guilty as hell, driving around with a corpse, the way this man's imagination was running. But weeks were too long a delay, and he'd have to be in town for the hearing. "No, that won't do. But I refuse to go tripping about town with a dead man as groom. He can't even get down to hold the horses, don't you know. I'll bring my godfather back if he insists."

Biggs spat on the ground. "Now, what good's some other swell going to do me?"

"Oh, didn't I say? My godfather's a magistrate. He's not the Lord High Magistrate of all of London, but I don't think this little matter is worth bothering Uncle Roderick, do you?"

Graydon's godfather didn't insist on seeing the body, naturally. "What, and ruin my appetite on a Sunday? It's that swine Whilton, you say? Good. Didn't kill him, did you, my boy? No? Good. See you at the wedding next week? Good. Your father's getting a fine wife. I dangled after Cleo Harracourt myself before she chose Whilton. Too bad the daughter's such a high stickler."

"Daphne? She's as game as a pebble!"

"Won't have a rake like you, I heard. Too bad."

When Graydon got back to the row house, Mrs. Biggs sent him off to the crematorium with a flea in his ear about care-for-naughts who didn't respect the Lord's day or His flowers.

Biggs apologized, once he had the certificate in his hand, all full of official stamps and seals. "And I can't do the job right away; the place is full of missionaries fresh off a boat what came from spreading God's words, and God knows what diseases. You wouldn't want your relation mixed in with that crowd."

"No, he might contaminate them. But take your time, as I said. Uncle Albert's in no hurry."

"May as well pick out an urn meantime; save you a trip back. M'brother runs the shop next door."

A trinket for Lady Whilton? Graydon wondered how she'd like a Grecian urn with handles, or maybe a brass one that looked like a spittoon. There were copper and silver ones, marble and jade, porcelain urns and plain earthenware crocks for ashes up the River Tick. One looked like a genie'd appear if you rubbed hard enough. Uncle Albert had already granted everyone's fondest wish by dying. It was a deuced hard choice. Graydon didn't want one with angels or flowers on the sides. Nehemiah Biggs didn't have any with a pair of dice on them.

The decision finally made, Graydon thought of returning to Hampshire that night, but his horses were tired and his father had given him a commission. All he had to do was wait for the shops to open Monday morning, so he passed the evening at his clubs, returning early to Howell House for a good night's sleep.

The gift for Lady Whilton was an easy selection, two ruby hearts joined by a diamond arrow. If that wasn't sincere, and expensive, nothing was. He couldn't properly give Daphne jewelry, although there were sapphires that almost begged to match her eyes. He reluctantly settled on a gold locket to replace the one he'd given her so long ago, another lifetime, it seemed, that she'd tromped on that fateful night. He'd offer it as a wedding gift, to celebrate the joining of the families. He told the clerk to hold the sapphires, too, in hopes of another joining.

To prove his constancy to Daffy, he picked out an extravagant diamond choker for Lady Seline Bowles. She'd know it for her *congé*, a parting gift. Unfortunately the clasp was faulty, and he didn't want to wait around to have it repaired.

"Oh, we can deliver it, my lord."

Yes, and bandy Seline's name and his all over Mayfair. "No, I have to return to town in a few days." He could deliver the necklace in person, which was the honorable thing to do anyway, while he fetched the urn. Seline's hysterics couldn't be any worse than toting around Albert's ashes.

If Jake were a cat, he'd be dead. Twice. As it was, he didn't know if he could survive another day of his nephews' company. He'd walk out on them, taking nothing but his dog and his cane, if he could walk. He couldn't, though; he needed a horse. A horse, his kinfolk for a horse. So he sent the boys out to steal him a mount, promising them one more try at the high toby.

Finding a field of hayburners was easy; catching one of them was a horse of a different color, gray, to be exact. Old Dan used to be chestnut, now he was just grizzled. The farmer only kept him around out of sentiment, and as a ride for his little grandchildren. All the other horses ran from the two thieves, who smelled of smoke, blood, and worse, but Old Dan didn't have a lot of run left in him. So he left with Sailor and Handy.

They hoisted Jake aboard and tied the dead

man's linen cravat around the horse's neck for Jake to hang on to, since there was no saddle, no reins. Then they led him back to that narrow stretch of roadway to wait for a carriage.

Jake was a real highwayman now. He had a horse, a pistol, a gang. He was proud. He was also delirious. The boys picked him up and put him back on Old Dan.

Unfortunately but not totally unexpectedly in the country, the next traveler wasn't a diamond-bedecked dowager in a fancy coach. It was a farmer. A pig farmer, to be exact, driving his herd from one place to another, right down the center of the highway. As Old Dan stepped aside without instruction, Jake called to the boys to watch out for little 'uns as might get lost. Sailor tried to lose one, but it squealed so loud, its mama chased him into the ditch at the side of the road. The farmer came and kicked Handy into the ditch, too, to make his point. The ditch being filled with muddy, stagnant water, and Jake for once not in it, he whistled in delight. Which was the sound the farmer made when he called the horses for supper.

Old Dan turned for home. Jake didn't. He didn't land in the ditch—hallelujah!—but he did land in the path of the prize sow, all three hundred mean, myopic pounds of her.

Sailor and Handy had to drag him home, through the ditch. Sal wouldn't come with them, they smelled so bad. When they got to the cottage, Jake was shaking so hard, he couldn't even hit the boys with his cane. "A fire," he croaked. "Light the fire."

But the fireplace smoked worse than before, so much that Jake couldn't breathe at all, not without moving his cracked ribs. He shoved his wet coat on the flames to douse the fire, which at least got him some steam. "Get up on the roof an' stick a branch down the chimbley," he gasped at his nephews. "Someat's stuck in there."

Jake waited until he heard a lot of noise above him before he raised his head to look up. First he saw sky through the holes in the roof. Then he saw Sailor's big foot. And Handy's little foot. Then *lots* more sky all of a sudden. "Oh, sh—"

Sailor carried him outside to a little clearing. Handy started him a fire out of the squirrel's nest they'd found, then tossed on parts of the roof as they cleared the debris out of the cottage.

When Jake was almost warm and dry, Sal returned from wherever she'd been, dripping water all over him again. But she also laid a fish in his lap. "My friend," Jake rasped as he impaled the fish on a stick with great effort and shakily held it to the fire. "My best friend." He hauled his bruised arm around the damp dog and buried his battered head in Sal's mangy fur while the fish cooked. "You're more like family than those two jackasses can ever be."

When it was ready, Jake split the fish and gave half to his best friend, his comfort and provider. Then he choked on a fish bone.

Chapter Seventeen

"*I* got me a shovel!" Sailor bragged. "I knew it would come in handy, Handy."

They couldn't take Jake into the village to be laid to rest in the churchyard. They couldn't afford the burial, and they couldn't afford to be recognized. Besides, Jake had never stepped foot in a church that either Sailor or Handy ever recalled.

"And he was happy here."

Handy nodded. "Best days o' his life."

So they planted him in that little clearing, not far away from the tumbledown cottage in the Woodhill Manor home woods. While Sailor dug, Handy gathered leaves and twigs and pebbles to cover over the grave so no one would notice. They thought of making a cross out of the rotten roof lumber, but that would have been too obvious, so they stuck the cane in the ground as a marker.

"Too bad we got no way to write his name on it."

"Couldn't spell it anyways."

As a final act of mourning, Handy picked a bouquet of wild violets—and stuck them in his buttonhole. Sailor did the same. They were free! It was time to go make their fortunes.

They gathered all their belongings, Jake's belongings, and the dead man's belongings, and left the cottage without a backward glance. And without Sal.

But Jake had warned them they had to get prettified before they could get hired on at any fancy house, and they still did not have the wherewithal for such luxuries as soap. Sailor was all for trying the bridle lay again. They still had the pistol, and he liked the sound of "Your shaving kit or your life." Handy thought they'd do better waiting till dark and breaking into the emporium in the village. They stood in the roadway arguing until they heard carriage wheels. As luck would have it, the painted wagon that trundled by belonged to the first of a Gypsy caravan that was headed toward the other side of the village. A fair was going to be set up to honor the earl's wedding, and to make a profit off his wealthy guests.

Gypsies being prodigious traders who asked few questions and gave out less information, the boys soon bartered the silver flask and the brass-fitted satchel for soap, razors, scissors, boot polish, and a soft leather tunic for Sailor.

"Giorgio roms go courting, eh?" The old Gypsy mother nodded and put some colorful ribbons in with the bundle. "For your sweethearts." When Handy reached for the package she grabbed his wrist and turned his palm up. "For free. Yes, a pretty fair-haired girl is in your future." For

Sailor: "A golden female will be sharing your bed."

This was getting better and better. They hurried off to the pool by the icehouse. It wasn't any hot-spring bath, but it was better than the ditchwater. And it was a good thing for Lady Whilton that it was springtime and not winter, or her ice would be black from their ablutions.

Clean, combed, and shaved (Sailor, at least), they each donned one of the clean shirts that had been in the baron's portmanteau. Sailor's just made it to his waist, Handy's fell to his bony knees. They put on the dead man's hose and surveyed the rest of the choices from Sal's clothesline foray. There was a pair of breeches from the blacksmith's laundry that almost fit Sailor. With his new tunic, no one would notice that the buttons didn't meet. But there was nothing that fit scrawny Handy without sliding down to his toes, except the blacksmith's daughter's skirts and petticoats. Sal was quick; she wasn't a genius.

Handy shrugged and donned the skirts, threading the Gypsy's ribbons through the long pale curls he hadn't cut off yet. "She said I'd have a fair-haired girl in my future."

"She didn't say you'd be one. Now if they take us on at that manor house, you'll have to sleep with the maids."

"Too bad, ain't it?"

The housekeeper at Woodhill Manor was in a dither. The guests were starting to arrive for the wedding, provisions were being delivered, and the house was not up to her standards. Lady Whilton was no help, with her head in the clouds all the time and the earl where he hadn't ought to be even so close to the wedding, in Mrs. Binder's considered opinion. Not that she'd whisper one word of disparagement about her mistress, but it didn't set a good example for Miss Daphne, nor for the silly maids who were giggling in corners so much they weren't getting half the work done. The footmen were worse, with their rolling eyes and knowing grins. At least the footmen were Ohlman's concern, for all the attention he was paying, what with spending half his time in the wine cellar and the icehouse. The guests weren't coming just to drink the cellars dry, for heaven's sake.

Not even Miss Daphne was up to her usual competent self, worried about that handsome devil staying in the guest wing, the housekeeper guessed. Now, if *that* rascal overstepped the line, Mrs. Binder'd have at him with her rolling pin, the same as she used to when he filched cookies from the kitchen. Meantime, Miss Daphne was losing her lists and changing her mind about the menus and room assignments, causing more work rather than less. Mrs. Binder would be sore glad when this marriage took place.

Thus it was that she was happy to see two clean, neat young persons apply for positions. She could use the help, if they proved worthy.

"We got references, ma'am," Sailor offered, handing over the forged letter.

Mrs. Binder read the glowing commendation, but frowned. "This here is for two brothers, Sailor and Handy."

The boys hadn't thought of that. "Well, he's Sailor, all right. And I'm ... I'm his sister Andy. T'other one stayed on at the last post."

Mrs. Binder wasn't happy. She peered at the pair in front of her. "You don't look like brother and sister."

"We don't look like brothers, neither," Handy muttered, but Sailor kicked him.

Mrs. Binder ignored both, her eyes narrowed. "I bet you're sweethearts, that's what. Well, I've got enough of that kind of nonsense already. If there's one thing I won't put up with, it's canoodling among my staff."

The boys swore they weren't, never did canoodle together, never would. Mrs. Binder didn't quite believe them, but she was desperate. She fixed Sailor with a steady glare. "One wink and you're out, understand?"

Sailor never had learned to wink, so he nodded.

Mrs. Binder went on: "I can't hire any footmen, that's Ohlman's province, but they're short at the stables, what with all the carriages they're expecting. Know anything about horses, boy?"

Sailor had just stolen one that week. He nodded.

"No matter, you're big enough to handle a shovel."

Sailor nodded again, grinning. He knew all about shovels.

"Good, go on with you and tell them I said you were to help. And you, girl," the housekeeper addressed Handy, "can you polish?"

He'd gotten that boot polish to darken Sailor's red hair all right, hadn't he? With visions of silver polish—and silver plates, silver candlesticks, and silver tea sets—floating in his mind, Handy swore he could polish with the best of them.

Mrs. Binder handed him an apron and some rags and escorted Handy to a narrow closet with row upon row of chamber pots. "Here, you're hired. Start polishing."

Relief, that's all it was, Daphne told herself, when Gray strode into the room, barely using his cane. He was returned safely and successfully, she gathered, from his wink in her direction and jaunty grin before he turned to greet her mother and the others. It could only be relief that made her spirits lift instantly and her heart start beating faster. She refused to entertain any other notion, although he was looking so devilishly handsome in his tight-fitting riding breeches with his dark curls all wind-tossed that her feet were itching to run her across the room and into his arms. Relief was a powerful emotion. Luckily she was serving tea.

Daphne was the first person Graydon saw when he entered the parlor. He thought she'd always be the first one he'd spot, no matter how many others were around, that his eyes would seek her out, instinctively knowing where she was. He winked so she'd know his mission was accomplished, then grinned when he saw how a cloud seemed to lift from her brow. She *was* happy he was back. Lud knew he was happy to be here.

His grin faded when he realized who else was there for tea. Of course. And he was sitting in her pocket, that dashed mushroom Miles. Graydon paid his respects to Lady Whilton and the other ladies, slipped a small package into his father's hands, and returned to take a seat on Daphne's other side.

"I say, Pomeroy, there's a curious noise out on the highway you might want to look into. Sounds like a wolf howling in the woods." It was a broad hint, but had merit.

"There are no more wolves in Hampshire. A lost dog or something."

"Well, I couldn't see anything from the road and couldn't leave my cattle, but I asked a field worker passing by to go see. In case the dog was in trouble, a trap or something, don't you know. Offered the fellow a coin, but he crossed himself and said it was a banshee, before he ran off."

Miles dabbed at his mouth with his handkerchief. "There are no banshees, either."

"Of course not. It's most likely just a lost dog, as you said, but the noise could frighten little children. Perhaps you should take a ride that way, if you have so much time on your hands." He stared pointedly at what else Miles had in his hands, a plate full of almond cake.

Miles resented being called to account by a Bond Street lounger, dressed to the nines and bang up to the mark, after a four- or five-hour curricle ride. He snapped, "I'm not the dogcatcher, by George."

Cousin Harriet grumbled, "You haven't caught a lot of anything else, either." She turned to the newcomer. "Howell, did you hear there's a gang of outlaws working the countryside, stealing anything not nailed down? Homer Riley says they even tried to get his pigs, right on the highway, in broad daylight."

And Graydon had driven along that same highway, his head in the clouds, with a fortune in a ruby brooch in his pocket. While Cousin Harriet nattered on about missing laundry, even before the Gypsies came to town, Graydon wondered when he could give Daffy the locket he had in his other pocket. He still wished it weren't such a trumpery bit, but she used to like the other one. She used to like him, too, he reminded himself.

She did seem pleased when, after Cousin Harriet went to fetch her needlework, he was able to recount his London adventure. Even Miles turned pleasant when the major told them how a London magistrate had signed an official death certificate. All was in order, he explained, right down to the blurred date of death.

"And there's no need to mention Albert's passing yet, since the ashes won't be back for days. The undertaker won't spread it around and neither will the magistrate, respecting the family's wishes."

"Then you don't think I should discuss it with Mama?" Daphne asked, looking toward her mother across the room.

Graydon's gaze followed hers to where the governor had his arm around Lady Whilton and was whispering in her ear while she giggled like a schoolgirl. The rubies had done the trick, then. "I'd hate to ruin their idyll. They seem so . . ." He couldn't think of the right words, but Daphne understood.

She nodded and smiled. "So . . ."

"So preposterous, if you ask me," Miles finished. "At their age! Dashed embarrassing, I'd say, and highly improper."

If Miles considered that a little cuddling was improper, Daphne thought, heaven help them if he found out about the earl's late night rambles. Perhaps Gray was right again and Miles was a trifle stiff-rumped. Well, he'd just have to learn to relax a little. He might start taking lessons from Graydon, who was grinning fondly at the older couple. No, then Miles might learn too many raffish ways. She'd rather have him this way, starch and all. She smiled at him and passed a box of chocolates.

Now that everything was all right and tight with the baron, Miss Whilton was looking better to Miles, downright appealing in fact, in a plain blue frock. Amazing what a crisis averted could do to a female's prospects. And if this leering son of an earl thought she was suitable to be a countess one day, Pomeroy supposed Daphne could learn to be an adequate squire's wife. With his mother's help and example, he could check her wilder starts. Get her breeding, he figured, that ought to do it. It calmed the mares down, anyway.

Lord Howell was contemplating similar notions as she smiled, but mares had no part in his musings. Damn, that jaconet muslin hugged a figure that any opera-dancer would envy. Those simple lines had to come from one of London's premier modistes, to be so demure yet so alluring at the same time. And the minx knew it, the way she was flirting with that maggot Miles, batting her eyes at him.

Those eyes *were* the color of sapphires, he mused, glad he'd had the jeweler put the set aside. He tried to picture Daffy in his sapphires, necklace, bracelet, and earbobs, and nothing else. The temperature in the room went up about ten degrees. Deuce take it, she was more luscious than a bonbon, half of which that pig Pomeroy was gobbling from the box Graydon had brought back from London.

Chapter Eighteen

"Don't get in my way, old man. I demand to see the magistrate. It's my right as a citizen." Terwent shoved past Ohlman into the parlor.

The valet was only partly subdued by all the faces turned to stare at him. He made a hasty bow, but his agitation was so great that he ignored the presence of earls and officers, ladies and the two lackeys Ohlman sent for, to toss him out. He went right up to Miles and shouted in his face, "Now you've got to do your dooty."

Miles flushed and told the man, "Stop your caterwauling. You're in a gentleman's house."

"I'm in *my* gentleman's house and he might right now be a-lying dead. In the village they're saying there's a spirit loose, some boggart moaning in the woods 'cause he ain't had proper burial."

"It's a dog, by Jupiter!"

"Did you go see it for yourself, then, Mr. Magistrate?"

Before Miles could answer, Graydon spoke up: "Did you, Mr., ah, Terwent?"

"Why no, I . . . ah, I . . ."

"Waited for the official inquiry. Highly commendable, I'm sure. As is this loyalty, this dedication. But to Whilton? My word, it beggars the imagination." Graydon helped himself to a bonbon.

Terwent didn't even try to bluster through his employer's good points; the baron had none. "He owes me my salary. And if he's gone and stuck his spoon in the wall, I want the pension he promised."

"Ah, such altruism. It makes more sense, at least. So what say you, Pomeroy? Shall we go take a look at this, ah, boggart in the woods?"

"It's a dog, blast it!" Miles looked regretfully at the remains of the tea, but got to his feet. "I suppose I'll have to, to stop all the yammering about haunted woods."

Howell thought he'd ride along, just out of curiosity, although he'd been driving since early morning.

"If you'll wait a few minutes, I'll change into my habit," Daphne said, and got up to leave.

"What's that, Miss Whilton? Oh, no, you mustn't come along. Highly unsuitable."

Daphne paused at the doorway. "What's unsuitable about my going for a ride, Miles? The woods are on Whilton property, after all."

Miles persisted. "But there's no saying what we might find. It's not the place for a lady."

"Nonsense, especially if you're looking for the lady's uncle!" She knew they wouldn't find Uncle Albert, but that didn't satisfy her curiosity either. "I'm going."

"I for—" She was gone. Miles sat down again, shaking his head.

Graydon gave him a pat on the shoulder and a complacent grin. "Not yours to order around yet, old boy. No saying but that Daffy'd listen anyway. Stubborn female, Miss Whilton, don't you know?"

Miles hadn't known, actually.

"Oh yes, needs a light hand on the bridle, else she digs her feet in and won't budge. I should know." Graydon also knew how much Daffy would hate being likened to a fractious filly, but he couldn't help needling his rival. "But why don't you go on; I'll wait here to escort her."

Miles wouldn't budge, mulish female or not.

They followed the eerie keening toward the old woodsman's cottage in the home woods. Daphne hadn't been there in years, her father having declared it off-limits since the place was in such dangerous disrepair. She made a note to have it torn down before someone got hurt. The noise was loud enough now to send chills down her spine. Daphne automatically turned to Graydon, riding beside her, for reassurance. He winked. It was all right then.

As they'd all suspected, there was a dog in the clearing, head back and howling. It didn't seem hurt, so Daphne left the old blankets tied on her saddle. She dismounted and started toward the scruffy tan cur.

Miles had his pistol out. "Stand back, Miss Whilton. It might be rabid."

"Nonsense, it's a she and she's just frightened. What happened, girl, did you lose your way?"

Then Terwent, who was riding pillion behind Daphne's groom, jumped down and shouted, "I knew it! I knew it! There's his cane."

And indeed, there was Uncle Albert's unmistakable bone-headed cane, sticking out of the ground. Graydon kicked some leaves and clutter aside to reveal freshly turned earth.

Miles was livid. "If this is some kind of joke, if you've been lying to me all along, leading me on, expecting me to be bought off like one of your lackeys when the—"

"Stubble it," Graydon ordered in his officer's voice. "You still have no idea who is buried here. You'd do better to send for some lads with shovels than stand around and rant."

"I'm not ranting!" But he directed the groom to ride back to Woodhill for a work crew and a cart, with Daphne's permission.

Daphne was still petting the dog. She hissed at Graydon while Pomeroy's back was turned. "You don't suppose . . . ?"

Howell shrugged. "I never checked the barrel when I got to London. But if Albert is here"—he jerked his head toward where Miles was using the cane to sweep the debris away from the grave site—"then who the hell are we having cremated?"

The men came, with extra shovels. Miles looked to Graydon, who just grinned. "Not my job."

Terwent crossed his bony arms. "Never."

So Miles Pomeroy took up one of the shovels and began digging. No one paid any attention to the tall stable hand next to him, the one who was sweating so badly, the boot polish was running from his hair down to his chin. If anyone did notice, they assumed it was dirt, from the grave. Sailor pulled his hat down lower over his hair and kept digging, and sweating.

Daphne had untied one of the blankets and sat down, the dog beside her. "Was this a friend of yours? Are you lonely? Hungry?" She crumpled a roll she'd stuffed in her pocket at the last minute, and fed it to the yellowish mongrel. "I bet you don't even know how to find food. Don't worry, someone in the stables will feed you, I'm sure, and give you a warm place to sleep."

So the Gypsy was right again: Sailor'd be sharing his bed with a golden-haired female. He kept digging.

When the body was nearly unearthed and Daphne would have stepped closer, Graydon put his arms on her shoulders and gently turned her away. "There's no need. You stay here."

It wasn't the baron, whoever he was. And he wasn't pretty. "Stay there," Graydon told Daphne, and for once she listened, to Pomeroy's chagrin.

Terwent had gone white, but he shouted, "I know him! It's that cutpurse from the tavern!" He turned, long nose twitching. "And that's the bloody, thieving dog!"

Daphne took her hand back from the hound's head.

"It must have been a falling out among crooks," Miles said, "though I don't see any bullet holes or knife wounds."

Graydon had been exploring while the men were digging. "More like a falling roof than a falling out." He pointed to the piles of rotten timbers, the roofless cottage. "That would explain why he looks so . . . battered."

"Yes, yes, I would have come to the same conclusion if I hadn't been busy digging." Miles was hot and sweaty from being out of shape, and filthy, while Howell was neat as a pin and impressing Miss Whilton with solving the case. Damn. "Yes, it appears that there was no foul play, just a criminal getting his just deserts. Unfortunately now the parish will have to pay to rebury the thatchgallows. I suppose it's cheaper than a trial and a hanging, but—" He had to pause to lift one of the stable-hands-turned-digger out of the hole where he'd suddenly fallen in. Big fellow, even dirtier than Miles felt. Miles took out his handkerchief to wipe his face, hoping he did not look like such a fool in front of Miss Whilton.

"But it should end your crime wave, Pomeroy. The man's accomplices must be long gone by now. They've cleaned the place out and moved on, at any rate. They didn't leave anything but the dead man."

"And the dog," Daphne added, coming closer now that the body had been wrapped in a blanket and loaded onto the cart. "They left the dog out here and alone, the heartless savages."

"The dog is a thief, Miss Whilton. I had more complaints about this animal stealing chickens and laundry than about the highwaymen. They seem to have stolen nothing."

"Perhaps you ought to arrest the hound then," Graydon said, "to show the local citizenry how conscientious you are."

Before Miles could respond, in kind or with a handful of dirt, Terwent spoke up: "They did, too, heist something. They got the baron's cane, didn't they? So where is he?"

"Yes, Howell, where is the baron, and how did his cane come to be marking a felon's grave? I'd like to hear your explanation for that myself," Miles said.

"Obviously the gang held him up when he left the Manor." When they rolled Albert out of the icehouse, to be exact, but Graydon didn't say that. Daphne was nodding her agreement.

Terwent was clutching the cane, polishing it with his sleeve as his beady eyes darted from one to the other. "They killed him, I know it!"

"No, I don't think so. We'd have found the body by now. What I bet happened was that some traveler chancing by saw the baron in distress and came to his aid, then took him up with them."

Daphne elaborated: "If he was unconscious, the baron couldn't have given his address, so perhaps the good Samaritan took Uncle Albert to his own house."

"He always had his calling cards in his pocket, for when he was, ah, temporarily disoriented."

"Drunk as a wheelbarrow, more like." Miles grumbled his disapproval, for the baron's drinking habits and for this whole unsavory mess. Good Samaritan, in a pig's eye.

"If he did have identification, this unknown benefactor must have driven him straight on to London, where the poor bastard might be lying in pain, waiting for his loyal valet. It would be just like Whilton to change his will when you don't show up. Don't you think so, Daffy?"

Terwent was already headed out of the woods when Daphne softly asked, "But what if he died on the way? You know Uncle Albert was not a healthy man. The shock . . ."

Miles snorted, but Graydon stroked his chin. "That's always a possibility. And it's also possible the thieves stole his card case. You know what, Terwent, if the baron is not at home when you get to London, you better check the morgues. And Bow Street. And don't worry about your salary. I'm sure

Lady Whilton will take care of your expenses. Don't you think so, Daffy?"

"Of course, Terwent. You'd be doing a, um, service to the family if you find my uncle."

So the valet got into the cart for the ride back to the village where the baron's own coach and driver were waiting. He sat up by the driver, not in the rear with Jake.

Pomeroy mounted and turned to follow. He wasn't even sorry to leave Miss Whilton alone with that glib-tongued Howell. Why, he felt like Adam, caught between Eve and the serpent. Too bad her dowry, and that twenty thousand pounds, was such a tempting apple. He left with a curt farewell.

Graydon tossed Daphne up onto her horse, and waited while she arranged the brown velvet of her habit. "Don't worry," he told her when she seemed distracted, her eyes following her stocky suitor. "He'll get over it."

Daphne wasn't so certain. That complete honesty that made Miles so strong and sure demanded nothing less in return. Everything that Miles was, everything he stood for, had just been belittled.

"He's not the man for you anyway, Daff. He'll never make you happy in the long run."

She looked down at the handsome face from her dreams, that laughing mouth that lied so easily. No, Miles might not be perfect, but he would never play her false, he would never break her heart.

Sailor and Handy had a bare half hour after dinner to escape Mrs. Binder's eagle eye and compare notes while they restored Sailor's hair coloring.

"They're puttin' Jake in a pauper's grave, no marker."

"But he's gettin' to the churchyard after all."

"And we're gettin' nowhere."

Mrs. Binder hardly let Handy out of her sight, and the head stableman kept Sailor busy from before dawn to after dusk, when Sailor collapsed onto his straw pallet. Neither one of them was ever permitted near anything worth stealing, unless you needed some manure or a chamber pot. Worse, Handy found out that a footman was on duty all night in the house. He used to drowse some, the maids' gossip went, but with that earl switching bedchambers at all hours, he didn't dare. Mrs. Binder would have the girls' hides for gossiping about their betters, but she didn't sleep with them, three to a bed.

"Maybe we should leave?"

It was a very warm bed. "Not yet, Sailor."

"Fine for you, you get to share with the maids. I get Sal in the straw. And she's got fleas."

"The food's good."

"An' no one's beatin' us on the head with his cane."

So they decided they may as well stay until the wedding. With more guests coming, there were bound to be more opportunities ... and more manure to manhandle, more commodes to clean.

Chapter Nineteen

"What can I do to help?" With only ten days or so before the wedding, there had to be something Graydon could do to relieve those little lines of concentration from Daphne's brow. She was so busy with her lists and errands and consultations with the gardeners, the cook, and the housekeeper, he hardly saw her at all, and never alone. They'd scraped through the highwayman business well together, but how was he to build on that friendship if he never spoke to her except at dinner, where she continued to wear that abstracted frown? He could only hope she wasn't pining because her cabbage-head of a country courtier hadn't been coming round so often.

By sheer luck and a rainy day, he'd tracked her down in the estate office room this morning. The library was receiving a thorough dusting, the billiards room was under renovation by carpenters, the music room was in the hands of the piano tuner, and the morning room had been taken over by a squad of seamstresses. The small parlor was being used by the older ladies to put the finishing touches on the new altar cloth for the church service, and the drawing room, all the vast expanse of Aubusson carpet, gilded chairbacks, and chinoiserie, was off-limits. The earl and Lady Whilton were "making plans." More like making cakes of themselves, Graydon thought, but fondly. He wasn't worried over the servants' gossip, only about the governor's heart. At this rate . . .

Daphne was fretting along similar lines, chewing on her pencil stub, when Graydon entered the office, hoping to find a quiet place to read the newspapers.

She put the pencil down and gave him a tentative smile. "Can you help? Well, yes, I suppose you are the only one I can ask. With so many guests arriving soon, the room assignments are getting complicated. This is a trifle indelicate, but do you suppose it would be beyond the pale for me to move your father into the master bedroom? I mean, Uncle Albert won't be coming, and the room would just sit there empty while we are getting overcrowded."

He laughed. "A trifle indelicate? Daffy, that's coming on too brown. What you mean is, there's a connecting door and you wish to cut down on the wear and tear on the hall carpet!"

She laughed back. "I was thinking more of saving Mama the embarrassment of having the guests see the earl in his nightcap before breakfast."

"I don't think your mother cares, Daffy, so do it if it will make things easier for you."

"Even though Uncle Albert died there?"

"I don't think those two would be distracted if a hundred barons died there. And they don't know anyway, do they?"

"No, I couldn't spoil Mama's happiness." She made some notations on her list, mostly to hide her blushes at the tone of the conversation. "Good, now that's done."

"See how much assistance I can be? What else shall I do for you?"

"Why, there's nothing, but thank you. Surely you have business of your own. Howell Hall, your correspondence." She nodded toward the papers in his hand. "The war news. I'm sorry if you cannot find a quiet spot. I can—"

"Botheration, Daffy, I don't need to read about the latest parliamentary debate over the price of ammunition. I want to help you!"

She stared at him, at the vehemence in his voice. "Well, I'm sure I—"

He leaned against the edge of the desk, looking down at her. "Listen, Daffy, I'm not very good at this. But, well, do you remember that harum-scarum little girl you used to be?" He didn't give a chance for her indignation to rise. "She was pluck to the backbone, but she was a sad romp. And you're not that little girl anymore."

"Certainly not! But that doesn't mean I'm hen-hearted or anything."

"Of course not, goose. I'd rather have you at my back than half the men in my regiment, but that's not my point. I just meant that you've changed. And I've changed, too. I'm not that unbroken colt intent on kicking over the traces anymore." He put

186

his hand over hers, on the desk. "I just want the chance to show you."

Daphne felt the tingle up to her shoulder, but she wasn't sure what she was hearing. "You want . . . ?"

"I want you not to rush into any bargain with the stodgy squire. I want . . . I suppose I want you to assign me some herculean task, to prove my worth." He withdrew his hand and ran it through his hair. "I want some time alone with you."

"That wouldn't be . . . that is, I don't think . . . Ah, but there is something you can help me with. The boys."

"The boys?"

"Yes, Eldart and Torrence, my cousins. They'll be home this afternoon, and I'm confused as to what to do with them."

He crossed his arms over his chest. If she wasn't offering cake, he'd accept the crumbs. "Well, if you put Dart in the master's suite, that'll be putting the cat among the pigeons for sure."

"No, no, they have their rooms in the nursery wing. I meant about telling them about their father. I'm not a good conspirator after all, I suppose, because I keep worrying that we've done something terrible, so disrespectful to Uncle Albert."

"Nonsense, the man was a rakeshame of the first order. He didn't deserve your respect."

"Yes, but what if Dart and Torry feel differently? I cannot lie to them, but I don't want them to feel guilty forever, or blame me, because we did not mourn their father properly."

"Then you'll just have to ask them what they want to do. Do you want me to go with you to explain? After all, I share whatever blame there might be."

Daphne eagerly accepted his assistance with this latest knotty problem, ignoring the new one he'd just given her. She'd think about the rest of his words later.

So they took the lads apart that afternoon after all the greetings had been made, the boys' new inches made much of, their school records praised or disregarded as befitted the marks.

Daphne explained how their father was sick, and without his medication. Graydon explained how anger and drink exacerbated his condition. "So he died."

The boys just stared, wide-eyed and open-mouthed.

Daphne and Graydon skipped the part about the wine cellar and the icehouse and the body snatchers, and went right to London and the cremation, on account of the wedding and all the company, and their aunt Cleo's happiness.

"But we'll hold a proper funeral right after the wedding, I promise, with all the pomp and ceremony befitting a baron."

"Do we have to?" asked Dart.

And, "Can we go riding now, Daffy?" asked Torry. So much for guilt, blame, and their sense of loss.

Graydon smiled over their heads at Daphne, who smiled back and said, "Yes, if Lord Howell will accompany you. There have been outlaws in the neighborhood. I don't want you out by yourselves."

The boys ran off with a whoop to put on their riding clothes, and Graydon glared at Daphne. "You said you wanted to help," she innocently replied to his raised eyebrow. Then grinned.

Hercules had it easy, Graydon thought in the ensuing days. He didn't have to bear-lead two wild young cubs who'd been shut in a schoolroom for months. They needed a man's influence, Daffy had pleaded. Their tutor was a scholar, she insisted, and could only keep them occupied for an hour or two in the mornings. They'd be bored and underfoot otherwise, she cajoled, and hadn't he offered to help?

It wasn't that he minded the boys. They were likable enough lads, who listened well to the major's lessons on shooting and fishing and riding, all the activities he remembered from his own youth and still enjoyed. Torry and Dart caught on quickly, just the way their cousin Daffy had. But they weren't Daffy. Graydon was no nearer to her—and his goal—than he'd been before.

That's what he thought. No Greek hero could have won Daphne's admiration more easily than by befriending her beloved cousins. As she watched through the windows Daphne marveled at how quickly he won the boys' affection, how kind and caring he was to devote so much time to them. And what a wonderful father Gray would be to his own sons, she thought with an ache in her heart caused only partially by yearning to go join their croquet match instead of selecting music with the church organist.

A few days later, Graydon received two messages among his correspondence sent down from Howell House in London: The diamond necklace and the baron were both awaiting his lordship's pleasure. His lordship, however, was finding uncommon pleasure in the Hampshire countryside and didn't wish to make the journey to London. Even if the trip took a mere two days, they were two days lost in his campaign to win Daffy's regard. Further, he was determined to instill in Dart and Torry a love for the land that they would keep forever. If Dart was to be baron, Graydon wanted to make sure he was better than the last, committed to his property and people instead of his own profligacy. Dart should know every inch of his grounds, every one of his tenants, the way Graydon would want his son to know, if he had a son.

The major's own father's benign absentee landlordship wasn't good enough. Graydon resented that his ancestral estates were being overseen by bailiffs, inhabited by strangers. As soon as that lease with Mr. Foggarty was over, he intended to take up residence. On the other hand, if Howell Hall wasn't rented, he and his father would have had to stay there, far away from Lady Whilton and her precious daughter.

No, he did not want to leave. And that trip to London boded ill on two counts: Seline the Moon Goddess's tantrums, and Terwent. So Graydon took the easy way out: he sent a message. Most of the staff at the Grosvenor Square house was off on holiday until after his father's honeymoon in Scotland, Graydon having decided to take up bachelor lodgings again if he came to Town. Still, he thought, there should be someone competent enough to complete two simple missions. *Deliver the package at Rundell's jeweler's,* he scrawled, *to Lady Seline*

Bowles with a note saying thank you, and bring the urn from the Biggs establishment to Hampshire as soon as possible.

A very junior footman received the note. The butler was out of town, the underbutler was away for two days, and the note, as far as James could cipher it out, indicated the young master wanted the pieces of work done instantly. So he fetched the two parcels, showing Lord Howell's note as his *bona fides*, and laboriously penned a message to the master's light-o'-love: *Thank you, and please—* James did a bit of editorializing—*bring the urn from the Biggs establishment to Hampshire as soon as possible.*

Lady Seline was packed and ready to go before the ink was dry on the footman's note. The diamonds were lovely, of course, but the invitation to join dear Graydon for his father's wedding was better. It was as good as a declaration, in her opinion. And Lady Seline was nothing if not opinionated.

Seline believed, for instance, that darling Howell's message could have been more loverlike, rather than the courteously worded note making her his lackey. She meant to take the dear boy to task, when she had a firmer commitment, of course. Like the ring that went with the choker, which she knew for a fact had been in Rundell's window just last week. Perhaps she'd tease him a bit about his rag manners before accepting the proposal she knew was coming. A man didn't invite his mistress to his former fiancée's house without good and honorable reason.

She'd forgive him for the last-minute invitation, of course. He'd had to test the waters, to make sure Miss Whilton's family wouldn't be offended. Seline supposed his gallantry owed the little country chit that much. And he was gallant, if not eloquent, sending a magnificent gift so she wouldn't feel slighted.

The poor dear must be finding it awkward, Seline considered, forced into company with the forward miss. Well, the discomfort would be over as soon as Seline got to Hampshire, for she'd see the two were never in each other's company. That's what she was invited for, wasn't it? To be at dearest Graydon's side. And to bring his father's wedding gift, of course.

The tall alabaster vase was an odd choice, she thought. She'd opened the crate as soon as her carriage left the city and headed toward country roads, the driver ordered to spring the horses. With her maid asleep on the opposite seat, and the precious crate nestled at Seline's side, what else was she to do? Besides, the top wasn't nailed down, and the straw packing lifted quite easily.

The raven-haired widow decided the thing must be a rare antique, or Napoleon's own, or something to make it more valuable than it seemed at first glance, although she did admire the cloudy swirls of black and gold in the grayish alabaster. (Graydon had settled on something smoky as the best match to the baron's character.) Then she tried to lift it, to see if there was an inscription or a date. The vase weighed so much, there must be something special indeed inside, for the top was sealed with wax and string. Seline didn't dare open the lid. Well, she would have, had the journey not come to a halt so soon. She was in Hampshire the same day she'd received dear Graydon's note. Wouldn't he be surprised?

Chapter Twenty

$\mathcal{C}$hanged? The man swore he'd changed? The only thing that changed was Daphne's room assignments. And without notice. He forgot, was all the blackguard could mumble. Forgot? In a toad's toenail! How in Heaven's name could he forget he'd invited this elegant, sophisticated woman of the world? His world. His mistress, by all that was holy! No, he hadn't forgotten; he'd been afraid of telling Daphne lest it ruin his current, pass the time till something better comes along, flirtation. With her! The lying, cheating, conniving scoundrel!

Daphne was almost as angry at herself because she hadn't changed enough, either. She was still the gullible little fool, almost believing his tender promises, his gentle touches, his affectionate smiles. They hadn't meant one blasted thing, not to him, at any rate. Did the leopard change its spots? No, not even when it was made into a lap robe, which was about as flat and dead as she was wishing Major Lord Howell at this very moment. How dare he make a May game out of her until his paramour arrived?

And bearing gifts, by Jupiter!

It wasn't enough that Daphne had to greet the stunning widow and welcome her to Woodhill while Graydon was struck all aheap at the woman's incredible beauty. No, she had to explain the urn, too, while he stood mumchance after removing the woman's silver-fox stole to reveal a diaphanous confection of the palest gray, with silver ribands under her magnificent breasts. Daphne threw her own barely adequate chest back, in her simple muslin.

And how could he have trusted Uncle Albert's ashes to a woman who used rouge and eye blacking? Daphne hadn't told Cousin Harriet, but he'd blabbed to his bird of paradise! If Lady Bowles was like all the other she-cats of her ilk, interested in nothing but the latest *on-dit*, the news would be all over London, with half the guests wondering if they were to attend a wedding or a funeral. And they'd be wondering at Mama's lack of mourning, chiding her for disrespect and breaking society's rules. Oh, how could he?

As easily as he'd agreed his father should move to the baron's suite, the sly dog. Well, if Graydon thought Daphne was moving Lady Bowles into the newly vacated room next to his, let him think again. Daphne would rot in hell first, which she was most likely going to, anyway, for all the lies she was telling.

"The vase? Oh, that's a surprise Graydon and I devised for you, Mama. Gray ordered it when he was in London last week."

Lady Bowles had insisted the urn be carried in by one of her own footmen, in her silver and black livery. She hefted it from him by the handles, and made a show of presenting it to the bridal pair, with her best wishes from "Dear Graydon." Lord Hollister almost dropped the unexpected weight, then handed it back to the footman with a questioning look toward his son. Knowing the ruby brooch had been his son's wedding gift, the earl was almost as astonished as Graydon, but not quite. Graydon still didn't say anything, his face gone almost as gray as the smoky urn. Daphne didn't notice his coloring, only that he'd selected a container to match his mistress's signature colors. And her eyes.

Daphne's own eyes were spitting fire as her mother turned to Graydon in delight. "Oh, I love surprises, dear, but I hate waiting. Won't you tell us what's inside now?"

Some gurgling noise came from Graydon's throat, that was all. Daphne poured him a glass of sherry, and kicked him when she handed it over.

"It's, ah, something special," he managed to say. "For when you get back from Scotland. The, ah, surprise won't be quite ready until then, will it, Daffy?"

She trod on his toes again, for calling her that silly name in front of Lady Seline. Daphne would wager her month's allowance that no one ever called the Moon Goddess Sally. Right now Her Moonship was casting a very big shadow on Daphne's life.

Meanwhile her mama was kissing the major's cheek for his thoughtfulness. She ought to kiss him twice, Daphne fumed, the two-faced dastard. At least he'd had the sense to snatch the urn away from the footman and try to place it inconspicuously on the mantel. He even dismissed the servant before any more tittle-tattle hit the servants' grapevine.

Lady Seline, of course, insisted the urn be given the place of honor among the other wedding gifts on display in the small parlor. She tucked her hand in Graydon's elbow and led him there, to exclaim over the Sevres bowls and ormolu clocks and silver platters that Lady Whilton and Lord Hollister needed about as much as they needed Uncle Albert's ashes. The widow cleared a space on the linen-draped table, right in the center.

"Now we can all take turns guessing at the secret contents," she cooed. "How utterly delicious." Lady Seline had not been happy to discover the vase was a joint venture between dearest Graydon and the country quiz. Nor was she happy when Lady Whilton suggested she might want to rest in her room this afternoon, or sit with the ladies at their sewing.

"Oh, goodness, no. You mustn't think I'm such a poor traveler." Or that much older than the fresh-faced Miss Whilton. She tapped Lord Howell's arm lightly with her long, manicured fingers. "I cannot wait to see the countryside now that I am here, and breathe the wholesome air. In fact, I was hoping you'd drive me out to see your own estate this afternoon, Graydon dear."

Graydon dear was watching his life pass before his eyes. He was drowning, and clutched at the only life ring he could think of. "It's leased," he gulped. "Can't barge in on the tenants."

"Oh, but I'm sure we can drive by. I so much want to view your childhood home." And measure it for alterations.

"Sorry, Lady Bowles. Hate to disappoint a lady

and all that, but I'm already engaged for the afternoon. My young cousins-to-be, you know. Down from school. I promised them a fishing trip today."

"Cousins?" Seline inquired. "I thought you had no close relations."

"He doesn't," Daphne replied, thinking the world was a better place without any more black-hearted Howells. "They are my cousins, and there is no reason for you not to escort Lady Bowles, Major. I can see to the boys for today." And from now on. She'd make sure the boys were never again exposed to such a shameless libertine. A male influence? Hah! She'd have done better taking them to watch the rams at work.

"No, no, a promise is a promise," Graydon insisted.

"Since when?" Daphne almost shouted, or cried.

Her mama stepped in and drew the widow aside. "No matter, Lady Bowles, you will get your chance to see Howell Hall this evening. We've been invited to dinner by Mr. Foggarty, the tenant. Perhaps you'd like to lie down after all. Daphne, do send off a note to the Hall that we'll be bringing an additional guest. No, no, Lady Bowles, I assure you Mr. Foggarty won't mind. He is everything gracious."

He might be the kindest man in the county, but his table was still going to be at sixes and sevens, like Daphne's room arrangements.

"I don't believe I know a Mr. Foggarty," Seline said.

"That's because he's not of the *ton*. He's just a retired merchant," Graydon commented, and noted Seline's pursed lips that she'd be asked to take her mutton with a Cit. "Perhaps you'd rather not attend, since the company is so plebeian."

Lady Bowles wasn't to be routed that easily. Their host could have been a coal-heaver and she'd go. "No, no, I'm assured country manners are more relaxed. When in Rome, and all that."

Both Daphne and Graydon were thinking that the Romans may have had a good idea, throwing their unwanted citizenry to the lions.

Lord Hollister was laughing. "That's the first time I've heard Full Pockets Foggarty called plebeian. Why, he's the richest man in four shires."

"I'm sure I'll be charmed."

"What do you mean, you didn't invite her?"

"Hush up, for goodness' sake. People are staring." They were at the rear of Howell Hall's music room, where the vicar's wife was performing at the pianoforte. Lady Bowles was seated next to their host, so Graydon could get away for his first words with Daphne since the widow's arrival, albeit they had to be quiet words.

Daphne pasted a polite smile on her face for Admiral Benbow, sitting nearby, and repeated, although in a lower tone of venom, "What do you mean, you didn't invite her? *I* didn't invite her. My mother didn't invite her. Your father didn't—"

"Blister it, Daffy, I know who *didn't* invite her. It was some curst footman at Howell House who did."

"A footman?" she squealed, and Graydon coughed to cover the noise.

"Will you lower your voice! We're in the briars as is, without ruining Foggarty's entertainment. And yes, a footman. I sent a message about bringing the ashes, with a separate note to be delivered to Lady Bowles about another matter entirely. The butler was on holiday, so some underling—if I ever find

199

out which one, he'll be under six feet of dirt—handled the errands. He garbled the notes."

"You expect me to believe that some untrained servant took it upon himself to invite your mistress to your father's wedding?"

"More or less, yes. And she's not my mistress!"

Admiral Benbow's eyebrows shot up. He wasn't quite that deaf. Daphne whispered, "Now who's shouting? And if she's not your mistress, why was she hanging on your sleeve all day and all through dinner? Why were you sending her messages? And why, my lord Mistruth, was she wearing your diamonds?"

Seline had appeared downstairs before they were to leave for Foggarty's wearing another gray gown, this one of sheerest silk, with a décolletage that ended where the waist began. Filling in that vast, milk-white expanse between neck and neckline was a diamond necklace so exquisite that even Lord Hollister had to notice. He hadn't looked at anyone but Cleo Whilton in weeks, but now he had trouble keeping his eyes above Seline's chin. "Lovely, my dear, lovely," he enthused, until Lady Whilton rapped his arm with her fan.

"Thank you, my lord. Doesn't your son have excellent taste?"

Lady Whilton dragged her betrothed out to the carriages before he could comment on Graydon's taste, in gems or in women.

Seline was telling the others: "And I've hardly had a chance to thank him."

Daphne wondered how the woman meant to express her gratitude, if not by plastering herself to Graydon's side as she seemed to be doing. Daphne also noted how Seline fiddled with the necklace all evening, drawing attention to it and her bosom, after which she would announce to everyone that dear Graydon had given it to her.

Daphne felt the complete dowd in her muslin and pearls, with a ribbon through her hair. The widow wore a matching gray turban on her head, with one black ostrich plume that complemented the one long black curl permitted to fall down her smooth, white, half-naked back.

"Not your mistress, hah! Next you'll be telling me your horse recites Shakespeare."

"She's not my mistress any longer, dash it. I never saw her when I went to London. The necklace was to be a farewell gift, an indication that the affair was over."

"I should think a handshake would have done better. Your subtlety seems to have been lost on Lady Bowles."

"Nothing subtle about it at all. These things are understood."

"I wouldn't know."

"Thank heaven."

"And neither, it seems, does the . . . lady."

The vicar's wife finished her piece. They applauded politely. Then Lady Bowles was persuaded to honor them with a few selections on the harp. It needed only that. "Get rid of her," Daphne demanded.

"I haven't even had a chance to speak to her in private. I couldn't very well announce to her in front of the company that her invitation was an error, could I? Be reasonable, Daffy; how can I ask her to leave now that she's here?"

Daphne was fanning herself, intent on the music.

"I promise I'll talk to her tonight, tell her the affair is finished."

"The affair? Is that what you think she traipsed out of London during the Season for? Don't flatter yourself, *dear* Graydon. It's your title and fortune that harpy's after now, not your—" More polite applause drowned out whatever Daphne almost said, happily.

Unhappily, Graydon insisted, "I never mentioned marriage to the woman, I swear. I never had the slightest honorable intention toward her."

"Then tell her. That should do the trick of getting rid of the witch, unless you're nodcock enough to present her with a diamond ring at the same time."

Somehow Graydon didn't think this was the appropriate moment to give Daffy that little gold locket.

He tried to convince Seline to leave, he honestly did. He knew he'd never get anywhere with Daffy while his mistress—his ex-mistress—was in the house. He never got her alone at Foggarty's, though, and his aunt shared their carriage on the way home. Graydon didn't dare leave it till morning, however; Daffy'd be in such a taking by then, he'd need years to win back her trust, the little shrew. The adorable, *jealous* little shrew.

Cheered by that thought, he was smiling when he scratched on Seline's door late that night, after everyone had gone to bed. She was waiting for him, an answering smile on her face and her arms outstretched.

Seline's smile turned to pure rage and one outstretched arm grabbed up a china cat from a nearby table when he explained his mission.

He ducked. "Be reasonable," he seemed to be repeating all night. It worked as well now as with Daphne. A perfume bottle followed the statue into the wall. "You know we never once discussed marriage." He caught the pillow, and the hairbrush. "I wouldn't have asked you to be my errand boy, so there was only one explanation for the necklace. We have to discuss this like adults."

The book from her bedside hit him on the side of his face, but it didn't hurt as much as her next words: "I'm not leaving."

He loosened his neckcloth. "Please, Seline, you are making this deuced awkward."

She folded her arms over her magnificent chest, still adorned with the necklace. "You invited me, sirrah, and I told that to all my friends when I made excuses not to attend their parties and such. I could never go back now without becoming a laughingstock."

"How would you like to go to Brighton then? I would stand the expenses, of course."

"With you?"

"No, dash it, that's the whole point."

"No, *chéri*, the whole point is Miss Daphne Whilton, isn't it? If you think I am going to simply step aside so you can have your bucolic belle, your attics are to let. Besides, a girl has to look out for her own interests."

"If it's the matching ring and earbobs you want . . ."

"Dear Graydon, you always were so generous. I'm sorry, darling, but now that I've set my sights on a higher target, nothing but a wedding ring will do. No, I'm not leaving. Mr. Foggarty seemed taken with me, didn't you think?"

Oh lud. How the hell was he going to explain this to Daffy?

Seline walked him to the door. "I'm truly sorry, dear boy; we would have suited, I think. But don't worry. Miss Whilton looks good in green." She planted a kiss where she'd hit him with the book and showed him out. "Good night, *mon cher* Major."

And that was the way Daphne saw him, in the hallway outside the black widow's door where she'd come to see what the commotion was about. Graydon's clothes were all mussed, he wore a dazed expression on his face and lip rouge on his cheek, and he smelled of the widow's scent.

"She's not leaving," he said.

So Daphne hauled off and hit him. It was no ladylike slap, but the full-fisted blow he'd taught her in case she ever had to defend her honor. Graydon supposed he was lucky she didn't employ the other defensive maneuver he'd taught her. He also supposed this wasn't a good time to give her the locket, either.

Chapter Twenty-one

$\mathcal{N}$ot only wouldn't Daphne believe the major's explanations, she wouldn't even listen to them. Nor did she feel the slightest remorse when he appeared downstairs the following day sporting a large black-and-blue mark on his jaw. Good. The black matched his heart, and the blue . . . well, the blue matched Daphne's spirits.

She threw herself with renewed vigor into the wedding plans. That way she wouldn't have to think about Graydon's perfidy or watch him drool down the demirep's dress, the way every other male was doing, from Lord Hollister to the lowest footman with an excuse to hold a door for her. Even Ohlman's breath came a little quicker when he poured the wine, from over Lady Seline's shoulder. To be fair-minded, Daphne admitted Graydon paid the Moon Goddess no more attention than the others did—but no less, either.

A rose on her pillow melted some of the ice wall around her heart, especially when she read the accompanying note: *She's not my mistress.* The message didn't say she never was, which would have made Miss Whilton happier, except that she'd know it for a lie. Daphne no longer expected abstemious morality from her childhood friend—she'd stopped believing in the White Knight and Father Christmas, too. At least Graydon hadn't thought she was that much of a gull.

"Did you get my message?" he asked hopefully when she passed in the hall, her nose in the air as though he'd brought the scent of the stable in with him, or the widow's, again.

"Don't waste the roses," was all she said. "We need them for the wedding."

That night there was a bouquet of violets, wild ones, from the woods. *She's not my mistress* appeared again. In fact, Daphne had to admit, he'd done his best to keep out of the widow's company.

Gray left the house before Seline was down in the morning, and at lunch he spoke to his father about handling his accounts while the earl was in Scotland. Then he rode out again with the boys, this time looking over properties for Mr. Foggarty to purchase, so the lease for Howell Hall could be terminated early. After tea he disappeared to discuss plans for a drainage problem at the Hall with Woodhill's bailiff, and later permitted Mr. Foggarty to take Seline into dinner. Afterward, at cards, he made sure to partner his aunt in a game with the vicar and his wife.

So if he wasn't Lady Seline's lover—Daphne stayed awake listening for sounds in the corridors; there were none—and wasn't her beloved either, what was the woman still doing here?

The answer had to be Mr. Foggarty. The poor man.

Then Miles started coming around again in his usual pattern of mealtime visits. Woodhill really had a superior kitchen, and his parents were nagging at him to make a match with Daphne and her dowry. Besides, he could puff off his letter of commendation from Bow Street. That villain they'd unearthed was a known felon on Bow Street's list of nuisance criminals, if not a hardened murderer. Now Miles had to warn the Woodhill staff to be on the lookout for the man's youthful accomplices, a tall redhead and a diminutive blond lad.

"And make sure you keep an eye on the dog. That's what clinched the identification," he told Daphne proudly as she walked with him into the parlor where the rest of the company was already at tea. "That animal is ... a Diamond of the first water."

"That scruffy mongrel?" No, Miles had caught his first glimpse of the Moon Goddess, in gossamer silver tonight, with sequined stars sewn to her skirts. Miles stared, struck speechless.

"Gets 'em all that way, the first time," Cousin Harriet snickered. "The blood all rushes from the brains to between their legs. Can't talk, can't think, can't see the hoity-toity miss gives off as much warmth as the moon she poses as."

Daphne made the introductions, and Miles made a cake over himself, to the point of ignoring the tea cakes. Daphne turned away in disgust, to see Graydon's gloating smile. "She's not my mistress," he silently mouthed in her direction.

And she'd never leave now, not with another handsome man to beguile. Of course, Pomeroy was no match for Mr. Foggarty for wealth, but he was younger, better-looking in a virile, rustic way, and came from decent family. She could polish him up nicely before parading him around London to prove her respectability at last. Only the highest sticklers would refuse her entry then. Now the lower sticklers were beginning to look askance on her affairs, her gaming, and her unpaid bills.

On the other hand, Foggarty could leave her a wealthier widow, sooner. And who was to say he couldn't use some of that fortune to buy himself a title for paying off Prinny's debts? Then she could have it all, her place in Society and the wherewithal to enjoy it. But squires needed wives, while rich old men mostly wanted bed-warmers. And Pomeroy was Miss Whilton's beau, which made him even more attractive. No, Seline wasn't budging.

And the wedding was getting closer. With the arrival of more guests, the earl's kinfolk, Mama's old schoolmates, Graydon's godparents, Lady Seline was not so conspicuous. Oh, she would always stick out as the brightest star in the night sky, but not so obviously as Graydon's mistress. He treated her with the same respect he gave his ancient relatives, and Seline flirted with him, Daphne noted, only when there were no other men around for her to practice her wiles upon. Or when Daphne was watching, the cat. If she hoped to make Miss Whilton jealous, she was meowing up the wrong tree.

Daphne was beginning to believe Gray's protestations of innocence. Not because flowers kept appearing in her bedroom, and not even because he seemed so indifferent to the widow and to her attentions to other men. No, what convinced Daphne that he might truly have ended the affair and its complications was how assiduously Lady Bowles was working at attaching another gentleman. If Seline had the least chance with Gray, with his looks, title, wealth, and charm, she'd never glance at Miles or Mr. Foggarty. No woman in her right mind would.

Cousin Harriet's gown needed last-minute alterations, Dart broke out in a rash from the starched collar on his new shirt. Torry skinned his knee, and the lobsters arrived lethargic. One of the guests' maids was thought to be increasing, the gardener cut off the tip of his finger instead of a bloom, and that dog swiped a whole haunch of venison to share with the stable hands. Two carriages collided on the way to the village, the vicar was developing a sore throat, and there were clouds. Lord Hollister had too much to drink the night before and couldn't remember where he'd put the wedding ring for safe-keeping, and Mama was having spasms that Uncle Albert would arrive to ruin everything. Daphne had a headache. Ohlman had another glass of sherry.

It was a lovely wedding.

The village church was filled, every seat taken with family and guests, with servants and local people standing in the back and outside waving branches of orange blossoms. There were flowers everywhere, inside and out, woven into garlands up the aisle, draped over the doorways, in massed arrangements of red, white, and pink roses.

The earl and his son stood by the vicar, next to the intricately wrought new altar cloth, waiting for the rest of the bridal party. Lord Hollister was elegant in black swallowtails and white satin breeches, with a red rose in his lapel. Graydon was the proud picture of British manhood in his scarlet regimentals, for the last time, he insisted. His papers would be processed by the end of the month. Torry escorted Cousin Harriet to her front-row seat at one side of the aisle; Dart walked with the earl's sister to the other side. The boys hated their white velvet coats and short pants, but wore them with resignation, Daphne having threatened them with a quick return to school if they protested once more.

Then Daphne walked down the aisle by herself, as maid of honor. She was radiant in soft pink, with a circlet of roses in her hair and ribbons trailing down her back. More than one of the congregants was heard to whisper that Miss Whilton looked like a bride herself, beautiful and beaming on everyone she passed. Daphne was so delighted this day was finally coming to pass, she could have cried.

Ohlman the butler *was* crying as he led Lady Whilton down the aisle. He'd argued against such a heresy, but Lady Whilton would not hear of his protests.

"Perhaps it wouldn't do in London where they are all such snobs, but here in Hampshire where we know everyone? There is no one else I would rather have, no one else who has looked after me so long or so loyally. I cannot very well ask my brother-in-law, can I?"

She certainly couldn't, so Ohlman accepted the honor, and wept with pride as he handed his mistress into the keeping of her new husband. Lady Whilton went gracefully, elegant in her rose-colored satin with the double-heart brooch pinned at the center of the neckline. Luckily they were rubies and matched her color scheme, all selected not to clash with Graydon's regimental jacket.

The vicar cleared his sore, scratchy throat. "Dearly beloved," he began.

Daphne let go a deep sigh. The roses had bloomed on time, the organist hadn't missed a note, the vicar's voice would last through the service if he cut the sermon short. The church smelled of flowers, and the boys had no mice, frogs, or snakes in their pockets.

It was such a lovely wedding that Ohlman wept throughout the entire ceremony. Cousin Harriet had to hand him her handkerchief.

All of the servants wanted to watch their mistress get married and their own Ohlman take his part in the ceremony. The kitchen staff had to stay behind, with the wedding breakfast to be held immediately after the service, but most of the other indoor servants were being permitted to attend. Not the newly hired, temporary staff, of course, for what did they care anyway? And someone had to stay behind.

In the stables, every driver and groom had been assigned to getting the company sorted into and out of their carriages to and from the church, holding horses during the ceremony, bearing the servants off in wagons, carting the massive floral tributes around. Again, only the newest hand was left behind to mind the remaining riding horses.

Opportunity was knocking, if not on the front door where one footman was left on duty, then on the rear parlor window, which Handy had open in a flash. Sailor was waiting on the other side with the wheelbarrow he used to cart the manure. Jake's gang was going to Heaven in a handcart, with Lady Whilton's wedding presents.

Handy had all of his possessions and two pillow slips hidden under his skirts. He hadn't dared approach the guest bedrooms above where jewel boxes waited on every vanity and bureau; too many of the visiting valets and maids were also waiting there to refurbish their employees between the service and the reception. The dining room with all its silverware was too near the kitchens, and the hired musicians were tuning up in the grand parlor.

The smaller room was empty of everything except a king's ransom in gifts, just as Handy's roommates had described it. The circumstances couldn't have been better if Jake had planned it. The only problem for Handy was deciding what to take.

Small and valuable, Jake always told them. Easy to hide and easy to sell. Gold letter openers, gold picture frames, gold candlesticks went into the first sack. Silver platters, silver bowls, silver candlesticks followed. Lots of silver candlesticks. Pearl-handled knives, gem-inlaid candy dishes, ivory inkstands, all got packed and handed out the window to Sailor, along with two dishes of sweetmeats left on tables nearby for when the company returned, and three cut-glass decanters from the mantel.

The last items were so Sailor and Handy could have a celebration of their own, since they'd be missing the servants' party later that night. Sailor had wanted to stay for the food and drink and a chance to dance with those little maids Handy kept crowing about, but they didn't dare make the heist, hide the plunder, and come back. The last time they buried something, Sal dug him up.

Sailor started on one of the decanters while Handy went back with the other pillowcase. There were the statues and vases: jade, porcelain, and crystal, all worth small fortunes to a boy raised in London streets. All went into the bag. A music box, a globe, three paperweights, and a marvelous egg that opened up to reveal a tiny bride and groom. Sailor wrapped that up special in his nightshirt, the same flannel nightshirt that had been the baron's, then Jake's. He stuffed in some more silver candlesticks, then spread the gifts remaining on the table around better, filling in empty spots, so no one would notice the theft too soon. It fair broke Handy's heart to leave so much, but they just couldn't carry those huge centerpieces or the tea services or the sets of rare books.

Jewelry sure would have been nice, Handy thought, a watch or a necklace or a gent's stickpin he could pop into his pocket, but these swells didn't give good stuff like that as wedding presents, it seemed. A bunch of the nipcheese ones just wrote letters, it looked like, for there was a pile of rolled-up parchments in an enameled bowl. Handy dumped the papers out and packed the bowl. Stock certificates, consols, acres in Jamaica, and a bill of sale for a thoroughbred mare rolled off the table. "Cheapskates," Handy muttered as he gathered them up again onto the table so the room still looked neat.

Church bells started to ring. Handy quickly handed the second bag of booty out to his brother, who tossed it onto the wheelbarrow. So much for the porcelain and the crystal. And now they had to leave in a hurry in case someone heard the sound of shattering giftware.

Handy gave one more look, and grabbed up the alabaster urn that was smack in the middle of the table. The maids said it was something special, with everyone guessing what was inside. God knew it was heavy enough to hold a pirate's horde. The nobs'd be sure to notice it was gone, though, so Handy snatched a vase of flowers that was about the same size off the mantel and put that in the urn's place. It didn't look right, so he took the flowers out. And took them along with the urn when he jumped out of the window. They'd look nice on Jake's new grave.

Chapter Twenty-two

*W*heelbarrows don't work so well in the woods. And maybe Jake would have figured a better plan for the getaway, rather than going back to that old fallen-in cottage. But they couldn't go trundling down the highway in broad daylight, and the loot had to be reapportioned before the broken crystal cut through the muslin pillowcase, and they had to do something about changing their disguises. And Handy demanded a bit of celebration, to catch up with his brother.

So they left the barrow at the icehouse and carried the plunder through the stands of oak and evergreen, Sailor complaining the whole way of the weight of that blasted urn Handy was making him carry as gentle as an infant.

"Jake allus said small and light. You have to go an' prig a bloomin' marble flowerpot with handles."

"Well, you went an' tossed the glass gewgaws. I had to find us somethin' else, didn't I? 'Sides, the maids was all in a swivet over the thing. Must be an antique or somethin'. Shut up and pass the bottle."

They arrived at their former hideaway thinking it was too bad Jake had been dug up, or they could have put the flowers on his grave right there, so he could join in the party.

Sailor wet his whistle, and then his hair to get rid of the blacking. They used the boot polish this time on Handy's new coif, once they hacked off his long blond hair. He was back in boy's clothes, too, with an improbable mustache drawn over his lip in an attempt to add to his manliness.

Sailor was not going to look like anything but a big carrot-topped sprout who kept pulling his cap down over his ears. He smelled so badly of manure, though, they figured no one would get close enough to recognize the footpad of his description.

Since they had to wait until dark to use the road, neither having enough confidence to attempt byways and deer tracks, they unpacked. It might have been wiser to get on their way, put as much distance as possible between themselves and the scene of the crime, but if they were wiser, Sailor mightn't smell of horse dung and Handy mightn't look like an underage pimp. If they were wiser still, they might have stolen some food to put in their stomachs, beneath the potent whiskey in the decanters. Then again, if wishes were horses, these two would likely wish for theirs well done.

Handy emptied one of the sacks of stolen goods out onto the bare dirt floor. If any of the rare Sevres or Dynasty ware had survived, they were potsherds now, tossed aside for some future Lord Elgin to weep over.

The ornately embellished egg didn't make the

journey, either. Handy took a few minutes to scrape the gold filigree and seed pearls off the shell, which had taken some poor, underpaid artisan a month to decorate. Disappointed, Handy tipped the other bag open. The silver and gold had taken a few nicks and dents, that was all. It was still sellable, still worth more money than either of the thieves had ever seen. They were on easy street, as soon as they could find it.

A few candies and brandies later, Sailor wanted to open the urn. "Why lug that ugly thing around if the good stuff is inside?" he asked.

Handy wanted to wait, to bring the whole package to Fred the Fence.

"Then you gots to carry it," his brother ordered, which was the deciding vote. Handy used one of the pearl-handled knives to slice through the wax that sealed on the lid, then pried the top off with a small gold pickle fork. He tipped the urn over, right there onto the dirt floor of the abandoned cottage.

Sailor stuck a finger in the gritty pile, licked it, shook his head, and sneezed. "Ashes."

Handy poked through the dark mound of finely ground rubble with the pickle fork. "Must be somethin' in here that needed special packing, like a diamond mine."

"No, you clunch, it's ashes."

"Why the hell give a jar of ashes for a weddin' present?" Handy wanted to know, as if his brother were a font of information.

Sailor shrugged and sneezed again. "Rich folks is different, that's all." Still, he kept sifting through the ashes, letting the stuff trickle through his thick fingers, until something didn't trickle. Something that looked a whole lot like a finger. Sailor jumped up, which scattered more of the ashes. "It's him!" he screamed. "The bloke what died! The one in the barrel. Now they got him in a flowerpot!"

Handy was halfway out the door. "Oh Lord, he's come back to haunt us. We're never goin' to be shut of the blighter!"

"Why's he after us? We wasn't the ones what had a thing against coffins. We would've got Jake a nice one, if the dibs was in tune."

"He's mad at us, is all. Maybe he wanted to stay in that icehouse, like a clause in his will or somethin', and we disturbed him. Spirits like their rest, they do." Handy looked around, saw the ashes all over the place. "He's going to be a whole lot madder now."

"Quick, get him back in the jar!"

So they scrabbled around trying to sweep up the ashes without a broom. They used the broken pottery shards to gather the piles together, and unavoidably gathered a lot of dirt from the cottage floor, too. And slivers of glass, chips of porcelain, crumbs from the broken eggshell, and a few chicken bones from their last meal here.

"What if we ain't got all of him? He'll come back to haunt us like one of them phantoms. You know, with a cape where his head was s'posed to be and only red gleams from what was eyes."

Handy's manly lip was trembling, fake mustache and all. "How're we going to get more of him? You went and sneezed on the poor bastard, scattered him from one corner of the place to t'other."

The drink was talking now in Sailor, and it was scared, too: "What if . . . what if it was his ballocks or somethin' that we lost? He'd be so mad, he'd come get ours."

"No way!"

"I swear he would. Wouldn't you, some fool tips your rocks on the ground?"

Handy was already feeling the cold hand of doom squeezing at his privates. So he ran outside and found two round stones, almost of a size and shape. "Here, maybe he won't notice." He stuffed some fish bones down the urn's mouth, too, in case the ghoul lost a toe or something. Sailor sacrificed his lucky marble, in case it was an eye he sneezed into the next county. Handy threw in those little seed pearls for teeth, unaware the baron's had been just as false. "There, good as new."

They crammed the top back on the urn as though that would keep the demon inside. But it wasn't going to work. The dead man's ghost already had them in its clutches and was giving them a good shake.

"We got to bring him back," Handy said, his voice even more high-pitched than ever.

"I ain't touchin' him." Sailor's hands were shaking so violently, they couldn't have touched his own poker to make sure it was still there.

"Well, I ain't."

"You took him."

"You sneezed on him."

"Maybe we could just put him in the ground with Jake?"

Handy gave the matter his full consideration, from across the room. "No, he must want to be with his loving fambly. They wouldn't've put him in the center of the table that way otherwise. We got to get him back. You're bigger. You can—"

"Not me. I ain't—"

* * *

Ohlman still had tears in his eyes halfway through the wedding reception at the Manor. He cleared his throat to catch Daphne's attention while she was organizing her cousins and some of the local children into teams for races on the lawn. Their elders sat on chairs under the canopies erected to shield delicate complexions from the sun, or they strolled around the gardens, relaxing after the lavishly abundant wedding breakfast, which, of course, did not start until after noon. It was a magnificent sight, Daphne thought, like a painting. All the ladies' pastel gowns dotted the landscape like flowers—except for Lady Seline's silver tulle, of course. And the men's more somber garb added contrast—except for Graydon's scarlet uniform, which made him the focal point of the composition wherever he happened to wander. Of course, he would have captured the imagination anyway, being so tall and athletically built and devastatingly handsome.

He was capturing Daphne's attention a lot more than she wished that afternoon as, almost against her will, she kept darting glances in his direction to see if he was worshiping at the Temple of the Moon like half the other men present. More often than not, he was circulating among the guests, greeting old friends, introducing the London visitors to the locals, playing host, making everyone comfortable and welcome. Ah, but she never denied he had charm.

Right now he was at Ohlman's side, waiting for her to finish with the children. Ohlman was weepy, and Graydon looked grim as he took her arm and led her a distance away from any of the clusters of guests.

"Trouble," he said, "but try to smile."

Ohlman was wringing his hands. "Nothing like this has ever happened in all my years of butling. And today of all days, when Lady Whilton, Lady Hollister, that is, put such faith in me."

Daphne had no problem smiling. "Are you still in a fidge over that? I've had nothing but compliments over the ceremony, and Mama is so happy." She looked around to find her mother in a circle of her bosom bows, laughing and giggling like a debutante.

"She won't be happy when she finds half her wedding gifts have been stolen!" It was a good thing Graydon had his arm under hers to catch her when she tripped.

"Ohlman?"

"I'm afraid so, Miss Daphne. While we were at the church, it seems. Mrs. Binder is beside herself, because two of the servants are missing also, the last two she hired as temporary help. They didn't go into the village with the rest."

"No, they stayed and robbed us blind!"

"Not quite, miss. Mrs. Binder is in the parlor right now, comparing the remaining gifts with the lists you've been keeping for the acknowledgments. I took the liberty of locking the door behind her, so no one wanders in and notices their present is not on display."

"Clever man. What would we do without you? Do you think most of the gifts are still there?"

"All of the important ones, from what I recall, Miss Daphne, and the written ones. Most of what seems to be missing are small knickknacks, tableware, candlesticks, and the like."

"Then there is nothing to worry about. Mama

didn't need any of those things anyway, so she won't notice that stuff gone. We won't have to tell her and ruin her wonderful day. We can thank the givers and they never need to know their silver jam jar or china creamer has done a flit either. See? Now, relax and tell Mrs. Binder she is not to blame. We can all make character misjudgments." She turned to Graydon, smiling. "Can't we?"

He didn't laugh at her teasing. "It gets worse."

"Worse? What could be worse than thieves stealing the presents on the day of the wedding with all these people in the house?"

"They stole the urn."

"The urn? *That* urn?"

Miles wasn't concerned with the theft of the gifts. He was more concerned that Mr. Foggarty was making headway with Lady Bowles whilst he was dragged aside by Daphne. "You should have posted a guard," was all he told her, his eyes on the widow.

"I did post a footman, and he made sure no one entered the house. One of the thieves was already inside, though. We think they were a brother and sister; at least that's what they told Mrs. Binder when she hired them. He was tall and dark, she was small and blond."

Miles wasn't listening. Foggarty was kissing Lady Seline's fingers, the lecher.

"So what are you going to do about it?"

"I'd plant him a facer if I thought it would— Oh, about the robbery? Nothing I can do now. The culprits are long gone. What, did you think they were going to sit around waiting to be arrested? Your cracksmen are too smart for that, if they planned this robbery so far in advance to get hired on as

222

servants. They're halfway to London by now to sell the goods. You can give me a list of the stolen properties tomorrow and I'll send it on to Bow Street, who'll keep an eye on the known fences."

"That's all? You're not even going to look for clues or call out dogs to follow their trail?"

"Now?" he squawked in agony as Foggarty led the widow off toward the maze. When they were out of sight he recalled himself enough to say, "Uh, that is, you were the one who didn't want to disturb your mother's wedding." Miles looked over his shoulders to make sure no one overheard. "Your uncle and all."

"They took him, too."

Miles looked so pitiful then, thinking of what a fool he'd appear in front of the dashing widow, chasing after the remains of a man not officially dead, that Daphne almost forgave him for his wavering affections. Almost. Miles Pomeroy was supposed to be waiting—anxiously—for her answer to his proposal. He was supposed to act like he cared. He was also supposed to put duty above pleasure and go searching for Uncle Albert. Was there no such thing as a man with a constant heart?

Chapter Twenty-three

$\mathcal{I}$t was the finest wedding the county had seen in years, so everyone agreed after the bridal couple left for Scotland amid shouts and cheers, ribald jokes, and rose petals. Then most of the local guests departed, the vicar to go rest his voice on Daphne's urging, because she was going to need his services in the not too distant future, she hoped. The vicar hoped she meant another wedding, to young Howell after all and not that fickle Pomeroy, who was busy making sheep eyes at a woman no better than she ought to be. He didn't say anything, of course; his voice was too weak.

The house guests were having their carriages brought round, too, in order to make London by nightfall, or the first stage of their journeys to some other country residence or fashionable retreat. The earl's sister was one of those leaving, setting off on a tour of the New World, now that her brother finally had someone to look after him.

Daphne and Graydon stood side by side at Woodhill's front door, accepting congratulations and wishing Godspeed as Ohlman and his minions handed over canes and hats and oversaw the loading of baggage. Pomeroy and Foggarty were among the last to leave, each trying to outstay the other. Daphne finally had to hint Miles away, saying, "I am sure you must be *yearn*ing to be on your way. *Earn*ing our regard with your devotion to duty. We'll be interested in *learn*ing the results of your investigation tomorrow."

Reluctantly Miles left to go beat the bushes in a halfhearted manner. The other half of his heart belonged to the most beautiful woman he'd ever seen, who unfortunately was not the woman whom he'd asked to wed. Pomeroy was a troubled man, so troubled that he never noticed the wheelbarrow by the icehouse or the tracks leading into the woods. He found nothing but a guilty conscience.

Foggarty took his leave with a wink and a leer— for Graydon. "Two beauties, eh? Lucky dog."

Then Daphne turned to Lady Bowles, who'd parked herself in the hallway as though she were family. "Should I have one of the grooms send for your carriage, my lady?"

Seline brushed aside the hint. "Oh, I sent my coach back when I arrived, sure that dear Graydon would escort me home. But don't worry, my dear, I won't rush off on you in your hour of need."

"Need? What need is that?" Daphne's tone was sour, as she was sure that Graydon had taken the widow into his confidence again.

"Your need for a chaperone, of course. Graydon's aunt is gone, and it would be highly improper for you two to be alone in the house."

"My cousin Harriet is here as my companion. I

225

assure you there is no need to put off your own plans. And if Gray has to accompany you . . ." She'd murder him, that's what.

Seline waved one graceful hand in the air. "But your cousin took to her rooms hours ago. Too much champagne, I believe. No, you need me to lend countenance, even though you are almost brother and sister now."

Daphne fumed but Graydon choked. A man didn't want to carry his sister upstairs and make mad, passionate love to her. Perhaps they needed a chaperone after all. But Seline Bowles playing propriety? When pigs grew wings. "Your new respect for the conventions mightn't have anything to do with a certain nabob, would it?"

"Don't be tiresome, dear boy, and I shan't be either." With that she floated up the stairs to plan her wardrobe for the coming days.

As one, Graydon and Daphne hurried to the small parlor. There was a neat inventory of missing items, with *Urn, alabaster, gift of Miss Daphne and Major Howell*, heading the list. Daphne sank onto a sofa and kicked her slippers off. "Uncle Albert is really gone again. Lud, how can we hold his funeral without him?"

Graydon poured them each a glass of wine from the solitary decanter remaining on the mantel. He handed one to Daphne and sat beside her. "A toast."

"Not to Uncle Albert, I hope."

"To the thieves. Can you imagine the poor cawkers' surprise when they realize what they've got?"

Daphne pretended to read from the list: "Ten candlesticks, silver; two figurines, jade; one baron, incinerated. Oh dear." She sipped at her wine, wondering why the man's presence made her forget to panic at the hobble they were in now. Gray was sitting so relaxed, with his coat unbuttoned and his carefully arranged curls falling onto his forehead. He always could make her feel safe and secure. When they were children he used to tell her not to be afraid of the thunder and lightning, that he'd protect her. She used to believe him, too. Daphne sighed.

The major heard her and said, "Don't worry, sweetheart, we'll come about."

There, he was doing it again, keeping the storm at bay.

Graydon reached into his pocket and pulled out a small box wrapped in tissue. He held it out to her. "Here, I've been wanting to give this to you for ages, but the time never seemed right. It's to celebrate our parents' wedding."

She unwrapped the package to reveal a gold heart on a chain, similar to the one she used to have. She swallowed the lump in her throat. "It's lovely, Gray. Thank you."

"It's just a token. I wish it could be fancier."

"Like Lady Seline's diamond necklace?"

"Brat," he replied with affection. "If I got you diamonds, your name would be a byword in the neighborhood, and well you know it. You deserve something better than this, though, for being such a trooper about this whole coil, and making the wedding such a success."

"No, the locket is perfect." She started to open the sections.

"A portrait inside would have been too egotistical, even for me. What was in the other one, any-way?"

"A lock of your hair your mother once gave me." Daphne fussed with the catch so he couldn't see her face. When she finally got the locket open, a tiny scrap of folded paper fell out. "What . . . ?" The message read: *She's not my mistress.* "You gud-geon."

"That not what I wanted to say, either, Daffy, but the time was always wrong."

Daphne's heart was hammering so loudly, she was surprised he didn't hear it. "What did you want to say?"

"I—"

The time was still wrong. Ohlman cleared his throat from the doorway. Daphne tucked her toes under her skirts so the butler wouldn't see she was barefoot.

"Pardon, Miss Daphne, but that Terwent person has returned. He insists on seeing you or Major Howell. I explained that you were resting after the wedding and all, but he is determined to wait on the doorstep until he sees you."

Graydon sighed. "You may as well show him in, Ohlman. The deuced chap is as hard to dislodge as a tick."

"And we don't want him feeding the gossip mills in the village either," Daphne agreed.

The valet hadn't improved in the days he was gone. He was still pinch-faced and prune-lipped, long-nosed and livid that he was being done out of his rightful share of whatever villainy was going on.

He'd been to Bow Street, it seemed, and all the morgues. Everyone knew of Awful Albert Whilton, but no one knew where he was. In desperation, Terwent had called on the magistrate, who allowed as how some soldier had kindly brought the baron's body to London some days back, with his identification on him. The family had been informed.

"Is it true?" Terwent demanded. "He was already cold when you sent me haring around town?"

The baron had been cold, all right, from the icehouse. Graydon reflected on the peripatetic barrel and truthfully admitted, "We were as confused as you about the whole matter. Of course, we weren't surprised to learn of his death, considering the baron's state when he left."

"And we did notify his man of business, who must have missed you in London." Daphne was careful not to say when they'd sent the letter. "So now we are merely awaiting the return of the ashes until we proceed."

"Ashes? You're not burying the bas—the baron?"

"No, the condition of the body, don't you know, and the amount of time gone by." Graydon studied his fingertips.

Terwent's nose was twitching; he was smelling a rat. No body, no funeral. No funeral, no reading of the will. And no reading of the will meant no pension for Terwent. He wasn't sure why these toffs were so determined to keep him from his due, but if they weren't up to something crooked, his name wasn't Sam Fink, which, in fact, it was. Close as inkle-weavers, these two, with her shoes under the sofa. They had more than their heads together, unless he missed his guess.

"Them ashes better be getting here in a hurry or I'll be knowing the reason why. I'll go straight to the magistrate, I will. And not that local bumbler who sits in your pocket"—with a glare toward Daphne—"but his nibs in London. He'll get to the bottom of this; see if he don't."

Lord Rivington should be back in town from the wedding by then, but Graydon saw no reason to have this unpleasant little leech disturb his godfather's rest. "The ashes will be here tomorrow, without fail." He tossed the valet some coins. "Why don't you put up at the Golden Crown again, and we'll send for you as soon as we know more details."

Daphne didn't want this man snooping around the house any more than Graydon did. "We'd offer you a room, but the Manor is still at sixes and sevens, with the guests and their servants."

Terwent left, still muttering about those ashes being there tomorrow or else. The moment the door was shut behind him, Daphne ran, without bothering to put on her shoes, over to the long table where the remaining gifts were displayed. She was studying the selection when Graydon reached over her shoulders and picked up a silver Russian samovar.

"This one, I think. It has a lid and handles."

"But it's got a spigot!"

"So the baron will think he's in a taproom and feel right at home."

The Wedgewood was too pretty, and the Ming too valuable. Daphne nodded and followed him to the fireplace, where they tried to fill the coffee urn with the ashes from the grate. Without a broom and dustpan, they had as much trouble as Sailor and Handy, at last resorting to tearing pages from the gift list book to serve as sweepers. Not enough volume, Graydon decided, and threw another log on the fire. Not enough weight, Daphne judged, and tossed her slippers into the flames. They were ruined anyway, and Uncle Albert had always been as tough as shoe leather.

By the time they were finished and the urn was back on the table, Graydon felt like a chimney sweep, but Daphne looked like Cinderella to him, all warm and rosy, with streaks of soot down her face, and dirty toes showing beneath her bedraggled skirts. Was there ever a prettier sight? He took out his handkerchief to wipe her flushed cheeks, stepping nearer to do a better job. And nearer, until there was hardly any space between them, and her cheeks were even pinker, and her blue, blue eyes were staring up at him.

"Ahem," said Ohlman from the doorway.

Graydon stepped back. "No, I can't find the speck in your eye, Daffy."

"Pardon, Miss Daphne, but Master Torrence is ailing. The nursemaid fears he had too much punch, but thought you should be called since the lad is feverish."

Torrence wasn't the only male with fevered brow, Ohlman reflected with satisfaction as Miss Daphne swept from the room with a hurried good night to the major. Her presence wasn't required in the nursery whatsoever. The boy's tutor was with him, and they'd already administered a sleeping draught, but Ohlman wasn't going to fail in his duty again, not twice in one day. Bare feet indeed!

Except for Ohlman and Mrs. Binder, who were consoling each other with the private stock in the housekeeper's apartment, the servants were all finished with their celebration and had gone to bed.

Tomorrow was the big cleaning day and they'd be up early, with headaches.

When the last candles were finally extinguished, Sailor and Handy crept out of the woods and slinked toward the house. They met Sal, who was patrolling the grounds for leftovers. She didn't bark at them, naturally. They were old friends, and her mouth was full.

Slowly, silently, like shadows at Stonehenge, the two bandits made their way to the colonnaded porch of Woodhill Manor. They inched their way up the marble stairs, each holding one handle of the urn. Since Handy was so much smaller than Sailor, the urn bumped a few times, chipping the alabaster and making enough noise to waken the dead. Luckily Uncle Albert was a heavy sleeper.

At last they were at the massive front door. The boys lowered the urn to the ground, banged on the knocker, then ran as if all the hounds in hell were at their heels.

It was only Sal, with half a roast duck to share.

Chapter Twenty-four

It is back. Such was the message in Ohlman's hand both Graydon and Daphne received with their morning hot water. They met at the top of the stairs and together hurried in search of the butler. He couldn't explain, other than that the container had been left on their doorstep last night, like an infant at the church gates. Now it was locked in the butler's pantry. Ohlman wasn't taking any more chances. They all went to look.

The alabaster was chipped and the lid was unsealed and the contents rattled.

"What's that noise? It never used to make noise." Graydon tried to look inside, but the neck was too narrow.

"My word, I wonder what they did, the thieves who took it."

"We'll never know. Maybe it's better that way. There are some peculiar people in the world."

"But what if it's not . . . ?"

"For all we know, Mr. Biggs could have sent us

one of the missionaries who were his previous clients. Don't think about it. Just be happy we have *someone* to show Terwent."

Ohlman nodded, then added, "It also feels lighter than it did." So they added some of the ashes from the samovar, shoe leather and all, and glued the lid on with sealing wax. They all watched as Ohlman locked the door behind them.

Then it was time to notify the vicar, tell the boys to put on their black armbands, and inform the rest of the household.

"Good." Cousin Harriet wasn't precisely grief-stricken. She refused to put on mourning for the dirty dish. "He wouldn't for me." Daphne couldn't argue with that.

Lady Bowles, on the other hand, wore perpetual mourning, so she was prepared.

"We'll understand if you choose to leave now," Daphne hinted. "With a funeral and mourning, this won't be a very lively house party, I'm afraid. We won't be entertaining, of course." She pointed to where the servants were draping hatchments over the doors and hanging crepe from the mirrors.

"Oh, but I couldn't desert you now. Furthermore, Mr. Foggarty is planning a lovely dinner. It would be a shame if we all had to cancel. Why, he'd have no company whatsoever. But don't worry, I'll make your excuses."

The few remaining guests hurried their departures when Daphne explained the situation. They didn't want to add to her burden, they said. They didn't want to perjure their souls by pretending to be sorry the old curmudgeon was dead, more like.

Daphne sent messengers round to all the houses in the neighborhood, the village, and the tenant farms. Not many chose to come to pay their respects to a man they didn't. What, give up a day's planting for that bastard what tried to raise the rent on them? Not likely.

So it was a small group that returned to the village chapel for the service. Miles may have come out of duty; Mr. Foggarty definitely came to see Seline, for Daphne could hear them chatting in the back row. A few locals did attend, mostly the grandmothers with nothing better to do. Two old men who remembered Uncle Albert as a nasty little boy came to gloat that they'd lived longer than the nasty piece of goods he'd turned out to be. Ohlman and Mrs. Binder were there representing the Woodhill staff. Terwent sat alone, weepers tied to his hat. And Mr. Rosten from the London solicitors' firm took a seat as the vicar opened his prayer book.

Daphne tried to pay attention, seated as she was in the front pew, and to set an example for Dart and Torry next to her. Her mind kept wandering, though, from the vicar's raspy voice to the man seated at the end of her pew, on Torry's other side.

How good he was, she thought, and not of Uncle Albert, whose urn was on the new altar cloth. Graydon had carried it there himself, to guarantee its arrival. Not many other men would go to such efforts for a wretch who wasn't even related, or work so hard to ease the boys' apprehensions. He wasn't wearing his uniform, but the midnight superfine stretched across his broad shoulders looked just as handsome. With the gleaming white stock and black brocaded waistcoat, he was a nonpareil, and Daphne felt even more blue-deviled at her own appearance.

She looked a frump. Her blacks were two years out of style, hot and heavy, and she looked ready for the coffin herself in the dreary ensemble, topped with an old black ruched bonnet of Mama's that hid every curl of hair. One week, that's all she'd give Uncle Albert of deep mourning. One week was seven days more than he deserved, and about how long it would take the village seamstress to stitch up some light muslins in gray or lavender. No, just lavender. Let the Moon Goddess keep her grays and silvers. Heaven forbid anyone think Daphne was trying to compete with the dashing widow.

Daphne's attention was recalled to the service when the vicar cut short the eulogy because his voice was reduced to a croak—and because he was reduced to lies, trying to find something good to say about the baron.

Finally they all trooped out to the graveyard and the family crypt. The boys pointed out the grave of the highwayman along the way. The newly dug plot had a bouquet on it, which curiously resembled the arrangement of flowers Daphne had done for the wedding reception. She shrugged and watched as the urn was placed on a shelf in the Whilton mausoleum. The vicar said a few last words, his voice miraculously restored, and they all gave heartfelt amens.

Graydon took Daphne's hand to lead her over the rough path back through the graveyard. "Do you think he'll stay put this time?" she asked.

"Definitely. I tipped the sexton to come back and nail the door shut."

Crime begets crime. That was Miles Pomeroy's favorite axiom, and it was true. Give malfeasance an inch, it would take a mile—of highway. The news around the darker side of London, mostly thanks to Terwent's panic-driven probes, was that there were easy pickings in Hampshire. Pigeons were just waiting to be plucked. So the hawks moved in.

There were five thugs waiting on the road Sailor and Handy had to take to get to London. Jake's boys had decided to stop first at the Gypsy camp to trade a candlestick or two for a pair of horses. Why should they walk the whole way when they were rich? The fact that they still couldn't ride a horse didn't bother them. Sailor was an expert on the species now, from cleaning their stalls.

But the Gypsies were gone, having heard that the magistrate was looking into current robberies. The caravan left before the blame, as it inevitably did, fell their way. Miles found the empty grounds, and the empty woodsman's hovel with its broken pottery and glassware. He was right, the bandits had come and gone. He could search the countryside from here till kingdom come—or till Lady Bowles ran off with Full Pockets Foggarty—without finding the culprits. They were halfway to London by now.

He was wrong. Sailor and Handy were no more than a mile from Woodhill when they were set upon by the London Mohocks. Now here was a gang Jake could have been proud of. Pop Bullitt's boys had guns, knives, and horses, and no morals to interfere with their chosen line of work. In no time at all they also had the two sacks of stolen goods from Sailor and Handy.

That wasn't enough. They wanted what was in the young men's pockets. Handy protested. What he actually said, in his high, girlish voice, was: "I'll sic my dog on you iffen you don't leave us alone."

The highwaymen laughed, and two of them dismounted to have at the runt who dared challenge them. One-eared Roger growled, "Thinks 'e's up to our weight, 'e does, the little bugger."

And Black Harry stomped toward Handy, huge fists dangling almost to the ground. "Seems top-heavy to me, anyways. I says we turn 'im upside down an' see what falls out."

Handy shrieked and Sailor jumped to his side. "He ain't heavy, he's my brother!" Fists started flying, so many that the mounted outlaws couldn't get off clean shots. Two more got off their horses and entered the fray.

Not even Sailor could withstand four antagonists with only Handy's screams to back him up. They were losing, and losing badly, when Sal came tearing up the road, barking and snarling, growling and slavering. She went right for the heels—of the horses. Pop Bullitt, the only gallows-bait still mounted, was having trouble staying on his pitching, rearing horse. There was no way he could hold any of the other terrified beasts.

"C'mon, the horses is boltin'. These two nancies ain't worth it."

The bullies ran down the road after their nags, Sal getting in a few last bites. Sailor and Handy dragged themselves off the road, under the hedges and into the woods.

They wouldn't have to worry about disguises for

a while. Not even their own mother would recognize them now, even if it hadn't been eight years since she'd left. Bruised and bloody, noses broken and one eye of each already swelling shut, the two once rich robbers huddled under some trees.

"Crime don't pay," Handy eventually sniveled.

"It sure as hell don't pay as good as shoveling horse dung." Sailor was removing his shoe and counting the pitiful horde of coins hidden there, tossed to him by gentlemen whose horses' stalls he'd cleaned.

"Think they'd take us back?"

"Yeah, when Jake writes us another reference."

Handy was emptying his pockets: a gold pickle fork, one pearl-handled knife, the tiny china bride and groom from inside the egg, some ribbons he'd saved from his feminine pose, the last bonbon, and the shilling every employee had been handed the morning of Lady Whilton's wedding. They hadn't stayed long enough to receive their pay.

"You almost got us kilt over that?" Sailor was so furious he blackened Handy's other eye. He would have done more damage, but Sal growled. The hound was carrying a silver candlestick that the highwaymen had dropped in their mad dash after their horses. She laid it at Sailor's feet.

"Good dog, Sal." He handed her that last bonbon. Handy didn't even protest.

They sat there, too tired, hurt, and discouraged to move, wondering if they were better off or worse from when they left London.

"At least we ain't got Jake beatin' us with a stick."

Handy's swollen-shut eyes couldn't see the improvement.

"An' they didn't take Sal." So they could start a flea circus.

"An' the weather's nice, so we don't got to worry about sleepin' outside."

It started to rain.

Mr. Rosten was ready to begin the reading of the will in the library. He looked over his spectacles to view the small audience, like an actor counting the house. It was almost a private performance.

Daphne was there, of course, in one of the comfortable leather armchairs, with Graydon standing behind. They had decided the boys didn't need to attend; even though they were most directly involved in the will's contents, they were too young to make any decisions, and Torry was still looking peaked. Miles was there in his capacity as justice of the peace, anxious to see this whole matter put to rest. Seline was there in her capacity as snoop. She refused to accept Daphne's polite hints to leave, thriving on the drama and Mr. Pomeroy's attention. Head-to-toe in black, Terwent hovered in the background like the vulture he was.

Mr. Rosten straightened his papers again. Then he adjusted his spectacles again. "Yes. Let me preface the reading of the will by saying that Lord Whilton had no interest in writing such a document."

"Most likely refused to believe he'd die," Graydon whispered in Daphne's ear. Mr. Rosten frowned.

"As the family's solicitors and financial consultants, however, the firm of Rosten and Turlow insisted that the baron express his wishes regarding the disposition of his estate and the guardianship of his minor sons. Lord Whilton finally agreed. His behests were conveyed herein." Mr. Rosten held up a torn sheet of paper with a few lines scrawled across it. "Which the firm of Rosten and Turlow dutifully transcribed into proper form." He held up a document of at least twenty pages. The major groaned.

"Quite. Now, this document"—he tapped the will—"is entirely legal, signed, witnessed, notarized, and filed with the proper authorities. This one"—the scrap of paper "—is not. Which shall I read, Miss Whilton?"

Daphne didn't need Graydon's hand squeezing on her shoulder to convince her to go for the shorter version. "The note, please, Mr. Rosten."

The solicitor fixed his spectacles more firmly in place. Then he looked up. "I shall, of course, leave a copy of the official will behind for your perusal."

Daphne nodded. Mr. Rosten cleared his throat. " 'Everything entailed,' " he read, " 'goes to the older boy. Everything not, to the younger. Make Daphne's husband guardian. Whoever the peagoose chooses, he's bound to be dull as ditchwater, but honest. Meantime, Rosten, you do the job.' My apologies, Miss Whilton, but those were your uncle's words."

Graydon was chuckling behind her, but her reply was drowned out by Terwent's voice: "What about my pension? Where's it say about my retirement he promised me?"

The valet had rushed forward to snatch up the legal papers, but Mr. Rosten put his hand atop them. "Your name was not mentioned, Mr. Terwent. Not verbally, not in his note. I believe your salary was owing, however. As guardian of the estate, I took the liberty of withdrawing such funds, and a month's bonus." He handed the valet a small pouch. "The firm shall write a reference, if you require."

"A reference? I wasn't going to have to work again! The old rotter promised! Why else do you think I stayed on with the miserable bastard?"

Mr. Rosten was ignoring the valet's tirade. He told Daphne, "I have seen that the London town house has been padlocked. It is customary to take such precautions when a death is announced and the residence is left empty." He did give a pointed glance to Terwent, who'd already removed a few items from the baron's rooms as soon as he heard the makebait was truly dead.

"Thank you, Mr. Rosten," Daphne was saying. "But about Torrence's portion . . ."

"I'm afraid the baron was a trifle optimistic. There doesn't seem to be any unentailed property left. In fact, the baron's personal debts will have to be paid out of the estate itself. Most improper, as I told him many times. Even if he had specified an amount for his servant, the funds would not have been available. Of course, as guardian, I shall set up a fund for Master Torrence, a percentage of the future income, shall we say. Unless you have my replacement already, ah, selected?"

Her cheeks going scarlet, Daphne stammered, "No, no, whatever you decide. I'm sure you'll do what's right. Thank you, Mr. Rosten. Would you like some wine?"

No one noticed when Terwent stormed out of the room. Ohlman and a footman did make sure he got in his hired rig and down the drive before shutting the door behind him.

* * *

242

No pension! Neither that stiff-rumped solicitor nor that blue-blooded bitch had suggested making good on the old whoreson's promise out of the estate, or out of their own pockets, for all Terwent cared. Blast, the French had the right idea! Get rid of all the aristos, so no poor bastard like himself had to spend the rest of his days powdering their butts. What, was he going to have to change his name again to find some doddering old fool willing to change his will? Damn and blast!

Terwent was so angry, he almost ran over two boys playing ball in the carriageway. Two boys that bitch cared about. Two boys who were getting *his* pension money! Terwent backed the hired gig around. He pulled out the pistol he'd taken from the baron's luggage. "Get in or I'll shoot."

Chapter Twenty-five

"Thank God that's over." Daphne may have said the words, but others shared the sentiment. Daphne was happy they'd squeaked through the wedding and the funeral without causing dear Mama a moment's grief.

Still chuckling over the baron's words, Graydon was pleased they hadn't misplaced Albert again. "Dull as ditchwater" indeed. The old rip must have thought she'd marry portly Pomeroy. Not a chance in hell, Howell mentally told him, addressing his comments to the right direction. The major took Mr. Rosten aside to discuss a few improvements that could be made in Woodhill's farming methods.

Lady Seline Bowles was delighted the reading had gone so quickly. Now she could spend the afternoon getting ready for her dinner with dear Fogey. Foggarty, she meant. And what delicious tidbits she'd have to share about the Woodhill will. Seline felt no remorse over gossiping about her hostess's family, not when Graydon still preferred that quiz in black bombazine to her own elegant self.

Miles was most relieved of all. No one had questioned the date of death, the cause of death, or the place of death. His career as magistrate was safe. His self-esteem as an honorable, law-abiding man was restored. So was his affection for Miss Whilton. That bit about ditchwater hadn't registered with Miles at all, only the fact of Daphne's husband getting to control this vast estate for years, until young Eldart came of age. They could even live here, so Miles wouldn't have the expense of setting up another household, for his mama wouldn't like those young boy cousins of Daphne's underfoot at holidays. Miles had also been relieved to see that, for all her faults, Miss Daphne had donned proper mourning. His mama would like that.

His mama had not approved of Lady Bowles. Fast, she'd declared, even for a widow. Wasn't she right now preparing for a dinner *à deux* with Foggarty? Miles felt his position demanded a wife above reproach, much less outright suspicion. Besides, he couldn't compete with the nabob. No, by light of day the Moon Goddess looked a little tawdry.

"Miss Whilton, a moment of your time, if I may?"

"Of course, Mr. Pomeroy. I'll just ring for the tea things, shall I, then we can have our chat." Daphne had noticed how his eyes followed Seline's every move. Who could blame him, as perfect as she looked? It was time and past Daphne put the poor man out of his misery and set him free to pursue the widow. Not that she thought he had much chance, not against Mr. Foggarty's purse, but it wasn't fair to keep Miles dangling.

When she told him of her decision, thanking him for the great honor of asking her to be his wife, but declining, Miles lost his appetite for once.

"It's not because I made a cake of myself over Lady Seline, is it?" Miles wanted to know.

She tried to convince him that she had decided they wouldn't suit, the widow notwithstanding.

"I know you set great store by such things, Miss Daphne. I admire you for it, I do. And I meant nothing but admiration for the lady. Deuced attractive female."

"Every man seems to find her so." Thinking of her as Graydon's mistress, in his arms, in his bed, made Daphne push her own cucumber sandwich aside.

Echoing her thoughts, Miles mused, "Don't suppose she's the type of female a man takes to be his wife, though."

"No, not a man like you, Miles. You deserve someone better, someone who would be happy in the country, raising dogs and children and roses. I don't think Lady Seline is cut out for such a life. She prefers London, the gossip and gambling and grand social events."

"Dashed expensive female, I guess."

Daphne pictured those diamonds around the widow's graceful neck. "Very."

Miles managed to take a bite of his buttered bread. "I don't suppose you'll reconsider? I mean, there's no reason to rush into a decision."

Daphne shook her head. "No, I shan't change my mind."

He saw how her eyes slid away, following Howell's movements. "So that's the way the wind blows, eh? Not surprised; Mama told me that's the way it's always been. I'd hoped . . . But there, enough said." He finished that piece of bread and reached for another, thinking of Admiral Benbow's unmarried niece. "Well, here's a piece of advice for you, then, my dear. Go ahead and take him. We're none of us perfect."

"No, no, you mistake the matter. We're just friends. How Major Howell chooses to live his life has nothing to do with me anymore, thank goodness."

Miles simply snorted and took his plate, now heavily laden since his future was once again clear, to the other side of the room to discuss a point of law with Mr. Rosten.

Graydon took Pomeroy's place at Daphne's side. "Deuce take it," he said as he accepted a cup of tea from her, "I can't take my eyes off you for ten minutes without you getting into a scrape."

"I don't know what you're talking about. Miles and I parted on the best of terms. There was no scrape."

"No? Then how come mealymouthed Miles left your side while there were still lemon tarts, hm? What, did he propose marriage again now that you are tied to another fortune?"

"That's none of your business, Graydon Howell!" But her blush gave her away. And Miles hadn't exactly brought the matter up this afternoon, she had.

He reached for a lemon tart and grinned. "Devil a bit, brat. Of course it's my business. We're partners in crime, don't you know."

"Yes, and I never thanked you properly for all you did."

"Fustian. You know you can count on me, don't

you, Daffy?" His face had gone serious, intent, his eyes trying to read her innermost emotions. She wasn't ready to let him see them, not sure of his feelings.

"Still, I don't know what I would have done without you."

"Likely married that prig Pomeroy."

He was right, she might have wed Miles if Graydon hadn't returned to remind her what it meant to love someone so deeply that you were almost—almost—ready to chance being hurt again and again, rather than let him walk out of your life another time. But he hadn't mentioned staying, now that the wedding and funeral were over. He hadn't mentioned anything but friendship.

Lest he see the moisture in her eyes, she stared out the window. "Oh dear, it's coming on to rain. I was afraid of that when the boys went out. Torry was still pale this morning, and it wouldn't do for him to catch a chill. I better go fetch them back."

But they weren't outside. They weren't inside either. They weren't anywhere that Daphne looked. Miles grumbled about ill-bred brats, playing ball while their father was fresh in the grave, or the urn as the case may be. "Besides, you spoil them." Daphne was well pleased she'd turned down his proposal.

"Breeding has nothing to do with it," Cousin Harriet insisted when she was consulted. "It's males. Always thinking of themselves and their own pleasure, not giving a rap for anyone else's fretting."

"They're only boys, Cousin. It's not like they've gone out on the town and forgotten the time. Most likely they decided to go visiting and they're taking

shelter with one of the tenants until the rain ends."
She tried not to let her worry show. They weren't
infants, but there had been criminals in the neighborhood, and she'd made them promise not to leave
the grounds.

Graydon patted her shoulder. "I'll give the
scamps an hour, then I'll go look for them. And I'll
give them a piece of my mind, too."

Lady Seline drifted past on her way to the carriage Mr. Foggarty had sent for her. She agreed to
ask the coachman to keep his eyes peeled for the
boys. "That's what comes of letting the beastly
creatures away from their tutors and nannies," she
said on her way out. "That's why they invented
boarding schools."

The hour went by and still Torry and Dart did not
come home. Daphne was thinking of giving the
wretches more than a piece of her mind when she
got her hands on them. Why did they have to disappear today of all days, with Mr. Rosten here? What
if he thought they weren't well supervised? He had
the authority to take them away entirely.

She wanted to ride out with Graydon, but he convinced her she'd do better waiting at home.
"There's no need for both of us to get wet when
they'll be straggling in any minute, needing dry
clothes and hot tea."

Miles went out, too, but with poor grace. "There's
no need to get in a fidge. Boys are always getting
up to mischief." He never had, but he wasn't one of
these wild Whiltons.

Miles and Graydon returned some time later,
cold and wet, and without the boys. "We'll change
horses and ride out again," Graydon told Daphne.
"And send the stable hands out with lanterns."

Darkness was falling. Torry and Dart should have been home ages ago, raining or not.

"Something's happened. I know it."

Gray didn't try to make light of her worries, he just put his arms around her, damp clothes and all. "We'll find them."

Then a window shattered. Amid the broken glass was a rock, with a note tied around it, a ransom note.

"Confound it," Miles swore. "Those Gypsies took them! I knew I should have run them off when I had the chance. Don't worry, Miss Daphne, I'll track them down. They can't have gone far with those slow wagons. Are you coming, Howell?"

Graydon was studying the note, which demanded the ransom money be placed near a crossroads halfway to London. "No, I believe not. I'll head in another direction, I think."

"Toward a warm fire, I suppose," Miles said with a sneer. He hadn't missed that cozy embrace. "I'll rouse up the sheriff and his men, miss. We'll get your cousins back before you have to lay out a shilling."

After he left, Daphne told Gray, "I'm going with you."

"And where is it we are going, my love?"

This wasn't the time to relish endearments. "After Terwent, of course. Gypsies don't steal children."

The major agreed. "Certainly not adolescent boys. They're more trouble than they are worth. No, it has to be Terwent. He was angry enough to pull a fool stunt like this, and he knows you'd do anything to get the boys back."

"Do you think he's taken them to London, then? They'll be hard to find."

"I think that if he were on his way to London, we'd have received this note by messenger or post, tomorrow or later. No, I think he must be right in the neighborhood, close enough to throw the rock himself."

"The old woodsman's cottage? He was with us when they dug up that body there. Do you think he'd be able to find his way back?"

There was only one way to find out, so they set off on horseback, with the pistols Ohlman had primed and ready.

Terwent had no intention of staying anywhere near Woodhill, not with his precious cargo. But he only had an open carriage, and two trussed boys were a bit of a giveaway on the open road. And it was raining. Even worse, one of the boys, the younger, was turning green and threatening to cast up his accounts. Terwent revised his plans.

That old tumbledown cottage was deep enough in the woods to be safe for one night. Once he'd sent his message, Terwent had only to wait until daylight, then head to the delivery place by himself. Unencumbered, he could pick up the ransom money and disappear into London's back alleys without any plaguey brats to watch over. Yes, this was a better plan.

Terwent decided he'd wait a day before sending a note telling the miserly solicitor where to find the devil's spawn. Maybe two. If the brats had an uncomfortable time of it before someone thought to look for them, well, Terwent had suffered enough in their father's service.

He made the older boy get down and lead the horse into the woods. A pistol to his brother's head bought Dart's compliance. "And I know the way, so don't be getting up to any tricks like your double-dealing father would pull."

At the cottage Terwent tied the boys' hands and feet with strips of torn shirts from his—the baron's—luggage. He could buy new ones tomorrow. Then he secured the boys to piles of fallen roof beams. They weren't going anywhere. The valet hefted a good-sized rock. He was.

Chapter Twenty-six

$\mathcal{J}$t was raining and they were hurt. Like whipped dogs, Sailor and Handy crawled back to the only shelter they'd known, that old hut in the woods. By the time they got close, after a few false turns, they were scratched from sticker bushes, sopping from falling into streams, and hungry.

And it was dark.

An eerie sound was coming from the area they knew the cottage to be, a moaning, crying sound.

"It's the wind in the trees." There wasn't any wind.

"It's water running off the rocks." There were no nearby brooks.

"It's him!" they both screamed at once, jumping into each other's arms.

"It's him," Handy squeaked, "come back to haunt us for gettin' his ashes all arsy-tarsy."

Sailor pushed him away. "What if it ain't that deader after all? What if it's Jake, come back to rail at us a'cause we lost the loot?"

"I told you not to step on his grave, you lummox!"

"Well, I ain't goin' in there."

"*I* ain't goin' in there neither."

Sal went in. She pushed past the brothers and bounded through the cottage's gaping door, then barked excitedly. Sailor and Handy heard someone say, "Good dog! Have you brought a search party? We'll get you a steak if you go for help."

Steak? Sailor and Handy went in. They saw two boys, not much younger than themselves, tied to beams. What Dart and Torry saw was much more frightening: two bloody, swollen-faced trolls come to make a meal of them. Dart screamed. Torry blubbered. Sal barked.

Sailor and Handy looked at each other and grinned. Someone was afraid of them! They started to untie the boys, using the pearl-handled knife to cut some of the knots, and asked what happened to them.

Reassured, Dart started to explain about a valet gone amok. If there was anything in this world Sailor and Handy understood, it was muck. Then the Whilton brothers wanted to know what had happened to their rescuers, to leave them in such conditions. Sailor didn't mention the wedding gifts, only the bridle culls on the road, all fifteen of them. They all agreed the world was a dangerous place.

The heirs to Woodhill Manor and the bastards from London's back alleys were soon fast friends. They had a lot in common: they were all orphans, and they were all hungry.

"I'm sure Daphne'll give you a reward for helping us get back home," Dart offered. "She's a great gun."

Sailor wasn't keen on going back to the Manor.

Even looking like a cart had rolled over them, he and Handy were too identifiable.

Torry was thinking. "I'll bet she'd pay you double if you help us catch Terwent. Otherwise he might just snabble us again for the ransom money."

That made sense to Sailor and Handy. Double was worth the risk. And the more grateful this Miss Daphne might be, the less likely she'd be to ask questions. So they were going to catch Terwent. No problem. There were four of them, weren't there?

But he had the gun. While the four youngsters were arguing how to plot the perfect ambush, there not being a lot of hiding places in a one-room, roofless cottage, Terwent snuck up on them and cocked his pistol.

"Which of you bastards wants to be first?"

Neither of the bastards volunteered, nor the sprigs of nobility either. No one moved while Terwent tried to decide what to do with this latest complication. No one was going to ransom these dregs of society, that was for sure. Just when he was figuring the easiest way of disposing of their bodies, Sal got tired of waiting for her steak. She went for his arm. Terwent went down. Sailor started bashing him with the silver candlestick, and Handy used the gold pickle fork on Terwent's flailing legs. Torry and Dart dove into the battle. The gun went off, hitting one of the few remaining rafters, which collapsed around them.

That's when Graydon and Daphne rushed into the cottage, pistols drawn, breath coming in gasps.

"What the devil is going on?" The major handed Daphne his pistol and started pulling beams away. He hauled Torry up, then Dart. Both seemed all right. Sailor was next. Graydon thought he recognized the heavyset youth from the stables under the blood and grime; Daphne was sure she recognized the candlestick. Handy crawled out from under a board, looking like the whole house had landed on him, not just one rotten log. "Who the hell . . . ?"

"They saved us, Daffy!" Both of her cousins were jumping up and down, shouting. "And we promised them a reward. You'll pay, won't you, Daff? We swore, word of a Whilton. Maybe we could find them jobs."

"I think they've already had jobs with us."

Graydon had finally uncovered Terwent, unconscious and like to remain so for a while. He started to tie up the valet with strips of linen Sailor handed him. One whiff of the lad convinced Graydon this was indeed the stableboy.

Handy was backing out the door, sure the jig was up. Daphne aimed one of the pistols at him.

"But Terwent would have killed us if it weren't for Sailor and Handy!" Torry claimed. "He said so!"

Daphne lowered the gun. What were a few candlesticks to her cousins' lives?

Graydon put both pistols in the pocket of his greatcoat and studied the heroic twosome. "I think your brave friends deserve more than jobs. And somehow I don't think they'd hold on to any reward money for long. No, a hot bath and a good meal, for sure, but then perhaps a change of scenery might suit them."

"Gorblimey, you ain't goin' to send us to gaol, is you?"

Torry and Dart and Daphne all protested, Daphne loudest of all, the waifs looked so pitiful.

"No, I was thinking more of finding you places on one of my family's shipping ventures. A little hard work, and then a new life in the New World. How does that sound?"

Sailor was thrilled. "I always wanted to go to sea!"

Handy wasn't. "I always wanted to marry a rich woman," he confessed.

Daphne couldn't see anything to appeal to anyone under those hideous bruises, but she wasn't going to spoil the boy's dreams. "Anything is possible in the colonies, I hear."

"Meantime you might like being a cabin boy. You'll have months to decide," Graydon told him.

Months when they couldn't get into any trouble that affected him, thank goodness.

When they got back to the house, Dart and Torry were taken off by their tutor and Cousin Harriet, and Sailor and Handy were taken in tow by Ohlman and Mrs. Binder, after a lecture on ethics of which the brothers understood two words out of five. Once they were clean and fed and bandaged, Mr. Rosten would see to their futures, far away from Woodhill Manor.

Miles appeared shortly after, ecstatic with his success. He hadn't found the boys—"I said they'd get home all right, didn't I?"—but he had managed to foil a highway robbery, and recover Lady Whilton's stolen wedding gifts. That should put an end once and for all to those London thugs' disrespect for country justice.

He and the sheriff and every able-bodied man in the village had set off after the Gypsies. Instead, they came upon Pop Bullitt's gang, which was in the process of holding up Foggarty's coach, which

257

was bringing Lady Bowles home. Mr. Foggarty was keeping the widow company inside the carriage, such good company that they were not aware of either the holdup or the rescue. The first they knew of danger, in fact, was when Miles threw open the carriage door and shouted, "You are safe, Lady Bowles."

Her skirts up, his breeches down, they'd never doubted it for a moment. And Admiral Benbow's niece was looking prettier by the minute to Miles, even if she did have a squint.

His minions took the red-handed rapscallions into the local gaol, and Miles came along to return the stolen goods. He was delighted to take Terwent in custody once he'd heard the whole, except for the parts about Sailor and Handy and the candlestick and the pickle fork and the ghosts. Daphne saw no reason to muddle the case, when Miles was so satisfied. Why, his corner of the county was so law-abiding now, Miles was claiming, he might take time for a jaunt to London, give the fellows there some pointers. Graydon agreed that might be a good idea.

Lady Bowles sailed in, and out again as soon as her bags were packed. Dear Foggarty was taking her to look at some property in Suffolk he was thinking of purchasing. He wanted her opinion, and la, they all knew what that meant. Daphne naively suggested it meant he wanted her opinion, but Graydon privately thought it meant Foggarty wanted a cozy armful for the weekend. He wished them both good luck, and good riddance.

They were all gone, every last one of the distractions, interruptions, and inconveniences. There were no weddings, funerals, robberies, or kidnappings to stop Graydon Howell from saying what he'd been waiting two years to say. There was only a lump in his throat the size of Gibraltar.

He poured himself a glass of wine, but put it down. He needed a clear head if he wasn't going to make a mull of the thing this time, not Dutch courage. "Daffy, I—"

"You were magnificent!"

She was sitting on the sofa, wearing a look he hadn't seen on her face since she was seventeen, when he'd rescued her kitten from a tree. Of course, he didn't deserve her admiration tonight. "Gammon, the youngsters had already saved themselves. I didn't do anything."

"Oh, I don't mean that, although you did look quite the hero, windblown hair, pistol at the ready. Scott could write a poem about you. What I meant was so magnificent, though, was how you didn't quibble about taking me along, how you handed me a gun, and how you let me decide how much to tell Miles. You didn't come the toplofty nobleman or the commanding officer even once."

"Pomeroy would have had seven kinds of fits, wouldn't he?"

"Eight. He'd never show me the respect of treating me like an equal."

"Is that what I did, treat you like one of the boys? Lud, Daffy, that's the last thing I wanted to do!"

And then, without so much as a by-your-leave, Graydon showed her what he *did* want to do, what he had been waiting all these months to do. He took her in his arms and kissed her till her knees turned to water and her blood turned to fire and her brain turned to mush from his touch—and lack of air.

Graydon forced his arms away. "No, I am going to do this right, which I suppose means that I cannot demand you marry me, or insist you have to after that, ah, demonstration of affection. You do love me, Daffy, don't you?"

"I thought we were just friends," she said, enjoying herself hugely now.

"Friends! You don't go around kissing your friends that way, brat. No, you love me," he said with assurance she could resent, but couldn't deny. "That kiss only proved it. You always have, but I wasn't worth it. And I never even knew how much it meant until you stopped."

"I never stopped, silly."

"But I didn't deserve your love, or you, Daffy. You were the best thing in my life, the only thing, and I didn't know it till it was too late. Then I tried to make you proud of me, tried to become someone you could admire. If I live to be a hundred, Daffy, I'll keep trying, but don't make me wait that long, sweetheart, please?"

"Please . . . ?"

He dropped to the floor at her feet. "One knee doesn't bend all that well." Then he took both her hands in his and stared up at her. "Please, Daffy, please say you'll marry me and truly make me the happiest of men."

Oh, how she wanted to say yes. But. "But what about the other women? I just couldn't bear it, Gray, if I had to share you."

"No other woman meant anything to me, sweetheart, and there will never be another one. I can't swear that my eyes will never wander—even if a fellow owns the finest Thoroughbred, he can't help admiring a fancy piece of blood and bone—but my body will never follow because my heart won't let it. I swear. And you don't have to be dull as ditchwater to be honest. Here."

Graydon reached into his pocket and retrieved a flat box. He opened it to show a necklace of perfect sapphires, with a diamond heart pendant in the middle.

"Good grief, that's even finer than Lady Seline's diamonds! It's a gift for a mistress, Gray!"

"I know." He lifted the necklace and handed her a folded paper. On the paper was written *You are my mistress. The mistress of my heart.*

Graydon raised the necklace and put it around her neck, where it looked absurd on the high-collared black gown, so he solemnly undid the collar, button by button. "The sapphires match your eyes, only they're not as beautiful."

There were tears in those eyes. "Oh, Gray, I have waited so long."

"Too long." He reached into another pocket and withdrew an official-looking document. "I ordered a special license when I sent for the necklace. Say you'll marry me, Daffy, and we can get the vicar here tomorrow."

"What, marry without Mama? I couldn't do that!"

"She said she'd be thrilled. I asked before they left. And I asked my father, too, in case you're thinking he's head of your household. He said it was about time. I'll ask Dart tomorrow if you want, since he's Baron Woodhill now, but he can't refuse my request, not if he wants to learn to drive my chestnuts."

Daphne pretended to frown, though her heart was smiling. "That's getting very autocratic of you.

You're not going to be dictatorial and overbearing like your father, are you?"

He kissed her nose. "You're not going to be high-strung and temperamental like your mother, are you?"

"No, I mean to keep my pistol loaded."

"We can do better than that, sweetheart. Let me show you." And he did, in a way that erased the last doubts Daphne ever had. Neither one of them might be perfect, but they'd have a perfect life together.

"Hmm," he purred some indecent time later. "Remember when you said you wouldn't marry me if I were the last man on earth?"

"I lied. But you are, for me. The first, last, and always."

"I love you, Daffy."

"And I love you. Just don't call me Daffy."

He unbuttoned another button.

Ohlman shut the door.

An Enchanted Affair

*To Stacy Seiden and Mark Siegal
in honor of your marriage.*

*May you be as happy
as any fairy-tale lovers,
forever after.*

Happy First Anniversary.

Chapter One

*L*isanne Neville was six years old before she realized no one else could talk to the fairies. No one else cared, either, so Lisanne was not concerned. She simply felt more special.

Her nanny was an old Cornishwoman, with superstitions bred into her blood since the Celts fled the mainland. Nanny Murtagh blamed the piskis for stealing her thimbles, for making holes in her stockings, and for causing her frequent bilious attacks. The medicinal tot of rum she added to her tea at night couldn't be contributing to her sore head and her upset stomach, ah, no. Didn't she leave a saucer of the brew on the windowsill every night to appease the wee folk, and didn't they drink it up by morning? If, by chance, an inordinate amount of pigeons fell off the roof at night, well, the pixies were a mischievous race indeed.

Nanny saw nothing unusual in her darling girl's knowing which herbs and meadow flowers made the most soothing tisane for a maudled digestion, or knowing how to bind a pigeon's broken wing. The Neville estate bordered on Sevrin Woods, didn't it?

Everyone knew the woods were bewitched. They were

not as dangerous as demon-filled Dartmoor, at Devonshire's other end, but bad enough that the locals wouldn't set foot under the ancient oaks and wide-spreading hollies. Not even Devon's intrepid smugglers used the forest's winding paths, nor did poachers follow its deer tracks. Neither group feared the Duke of St. Sevrin or his minions, for His Grace was away in London dissipating what little remained of the family's fortune, and St. Sevrin Priory was going to wrack and ruin without benefit of housekeeper, gatekeeper, or gamekeeper. What would-be trespassers feared was magic, witchcraft, sorcery. A bit of venison or a tickled trout wasn't worth the risk of being turned into a toad or getting elf-led off the paths to wander for enchanted eternity.

The vicar's harangues against paganism didn't open a single closed mind, nor did the fact that Lord Neville's little girl played in the woods all the time without coming to harm. The housemaids and stable boys at Neville Hall simply crossed themselves when Lisanne claimed the forest folk weren't evil, that they'd never hurt anybody.

As for Lisanne's parents, Lord Neville had married late in life, and his wife had conceived even later in their marriage. After Lisanne's difficult birth, the physicians had warned the baron that there would be no more children. Lord Neville was content. His barony was one of those archaic land grants by which title and property could pass through the female line if necessary. The papers were drawn, the succession was secure, and the baron could return to his translations of the early Greeks and Romans.

To say that Lisanne was the apple of her father's eye would be an understatement. She was the whole orchard, with nary a blight or a blemish to spoil his satisfaction. So when his little golden-haired cherub climbed on her papa's knee and babbled about her friends in the forest, Tug and Moss, Alon and baby Rimtim, Lord Neville was delighted. What a bright puss she was, his precious poppet, creative and clever. She was already learning the

Greek alphabet along with her ABC's. Best of all, she was happy to play for hours at the far side of Neville Hall's sloping lawns, past the formal gardens and the maze. She did not interfere with her papa's concentration on a difficult passage, but was right there when he looked up and out his library's windows. The baron could always spot his jewel of a daughter, laughing and dancing and skipping around while Nanny sat with her knitting on a nearby bench, there at the edge of Sevrin Woods. As Nanny Murtagh would have said, the sight warmed the cockles of his heart.

Lady Neville's cockles were not quite so contented, although she loved her daughter none the less. It was a lonely child who created imaginary playmates, the baroness believed, an only child. Whenever she saw Lisanne frolicking with sunbeams at the edge of the forest, Lady Neville's heart ached. When she heard Lisanne's bedtime recital of her day's adventures with her little friends, the baroness nodded and smiled and agreed that the forest people were the happiest, wisest, most amusing companions a child could have, and wasn't Lisanne lucky they'd chosen her. Inside, Lady Neville grieved for the sisters and brothers Lisanne would never have.

There were no wellborn children of an age with Lisanne in the neighborhood, and the tenants' children were too busy with chores, the village youngsters too rough. Neither Lady Neville nor the baron, of course, would ever entertain the notion of sending their treasure away to school with other daughters of the nobility. Perhaps when she got older, they'd tell each other, never intending to part with their dearest joy.

Of frail constitution herself, the baroness never considered joining her daughter for rambles through the woods. She also never considered how such a little girl seemed to know the name of every wildflower, which berries were safe to eat, or when a storm was coming. Perhaps old

Nanny Murtagh was teaching her, or the gardeners. The gardeners? Heaven forfend the future Lady Neville was reduced to befriending the servants. Imaginary playmates were better, even if they were fairies.

So Lady Neville took matters into her own frail hands. It wasn't what she would have wished, but for her daughter's sake the baroness was willing to make the sacrifice. She invited her brother and his hopeful family to spend the summer at Neville Hall.

Sir Alfred Findley was hopeful of separating his scholarly brother-in-law from a portion of the Neville fortune. Findley was a baronet of very minor gentry as was his father before him, and as his son Nigel would be after him, with a barely adequate competence. Sir Alfred's baroness sister, however, had risen to the nobility—the wealthy, landed, idle, and inbred nobility. Sir Alfred bitterly resented this fact, which was one reason traffic between the two families was so infrequent. The other was that Lord Neville considered his in-laws nothing but a clump of ignorant mushrooms.

Still, the invitation went out and was accepted. The Findley *familia* arrived and settled in.

"Why don't you show your cousins around, dearest," her mother directed Lisanne the next morning. "They might enjoy the maze and the gardens. Nigel can roll his hoop on the lawns, and you and Esmé can have a tea party in the gazebo."

Nigel was a year older than Lisanne and didn't want to play with girls. Esmeralda, Esmé as she was called, was a year younger than Lisanne and didn't want to get her slippers wet in the damp grass. They went anyway, following the stern direction of their father and the nervous cautions of their city-bred mother. Lisanne promptly lost them in the woods.

She didn't mean to, of course. She merely intended to introduce her cousins to her other playmates. The cousins couldn't see them, of course.

4

"I don't understand," Lisanne complained to her friend Moss, who was reclining beneath a dandelion.

Moss stood and puffed out his cheeks and blew until the dandelion fuzz drifted away. "That's what they have between their ears, your cousins, nothing but fluff. A toadstool has more imagination. Who wants to talk to lumpish, loutish children like them?"

Lisanne turned back to her guests. Nigel was tossing stones at the crows jabbering above them. "This is boring," he whined when he didn't hit any.

Esmé was brushing a smudge off her pinafore and sniveling, "I want to go home."

"See?" Moss asked. "You're not like them. You're special. Now, come, the vixen just had her babies in the meadow."

Lisanne politely invited her guests along to see the new fox kits.

"Mama said we weren't to get out of sight of the house," Esmé dutifully reminded, "and it's nearly time for tea."

Nigel sneered at his cousin. "You can't know there's any such thing in the meadow. And no fox is going to let you play with her babies. We should go find the head huntsman, anyway, so he can drown the vermin or take the young hounds cubbing."

Moss just laughed, shaking the tiny bells on his cap. Lisanne looked from her glum-faced cousins to her smiling friend. There was no competition. She waved to Nigel and Esmé and ran laughing after the tinkling chimes. "Wait for me!"

Esmé would have been happy to go back to the house, but Nigel was having none of it. What, get shown up by a mere girl? He grabbed his sister's hand and pulled her along the faint path Lisanne had taken. Then he dragged her through briars and brambles and a stream. It was the stream that did it. Esmé set up such a howling that Nigel relented. "Very well, you sissy, we'll go home." Except that Nigel had no idea of where home was.

Lady Findley lay prostrate on the sofa while her maid burned feathers under her nose. Sir Alfred was all for calling out the stable hands, the tenant farmers, the militia. Even Lisanne's fond papa was a tad concerned when his poppet ambled out of the woods some hours later, leaves in her braids, mud on her skirts, and berry juice on her chin, sans cousins.

Matters were not helped any when Lisanne was able to lead the searchers through the woods on a direct route to the missing children. Nigel and Esmé were huddled under a juniper bush, damp, cold, and frightened out of what wits they possessed. Sobbing, Nigel shoved his sister aside to be first into his father's arms. Then he remembered he was a boy.

"She did it," he screamed, pointing at Lisanne, the cause of his shameful tears. "She led us into the woods saying we'd see wonderful things. Then she left us alone so we couldn't get back. She pretended to talk to someone who wasn't there, just to frighten us."

"No, Papa, I never did. They didn't want to come with Moss and me, so I left them in the gardens."

"Moss? Who's this Moss?" Uncle Alfred demanded. "Nigel said there was no one else around."

Lord Neville could only shrug, but Nigel hopped up and down. "There wasn't, Pa, I swear. She was talking to a dandelion. Lisanne's a loony, Pa. Addled Annie, they should call her."

And Esmé, now that she was safe in her father's arms, chanted, "Addled Annie, Addled Annie," all the way home.

Suddenly, being special wasn't quite so much fun.

Sir Alfred raged at his sister while his wife saw to the packing. "You always were a weakling, Elizabeth. And now you're raising a mooncalf because you're too feeble to do anything about it. You are letting some half-mad Cornishwoman raise your daughter, and look what it's gotten you. Why, the woman didn't even know the children had wandered off. Drunk, I don't doubt."

Lady Neville wiped at her eyes with a delicate scrap of lace. "Nanny Murtagh? Never."

"Hah! That's how much attention you pay to your household. I could smell Blue Ruin on her breath the instant I arrived."

Since Lady Neville would not have recognized Blue Ruin from a blue moon, she could only sniff some more.

"And what's she teaching the chit, that's what I want to know," Alfred ranted on. "Dash it, the gel could snabble a duke if she's reared properly. My girl's younger, and she's had a governess for two years, not a cloth-headed nanny. Of course Nigel has a tutor, but that's irrelevant. Watercolors, your girl needs, and pianoforte lessons, dance instruction. She should be sewing samplers instead of wandering around in haunted woods."

Lady Neville did not think this was the time to inform her brother that Lisanne had already read every book in the nursery and was starting on her father's library, Greek and Latin volumes included. Not when they'd all had to suffer through an hour the previous afternoon watching Esmé blot her way through signing her name, and listen to Nigel stutter over a short paragraph in his primer. Perhaps Alfred was right, though, that parts of Lisanne's education were being neglected. Heaven knew Elizabeth had endured hours with a backboard, and she'd won herself a baron. Lady Neville promised to consider hiring a governess for her daughter.

"What, some down-at-heels parson's daughter from the next village? Your gel's a hoyden, a dreamer, a scheming liar, if she's not knocked-in-the-cradle altogether. Are you sure that Murtagh woman didn't drop her on her head? For certain she filled Lisanne's mind with all that fairy-tale tripe. What the little baggage needs now

7

is a firm hand on the reins. Someone who's up to every rig and row, and knows her way around the ton besides. I'll look into it on my way through London. The chit has to be ready to take her place where she belongs, in Town, not in a benighted blueberry patch."

Someone had to plan for the girl's glorious future, Alfred told himself. A well-bred, titled heiress would have the eligibles buzzing around her like flies on fruit. And he meant for his Esmeralda to be at Lisanne's side, and his Nigel at her feet. "It's never too early to start," Alfred told his sister as he climbed into the baron's luxurious coach for the ride back to his own pawky property. Alfred lovingly rubbed his hand over the bright lacquerwork of the carriage door. No, it was never too early to start.

"Nice holiday, what?" Lord Neville asked his wife, putting his arm around her thin shoulders as the coach pulled away. "Just the way I like visits from your family. Short."

Chapter Two

The new governess arrived. Sir Alfred had done his job well. Miss Armbruster was the most widely recommended instructress of young females in all of London. Her blood was the bluest, with an earl for an uncle, albeit said earl was currently languishing in the Fleet debtors' prison. Miss Armbruster was also intelligent, reliable, and the highest paid governess currently on the market, which iced Sir Alfred's cake, since her wages were coming out of Lord Neville's deep pockets, not his own.

Miss Armbruster was a female of a certain age who was certain in her notions. When Sir Alfred cautiously mentioned that the nearby woods were said to be haunted, Miss Armbruster replied, "Bosh. There is no such thing." Warned that her charge was considered fey in the neighborhood, she answered, "Nonsense. The child simply needs discipline." A difficult charge? Miss Armbruster hadn't met one yet.

Nanny Murtagh was pensioned off to a cottage back in Lostwithiel, and Miss Armbruster took over Lisanne's education. She tried, anyway.

Lessons. That was the key, Miss Armbruster declared to Lady Neville. Prayers before breakfast, then grammar, composition, and mathematics, with history and geography on alternate days. After luncheon, healthful exercise: nature walks in the formal gardens on pleasant days, to be combined with science and sketching, or laps around the portrait gallery on inclement afternoons for more history and heritage. French before tea, etiquette and elocution during. The interval between tea and supper would be reserved for music instruction, voice and instrument, with dance to be added later. Needlework could be accomplished after the meal, in the hour before the child's bedtime. If not, they could rise earlier in the mornings.

Sunday afternoons, Miss Armbruster continued, were to be her half days, and she had one full-day holiday per month; but, the governess assured Lady Neville, she would leave enough assignments behind that Lady Lisanne would not have a moment free to get into any trouble.

Lady Neville took to her bed.

Lisanne took to the new regime the way a crocodile waltzes, which is to say not at all. No time for her friends? No time for her books? No time for the wonders of Sevrin Woods? No way. Being a polite, obedient, cheerful child, Lisanne did not throw herself on the floor in a tantrum, run away from home, or hold her breath until she turned blue. She merely cried. She didn't even cry on her papa's waistcoat or, worse, on his translation of Ovid. She simply sobbed in her bed at night and came to breakfast with red, swollen eyes. Then she silently wept through luncheon. If ever there was a doting father who could see his little girl's misery and not be moved to rehang the moon for her, it was not Lord Neville. He took another look at the new governess.

Sir Alfred had outsmarted himself in finding such an intelligent, competent, expensive female to bear-lead his peculiar niece onto a more conventional path. Miss Armbruster was intelligent enough to see which way the wind blew. She was most definitely competent to recognize precisely who it was who paid that exorbitant salary—the same quiet and bookish gentleman who wouldn't hesitate to throw her out on her aristocratic ear if his little darling was unhappy.

So there was a compromise. In the mornings Lisanne was expected in the schoolroom with completed assignments. In the afternoons, well, in the afternoons Miss Armbruster suddenly found it necessary to work on the reference book she was compiling for the education of young females. Lisanne was to return for tea, dinner at the very latest, having practiced at least one ladylike skill to show off to her proud parents. And she was never, not in public, not in private, to mention fairies, little people, pixies, or elves.

Miss Armbruster was happy. This was the easiest position she had ever held, and the child was bright, inquisitive, and quite endearing, so long as one didn't inquire too closely as to where she went of an afternoon. Since that involved forbidden topics, Miss Armbruster was able to ignore what she considered the odd kick in Lisanne's gallop. Over the years of her tenure, she was able to complete three volumes of her textbook, which were very well received in academic circles.

Lisanne was happy. She had friends, freedom, her parents' affection, and her governess's approval.

Lord Neville was happy, too, until he died.

The doctors would not let Lisanne near the sickroom. They wouldn't listen to her rantings about willow bark tea and foxglove infusions. The Honorable Lisanne Neville had all of twelve years in her dish by now. She had no business with possets and potions.

What did a child, a feebleminded one at that, if rumor was to be believed, know about the healing arts? the consulting London surgeons asked each other. Herbal quackery, that was all she proposed, likely from some ancient crone who lived in a hollow tree stump and stole pennies from the poor with a handful of dried weeds. Next the chit would be bringing the learned physicians eye of newt or some such thing from an old household book of simples.

The medical scientists cupped the baron, bled the baron, and purged the baron. They killed the baron.

Lady Neville could not survive on her own. The grief, the details of the estate, the uncertainty of her future were too much for the baroness. She never had been strong in will or in body, but without the baron, Lady Neville was too weak to get out of bed. Then she was too weak to keep waking up in the morning. One morning she didn't.

No one was going to see Lisanne's tears and make things right. Not even her friends in the woods could make this right. What did they know of death? They lived forever. So Lisanne stopped crying. Miss Armbruster was concerned: a child needed to grieve instead of wandering alone through the corridors of an empty manor house. But nothing in all of the governess's book learning or learning books could change matters, either.

And then Lisanne wasn't quite so alone. Uncle Alfred and his family came. To stay.

Since the nearest Neville relation was so distant that the baron had never met the chap, Lord Neville had reluctantly named his wife's brother as guardian for his daughter and heiress. Alfred Findley might be family, but the baron made sure to appoint his own London solicitor as trustee of Lisanne's vast estate.

Sometimes no family was better than the family one had. Uncle Alfred's first order of business, after moving himself and his vaporish wife, Cherise, into the master suite, was to get rid of Miss Armbruster. Now that Sir Alfred was paying the household bills—and pocketing what he could scrape off the accountings—he saw no need to keep the pricey dragoness. Esmé's governess was good enough for Annie, too. Mrs. Graybow wouldn't stand for any of this wandering off alone, playing in forbidden

12

woods like some savage or grubbing about in the dirt for roots and stuff. Widow of an infantry sergeant, built like a cavalry horse, Mrs. Graybow would shape the new baroness into a proper lady, one way or another.

Miss Armbruster had amassed a tidy sum from her years at Neville Hall, both from her generous salary, frequent bonuses, and profits from her books. She had enough money put by that she could either live quietly at a respectable boardinghouse for the rest of her days, or she could use her savings to found a school for young ladies. One look at Sir Alfred's unprepossessing daughter convinced her on the boardinghouse. Too bad they couldn't all be like Lisanne.

Lisanne didn't cry when Miss Armbruster left, promising frequent letters. Nor did she weep when her uncle and Mrs. Graybow forbade her the woods. There were no more tears in her. Lisanne simply disobeyed and disappeared into her beloved woods for hours on end. So Mrs. Graybow boxed her ears. Then she rapped her knuckles with a ruler. Then she whipped her with a switch.

Lisanne wouldn't cry, and she wouldn't promise not to go off again.

So Uncle Alfred beat her. Years of bitter rancor went into every stroke: anger at his dead sister's elevating marriage, anger at the terms of the dead baron's will, and anger at fate, that put such a fortune into the hands of a city shyster instead of the much worthier ones of the brat's uncle. The exercise might have relieved some of the baronet's ingrained resentment, but it had no effect on Annie, as the family now called her, beyond the obvious. As soon as she recovered, Lisanne left the house and stayed away for two days and a night.

When she returned, Sir Alfred had Mrs. Graybow lock her in her bedroom. Lisanne climbed out the window onto the trellised vines. They locked her in the butler's pantry. The Hall's old butler would never have stood for seeing his mistress so abused, but the Findleys' own major domo held sway now. Sir Alfred had given all the Neville staff the sack, saying he preferred his own loyal retainers. These servants just happened to be used to more niggardly wages—not that Alfred needed to mention that fact to Lisanne's London solicitor. Alfred rented out his own small property near London, preferring to put up at a hotel when visiting the City on his niece's business—and on her expense account.

No one, therefore, protested as Lisanne spent hour after hour in the small dark room. She was hauled out three times a day for meals, Mrs. Graybow deeming tea unnecessary for a disobedient child. At those meals Lisanne was given the chance to swear on her honor not to leave the property. Now she not only stopped crying, she stopped talking, and stopped eating.

Rescue came from an unexpected source. Aunt Cherise was having palpitations. Not only was she forced into the country away from the shops and entertainments of the City, but she was too embarrassed to venture into local society. "The child is going to die if you keep this up, Alfred. Look at her, she's skin and bones already." And bruises, but Aunt Cherise turned her eyes. "I can not accept invitations because we are in mourning, but what will people say?"

Sir Alfred didn't care what a parcel of country nobodies said. He did care what that blasted will said. If she died, the little baroness, that distant Neville cousin inherited everything, all those trust-fund earnings, all those rent rolls. Findley wasn't about to let his meal ticket waste away over a bit of hoydenish behavior the chit would likely outgrow anyway.

The baronet rubbed his weak chin. After all, there was no chance his own daughter would be contaminated with Annie's disobedience. Esmé treated her cousin as a *grande dame* would a noxious puddle, pulling her skirts aside and ignoring the mess. Esmeralda would never set foot in those bothersome woods again if her life depended on it, even if she was assured her slippers wouldn't get soiled. Nigel tried once when they first arrived, taking his gun into the woods after a deer. He got lost again, which had to have been Annie's fault, he swore, since she eventually came to lead him home.

Although he never mentioned it to anyone, Sir Alfred went into the forest one day, determined to drag Annie back by her hair if necessary. But under the great trees he found a dark, forbidding atmosphere with odd, earthy scents. The baronet even thought he heard voices laughing at him where no one was. He'd turned around while he could still see the chimneys of Neville Hall.

"It's not as if any of the neighbors are going to spot her outside without an escort or a bonnet," Aunt Cherise urged, to get the impossible child out of the house.

No, none of the neighbors were about to spy on his niece whatever the brat did in those woods. Annie could take her clothes off and dance naked in a Black Sabbath. No one would know, because no one ever ventured a toe into Sevrin Woods. And she was still only a little girl.

So there was another compromise, of sorts. Sir Alfred and his family lived in Lisanne's house, off her income, and ignored her presence as well as her absence. This suited the young baroness just fine.

Lisanne kept away from the house and away from its surly servants as much as she could. When she was at home, she read in her papa's library, where there was small chance of encountering any of her relations. She also kept up with her studies in the woods, the stillroom, and the herb gardens. And she still nursed the injured birds and orphaned rabbits that came her way.

One other duty kept her from the forest on occasion: her responsibility to the Neville tenants. Sir Alfred wasn't able to replace the bailiff, so those dependent on the barony were not subject to his penny-pinching ways. Neither were they well served by him or his wife. The Findleys made frequent trips to London, nary a one to the thatch-roofed cottages. It was Annie, remembering her father's gentle teachings, who brought baskets of food when the crops were meager, blankets when the winter was severe. She had an elixir for old man Jenkins's rheumatics, and a syrup for Neddy Broome's cough. Soon the household servants started coming to her with toothaches and such. For sure Sir Alfred wouldn't pay out the fee for a doctor's visit. They might make the sign to ward off the evil eye when Annie was through, but they brought her their sniffles and spasms.

Annie could doctor simple ailments, but she was better with animals. Soon the tenants were asking her to look at a sow that wouldn't farrow, a cow that gave no milk. And gardens, why, the slip of a girl could sniff at a handful of dirt and tell why the roses didn't bloom or when the peas should be planted.

Lisanne's reputation grew, despite all of her uncle's efforts to curb it. While there was respect for the child's learning, there was suspicion, too. That was a powerful lot of knowledge for such a young head, the rumors went. And where did she come by guessing whether Rob Fleck's next babe was a boy or a girl—and getting it right year after year? No one could have taught her, for the servants said she had no schooling. The Devonshire folks shook their heads. They never let any of *their* children play in Sevrin Woods. Whispers of Addled Annie followed Lady Lisanne's visits.

Uncle Alfred was furious. His fortune, his plans, his dreams of having Esmé and Nigel marry fortunes and titles, were all going up in smoke with one of Annie's reeking concoctions. The girl wasn't outgrowing that claptrap about fairy friends; she just wasn't talking about it. Her silence, in turn, made the locals wonder all the more how she came by her knowledge. It wasn't normal, they said, crossing themselves. It wasn't natural. And wasn't there a peculiar vagueness behind the girl's blue-eyed stare, almost as if she were seeing other sights, hearing other voices?

Sir Alfred decided to send Annie away to school, away from the gossip, away from those thrice-cursed woods. One of those strict seminaries would know what to do about making a lady out of a chit who constantly looked as if she'd been pulled through a thicket backward. Esmé could go along as companion. On Annie's account, of course.

When informed of the treat in store for her, Lisanne stared down at the hands correctly folded in her lap, not seeing the dirt under her fingernails that made Aunt Cherise wince. She quietly, politely, ever so assuredly, informed her guardian that she would find a way to run away from whatever school he chose. She'd live in the woods, and he'd never see her again . . . or a groat more of her income. Lisanne wasn't half as vague as everyone thought. She'd managed to read her father's will as well as most of the communications from the London solicitor. She knew her worth to the ha'penny, and knew how much of it was going into Uncle Alfred's pockets.

Sir Alfred believed the little witch would do what she said, disappear forever just to spite him. So he bit his lip and let her be. As she turned fourteen, then fifteen, and neared sixteen—almost of an age for a presentation—he gnawed on his own frustrations.

How could he bring Annie to London to make a grand match that would benefit him and his children? Even if he could get her there, Annie wouldn't take. She never cared about her clothes, wearing whatever she found in her closet. Since these were usually the taller, plumper Esmé's castoffs, Sir Alfred hadn't complained at Annie's dowdiness, not in light of the expenses saved. The chit still wore her hair in braids down her back, while Esmé was already nagging her mother to have hers put up. Annie's skin was browned from the sun, she ran barefoot half the time, and to his knowledge she had no drawing-room skills or conversation. Wouldn't the Almack's patronesses just love to chat about Farmer Goode's infected thumb? What man of means would look twice at a filthy, dreamy, waiflike female? What nobleman would chance begetting an heir with attics to let? None.

Chapter Three

*N*o man in his right mind was going to marry a woman who wasn't in her right mind. Sir Alfred slowly repeated that obvious fact to himself, in wonder. It was almost as if the skies had opened up and the heavenly host presented him with a divine revelation. No one was ever going to marry Lisanne Neville, not even the most desperate fortune hunter. All these years Alfred had been thinking of the grand marriage he'd arrange for Annie—and for his own advancement. But if she never married, he didn't have to relinquish her guardianship for ten more years, not until she turned five and twenty. If, by some happenstance, he could then show that the poor, unfortunate lackwit needed a keeper, well, perhaps he could spend the rest of his days in clover.

Yes, Sir Alfred liked this new idea very much indeed. He let Annie go her own way, higgledy-piggledy adding to her reputation as an eccentric or worse. He encouraged the local gossip, and even added some of his own when in Town, laying the groundwork with the deceased baron's old acquaintances.

"Dreadful news about Neville's daughter." Sir Alfred sighed. "Why, the poor dear is as queer as Dick's hatband, don't you know. The death of both parents was too much for her, such a fragile little thing. Her mind must have snapped."

He gravely accepted the condolences of Lord Harrington, the biggest rattle in Town. "Sad fate for a noble family to end that way. Nothing to be done, eh?"

Findley shook his head. "Unfortunately not. She lives in a fantasy world, dabbling in herbalism and woodlore so she doesn't have to face the harsh reality of her loss. It's all harmless, you understand, but not the thing for a proper young female. She simply cannot be taught any of the usual accomplishments."

"You've had her to the sawbones, of course. Don't suppose they did her any good. Can't cure the king, after all."

Another sigh. "The professionals have given up. It's a hopeless case. Besides, all they advised was to bleed her or put her in restraints, or drill holes in her head. We couldn't put the dear child through that."

Harrington shuddered. "Nothing left but to send her to Bethlehem Hospital."

"What, declare my own sister's child a bedlamite? I couldn't betray the baron's trust in me that way. No, we'll keep her safe at home." Alfred put his hand over where his heart would be, if he had one. "Her loving family will stand by her."

Of course they would.

"Pa, I don't see why you can't make Annie show me the way through Sevrin Woods. It ain't as if it's hers or anything."

Nigel had been sent down from school again. This was the last time, for Sir Alfred knew better than to send good money after bad. They were at the breakfast table on a gloomy, rainy day. The eggs were runny and the rashers were greasy. Sir Alfred had the newspaper propped in front of him in hopes of avoiding the morning brangling between his children and the carping demands of his wife. He looked over the newspaper and said, "Why don't you ask her yourself? She's sitting across the table from you."

Lisanne was taking one of her infrequent meals with the family because it was raining too hard to venture out, and the current cook refused to permit any hell-born babe in her kitchens lest her bread stop rising. As usual, the family ignored Lisanne's presence in their midst, except for Aunt Cherise's calling for her sal volatile when she saw her niece's apparel. Tired of Esmé's billowy castoffs that snagged on every bush and briar, Lisanne had taken to wearing Nigel's.

"Tell her she must not appear in the public rooms in such attire, Alfred. I have a hard enough time holding my head up in this neighborhood as is."

Alfred pointedly nodded to where Lisanne was placidly nibbling at a sweet roll, and went back to his paper.

Esmé took up the complaint: "Well, I don't see why I have to have lessons anymore when Annie doesn't. She's only a year older than me, and she's been out of the classroom forever."

"Than I, Esmé," Sir Alfred wearily corrected without looking up. "And if you knew that, perhaps you wouldn't need schooling any longer, either."

Nigel reached across the table for the jam pot. "But, Pa, I have to hunt in Sevrin Woods. You know the bailiff won't let me shoot on Neville grounds."

"That's because you shot two goats and a chicken last time." Esmé snickered before returning to her claims of injustice. "I think you should make Annie practice the pianoforte at least, Papa. It's not fair that I have to play when the church ladies come visit and Annie doesn't."

"What, have her in the parlor when company comes?" Lady Cherise screeched before falling back in her seat, clutching her chest. "Tell her she cannot, Alfred."

Sir Alfred tossed down his papers. He couldn't recall the last occasion he'd been able to tell his niece anything but the time of day.

Lessons? Hah! Even Mrs. Graybow had confessed years ago that there wasn't a blessed thing she could teach the chit, and a lot she could learn from her. Trust that fusty old Neville to spawn a brilliant child, while Alfred's two progenies hadn't a brain to share between them. It suited the baronet's purposes to have everyone consider Annie an unlettered wantwit, however, so he kept mum about her abilities, although a bluestocking was nearly as unmarkable as an imbecile on the marriage block. As for music, heaven only knew what language the chit would sing if she ever opened her mouth. Annie must know six or seven languages by now, the governess reported after spying in her room. Chances were the gel had the voice of an angel, too, to show up Esmé's cater-wauling. The devil knew she understood farming better than Alfred did, and horses, too.

As for making Annie do what she didn't choose, such as taking Nigel hunting, or wearing proper dress, or practicing some mind-numbing set piece, well, Findley might as soon whistle for the wind. And Alfred hated to whistle; it was common. The deuced chit was like a thorn in his side, though, going her own quiet way. Nigel could be kept on a short lead by threatening his allowance or a caning, and Esmé would jump through burning hoops for some new gewgaw or other. It was only Annie that Findley couldn't control. The very thought gave Sir Alfred dyspepsia. He pushed his chair back and stood up. "Dash it all, can't a man have any peace at his own breakfast table?"

"I believe it is *my* breakfast table, sir."

Six pairs of eyes turned to stare at Lisanne: four Findleys and two servants. It was the first time in ages any of them had heard her voluntarily enter a dialogue. She spoke to the tenants, she made requests of the servants, but Lisanne did not often speak to her family.

Sir Alfred sat down again. "What, you've blessed us with your presence and now you're going to extend us the gift of your conversation?"

Lisanne sipped at her chocolate.

"Come now, Annie, surely you have more to say than to claim a piece of mahogany."

"Yes, sir. I wish to tell Nigel that he must not hunt in Sevrin Woods."

"Dash it all, Annie, it's not yours to say me aye or nay. Is it, Pa?"

Lisanne stared at her cup. "The animals and birds there have never been hunted. They're tame."

Giggling, Esmé taunted, "Then maybe he can hit something."

Nigel's face got red, but he spat back, "Shut up, brat. And what's the difference, I say. A deer's a deer, no matter where it lives."

"It wouldn't be sportsmanlike" was all Lisanne said, finally staring Nigel in the eyes, daring her cousin to admit he was less than a gentleman. His adolescent amour propre could not let him confess to such a thing in front of his disdainful father or his sniggling sister. He might feel that there was nothing wrong with shooting ducks in a barrel, either, as long as you managed to hit one, but he knew better than to admit it. Nigel looked away first.

Lisanne nodded. "Besides, you would be poaching on Lord St. Sevrin's preserves. His Grace might be in London, but he is still the owner of the property."

"Then how come you get to wander on his land free and clear?" Nigel wanted to know, his voice cracking in his agitation.

"I never harm anything," Lisanne answered in her quiet way.

Esmé couldn't resist adding: "Neither would Nigel, the way he shoots."

Ignoring his sister, Nigel tried to shake Lisanne's composure. The fact that his cousin was so poised and confident when she was the one dicked in the nob infuriated him. "Harm, my foot! What's that to the matter? It's still trespassing! You've never met St. Sevrin. For sure the duke never gave permission for no loony to ramble around his estate."

"I did meet His Grace once, when I was very small. He put some of the Priory's furnishings up for auction. Papa took me when he went to look at the books."

"I daresay the man was run off his feet even then," Aunt Cherise put in, addressing the table at large. She knew everything about everyone in the ton, being an avid reader of the gossip pages and a faithful correspondent to her like-minded London acquaintances. "They say he took to drink right after his wife died, well before Annie could have been born, and started gambling away his fortune. I'd always heard he was a dirty dish."

"He was pleasant to me," Lisanne said, smiling at the memory. "I told him he had the loveliest wildflowers growing in his wood, and he said I may as well pick all I wanted, for he couldn't make any profit off them." She turned to Nigel. "So you see, I do have His Grace's permission to be on the property."

"Not anymore you don't, missy." Uncle Alfred tapped the newspaper that was next to his plate. "The old duke is dead. Shot in a duel over a Covent Garden whore."

"Sir Alfred!" Aunt Cherise nodded in Esmé's direction. "Little pitchers."

The baronet shrugged. "You're the one who said the chit was almost ready for a London come-out. She'll hear a lot worse there."

Lisanne was burning to snatch up the newspaper and run to her room with it, but her uncle still held the folded pages. "The article says the heir is being notified. He's with the army in the Peninsula. I suppose he'll have to re-

24

sign his commission and settle the estate, what there is left of it."

Aunt Cherise sniffed. "It's more likely Viscount Shearingham will take up where his father left off. The young man already has a reputation for wildness. There were rumors of his being turned away from various clubs before he purchased his colors." Aunt Cherise had to stop and think. "Money from his mother's side, I believe. There was not enough left of his patrimony to purchase a corncob pipe, much less a coronetcy."

Lisanne excused herself, although no one noticed when she left. The footman did not even pull her seat back, she got up in such a hurry, eager to get to the bundle of old newspapers that was always stored in the polishing room. Yes, there he was, Major Lord Shearingham, mentioned in the dispatches. The viscount was on Wellesley's own staff, and it seemed, from the tittle-tattle columns, that he'd made a career of equal parts daring and debauchery.

From that day on, Lisanne made sure she saw the daily newspapers, even if they were two days late from London. She skimmed the war news, the political reporting, and the financial sections, but she studied the *on dits* with as much intensity as her father had studied his Greek tomes. She even paid attention to Aunt Cherise's gleanings from her gabble-grinding correspondents.

The new Duke of St. Sevrin was frequently mentioned for his acts of bravery, his commendations and medals. It was duly noted that he refused to sell out in the middle of the war. According to Aunt Cherise's informants, from whom Wellesley could have learned a thing or two, His Grace hired a London man of business to engage a new bailiff, to handle the income, and to make investments until St. Sevrin was good and ready to take up the domestic reins.

An infected saber wound wasn't good, but it made St. Sevrin ready to leave the front a year or so later. Lisanne read the papers even more avidly. Now the news was of the swath St. Sevrin was cutting through London's *demi monde*, instead of through the French forces. He seemed to favor opera dancers, from all she could gather. If Aunt Cherise and the budding debutante Esmé were examples of the females in Society, Lisanne didn't blame him. Weighed against the rest of the gossip she read, Sloane St. Sevrin didn't seem much worse than any other London profligate—certainly no worse than his own father. No better, either.

Tongues wagged and turbaned heads shook in disapproval, but not Lisanne's. She didn't care a jot about St. Sevrin's morals. In fact, she wished him joy of his birds of paradise, his gaming hells, his dockside brawls, whatever it took to keep him happy in London—and away from St. Sevrin Priory.

Chapter Four

Sloane Shearingham, late of Her Majesty's First Hussars, only son of the late fifth Duke of St. Sevrin, and perpetually late with the rent, was not happy in London. Not at all. The gossip mills might lump him with the other idle pleasure-seekers of his class, but the sixth Duke of St. Sevrin was getting deuced little pleasure out of the constant rounds of gambling, drinking, and wenching.

It wasn't that he missed the army. Zeus knew he'd hated the bloody war. Sloane still woke in the middle of the night bathed in sweat from the memories of cannons and fallen comrades, screaming horses and the stench of blood. He still ached where the Frenchie's saber had sliced across his chest and under his left arm, which the sawbones warned would always be weak. If Sloane's right arm hadn't been so strong around the surgeon's neck, the medico would have removed the left one altogether, so Sloane should have considered himself lucky.

Lucky, hah! He'd come home to find that his man of business had played ducks and drakes with whatever income the swindling bailiff had sent on to London. There was nothing left of his inheritance but bills. The estates had been bled dry and weren't about to see a profit

27

without a major investment of capital that His Grace simply did not possess. St. Sevrin would have broken the entail in an instant, sold off half the property to maintain the other half, or at least let himself live in comfort. Half the time he was shivering with the return of the fevers just because there wasn't enough blunt to waste on coal.

But the new duke couldn't break the entail. His cousin and presumed heir Humbert Shearingham had made sure of that. Bertie didn't need the unprofitable Priory acres; he didn't even need the blunt the sale would bring. He wanted the title. He sat like a spider that had built its web, waiting for the unwary bug. Bertie had agreed to pay off the mortgages, Sloane's new solicitor reported, and to restore the estate. He'd even make Sloane a handsome annuity. All St. Sevrin had to do was renounce the title in his cousin's favor.

Well, Napoleon Bonaparte hadn't succeeded in giving Humbert the dukedom. Be damned if Sloane would, either.

So the former officer was living on his wits and luck, and feeling more every day that both had gone begging. He lived in three rooms of St. Sevrin House in Berkeley Square with his retired batman Kelly as his only servant. He paid his expenses, when he managed to pay at all, with his gaming winnings.

Unfortunately the men he gambled with—not always gentlemen, either—were heavy drinkers. Anyone more sober than themselves was suspected of being a Captain Sharp, as was anyone who won too often or too much. The drink kept St. Sevrin from being distrusted—and from being a successful gamester.

It was easier to stay drunk than to face the piles of bills, as well as the pity and disdain on his fellow peers' faces. Soon the doors of polite Society were closing in his face, except for a few that remained open on account of his war record. St. Sevrin didn't give a rap for the

Quality, save that they were easier to pry loose from their blunt.

A good cardplayer, though no wizard with the pasteboards, St. Sevrin managed to keep his head above water, barely. There was nothing left to sink back into the estates, so there was no hope, therefore, of His Grace's seeing a shilling from his fine inheritance.

There was nothing his father hadn't mortgaged, nothing unentailed that the old rip hadn't sold. Sloane was desperate, and the vultures knew it. A man on the edge couldn't wager recklessly because he couldn't afford to lose. Time and again Sloane had warned his young recruits not to play where they couldn't pay. Now he was doing the same thing, finding himself deeper in debt every day.

The war may have been a nightmare, but at least Sloane had felt he was getting a job done. Here in London he was accomplishing nothing, and it was taking all day and night to do it. He was exhausted and dejected, but not yet ready to admit defeat.

"I have a new plan," he announced to his valet-butler-groom one morning. It was actually more like late afternoon when St. Sevrin opened his eyes for the second time that day. The first time he'd seen nothing but the walls swaying, so he'd shut them again. Now the pounding headache was almost endurable.

"What, are we going to go on the high toby? Might be more profitable holding up coaches. And hanging might be quicker'n freezing to death in this place." Kelly placed a cup of coffee near his master's hand, his right hand. Kelly was tired of mopping up when the major, what was now His Grace if Kelly could only remember, tried to use that left arm. The old infantryman's joints were too sore for all that bending.

"Freezing be damned. It's spring. We don't need fires."

"Then why are you sleeping under your greatcoat?" Kelly had been with the major through Coruña, Oporto, and Cifuente. He'd dragged him off the fields of Talavera to the hospital tents. With all the gray hairs Kelly'd sprouted on the major's behalf, he could deuced well complain about the conditions in Berkeley Square, and frequently did.

St. Sevrin as frequently ignored the older man's grousing. He'd promised Kelly a glowing recommendation if the batman wanted to find other employment, but Kelly chose to stay on, for which the duke felt grateful, and guilty as hell. "You can borrow my greatcoat tonight," he offered now, taking a gulp of the coffee to help clear his mind. The coffee had been sitting on the stove all day for just that eventuality, though. Now it was scalding, bitter, and thick as boot polish. In fact, it could have been boot polish. The duke spit out the brew and fell back on his pillows. "Thunderation, what does it take to get a decent cup of coffee?"

"Let me think . . . some fresh beans, 'haps a grinder what works, a pot without rust, one of them modern stoves. Oh, and maybe a real cook what gets paid. Yessir, Yer Grace, that ought to do the trick."

So the duke threw one of his pillows at his longtime, long-suffering servant and companion. "Stubble it. I know you're doing the best you can."

Kelly picked up the pillow and His Grace's discarded clothes from the evening before. "A'course, I could go out to the coffeehouse and bring you back some fresh-brewed and a meat pasty or such, was the dibs in tune." He shook the duke's coat, hoping to hear the rustle of paper money and the jingle of coins. All he heard was his own stomach grumbling that they'd have to eat his own cooking again. "So what's the new idea?"

"We're going to Devon, Kelly, that's what." St. Sevrin felt better just thinking of getting out of the stinking City, especially with the weather turning toward spring. In London all one noticed was a warmer fog.

"Devon, eh? We taking up smuggling, then?"

"Dash it all, I know you don't approve of my making a living at the baize table, but it's not as if I've been shaving the deck or anything. And this plan is strictly legitimate." The coffee was cool enough to drink now. St. Sevrin tried to make it more palatable by pouring in a dollop of brandy from the bottle at his bedside. "We're going home, if you can call St. Sevrin Priory my home."

"You usually dub the place the millstone around your neck."

"Yes, well, it is the ducal seat, even if I've only been back there a handful of times since I was out of short pants."

His Grace did not have fond memories of those visits, either. He'd been sent off to boarding school when he was six, unfazed at the petty cruelties there. The schoolyard brawls were as nothing compared to the arguments between his parents. Theirs had been an arranged match, the old story of the groom's title and the bride's wealth. Fiona's father was an Irish shipbuilder who'd amassed a fortune that he left to his daughter, so pleased was he that his little lassie was to be a duchess.

Sloane's mother died after his seventh birthday, and his father began a quick descent into dissipation. It wasn't grief that sent the fifth duke into his decline; it was the freedom from his duchess's shrewish tongue and her hand controlling the purse strings.

The heir was sent to relatives during vacations at first, when his father remembered to make arrangements. The few times the young viscount did return to his birthplace, he found the ancient building depressingly run-down, ill-staffed, and damp. His father was usually passed out from drink, or entertaining the kitchen wenches in the ducal suite. The duke's bed must have been the only warm thing in the house; surely the food never arrived hot. After that, Viscount Shearingham managed to sidestep Devon and the duke as much as possible. He planned walking tours or tutorials during school breaks, and accepted friends' invitations for the long holidays.

Upon graduation, when his classmates were eager to acquire a veneer of Town bronze, Sloane was only eager to avoid his father's dissolute presence. He purchased his colors as soon as he came down from university, and hadn't been back to the Priory since. He wasn't looking forward to this trip, either.

Kelly knew the major never spoke of home or family, so the batman wasn't ready to commit himself to an opinion. He hadn't heard the rest of the plan. He did move the bottle of spirits farther out of reach, making room on the bedside table for His Grace's shaving lather. "I hear Devon's pretty countryside. Good farmland. Cows and sheep."

"Pretty be damned. And if there was a cow or a sheep on the property, the thieving bastard I had as bailiff would have eaten it by now."

"Then what? We're going on a repairing lease to St. Sevrin Priory? The footman next door says as how it's in the guidebooks."

"As a location to avoid, I'm sure. The house is not worth saving for dry rot and termites, the staff decamped ages ago, and the whole pile is supposed to be haunted. This place is a regular palace compared to what we might find there."

"And I was just telling myself a tent in the mud and dust of Portugal would look good about now. So why are we going to Devon?"

Sloane was happy to hear the "we." Despite his complaints, Kelly was the best forager St. Sevrin had ever known. And the most loyal. The duke tipped his cup in salute—without spilling any when he saw Kelly wince. "We are going to the ancestral abode," he declared after a swallow and a cough, "because we are at *point non plus* here. We'll be reduced to burning the banisters for the cookstove, which will only bring my cousin Humbert breathing down my neck. Every rung and railing is part of the entail. I checked. If they weren't, the pater would have sold them for kindling the way he did the Hepplewhite chairs."

"Maybe the gudgeon's hot air would keep us warm." Kelly didn't think much of Humbert's Corinthian set: wealthy, active, sportive young men who'd be better employed facing Boney's artillery like honest Englishmen. He started to strop the razor in angry swipes that had St. Sevrin's bloodshot eyes blinking rapidly.

"We'll be warm, I swear. For there is one thing at St. Sevrin Priory that my esteemed parent didn't manage to sell. If I can get a decent price, it might just see us through the next winter at least. I'd have a stake to bet with, or I could buy back my commission."

"Can't say as I'd rather face the frogs again, iffen I had my druthers."

"Yes, well, I doubt Whitehall would let me go, with this confounded weak arm of mine, although old Humbert would take the medical exam for me if he could."

Kelly approached with the razor and lather and a sour expression. The duke thought he'd better have another sip of fortification first. "They reminded me over at Horse Guards that Prinny didn't approve of his nobles going over as cannon fodder until they've ensured their successions. I don't count Humbert, so we're likely stuck in England anyway."

"In a moldering heap what's been deserted by everyone except the rats and the ghosts of them long-gone monks?"

"Only temporarily. And we'll be warm, remember? Because the one thing the old man left intact is the home woods."

Kelly was not impressed by his master's pronouncement. "I thought all the land was entailed. That's why an officer and a gentleman is living worse off than a coal heaver. Leastways that's how you explained it."

"And it's true. I can't sell off the land because it's actually held in trust for my heirs and their heirs, ad infinitum. But what's on it isn't. I checked with the solicitor. He says I can go ahead with the sale. There's I don't know how many acres of prime timber in the home woods. I'd have to check the estate maps to be sure. And it's never been cut, as far as I know. The lumber is bound to bring in a pretty penny, the solicitor thinks. Maybe I'll invest in turnip seeds and become a farmer. What do you think?"

Kelly'd been a farmer's son before he became a duke's batman. He'd eaten better then. Spreading lather on the duke's cheeks, he asked, "When do we leave?"

Chapter Five

"*Your* uncle wants to see you, miss," the maid said when she brought Lisanne's hot water in the morning, an hour earlier than usual. "In a huff, he is. Says he looked for you all day yesterday. Made me get up before I'd had my sleep out, he did, to make sure you didn't leave the house without seeing him." The maid wasn't best pleased, either, it sounded.

Lisanne didn't listen. Birds were singing, trees were budding. It was spring. There was no reason to stay in the house and every reason to be gone, not the least of which was that it was warmer out-of-doors than in. Uncle Alfred was another who subscribed to the notion that fires were not necessary after the first of March. His belief stemmed from parsimony rather than need, and did not, of course, extend to his own bedchamber or the parlor, where he sat of an evening.

But it was the birthing season, the planting season, a time when everything burst into new life. That was outside. Inside Neville Hall, the Findleys stagnated in the same fetid pool of their discontent, only louder than ever, like bullfrogs with the colic.

Esmé wanted to be a lady now that she was seventeen.

She demanded a social life, a London Season, and every new whim that whistled on fashion's fickle breeze. She also wanted that stable boy, Diccon. Tears and tantrums erupted at each meal or family gathering.

Nigel saw no reason he shouldn't have digs of his own in Town now that he was done with schooling. He was nineteen, a real man. Since Nigel found ways aplenty to overspend his allowance, overturn the carriages, and overset his mama's notions of propriety right here in Devon, Uncle Alfred wasn't about to loose such an expensive piece of goods on the metropolis. Nigel pouted and pounded the table and flicked peas at his sister. A real man.

Aunt Cherise still resorted to her smelling salts at every raised voice. Most mealtimes were interrupted for the burning of feathers or the waving of a vinaigrette. The family should invest in the apothecary business, Lisanne thought, but not even that windfall would be enough to satisfy her greedy, grasping relations.

Lisanne usually ate in the kitchens, where she'd come to terms with the latest cook after curing the old woman's asthma. Curing the ailment was simple: Lisanne had merely ordered the kitchen cats outside and the room aired. Winning Cook's trust was another matter. The woman still made the sign of the cross when Lisanne entered her precincts. Lisanne shrugged. So what if everyone thought she was a witch, a wantwit, a lunatic? She was free to come and go as she pleased, to live her life without the constant nerve-gnawing that passed for family feeling among the Findleys.

But not this morning. Of course Lisanne could disobey her uncle's demand for her presence. She could go down the back stairs and not return till the candle in the master bedroom was snuffed at night. But years of experience had taught her that Uncle Alfred would only take his ire out on the servants. The poor maid who brought the message would be blamed. She might even lose her position, lowly as it was. Besides, Lisanne was curious to find what was so important that her uncle deigned to tell her. He never mentioned how her income was being invested—she had to find that out from the solicitor's letters on his desk—or what plans were afoot for the farms and fields of the Neville holdings. The bailiff gave her that information, being one of the few retainers who still respected the Neville barony, if not the current bizarre baroness.

Lisanne donned the dress the maid laid out for her. It was another of Esmé's castoffs, but since that spoiled miss was notoriously fussy and hard to please, the gowns in Lisanne's closet were nearly new, not that she cared. Rid of all the bows and lace frills, taken up six inches in the hem, the dresses were not half bad, especially since a sash at the high waist could gather in the extra material. Besides, Nigel's outgrown clothes were instantly burned. Those were Aunt Cherise's orders, so Lisanne had no choice unless she wanted to shop with her cousin for fabric, ponder fashion magazines for the perfect designs, then stand for hours being pinned. Esmé's muslins were good enough. And they'd soon have spots and stains on them, anyway, from the days Lisanne spent in the fields and forest, the garden and the stillroom.

The maid didn't bother with a hat or gloves or reticule, for everyone knew Miss Annie would only lose them by lunchtime, poor thing. At least she wore shoes now, most times, anyway.

Lisanne twisted her long hair into a braid that hung neatly down her back. It wouldn't stay that way, of course, so she crammed a ribbon into her pocket for later. A knife followed, and scissors, a needle and thread, a handful of handkerchiefs, that jar with the butterfly larva, the packet of seeds from the wild orchid, a book with the spiderweb from the windowsill pressed between its pages, and a small, meticulously carved flute. The maid rolled her eyes behind Lisanne's back.

Sir Alfred cleared his throat. The footmen serving the breakfast snapped to attention, but of the family only Lisanne looked up from her muffin and chocolate. Esmé and Nigel continued their bickering over the last rasher of bacon.

"I have news," Sir Alfred pronounced. When that gained him no more notice, he slammed his fist on the table and shouted, "Dash it, I will have your silence when I speak."

Aunt Cherise, picking at her invalid's fare of weak tea and dry toast, cringed. "Not so loud, Sir Alfred. My nerves, you know."

The baronet didn't apologize, he just forged on, now that the small group in the morning room, family and servants alike, was listening. "I want all of you to pay close heed. I heard some important news in the village yesterday. I wanted to mention it sooner." At this point he glared at Lisanne for not being where he could issue his orders. "At any rate, the news was confirmed by Squire Pemberton last night. St. Sevrin is in residence."

Lisanne's cup shook in her hand, spilling a trail of chocolate down her badly altered gown. Lisanne didn't notice. For once, neither did Aunt Cherise.

"That awful Sloane Shearingham? Why, he's not received anywhere anymore. All the important houses have been closed to him since the duns started knocking on his door. Now, why didn't my cousin write and tell me that knave was coming to Devon on a repairing lease? We could have been long gone on our way elsewhere."

"What, madam, should we run away from our home?" her husband asked, amazed.

"But what if he comes to church?" Lady Findley was in a fidge of indecision. "Should we recognize him or give him the cut? He's a rakehell, for sure, but a duke still and all. Oh, how I wish I knew what the ladies of London had decided about the dratted man. One wouldn't want to be blamed for lending countenance to such licentious behavior, but neither should one be behind times in courtesy to our noble neighbor."

Her husband had no patience for such niceties. "He isn't coming to church, you can be certain of that. I doubt His Grace St. Sevrin could even recognize the inside of one. Besides, sots like him are never out of bed in time for services."

"Can we go call on him, then, Pa?" Nigel wanted to know. "Can we? I hear he's a regular Trojan, a real hero."

"He's a wastrel." The last thing Sir Alfred needed was for his gudgeon of a son to pattern himself after a cardsharp and a basket scrambler. "He most likely plucks green pigeons like you as an appetizer before he gets down to serious wagering. Pray you stay out of his clutches."

Esmé wasn't listening. "*I* think it's the most romantic thing in the world, a real live hero right on our doorstep. Perhaps the duke drinks to forget a lost love who wouldn't wait for him to come home from the wars. Or some injury that makes their marriage impossible."

Nigel groaned. "Just like you to make a Cheltenham tragedy out of a chap's tossing back a few. Next you'll be offering to bathe his fevered brow. Now, if that ain't what every soldier dreams of, some plump little schoolgirl's pity."

Before Esmé could retaliate, their father pounded the table again. "The man is a libertine, I say. You will not make him out to be any kind of Minerva Press hero. Heroes are just bloody fools who don't care about their own hides anyhow. This one is a dashed loose screw drowning on River Tick. Not even rich cits will look at him for a son-in-law, that's how low he's fallen. The father was a rakehell; the son's a rakehell."

But he was Esmé's first rakehell and, like the first taste of champagne, irresistible. She had every intention of trotting her old mare back and forth in front of the

Priory's gates in case the duke rode out. "Do you think he'll attend the assembly at Honiton? You said I could go, remember, Pa?"

"I think he'd attend his own funeral before doing the pretty with a hall full of provincials. But that's no matter. You are not going to meet him, you are not going to speak to him if you do see him, and you are not going to go out of the house while he's here. It's just a day or two, according to the squire, while St. Sevrin transacts some business."

Lady Findley was nodding vigorously. "A girl can't be too careful of her reputation, Esmé. You wouldn't want to be tarred with the same brush."

"And that goes for you, too, missy," Uncle Alfred told Lisanne, as usual not minding his tongue in front of the servants. "I don't want you in his woods or on his land. I don't want you anywhere St. Sevrin might happen to be." He took a look at his niece's suntanned face, the childish braid, the bunched-up and besmirched gown, whose neckline fell much lower on her than it had on the more rounded Esmé. Damn, but the chit was turning into a tempting morsel. "He's liable to mistake you for a dairy-maid and tumble you in the grass. And I'm not about to call him out over your honor. They say he hasn't got any, when it comes to wenches."

Aunt Cherise was near to swooning. The well-practiced footmen stood on either side of her chair ready to catch her. "Oh, my word, the scandal."

"Precisely. And it's the last thing we need just when we're going to be bringing Esmé out next fall. Everything has to be perfect. I don't want word getting back to London that my niece is fast, chasing after a rank libertine on his own grounds."

No, Lisanne thought, it was all right for people to think she was a lunatic, but not immoral. She wouldn't set foot in the London marriage mart for anything, which suited her uncle's plans to a cow's thumb. She knew he intended

40

to claim she was supposed to share Esmé's Season. Actually Esmé was supposed to share Lisanne's; that's how Uncle Alfred could justify opening Neville House, which was much larger and more fashionably situated than the Findleys' own leased town house. Then he'd tell everyone that his poor niece had come down with something. That's what he wrote to her London trustee last year, explaining why she was not making her come-out with other girls her age. A sickly child, don't you know. This year he might bruit it about that she was too emotionally unstable to handle the pressure of curtsying at a court presentation, undergoing the scrutiny of the Almack's patronesses, or having to impress the eligible *partis*. Since those were the last things Lisanne wanted or desired, she didn't mind not going to London with her relations.

The Findleys would all be leaving, and their servants with them. That was enough. For once Lisanne could have her home to herself. She didn't need London when everything that mattered was here. The problem was that half of what mattered to her was on St. Sevrin property.

"Thunderation, girl, stop your air-dreaming for once and pay attention! It's for your own safety, too. The man might go out hunting and never know you're about."

Nigel was muttering about the unfairness that St. Sevrin should get to hunt those well-stocked woods, when he'd never been allowed.

"They're his woods, you nodcock," Sir Alfred ground out before turning back to Lisanne. "I don't want you out of the house, Annie, and I mean it. You've always been the most stubborn, disobedient child I've ever known, and I can't imagine you're any different now that you are eighteen. But that's not too old to beat, I swear."

Lisanne just looked at him with that clear blue gaze that seemed to read Alfred's soul, and to know how much guilty pleasure he'd get from laying his hands on her. Findley flushed and looked away. They both also knew a beating wouldn't gain him one iota of respect—or obedience. Lisanne didn't even respect him enough to be afraid.

"I'll lock you up," he blustered. "I swear I'll . . . I'll . . ." Sir Alfred looked around for inspiration, something that might make her comply with his orders, for once. "I'll burn the library. That's what I'll do. I'll have all your precious books taken out and burned if you put one foot out of this door."

"They are part of the estate," Lisanne reminded her uncle in the usual composed, reasonable way she had that aggravated the baronet to no end. "How will you explain such wanton destruction to the trustees?"

Thunderation, the blasted chit was too smart for Alfred's liking. "I'll go ask St. Sevrin's permission, then, to go out hunting with him. I'll shoot down every animal in those cursed woods of his."

Nigel's mouth was open, and Lady Cherise was mopping her forehead with lavender water, but Lisanne knew Uncle Alfred wouldn't dare step an inch into the forest. She asked the footman for more chocolate, effectively showing the baronet what she thought of his tirade.

Findley knew his niece recognized him for a coward and hated her the more. "Then I'll take my gun and shoot that deuced dog of yours." He smiled when he finally saw the stricken look on her face. So the chit wasn't made entirely of ice water after all. "Yes, that's what I'll do."

Lisanne knew her uncle just might, out of meanness alone, if he could find Becka. She got up to take her pet into the woods. Since Aunt Cherise did not allow animals in the house, Becka was used to being out alone. The big dog was used to the woods, too, and would stay there until Lisanne came for her. Before she left the breakfast parlor, Lisanne thought to ask: "Did the squire happen to say what business St. Sevrin has at the Priory?"

"Oh, did I forget to mention it?" Sir Alfred smiled, showing his yellowed teeth. Almost ten years of aggrava-

42

tion were about to be repaid. Satisfaction sat sweetly on his lips. "Why, the duke is here to get bids from various lumber mills. He's selling off your precious forest."

Chapter Six

The old ways were dying. No one believed, no one cared. Without that ancient forest, so full of history, so full of mystery, a bit more of the world's magic would be lost. And a lot more of Lisanne Neville's world. Wealth and title, fame and social standing, reputation and the respect of those around her—none mattered to Lisanne as much as Sevrin Woods. She didn't count her personal safety or her personal appearance, only the woods.

Now the forest was threatened, to pay some scapegrace's gambling debts. It just couldn't happen. Lisanne couldn't let it happen. She was the one who understood, the special one, so she had to do something. But what?

She stayed in her room that day, thinking. Uncle Alfred had footmen stationed in the hall outside her room, and groundskeepers working close to the house. Lisanne wondered what they would do if she just strolled past them and kept going. Most of the staff was afraid of her, she knew. They wouldn't be too anxious to chase her down and bring her back by force, for fear she'd lay a curse on them or contaminate them with her strangeness. Most likely they would simply send for Uncle Alfred.

Becka was safe enough. Lisanne had gone to the stables

after breakfast and taken the animal out for exercise. She managed to "lose" the dog at the edge of the Neville lawns where they met the forest. After that she'd had all day to pace the confines of her room, making plans. If the squire knew of the duke's intentions, everyone in the countryside knew, so Lisanne didn't have to hurry to give warning. No harm could be done immediately, anyway, not if the dastard was first sending for lumbermen.

How could he? Such arrant waste and disregard for a place of beauty was appalling. Lisanne knew how the foresters operated, for she'd seen it often enough on Neville property under Sir Alfred's care. The men would come in with their huge wagons and teams of heavy workhorses, their ropes and saws and axes, and they'd begin chopping away. They wouldn't take only the fallen, diseased, or overcrowded trees, giving the others more room to grow. No, that took too long, required too many men, didn't yield enough profit. Instead they'd cut everything in sight, leaving nothing but ugly stumps as a mark of shame and greed on the landscape.

All the animals, the precious wildflowers, the secrets in the soil—those things could never survive, could never be replaced. There wouldn't even be birdsong if the sparrows had nowhere to nest.

And then there were the trees themselves. Despite his current low tide, the duke was likely some high-nosed blue blood, claiming his family came over with William the Conqueror. But the trees would have been here to greet the invaders, to give them shelter, firewood, and fruit. The trees had blood and life, too, besides nurturing the souls of other ancient races.

The forest would die, and everything with it. Oh, some creatures could find other roosts, other dens, but not those whose very spirits were tied to Sevrin Woods. There was no place else for them to go.

Lisanne couldn't let it happen. Neither could she buy the woods or offer to pay the dreadful duke's bills. She didn't control her own income and wouldn't until she was five and twenty, if she managed to wrest the guardianship from Uncle Alfred's grasping fingers then. For the first time Lisanne wished that she'd cared more about worldly matters, that she'd written to her solicitors herself to tell them what was happening. Now it was too late. Her pocket money wouldn't keep a mare in oats, much less a spendthrift sot in London, where he belonged.

Uncle Alfred finally went to sleep. His valet had crept down the silent hall ages ago, but candlelight still shone under the baronet's door. Lisanne waited another half hour after the light went out.

She knew one of the gardeners still patrolled the grounds, because she could see him and his lantern pass under her room every fifteen minutes or so. That was enough time for Lisanne to lift her window and scurry down the trellis, then scamper across the lawns to the boxwood maze. She could have made her escape in pitch darkness, so many times had she taken the same route, but tonight, when she didn't need it, the moon lit up her path through the ornamental gardens. Still wearing Esmé's light-colored muslin, with an old woolen shawl hurriedly tied around her shoulders against the chill night air, she'd stick out like a lighthouse at sea. She pulled the shawl over her blond hair and waited behind a topiary unicorn for the guard to pass by again before entering the maze. Then, racing through its twists and turns past the fountain at the center, she exited at the opposite side, where the maze's high hedges would block her flight across the lawns and into Sevrin Woods.

Only Becka greeted Lisanne, joyous to see her mistress and the rolls she had stuffed in her pockets. Everything else was hushed except for the mist that dripped steadily off just-budded branches. 'Twas almost as if the trees themselves were weeping.

No one answered Lisanne's call, or came tumbling out of the mist when she played a tune on her little flute. They knew. She could already feel their pain.

"No!" she shouted into the empty night, and "No!" again. Becka set up a howl that had the Neville Hall groundsman dropping his staff and his lantern and heading for the next county.

Sloane Shearingham was drunk. There was nothing unusual in that except for the location. Tonight he was castaway in three barely habitable rooms of St. Sevrin Priory in Devon instead of three barely habitable rooms of St. Sevrin House in London.

He and Kelly had arrived the afternoon before, enough time, thank goodness, for a hasty inspection of the centuries-old building to see if it was liable to fall down around their ears as they slept. While Kelly unpacked and tried to find chimneys that weren't blocked by squirrel nests and mattresses that weren't burrowed through by mice, Sloane had made a quick trip to the village to arrange for a delivery of fodder for the horses. If Kelly couldn't find them reasonably comfortable billets in the house, at least they'd have fresh hay to sleep on in the nearly intact stables. It wouldn't be the first time Sloane and his batman had bedded down with their mounts.

When Sloane returned, pockets slightly emptier since the liveryman wouldn't extend credit to any St. Sevrin, he rubbed the tired horses down himself, and discovered where some chickens had taken up housekeeping in one of the stalls. He relieved the hens of a clutch of eggs, helped Kelly fire the antique stove in the kitchen, and sat down to a halfway decent omelette. Theirs was such a hand-to-mouth existence, he thought, that those chickens should be making out their wills.

At least they wouldn't be cold. There was firewood lying all over the place from fallen trees, broken shutters, wrecked carriages. Better yet, the duke unearthed a case of old brandy in a far corner of the wine cellar that the servants or squatters or his sire had overlooked. 'Twas better to stay drunk, His Grace decided, for St. Sevrin Priory was indeed haunted, if only with the ghosts of the past. A mass of murdered monks would have been good company by comparison.

Asleep Sloane had nightmares of battle, of fallen comrades he couldn't raise, of devastated Spanish villages after the French had been through. He saw the eyes of the children there, beseeching him, accusing him. By day, he had the shambles of his life to torment him. This morning he'd made inquiries about lumber mills, then he'd ridden across parts of his estate to see firsthand what years of neglect and avarice had wrought. He'd seen the bare fields, the tumbled cottages, the abandoned gristmill. The children of his own tenants—the ones who'd remained at St. Sevrin because they had nowhere else to go—had those same pleading eyes.

When Sloane returned from his inspection, he'd started drinking the brandy. Now it was well after dinner—chicken, as expected—and he wasn't done yet. No, he was still sober enough to see the damp spots on the ceilings of the Priory, the warped floors where priceless Aubusson carpets used to lie, the empty gallery walls, the boarded windows. Worse, he could hear his mother crying.

Hell and damnation, he'd hated everything his father was. Now he was his father.

Two hours later the Duke of St. Sevrin was propped against one of the windows that still had glass in it, in one of the parlors of the Priory's modern section. This addition was only one century old instead of two or three, and it overlooked the rear of the Priory, toward the home woods. He could just make out the distant trees in the hazy moonlight, spreading as far as he could see in either direction. The next duke, he told himself, Humbert or whoever, would likely be looking out this very window right at Neville Hall. The two estates weren't all that close, but the land was flat. 'Twould be just like Humbert to purchase a telescope to peek in his neighbor's bedrooms.

Sloane had long since dispensed with the glass; but the bottle of brandy, the second bottle of brandy, dangled from his right hand. He wouldn't trust his unreliable left arm with such a fine vintage, such a fine, mind-numbing companion. When he saw the ghost walk from the woods, the bottle slid, unnoticed, to the floor anyway.

St. Sevrin blinked to try to clear his eyes, but the figure didn't disappear. It was definitely a woman, her light-colored skirts billowing around her in the breeze. She couldn't be real, of course. Women did not float out of forests in the middle of the night, not even in Devon. The Priory ghosts were all said to be monks, so those old stories of the woods being enchanted must be correct after all. A fairy creature was coming to visit. Either that or he'd finally had too much to drink. Sloane rather hoped it was the brandy.

The woman held neither lantern nor torch, yet she was walking directly toward him across the unscythed lawns. Her hair looked silvery by the moonlight, and his experienced eye told him she must be small-boned and thin, perhaps still a girl.

She kept coming closer until she stood just outside his window. St. Sevrin did the only thing possible, of course, for a gentleman so deep in his cups. He opened the window, not without a struggle with the rusted latch. " 'Well met by moonlight, proud Titania,' " he greeted her.

"That's 'Ill met,' " she corrected automatically, worried lest the real quote prove true.

Sloane held out his hand. "Won't you join me anyway, sweet fairy queen? There's a fire, and wine."

Lisanne was suddenly undecided. She'd come this far out of necessity, but her courage was failing her at actually facing the rogue. He was large and broad-shouldered, wearing a shirt with an open collar, no neck cloth. With his reddish hair fallen over his forehead, he looked sleepy, unfinished. Mayhaps this was a bad idea after all.

While Lisanne was studying the duke, St. Sevrin was owlishly peering out the window at her. "No, you cannot be Titania, for surely you haven't enough years in your dish to be queen of the ether. But come in out of the chill, fairy child."

For a moment Lisanne's heart soared. He understood! He knew about the woods! But no, she realized, he was only teasing, flirting with her. He was a rake, after all.

St. Sevrin watched the expressions flitter across the beautiful face. That smile lit her whole being, as if the moon rivaled the sun when she was happy. Sloane thought he'd move mountains to bring it back. "Come, sweetings, do."

Lisanne thought the clunch would fall out of the window if he leaned any farther out. She could smell the spirits on his breath even from where she stood. But she had no choice. Muttering under her breath, *"Ave atque, Caesar, mortituri est te salutamus,"* she raised her arms to be hoisted through the window.

When he lifted her, Sloane was surprised to find that his guest was flesh and blood after all, although she weighed about as much as a moonbeam, and her hand trembled in his like a captured butterfly. But her eyes never wavered from his and that clear blue gaze seemed to sear his very soul, like the eyes of the children of war, the children of poverty. St. Sevrin prayed this angel-child would find what she came for. Lud knew he had little enough to offer.

He kicked the fallen bottle aside and made a fairly creditable bow, for a fellow half seas over. "St. Sevrin, at your service."

Lisanne bobbed an awkward curtsy, being out of practice since Miss Armbruster had left. She had to stifle a nervous giggle to think of worrying over drawing-room manners at a time like this. Then she took a deep breath and poured forth her prepared speech: "I am Lisanne Neville, and you can have my fortune if you'll marry me."

St. Sevrin decided he really had to give up drinking.

Chapter Seven

St. Sevrin sank down in a chair. It wasn't the polite thing to do, of course, sitting before a lady, but he felt it was more courteous than falling in a heap at her feet. Many years had passed since he'd been knocked so cock-a-hoop. "Could you repeat that?"

The girl cleared her throat. "I am Lisanne Neville." She jerked one angular shoulder toward the woods and beyond. "I am very wealthy, and I . . . I should like to marry you."

Now there, he thought, that made everything clear. Clear as Kelly's coffee. The outrageous chit just stood near the window, ready to flee, he thought, but giving him time to recover his wits and look his fill.

Miss Lisanne Neville was a tiny scrap of a thing, bird-bone thin. Those big blue eyes gave her an even more waiflike appearance as they made their own inspection. She didn't like what she saw, he could tell by the downward pull to her soft lips, but she held her ground, only the clenched hands and white knuckles betraying her fear. Sloane had seen seasoned foot soldiers show less courage. Whatever her mission, the girl had bottom.

She also had dirt on her hem, twigs in her skirts, and

smudges down the front of her poorly fitted gown. There were leaves in her streaked blond hair, which was every which way around her face and down her back. No wonder he took her for some elven being; she even smelled of forest and earth. At least Miss Neville didn't chatter on like most other females of his acquaintance, highborn or low.

Of course she didn't blather; Lisanne was struck dumb now that she was face-to-face with the duke. He was everything she'd been warned about, and worse. No one had mentioned he might be half dressed. Naturally no one thought she'd come to call after midnight, either. No one had warned her he was such a firm, muscular man, obvious under the form-fitting breeches and the white shirt that was open enough to reveal reddish hairs on his chest. Did all men have hair on their chest, or only the devilish ones? Lisanne made herself look away from his body. It was even more unnerving than his frown.

Returning her gaze to his face, she could see the firm chin and well-defined planes of the hero; she could also see the lines of dissipation, the sallow complexion, the bloodshot, puffy eyes of the libertine. The duke's auburn hair had no shine to it, and those eyes, hazel, she thought from this distance, seemed cold and weary, empty.

St. Sevrin, meanwhile, was trying to recall what he'd heard of the Neville offspring. The parents were dead of course; that was ages ago. Were there more children? He thought not. And there was something, some rumor or other that hadn't mattered at the time, about the daughter. He'd only listened because the Nevilles were old neighbors. Was it that she was sickly? The chit didn't look febrile despite her thinness. She had a golden outdoor tan, unless that was dirt on her face. And the talk couldn't have been that she was a simpleton, for she'd quoted Latin and Shakespeare back at him. Most likely someone had mentioned she was a wayward baggage, hot to hand. What else could she be, wandering around the countryside at night, visiting bachelor quarters? Most likely this was some schoolroom prank, or a dare from her giddy girlfriends, who were undoubtedly safe asleep in their warm beds while this little wren was flitting through the forest at night.

No matter, the gossip would come to him later. For now he had to get the infant home before her guardians tossed a gauntlet in his face, or whatever it was that rustics did when great hulking lechers besmirched their innocent womenfolk. For if there was anything St. Sevrin knew, it was that this little girl wore the face of innocence.

"I'm sorry, sweetings," he told her, deliberately drawing the words out, "you might have a yearning to be a duchess, but I'm not in the market for a bride. If I were, I most decidedly would not choose a hobbledehoy urchin."

"That's a hobbledehoy baroness, sirrah," she retorted, "and the least you could do is listen to my proposition." Her eyes ran around the room, noting the moth-eaten drapes, the water stains on the paneling. "I don't see where you have much to lose."

Some of the old baronies were like that, St. Sevrin knew, passing through the female lines. "Very well, Baroness, I acquit you of coveting my title. You still have to leave. It's past your bedtime."

Lisanne drew herself up to her five feet naught height, the naught giving her dignity. "I am eight and ten, Your Grace, not a child."

"Forgive me, Baroness, but you appear to be no more than fifteen."

"And you are said to be twenty and seven, yet you look nearly forty."

"Touché," he acknowledged. "Very well, you are not a child. Therefore, you know you have no business here. For one thing, the woods can be a dangerous place at night. I suppose you must have played there all your life, but there are unseen hazards in the darkness."

That earned him a disdainful look. Compared to her uncle's wrath and this gentleman's uncertain temper, Sevrin Woods was the last danger she had to worry about.

"Bats? Spiders? Poachers?" She didn't flinch. It was a peculiar female he had on his hands, but St. Sevrin was determined to make his point. "What about the witch who's supposed to live there, casting spells?"

Lisanne laughed. *She* was the enchantress everyone feared! Then she laughed again, in relief. The duke wasn't a total ogre, not if he cared about her well-being. She found a chair whose seat cover wasn't totally ripped and sat down.

Her laughter was like honey, sweet and soft. The duke let it flow around him, but he wasn't to be swayed. "Don't get comfortable, my intrepid lady, for there's still a matter of reputation."

"Yours or mine?"

"Both. Someone has sullied your tender ears with mine, I'm certain." He quirked an eyebrow in inquiry; Lisanne nodded. "Therefore the meanest intelligence could calculate the damage this visit could do to yours."

Lisanne brushed that aside. "I have no reputation to speak of, and no one whose high esteem I desire."

Thunderation, Sloane wished he'd listened harder to the gossip about this chit. "What, have you blotted your copybook so badly that you were denied vouchers at Almack's? If you are of age, you should have been presented at court this past year." The duke was sure he would have remembered that. Gossip about a debutante baroness would have penetrated even his alcoholic fog. "You should be in London now, dancing at balls in silk gowns, having mooncalves write sonnets to your eyebrows." They were very fetching eyebrows, he couldn't help noticing, a bit ragged, as though his fingers could smooth the golden hairs into line.

"Is that what those cabbage-heads do? I'm even more

glad I never went, then. My cousin Esmé comes out in the fall. She'll be thrilled, although I'm not sure . . ."

"Platter-faced, is she?"

"Spots," Lisanne confided. "Uncle Alfred and Aunt Cherise are hopeful she'll outgrow them over the summer."

St. Sevrin was positive the spotted Esmé wore silks and lace. "What about you? Shall you go to Town with them?"

"Oh, no, I don't want to, and Uncle does not want to lay out the expenses for a Season for me, so we are agreed for once."

"Ah, the wicked uncle. I knew there had to be a villain in this piece."

Lisanne gave her answer serious consideration. Actually the man in front of her was the villain, but she didn't think she ought to say that.

He seemed to read her thoughts. "No, no, sweetings. I cannot be the villain and the hero both. You did come to me for rescuing, didn't you?"

"I don't think Uncle Alfred is wicked, precisely. He is greedy, certainly, and miserly. Mostly he is discontented that the Nevilles have so much and the Findleys—that's Uncle Arthur's family—have so little."

"I believe certain Frenchmen felt the same way about their monarchs, and look what happened there. You are very forgiving, Baroness."

St. Sevrin wasn't. He already despised this unknown Alfred Findley for keeping his niece in rags and letting her go unguarded, hidden away in Devonshire. The man should be finding a splendid young husband for his ward, someone of equal rank and fortune to cherish her and protect her from evil beasts like the Duke of St. Sevrin.

"Go home, sweetheart. You've got your fairy tale all wrong. The dragon isn't allowed to rescue the damsel in distress." He closed his eyes and leaned his head back on the chair.

A moment later he felt a gossamer touch on his shoulder. "Sir? Your Grace?"

She was so close Sloane could smell rose water under the other, more earthy scents. He opened his eyes. "What, still here, Baroness? You are a stubborn little thing, aren't you?"

"When I have to be, Your Grace. Won't you hear me out?"

"Will you go home after?"

She nodded.

"Then bring me the bottle over there, child, and let's have your story."

Lisanne found the bottle on the floor near the window, with some brandy miraculously still in it, and handed it to the duke. She searched for a glass.

"But I'm not half civilized, Baroness, haven't you heard?" He tipped the bottle to his lips and swallowed. "I'd offer you some, but I'm sure one of us ought to stay sober."

Drunk, unmannerly, bitter . . . could she bear this in a man? She'd have to. Lisanne found the glass where it had fallen behind a chair still in holland covers. She took the bottle from his limp fingers and poured out a scant thimbleful. "I'd think you'd want a clear head to hear my proposition," she told him, handing over the glass instead of the bottle.

"If I had a clear head, *chérie*, you'd be home in your bed, or upstairs in mine. Now, say your piece, little lady, and get out."

Lisanne put the bottle out of his reach and pulled her chair a little closer. She closed her eyes a moment. "I am the only child of Lord and Lady Neville," she began. "When they died, I inherited the title and great wealth. I cannot give you exact amounts, for no one shows me the account books, but I believe my fortune to be over a hundred thousand pounds."

He whistled. "Now, that's a number to gain any man's attention."

"That's without the income from Neville Hall, which has been earning a handsome profit, and the returns on Papa's investments, which fluctuate. My solicitors in London could give you the precise details. They hold the funds while Uncle Alfred . . . holds me, until I marry or reach five and twenty. But I think—no, I know—that he has plans to extend his control by legal means after I reach my majority."

"What, does the dirty dish want you to marry his nephew or something, to keep the money in the family?"

"No, I think he intends that I never marry."

"What, never give his permission? Never let you go into Society?"

"That needn't concern you, Your Grace. What must is that I have all these funds I don't need and cannot touch, and you have none."

It would be useless to deny the obvious. St. Sevrin stared at the minute amount of wine in his glass. "Why me? A hundred thousand pounds could net you any number of handsome young beaux ready to sweep you away from Uncle Alfred and off to Gretna Green. What could I possibly have that you'd want? A crumbling monastery, a hellish reputation, a mountain of bills? Perhaps this old, battered body?"

If he thought to put her to the blush, he was wrong. "Sevrin Woods" was all Lisanne said.

"Excuse me?"

"Sevrin Woods. That's what you have that I want. I can put a fortune in your hands, if you'll give me Sevrin Woods."

Sloane thought he must be more foxed than he realized—or she was. "Sweetings, if I could sell Sevrin Woods or any part of this monstrosity I've inherited, I wouldn't need your fortune."

She brushed his objection aside impatiently. "I know

58

you cannot sell the property; I wasn't born yesterday. It's what's on it that I want, what's in the woods. I cannot simply buy the trees and such like the lumber mills can. I told you, I cannot touch my moneys. But Sevrin Woods could be written into the marriage settlements, that the woods are to be mine, absolutely inviolate in perpetuity."

"Trade a king's ransom for marriage to a curst rum touch like me—to get a forestful of trees? Lady, you're crazy!"

Lisanne jumped to her feet, fists clenched at her sides. "Never, ever, say that to me!"

He watched her through narrowed eyes. "And prickly as a hedgehog. Almost as grubby, too. Well, I wasn't born yesterday, either. What's in Sevrin Woods you want so badly, you're willing to marry me to get? Did you find gold under the surface? A diamond mine? The fountain of youth in one of the streams?"

"It's nothing like that." Lisanne stared at the mud on her shoes. "It's hard to explain. I spent my childhood playing among the trees. After my parents died my only friends were the, ah, sylvan creatures."

Although Sloane had spent his childhood at schools or being passed from relative to relative, he sympathized with her. "Poor puss."

"No, no, I was never sad in the forest. My happiest memories are there. That's why I cannot bear to see it all destroyed to pay your gaming debts. No, I shouldn't have said that. I know you inherited debts and mortgages you could never have repaid. I don't blame you, truly, but I can help."

"What did you say your name was?"

Chapter Eight

*H*e was listening! More important, he was hearing her! Self-interest was a wondrous tool sometimes, Lisanne decided, and who could be more self-centered than a hedonistic, care-for-nothing rake? Instead of disdaining the duke for his profligate ways, she was relieved. Given enough time and his favorite peppermint drops, even Lester Roarke's most cantankerous bull could be gentled a bit.

"My name is Lisanne. Lisanne Margaret Finella Neville. My cousins call me Annie, but I hate it."

"As do I. It's common. Lisanne suits you, something that's a combination of many things, but with its own flow, its own grace."

That may have been the first compliment Lisanne ever received from a man. She didn't need flattery from this cup-shot stranger, only his cooperation, but she was pleased all the same. "And you, Your Grace? Do you prefer something to your title? Or does that suit your consequence?"

"Consequence be damned. My father made sure there was no distinction in those ducal strawberry leaves. I've only continued the slide. I was born Sloane Jarrett Shelton Shearingham, with more titles and dignities than I can recite now. My fellow officers used to call me Sherry. I was Lieutenant Shearingham at the time, you see, so it was natural, given the reddish color of my hair and my fondness for the grape."

She looked at the bottle. No, she would not call him Sherry. "St. Sevrin fits you better. Or Sloane."

"Slow to pay what's owed? Securing a loan? No, don't answer. Call me whatever you will. After all, we should be on a more familiar footing. It's not every day a chap has an offer of marriage. Or an offer for his home woods, since that's what this so flattering proposition amounts to. No, no, I'm not offended," he said when she would reply, holding up his hand with the glass. A drop or two spilled on the threadbare carpet. "I admire your honesty."

"In that case I'd better tell you that I do have a few other conditions."

"Ah, now, why am I not surprised?"

"But these are negotiable, of course."

"Unlike the deed to the woods, which is to be bound in a blood oath and witnessed by an archangel."

"The rest are nothing so terrible." Lisanne fished in her skirt pockets, pulling out her usual hodgepodge of stuff, until she found a folded paper.

To St. Sevrin's amusement, she shoved the rest of the junk willy-nilly back in her pockets till she looked like a tattered Elizabethan doll with panniers. This ragamuffin thought she could be a duchess? As she smoothed the page on her lap, Sloane noted, "I can see you've put some thought into this, at least."

"Oh, I thought and thought. I would not have come to you if there was another way."

"Thank you for that, my lady."

Lisanne colored up again. "I'm sorry. I'm not in the habit of dissembling."

"Never learn, sweetings. Go on, let me hear the rest of your terms."

She consulted the paper, as if trying to decide which stipulation he'd find least insulting. "Firstly, I should wish part of the money to go to restore the Priory. This must have been a wondrous place. It shouldn't be allowed to crumble into dust."

"I am not comfortable in such conditions, you may be assured. This rubbish heap makes Portugal look like a well-run hostelry. The London house needs refurbishing, too."

"And the farms?"

"A given. It only makes sense to invest some of the ready back into the land so it can turn a profit. What's next?"

She had to moisten her lips with her tongue. "I would want a portion of the moneys, perhaps the income from Neville Hall, to be kept separate for my use."

"I thought you said you didn't need the blunt, *chérie*. Never tell me you're going to turn into one of those fashionable belles who spend their husbands' incomes on feathers and furbelows? Hiding your fashion sense under a bushel, are you? Or do you hanker for jewels, perhaps a diamond tiara to go with the leaves in your hair?"

Lisanne reached up to remove the offending articles, disarranging what remained of the braid. She pulled the ribbon away and shook out the rest of her long blond hair, over her shoulders and past her breasts. St. Sevrin watched her unconscious sensuality and shook his head. Zounds, the chit didn't even know what she could do to a man. She could unman him with her words, too.

"I want a sum settled on me, perhaps the amount my dowry would have been, so that you cannot gamble it away if you manage to lose all the rest."

At his indrawn breath, Lisanne glanced toward the window, gauging the distance if she had to escape. "You said I should be honest."

So his little hedgehog had teeth, too. "Fencing with naked swords, are we, Baroness?"

He had reverted back to formal titles. So be it. "I wouldn't want my children going hungry, Your Grace, or reduced to living in the gamekeeper's cottage when you get yourself killed in some brothel brawl. My children's future must not depend on which horse wins at Epsom."

"Oh, so there are to be children of this union? S'truth, I thought it was to be a financial transaction, accrued interest the only outcome."

There was no blush this time, just the matter-of-fact: "You need an heir. And yes, I would like children . . . someday. After we know each other better."

And after she had a bath. "I would derive great satisfaction in eliminating my current heir, my cousin Humbert, from the succession." St. Sevrin also thought he might find a bit of satisfaction in introducing this hurly-burly baroness to the joys of lovemaking.

"Then why haven't you married?" she asked in that disconcertingly straightforward manner of hers.

Because he couldn't ask a decent female to share his miserable life; because if he could have fed another mouth, he'd have bought a racehorse; because he hadn't yet met a woman who didn't bore him to death after twenty minutes, ten if he was in a hurry.

Until tonight. Tonight this female was full of surprises. Sloane didn't think she could ever bore him, with her eccentric mix of worldly wisdom and naïveté. Lady Lisanne was the one who let her thoughts rule her tongue, however, not him. Sloane was used to keeping his cards close to his chest, so his answer was, "What, marry and settle on one woman?"

Lisanne nodded. "I've thought of that also, and I promise not to interfere with your life. I know you have other interests, and I don't mean to hang on your sleeve, you know. I don't care if I never go to London, and you don't have to dance attendance on me here."

"You have an odd notion of where the heir is coming from, then, my dear, if we live separate lives."

Lisanne refused to be embarrassed. "I believe it's done all the time in arranged marriages. I wouldn't care, as long as you do not embarrass me. I realize you haven't had reason to be discreet in the past. I understand, truly."

"You do?" Then she understood more than Sloane could himself. He didn't want to continue this particular line of conversation. "Is that it, then? Have you finished your shopping list? Let me reiterate, Baroness, to make sure I have it correct. You want the woods, or what's in them."

"Sworn and inviolate. Forever."

"Right, forever. Marriage to me would get you Sevrin Woods and get you out from under Uncle Alfred's thumb, with a substantial amount settled on you and your children. For a rainy day, of course." At her nod he continued: "In return, I get my bills paid, my property restored, a fortune to fritter away, and my freedom, as long as I don't embarrass you. I also increase my holdings with Neville Hall and your father's investments."

"There's a town house in London, too. It's part of the entail so cannot be sold, but you could lease it out."

"Rental income," he said, ticking another bonus off on his fingers. "And, of course, a wife and heirs, sometime in the future. I think I have covered everything."

Sloane reached over for the bottle, about to pour a healthy amount of the brandy into his glass.

"There is one more thing." Lisanne stared at the paper in her hand. "You must promise . . . never to lock me up."

The glass's stem snapped off in the duke's left hand. "That bastard. Is that what he threatened you with if you went to the magistrate, that he'd send you to Bedlam? Is that how he was going to keep your fortune when you came of age? Snakes like that should be boiled in oil."

Lisanne was rummaging in her pockets again. She found what she wanted, a clean handkerchief, and poured brandy onto the linen square. She reached for the duke's hand.

"What? Oh." St. Sevrin hadn't felt the cut or seen the blood. "Hold now, that's expensive brandy!"

"And it will do you more good outside than inside." When Lisanne was finished cleaning the wound, making sure no glass remained, she went back to her pocket for the small book. She opened its pages and carefully removed a spiderweb.

"What the deuce . . . ?"

"It helps stop the bleeding, Your Grace, and holds the cut edges together so they don't need to be sewn. And the spider doesn't need it anymore. She makes a new one each night."

The spider doesn't need it? Sewn? No, he would not be bored with Lady Lisanne Neville. While she was busy tying yet another handkerchief around his hand, he apologized for his clumsiness. "That was just my bad arm, weakened from a war wound that never healed right."

"I might be able to help. I know a lot of remedies, oils, potions, that sort of thing." She started to lift his shirt.

He clamped his good right hand over hers. "Here now, none of that until we're wed."

Lisanne's whole face lit up. "Then you agree to marry me? You'll really do it?"

St. Sevrin leaned his head back and let his eyes drift closed, but he kept his hand over hers, on his warm shoulder. "Devil a bit, poppet, I don't know. I suppose I need time to think on it. It's an offer that could tempt a saint, which I never pretended to be, but I still have some honor. I cannot take advantage of a tender little bud like you."

"How could it be taking advantage when it's what I want?"

"When you're too young and innocent to know what's best for you, that's how. I'll call on your uncle tomorrow, to sound him out on plans for your future. Perhaps he has some likely candidate for your hand waiting in the wings."

"No, you mustn't do that! He'll never tell you the truth anyway. And he'll forbid you to call."

"My title ought to be enough to have him consider my suit, should I decide to make the offer for his ward's hand."

She moaned. "What's a title for me compared to control of all my money, for him? No, he'd find a way to ruin everything. We have to present him with a fait accompli. It's better for you to go speak to my London trustee, to make sure he'll release the estate to you." She took her hand back to search through the pockets again. "I wrote Mr. Mackensie a letter, telling him my wishes."

"Sure of your charms, were you?"

"Sure of my worth, rather, and sure of your need. Your Grace, Sloane, marriages are made for much worse reasons all the time. I know I'm not any Society Toast. I'll never make a political hostess. And I'm not a beauty, tall and willowy or all rounded like the current mode. Aunt Cherise despairs of me in a polite drawing room. But I would try my hardest to manage your household and make your children happy."

"And me? Would you try to make me happy?"

"I . . . I wouldn't know how to begin." It had never occurred to Lisanne that he might want something from her beyond the monetary, beyond that other marital duty. "Yes, I'd try, if you wished."

"And you? I suppose you'd be happy here, with children and a great forest to romp in. You wouldn't even need me, would you? No, don't answer. Leave a man some pride." He sighed. "Very well, I promise to consider this mad bargain. If it doesn't all turn into a whiskey dream when I wake up, I'll travel back to London and talk to your man. He'll likely throw me out on my ear. I would. But now it's time for you to go. Let me get my coat and a lantern."

"Oh, you needn't accompany me."

"What, you only need a husband, not an escort through haunted forests in the middle of the night?"

"The forests aren't haunted. You know there's nothing in them to fear."

"Still, I cannot let you go alone."

"But I'm not alone." The cavernous pockets yielded a carved flute this time. Lisanne played three high lilting notes, then repeated them.

In moments a great lumbering black beast galloped out of the forest, across the field of onetime-lawn, and through the open window without breaking stride. The shaggy monster took up a stance in front of Lisanne, blocking all but her upper body, and slavering in Sloane's direction.

"This is Becka."

St. Sevrin knew better than to step forward or to raise his voice. "What *is* Becka? I've seen handsomer creatures at the bottom of a bottle of Blue Ruin."

"Becka is beautiful! Her mother was Homer Phelps's prize mastiff bitch."

"What was her father, a troll from under a bridge?"

Lisanne shrugged. "Homer thought so, too. He tried to drown the puppies. Becka was the only one I could save."

St. Sevrin could foresee a lifetime of rescued kittens and orphaned lambs. Was he to be one of her acts of charity? "You're too soft, Lady Lisanne."

"No, I am strong, Your Grace, like Becka. Strong enough to make Homer Phelps swim into the pond to get her out. Strong enough to be your duchess."

"We'll see."

Lisanne flitted out the window before he could go to assist, the oversize dog right behind her. St. Sevrin watched the baroness scampering across the moonlit lawn toward the woods, just like some fairy sprite.

Maybe it was all a dream.

Chapter Nine

$\mathcal{E}$ighteen years old. Lud, St. Sevrin didn't even remember being eighteen. He must have been so young, somewhere in the murky past. And it was true, many chits the baroness's age were already married and breeding. Some of them were even married to men older than he was. It wasn't as if he were losing his hair or his teeth, either, Sloane told himself, standing by the window as he watched his visitor disappear into the woods. He could still cross swords with the best of the fencers at Antoine's, and go a few rounds with Gentleman Jackson himself despite his weak left punch. No, ten years wasn't such a big difference, until you measured it in experience.

Every scrap of honor he had left told Sloane to stay away from Lisanne Neville. Boys don't pull wings off butterflies; men don't destroy innocence.

But she already knew about him: the drinking, the gaming, the whoring, things no decent female acknowledged. The baroness acknowledged, accepted, forgave, and gave him future permission to repeat his sins. She wasn't a lovesick peagoose who'd wake up three months into the marriage to discover she was wed to a cad.

Maybe she really wouldn't mind living alone here in seclusion when Sloane resumed his dissolute life in London as he was bound to. And maybe pigs would fly.

She had come to him. That had to count for something, such as how desperate she was. Sloane could no more make a chit like Lisanne a decent husband than he could make his horse do somersaults. But if her alternative was no husband at all, no family of her own but that mawworm Findley, then maybe the Duke of St. Sevrin wasn't so bad a choice. Lisanne had offered Sloane his freedom in the union, but maybe it was her own she was seeking. Money of her own, an absentee husband—a lot of chits did far worse in marriage. Lisanne Neville looked to be doing far worse now.

Unfortunately St. Sevrin wasn't the one in the business of rescuing fallen sparrows. Lud, what was he thinking of, to entertain the notion of wedding the appealing little waif? Worse, what was he thinking of to let her go home alone through the woods? She didn't even have a light. St. Sevrin pushed himself away from the window and went to the kitchen, where his greatcoat hung on a peg.

Kelly was sitting at the scarred table, having a cup of well-fortified tea. Another of those precious bottles of brandy sat half empty next to him.

"You went into the village today," St. Sevrin casually remarked. "Did you happen to hear anything about a Miss Neville, the baron's daughter?"

Kelly whistled. "What, we been here a whole day now and you're tumbling into trouble already?" The ex-soldier shook his grizzled head. "I don't see how you do it, Yer Grace. I swear I don't."

The duke frowned. "What do you mean, trouble?"

"The Neville gal. She's trouble. You've hardly been out of your own stable, and you're up to your neck in manure already."

"Come on, old man, what have you heard?"

"The chit's all they find to talk about around here. Except you, a'course. But after trying to get me to open my budget about Yer Grace, which I ain't about to, a'course, it's Lady Annie this and Lady Neville that. Or worse."

St. Sevrin left his coat on the hook and took a seat across from his manservant, who got up and found another chipped cup. The baroness would be long gone into the woods, Sloane realized, and he'd never find her in the dark. He'd just have to trust in that dog to see her home safely.

"But what are they saying about her, Kelly?" he asked.

"Fey."

"Faye? No, her name is Lisanne."

"Fey. Touched. Fairy-dusted. Pixilated."

"That's absurd. There's no such thing, just ignorant folks trying to explain away someone else's peculiarities."

"A wee lass what can charm birds down from the trees sounds a tad peculiar to me, too." Kelly scratched his head. "But there's others who say she's a natural. You know, simpleminded."

"They're far off the mark there. The lady quoted me Latin, French, and Shakespeare."

Kelly slapped his hands down on the table, jostling the cups and bottle. "I knew it. You've gone and met the female somehow, not hours after that guardian of hers spread word around the village that he'd have your hide if you so much as looked at the chit. Warned all the locals to lock their daughters up, too."

"What, did he think I was in the habit of ravishing milkmaids and dressmakers' assistants? Forget about Findley for now. What else do they say about the baroness?"

"One man claimed he'd never heard her speak a word in ten years."

"Nonsense. She most likely had nothing to say to the dolt." She'd had plenty to say to St. Sevrin tonight. "Anything else?"

"Well, they was all agreed she had the healing hands." Kelly stared at the handkerchief wrapped and neatly tied around the duke's hand. "But you wouldn't be knowing nothing about that neither, would you?"

"What a lot of claptrap. I forgot how narrow-minded and superstitious people were in these small villages and outlying shires. Did anyone happen to mention anything about the Neville inheritance? How it was divided, that kind of thing."

"Weren't divided at all. Every last farthing comes to this female, what the uncle doesn't manage to skim off. He's too smart to let the land go to waste, unlike some others I could name, but that handsome profit the bailiff collects ain't all making it to the London bank. They might split hairs about the girl, but no one hereabouts has a decent word to say about the uncle. A regular dirty dish, I figure. Miserly and mean, he turned off all the Neville staff without a groat when he took over. Brought in London servants. What with the Priory gone to the dogs, there's a heap of folks nearby on the dole."

"A few more hints like that, old man, and you could be joining them."

Kelly ignored his employer, as usual. "They say the old baron was a downy cove what tied up most of his fortune with a London solicitor so Findley couldn't get at it. So now the scurvy bastard makes money by charging a fee to anyone doing business at the Hall. You know, the carter, the coal man, the chandler. Some London butlers pull that rig. First I heard of the gentry doing it."

St. Sevrin was staring at his cup. "I don't suppose the solicitor is aware of any of this. I've a good mind to go tell him."

"Now, why would you want to go and stick your nose in someone else's business? It'll just get bitten off. And ain't we got enough in our dish right now?"

"Yes, but there's a lady who needs rescuing, and she

just might be the salvation of us all." Sloane took a swallow. "Tell me, old man, do you think I'm beyond hope?"

"The devil hisself is not beyond hope. They call it religion. Why don't you try going to church instead of to that accountant bloke?"

"I wasn't thinking of divine intervention. Let's start off with small miracles."

"Oh, dear; oh, dear. This is all my fault." Mr. Mackensie had been shocked when the Duke of St. Sevrin sent in his card that morning, asking for an interview with the Neville solicitor. From what Mackensie heard, the duke never took the time nor made an effort on anyone's behalf but his own.

"I remembered the baron and his lady fondly from my own childhood," Sloane lied when he read the suspicion on the elderly gentleman's face. "I thought it my duty to help their daughter. As a concerned neighbor, don't you know."

"Much obliged, Your Grace, to be sure. And you say things aren't what they ought to be?"

Mr. Mackensie was even more shocked after he'd listened to St. Sevrin's claims against Sir Arthur, but not precisely surprised, Sloane thought.

"I should have gone in person," the solicitor bemoaned, "when I first heard those rumors. But . . ."

St. Sevrin understood. Mr. Mackensie was a white-haired, bespectacled old man, with fingers bent and swollen with arthritis. Two canes were propped against his desk in the well-appointed office. The roomful of clerks in the outer office would run all of the gentleman's errands here in Town, but he could never have traveled to Devon. "I'm sure you did not want to give credence to idle rumor."

Mr. Mackensie nodded, thankful for the rescue. "I did send one of my assistants with some papers to be signed some years back. I could have put them in the post, of course, but I asked the lad to look around. He found everything in order."

"Did he actually see Lady Lisanne? Speak to her?"

"Unfortunately no, she had a putrid sore throat at the time. The baronet was very concerned. He wrote me as soon as she was recovered."

"I'm sure he included a tidy bundle of doctor's fees, too. I doubt the chit ever saw a physician. She's the one the villagers call on for their aches and pains."

"But my clerk saw nothing untoward."

"Possibly he was gulled, but more likely greedy. Sir Alfred would have given him a handsome douceur to insure a good report."

"I take it you have no high regard for human nature, Your Grace."

St. Sevrin brushed that aside. It was a fact. "Did that clerk stay in your employ? Is he here now? Can we speak to him?"

"Unhappily I had to dismiss him from my employ several years ago for irregularities in his accounts." Mr. Mackensie was looking even more old and pained. He kept rubbing at his swollen fingers. "I should have sent another when I started to hear those disturbing rumors. One of my other clients told me word was going around the clubs that the child was sickly. Her mother was, do you recall?"

St. Sevrin could honestly say no. He had no memory of Lady Neville whatsoever, and still hadn't remembered the gossip he had more recently heard. "I daresay that Lady Lisanne is in better health than either of us, sir."

Mr. Mackensie smiled, reassured. "Then there was talk that the heiress was high-strung, of a nervous disposition. I didn't know what to think. An old bachelor like me, what did I understand about children, female children besides? I thought her aunt and uncle would know what was best for her."

"I fear, sir, that they were worrying about what was best for themselves."

Mr. Mackensie removed his spectacles and painstakingly wiped them with his handkerchief. Not until he was done and the glasses were back on his nose did he continue. "I was relieved when Sir Alfred sent notice that he was bringing my client to Town for the coming fall Little Season. It's more than time. I don't know why he's putting it off so long; most debutantes make their curtsies in the spring. I suggested my staff could have Neville House opened, aired, and ready by mid-April."

"Most likely his own daughter is still too young."

"Yes, well, I thought I could see Lady Lisanne for myself, then talk to the poor dear."

"I seriously doubt you'd have been given the chance. Lady Lisanne believes she would not be permitted to come to Town if she had intentions of doing so. Findley will give some excuse or other: a lasting fever, a broken ankle. Frankly, sir, she is not ready to make a come-out. From what I saw, the baroness has no wardrobe, no care for her appearance, no drawing-room accomplishments, no sense of decorum." Hell, if he told this old gent how she climbed through bachelor windows in the middle of the night, the solicitor was liable to have apoplexy right there, and St. Sevrin needed him safe and sound.

"But the estate has been paying for expensive governesses for years," Mr. Mackensie protested.

"I'd wager the estate has been paying for a great many things Lady Lisanne never received. Oh, there may have been an instructress—for the younger girl. No governess worth her salt would turn out a hoyden like the baroness; she'd never find another position with such a recommendation. Lady Lisanne's education does not seem lacking, just her social skills. The villagers say she hardly speaks, she runs barefoot in the woods . . ."

"Oh, my; oh, my. I'll have to send someone. Perhaps two so they cannot be suborned if what you surmise is correct. But with the Findleys named my lady's legal guardians, it would mean a scandalous court case to have them declared unfit. I cannot think that will help Lady Lisanne's chances of making an eligible match. And there is no one else, no other family on either side except very distant cousins. I know of no one who could arrange the proper introductions and smooth her path."

"I thought perhaps a match might have been arranged in infancy or some such, since Sir Alfred does not seem concerned with putting his ward in the way of eligible gentlemen. Maybe he's contracted with a wellborn family in Devon."

"Oh, no, I would have been notified at once. The settlements, don't you know. And there was nothing like that in Lord Neville's will, you may be assured. You say she is eighteen and has never been to a local assembly?"

"She is past eighteen, plaits her hair in schoolgirl braids, and wears her cousin's castoffs."

Mr. Mackensie pawed through a thick folder of papers. "But these are dressmakers' bills from this past quarter."

"I'm sure they are. Sir Arthur's wife and daughter are very à la mode, according to the local vicar. I spoke with him because I wanted to verify my facts before coming to you, without stirring up a hornet's nest."

"Oh, dear, what is to be done now?"

St. Sevrin handed over Lisanne's letter.

The poor old solicitor almost fell off his seat. If things were bad before, this was disastrous. "Oh, my stars. She wants to marry—you?"

St. Sevrin inspected his boots. "As they say, there's no accounting for tastes."

"This is a love match?" Mackensie asked hopefully.

"Don't be ridiculous, man. I hardly know the chit. The union's to her advantage, though. She's positive no one else will be allowed near her until she's twenty-five. She'll be firmly on the shelf by then, and so set in freakish ways that no one will have her, no matter how large the fortune."

"But, Your Grace . . ."

"I know, Mr. Mackensie. I wouldn't wish a female in my care to throw herself away on a loose screw like myself, either. But Lady Lisanne wishes it. She needs it. And I'm not fool enough to turn her down. I know you have no reason to trust me and years of indiscretions not to, but I do mean to improve. Furthermore, you shall see that her settlements are so securely tied that Lisanne will never be at the mercy of any man again, myself or any other. Neville Hall is to remain hers and her issue's, along with its income. Whatever would have been her dowry joins her portion. You might have to stay on until she is of age to satisfy the law, but the money is hers, to do with as she wishes."

"Ahem. That's very generous, Your Grace."

"I need to pay my bills and mortgages. I need to reclaim my estates from bankruptcy. I do not need to look in my mirror every morning and see a fortune hunter looking back. As soon as my own property turns a profit, I will pay her back. I swear to you Lisanne will want for nothing."

Except a decent man as husband. Mr. Mackensie could foresee the little baroness abandoned within a month of the wedding, in favor of the card tables. Leopards didn't change their spots. "And you'll bring her to court for presentation, as her parents would have wished?" he tried.

"If she is willing, yes, I can do it. There are certain advantages to playing cards with Prinny, don't you know. The lady is much happier decocting herbal remedies and going for walks with her dog, though. I cannot imagine what the polite world will make of a lady with snails and spiderwebs in her pocket, but I can try. It would not suit me to have my duchess outcast from Society." Actually it wouldn't bother him a whit—Society be damned—but

77

St. Sevrin was of a mind to rub Sir Alfred's nose in the mud, and Cousin Humbert's, too.

Mr. Mackensie sighed. "I can't see how I can refuse if it is what my lady wants."

"That's how I looked at it."

Chapter Ten

Alone. Alone. Alone.

St. Sevrin had gone back to London. Lisanne's uncle had gone back to ignoring her. And she had gone back to the forest, where silence reverberated in her mind.

Lisanne visited all the secret places, called all the names, played all the songs on her flute. No one came, no one answered. She was alone.

In her mind she'd known how it would be. You can't play cards with the devil and not come away smelling of fire and brimstone. St. Sevrin had gone to London, so there was hope that she'd won; but, either way, she'd lost. She'd lost her innocence by selling herself, even if it was for the best of causes.

Besides, she was too old. Fairy tales were for children, with their wide-eyed sense of wonder. Children knew how to play; adults forgot.

In Lisanne's mind she understood. She even knew she'd been fortunate longer than most. In her heart, though, she felt abandoned. "It isn't fair," she cried the eternal lament into the void. "I did it for you. Please don't leave me alone like this! I cannot help growing older. Please. Without you I have nothing."

Under the ages-old trees, where violets tried to find a patch of sunlight, Lisanne cried for her lost parents, her lost childhood. She faced a terrifying future with a dangerous stranger, or an equally uncertain future without him, under her uncle's domination. The only creature in the world who cared about her was her dog, whose motley fur was soon damp with the first tears Lisanne had cried since her mother's death.

Like a newborn crying at being thrust from her safe womb into the world for the first time, Lisanne lay on the forest floor and sobbed her heartbreak.

She didn't know how long she wept there, and she never heard his footsteps. Becka didn't even growl when strong arms reached for Lisanne and lifted her into his lap, cuddling her against his chest while he leaned back against a tree trunk. St. Sevrin let her cry her fill, even though her tears were soaking through his shirt in front, and the tree's rough bark was digging into his skin in back. And Becka was drooling on his Hessian boots.

"Everyone has left me" was all he could understand between her wrenching sobs.

"Ah, and I feared you were crying because I came back."

"But, but my friends are all gone." She tried to move from his embrace to find a handkerchief, but he already had one to hand, knowing how long it would take her to sort through the clutter in her pockets.

He gently wiped her eyes. "I'll be your friend, sweetings. I haven't much practice at it, but I'll try."

She took the cloth from him and blew her nose, not a delicate gesture. Since she was already covered in dirt and debris from the forest floor—as was St. Sevrin now—one more inelegance didn't count, to Sloane's thinking.

Coming upon her crying in the woods, all splotchy-faced and disheveled, St. Sevrin felt something twist in his guts. Women's tears hadn't moved him in ages, manipulative and on cue as they usually were, yet these sobs had brought him to his knees literally and figuratively. He didn't know the problem, only that he had to protect her, even if from himself. Whatever was wrong, he'd make right.

This new feeling of protectiveness wasn't passion, which the duke was used to, or even casual attraction. It was more like brotherly affection, paternal almost, which was not a comfortable role for him. Sloane did not want to think of Lisanne as a child, as too young for his attentions. If comforting was what she needed, however, comforting was what she'd get.

As she sat there in his lap with his arms around her, though, Sloane could feel her rounded bottom against his thighs, her softness against his chest. She was not a child, he told himself. It was her small stature that was deceiving, and her thinness. Lady Lisanne was not his sister, daughter, or ward. She was the woman he was prepared to marry if she'd still have him, if she wasn't crying at the mare's nest she'd dug up with her offer.

"What, is the idea of being a duchess so terrible, then?" he asked. "Or just my duchess?"

She sniffed and squirmed off his lap to a position across from him, sitting cross-legged in the leaf mold, her skirts hiked up past her ankles. "You decided, then."

"Only if you're still sure it's what you want. You can back out now, Baroness, and I'll understand."

The magic was lost to her either way, but the forest would be safe. She didn't even hesitate, especially when the duke had shown how gentle he could be holding her. If there was an ounce of tenderness in this war hero turned rake, that was one ounce more than Uncle Alfred possessed. "I am sure."

"Then, here." He reached into his coat pocket for a small jewel box and opened it to show her a gold ring with a pearl surrounded by tiny diamonds. "It's the lightest ring in the St. Sevrin collection. The emeralds would have weighed you down, *ma petite.*"

"It's lovely." Lisanne started to admire the ring on her finger until she realized the duke was trying not to laugh at her dirty hands and ragged fingernails. She hid both hands and ring in her skirts. "But do you mean you have a fortune in gems somewhere? Why ever didn't you sell them to pay your bills?"

"The entail, of course. Cousin Humbert would be after me with a court order before the ink was dry on the jeweler's check. I did take the lot 'round to Rundell and Bridges for cleaning while I was at the vault, to make sure my esteemed father hadn't switched them for paste. You can have them reset later. And Mackensie says he's holding a box full of your mother's jewelry for your request, too, so you'll outshine all the other sprites in your forest."

Lisanne didn't want to talk about the forest. "Then he gave his permission?"

"Reluctantly, but yes. Your estate was even larger than you thought, so a goodly portion of it is being tied up for you and your progeny, besides Neville Hall and its income. I told him to add a codicil to keep your father's title from being absorbed into the dukedom, naming our second son to the barony."

"Or daughter."

"Or daughter," he agreed. "See? I'm really an easy fellow to get along with." Especially when handed a fortune to rival Golden Ball's.

"And Sevrin Woods?" she had to ask.

"Mackensie's writing a book, it seems. I'd be surprised if a crow will be allowed to nest in one of the trees without your permission when he's done."

"That's it, then." She was relieved, of course, but anxious. "When? That is, how soon . . . ?"

"Until the execution? Poor poppet, between the devil and the deep blue sea, are you?"

"Oh, no, you mustn't think I'm having second thoughts."

"Third and fourth ones, too, if you've any common sense." He patted his inside pocket. "The venerable Mr. Mackensie helped me get a special license. We can be wed as soon as you wish."

"Soon, then. You'll be wanting to settle your accounts and start the renovations."

"No fancy June wedding?" He couldn't imagine this ragtag urchin at a grand social event at St. George's, but it was her money, her wedding. He had to ask.

"No, if we marry now, there's still time for spring planting if you get the tenant farmers back."

He nodded. "Practical little puss. I'll go speak to Uncle Alfred this very afternoon."

"No, you mustn't! He won't allow it."

"He cannot stop it. And I'm not about to steal you away from him like a thief in the night. I don't want the sheriff coming after me for kidnapping an heiress, and I don't want anyone thinking this was some hole-in-corner affair."

"But he'll ruin everything. You don't know him."

"No, Baroness, he doesn't know me. If he causes any problems, we'll make other plans. Don't look for trouble." The marriage itself was going to be hard enough, heaven knew. "Now come, sweetings, a smile. I hear you can charm the birds out of the trees. Is it true?"

Lisanne did manage a wan smile. She pulled a heel of bread out of her pocket and played a few notes on her flute. "Be very quiet." Soon enough, little black and white birds came and took crumbs out of her hand.

When the crumbs were all gone, St. Sevrin kissed her hand, dirt and all. "I bet no other duchess can do that."

He stood to leave, brushing at the damp spot where he'd been sitting. Now he'd have to go back to the Priory and change clothes before calling on Sir Alfred. Kelly was going to have a fit.

As he turned to go, Lisanne asked, "How did you find me? No one else ever comes through the forest. I could have been anywhere."

"It wasn't hard. There was a path right from the edge of the Priory's old lawns. I can't imagine how I missed it the morning after your visit."

Lisanne could. It hadn't been there then. So she wasn't quite alone after all.

The duke sent his card in. Then, to make sure Sir Alfred didn't deny his presence, he followed the niffy-naffy butler into an airy parlor done in the Chinese style. An older woman was pouring tea for Findley, a chinless youth, and a plump miss who was obviously and unfortunately the spotted Esmé, all rigged out in the height of fashion. The ladies' gowns were made in London by a French modiste, if Sloane didn't miss his guess.

Findley took the card from the butler's silver salver and cursed when he read the name. "St. Sevrin, damn his effrontery in calling at a decent house. Pomfrey, tell the makebait I'm not—" Sir Alfred stood abruptly when he saw who stood behind the butler in the doorway. "Why, Your Grace, what an unexpected pleasure."

St. Sevrin made his bows, murmuring some fustian about calling on neighbors, while Sir Alfred begrudged the introductions without offering tea. Out of spite, Sloane raised Esmé's hand to his lips and lingered over her baby-fat fingers. Not until he thought Lady Cherise was about to have palpitations and Sir Alfred to have conniptions, did he release the pudgy hand. At least the chit's face was now so red you couldn't see the spots. Sloane asked for a moment of the baronet's time, on a private matter. Sir Alfred was only too happy to get him away from his starry-eyed peagoose of a daughter.

There was no sign of Lisanne until they moved to a small room, apparently the estate office. St. Sevrin could spot the baroness out of the corner of his eye, standing behind a large potted fern in the hall. She'd changed her gown to another unhappy selection, an ill-fitted beige lutestring that looked like a grain sack with a bow around it, an unevenly tied, frayed bow at that. Her uncle didn't acknowledge her presence, didn't bother making an introduction, as if she were a servant. Of course the servants all wore immaculate livery, not rags.

Sloane noted how everything in the house was of the first stare, right down to the smuggled cognac Sir Alfred offered. He declined in favor of keeping a clear head, but he did accept a seat opposite the baronet at the handsome cherry-wood desk.

"I hear you are interested in selling off your timber." Sir Alfred was making conversation while letting his own glass of cognac settle his nerves. "Sorry I can't be of service, but the man in Honiton is supposed to be reputable. He'll give you a fair price."

St. Sevrin adjusted his cuffs. "Oh, I am no longer interested in selling off the home woods. I won't need to, after I marry your niece."

Sir Alfred jumped up, overturning the inkwell on the desk. "What did you say? Never! I wouldn't give permission for a basket scrambler like you to get within five feet of her. I know my duty to my dead sister's child better than that." He stomped over to the door and called for a servant. "Clean this mess. And show this man out."

The footman who entered looked at the spreading black puddle, then he looked at the black expression on the duke's face. "I'll be fetching some rags, milord."

He didn't come back, which St. Sevrin thought was a shame; it really was a lovely old desk. "I have Mackensie's permission, you know. I am here only for the formality of the thing."

85

"He's not her guardian!" Sir Alfred was growing red in the face. "He cannot make that decision."

Lisanne came in then. She did not look at the duke, but addressed her uncle. "Mr. Mackensie didn't make the decision, sir. I did."

"What? You? How the deuce did you ever see him? I'll have your hide for disobeying me, you wretched brat. I told you to stay away."

"I wouldn't advise such intemperance, Findley. I do protect what is mine, you know." No emotion showed on the duke's face now, but his voice was quiet, sinister.

Findley didn't take the warning. "She's not yours, blast you, and never will be! What, are you going to claim you've fallen top over trees with this . . . this ragamuffin? The dustman wouldn't have her!"

Sloane took his eyes from Findley's beaked nose, which he was going to flatten if the man didn't shut up soon. He glanced at Lisanne, who had gone pale enough that a row of freckles stood out on her cheeks and her eyes were wide with distress. He saw all those other children who haunted his nightmares, their hungry, hopeless eyes.

"Nevertheless, I aim to have her."

"Over my dead body!"

"It's coming to that, you clodpole," the duke muttered under his breath, but Sir Alfred was too enraged to hear. He turned to Lisanne with his ranting: "And you, Annie, do you want to tie yourself to a rake and a wastrel, a degenerate womanizer? Why, the man's nothing but a fortune hunter. You'd be penniless in a month. He'll have his whores at your breakfast table, wager your house or your services on the turn of a card."

St. Sevrin stood and leaned threateningly over the desk, one hand on either side of the ink blot, prepared to slam this maggot's face into the mess.

It was Lisanne, though, who quietly interjected: "He

may be all of those things, and worse, Uncle, but I doubt he has ever struck a woman."

Findley's face turned purple now, and St. Sevrin had all he could do not to strangle the man as the import of her words sank in. "Enough, sirrah. Lady Lisanne and I have come to an agreement that suits both our needs. We do not require your blessing. At this point I do not even care for your presence at the wedding. I have fulfilled my honor-bound duty in advising you." He stepped back to leave.

Sir Alfred called him back. "I'll fulfill mine, Duke, by telling you what a Smithfield bargain you'll be getting. What do you think, that Annie is some pretty little rustic tomboy you can dress up and teach to make polite conversation? Well, it can't be done. God knows I've tried. Annie's no hoyden, no high-spirited filly. She's a lunatic, that's what!"

Now he remembered the rumors. Sloane stared at Lisanne while her uncle continued his harangue. Damn, he knew this deal was too good to be true. He murmured to himself, *"Timeo Danaos et dona ferentes."*

Lisanne snapped back, "Then never look a gift horse in the mouth."

"She's insane," Sir Alfred raged on. "She talks to fairies. She lives in a dreamworld in that forest of yours. Addled Annie, everyone calls her. The only reason I never saw fit to lock her away is that she seemed harmless enough. Now look what my kindheartedness has done."

"You didn't lock me up, Uncle, because then you'd have no excuse to stay at Neville Hall at my expense. If asylum fees were paid from my estate, there'd be no need for a well-fed, well-kept guardian and his family. And I might have died in such a place. Most bedlamites do, don't they? Then you'd never see a groat of my income."

"You see, Duke? See what madness she speaks? No

child in her right mind would so accuse her loving guardian. With such suspicions, she'll see a plot to assassinate her next." Sir Alfred was practically frothing. Beads of spittle had joined the ink on the desktop.

St. Sevrin turned to Lisanne. "Are you insane?"

"Can you afford to be so particular?" she replied, pointed chin raised, blue eyes flashing.

"Dash it, girl, I'm on your side!"

Findley pounded the desk, sending droplets of ink and saliva flying. "You may as well ask a liar if he's telling the truth. That's what makes a crazy person crazy, isn't it? A lunatic doesn't know reality from cloud-cuckoo land."

"They say the king knows when he is having one of his spells. It upsets him, but he realizes when he is all about in his head. I think the baroness knows very well the state of her mind. What say you, my lady?"

"I am not daft. Sir Alfred chooses to make me out to be for his own purposes."

Sloane stared into her eyes. There was no guile in their blue depths, no blank look he'd seen on soldiers with head injuries, only intelligence, bravery, and a plea for help. He nodded. "The marriage will take place tomorrow morning. I'll make arrangements with the vicar. See that my bride has a clean gown to wear at least, Findley, or you'll be wearing your teeth on your tonsils."

"Are you threatening me?"

"Of course not. I never waste my time threatening pigs like you. That was a promise."

"I'm not afraid of you, Duke," Sir Alfred sputtered.

St. Sevrin shrugged. "Then you're a fool besides a blackguard." He stepped closer to Lisanne and clasped her hand, where she was shredding the already frayed ribbon on her gown. He made sure Sir Alfred saw the ring before he brought her fingers up to his lips. "Mine."

No one in the room made the mistake of thinking he meant the ring.

"*A demain, chérie.*"

Chapter Eleven

"Oh, the shame of it! Oh, the disgrace of being connected to that family!" moaned Aunt Cherise.

"Oh, shut up," snarled Uncle Alfred back.

The rest of the family had rushed into the estate room as soon as the duke left, leaving their tea in the parlor. Aunt Cherise wanted to know what all the yelling was about. What could a bounder like St. Sevrin want with Sir Alfred?

"He what?" she shrieked, clutching her vinaigrette. "My nerves cannot take such a calamity, Sir Alfred, I tell you. I'm sure to be laid in my bed for a week."

"Stubble it, woman. He means to have the plaguey chit, your nerves or not, blast him to perdition! Wants me to buy her a trousseau, no less!"

The plaguey chit was standing near the fireplace, as far from the Findleys as she could get. If Nigel and Esmé hadn't been crowded in the doorway, she would have fled lest Sir Alfred decide to ignore the duke's warning and take his ire out on her, as usual.

This time it was Aunt Cherise who turned on Lisanne before she could make her escape. "You ungrateful child! How could you do this to us? Why, that man is not acknowledged among the best houses. With that connection we'll never be received by the highest sticklers. Dear Esmeralda won't receive invitations to the best parties, where she can meet the most eligible *partis*."

"What about Almack's, Ma? I'll still get my vouchers there, won't I?" Esmé demanded.

"Oh, my precious, I fear not."

"What?" screamed that devastated miss, who'd secretly harbored the notion that the dashing rake had come to ask Papa permission to pay his addresses to her, Esmé. "Why, you jade, Annie! You've ruined everything! I hate you! I hate you! If I can't go to Almack's, my come-out will be a failure. I may as well stay in Devon!"

"Where?" Sir Alfred snidely asked. "You cannot have thought, miss, nor you, madame," he said with a nod toward his wife. "Neville Hall will become the duke's property. And it's not merely a matter of receiving the proper invitations to those dreary subscription balls when we go to London; we cannot go to London! In case you forgot, the site of that grand debutante ball you've been planning for months, Neville House in Cavendish Square, will belong to the dastard also!"

Aunt Cherise fainted into Nigel's arms, never yet swooning when no one was nearby to catch her. Nigel quickly lowered his mama's bulk to a leather-covered chair. Esmé was drumming her feet into the carpet, screaming that her life was over, that she hated all of them.

"Neville House is to be mine. Mr. Mackensie is drawing up the papers." Lisanne ignored her uncle's narrowed eyes, his fury at how much she had done behind his back, and addressed Esmé. "You may still have your ball there. His Grace has a home of his own in London. He cannot live in two houses at once."

Aunt Cherise sat up, and Esmé sniffed, "Well, that's the least you could do."

"And the most, I'm afraid. His Grace will naturally

control the bulk of the estate. You'll have to bear the expenses yourself, Uncle. Unless, of course, you wish to ask my lord St. Sevrin to sponsor your daughter's come-out."

Aunt Cherise fainted again. Sir Alfred pushed past his children and out the door, slamming it behind him. No one mentioned Lisanne's trousseau.

Lisanne took dinner on a tray in her room, what little she could eat atop the knot of uncertainty in her stomach. She thought of asking the serving girl to help her find a gown, but the maid was already rushed off her feet since Aunt Cherise and Esmé had also requested trays, tisanes, and soothing teas. Findley and Nigel were left alone in the dining room to bedevil the other servants with their ill temper.

Searching through her closet brought Lisanne no closer to an acceptable gown in which to be married. For her own sake, she couldn't see what the to-do was about a dress. The wedding was a formality only, a ritual binding of the arranged contract. Any of the serviceable gowns in her closet should have done, spots, stains, gathered seams and all. But His Grace had requested a clean, decent gown. Appearances obviously meant more to him. The veneer of a proper bride must suit his self-consequence, although Lisanne knew she was no such thing. St. Sevrin must be worrying over his decision as mightily as she was hers, Lisanne thought, so she owed him the attempt to satisfy his wishes.

She would not think about what other desires of his might need satisfying. She would not think about tomorrow at all. He had stood up for her—for his own reasons, she must never forget—and he wanted a conventional bride. So a dress was her mission for the evening, not fretting herself to flinders over decisions already made.

Scratching on Esmé's door produced nothing but more

vitriol. "Go away, you loony. I hate you! You've ruined my life."

Her aunt's French dresser opened the door to Lisanne's knock, took one look at who called, and shut the door in her face. "Madame is prostrate with *une crise de nerfs.* Good night, mademoiselle.

So Lisanne took herself upstairs past the servants' quarters, to the attics. It took some time for her to find what she wanted in the dim light of two small wall lamps and the candle she carried. Even after she found the right trunks, she had to struggle to uncover them, to move heavier items off their lids. For once she wasn't concerned with collecting cobwebs, although her hair and hands did a good job of it. At last she gave up trying to drag the weighty trunks toward better light and just started opening them. First she wiped her hands on her already filthy skirts.

Gowns were fuller in her mother's time, she quickly realized, pulling out one opulent gown after another, trying to ignore the smell of camphor. They were meant to be worn over the voluminous crinolines that filled a nearby trunk. Contrary to Aunt Cherise's estimate, Lisanne could ply a pretty needle indeed—she had to, to mend broken wings and injured paws. But remodeling one of these gowns was entirely beyond her. Why, it would take all night just to hem the wide skirts.

She kept opening more trunks, almost in despair, when she came upon her mother's undergarments and night rail. Silk and lawn, they were, the finest muslin with lace and embroidery. One white silk nightgown had a rounded neckline, a high waist, and small puffed sleeves, similar to the muslins Esmé wore year-round. It was a narrow slip of a gown, meant to be worn under a satin robe with matching embroidery. It was the embroidery that caught Lisanne's eye. Flowers of all hues and tints twined around the entire bodice and trailed down the skirt, with here and there a butterfly sewn into the design. Perfect.

Of course the gown was almost transparent, so Lisanne unpacked the trunk onto a blanket she placed on the floor until she found a silk slip, a batiste shift, and an entire layer of neatly folded stockings. She left the whalebone corsets in the bottom of the trunk. Not even for His Grace would she lace herself into one of those contraptions.

There was a pier glass in the attic, its silvered mirror turned cloudy. Still, it was better than going downstairs to try on her finds, then returning to the attics if she wasn't satisfied. Lisanne quickly undressed—there was no heat here in the attics—and drew on the gown. Her mother had been thin, so the fit was better than Esmé's rejects, although the hem would need to be taken up.

An old sewing box leaned against a dressmaker's dummy near the mirror, so Lisanne held the skirt off the floor and went to search for pins to mark the hem before removing what was to be her wedding gown. There were a few pins, not even rusted.

It was when she bent down to fold the fabric under that Lisanne heard voices. At first she thought she must be hearing the servants in their nearby rooms, but the voices sounded like Uncle Alfred's and Aunt Cherise's. Looking around to get her bearings, Lisanne realized she must be directly over the master suite, which her aunt and uncle would *not* have after her marriage. They might stay until they removed to London in the fall, but that was the end of her charity, and her patience.

She was gathering up a handful of pins and the other items she had selected from her mother's trunks, thinking to take them back to her room since she had no desire whatsoever to be privy to her relatives' bedroom conversations traveling up the chimney flue. As she bent to retrieve the dress she'd been wearing, though, she heard Uncle Alfred's voice clearly state: "I tell you, the wedding will not occur."

Lisanne sat on top of one of the trunks.

"What do you mean?" Aunt Cherise asked. "St. Sevrin

has a special license and permission from that awful man in London. He doesn't need her guardian's approval, so how are you going to stop it?"

Lisanne could hear her uncle chuckle. "Oh, Nigel has his orders. He'll take care of things."

"Nigel?" shrieked Aunt Cherise loudly enough to be heard down in the kitchens. "He's not going to challenge that disgusting man to a duel, is he? They say St. Sevrin never misses his mark. And he's a master swordsman. My baby will be killed!"

"Don't be absurd. Nigel will merely make sure that the chit is, shall we say, less desirable."

"Less desirable? I don't understand. You said that reprobate wants her for her money, not her appearance. Annie's already an unkempt, unmanageable sort of female. However could Nigel make her any less appealing?"

Lisanne wanted to know, too, but she had an idea. Her suspicions were confirmed when Uncle Alfred's voice rose through the flooring: "If you cannot understand, madame, then I suggest you put your head to it. Not even Satyr St. Sevrin will take used goods for his duchess. He might spend his life whore-mongering, but he won't marry one of them."

There was a gasp. Lisanne didn't know if it came from her own mouth or Aunt Cherise's.

Sir Alfred was going on: "Nigel will make sure of it tonight."

"I don't want to hear anymore!" Lady Findley cried. Lisanne could picture Aunt Cherise pulling her sleeping cap down over her ears.

"It's a masterful plan," Sir Alfred boasted, ignoring his wife's mewling sounds of distress. "I don't know why I didn't think of it years ago, except there was no need. Who would have thought that any man, no matter how badly dipped, would marry that farouche female? No, she'll just have to marry Nigel. That way all her lovely blunt stays in the family where it belongs. The curst solicitor will have to give his permission. He'll understand Annie'll be ruined, else."

"But . . . but my baby is a good boy. He wouldn't want to . . . to . . ."

"Oh, wouldn't he just. Our niece is turning into a dashed attractive female, if one doesn't mind a little muck and mire. Some men might even find that attractive in a primitive, earthy way. Besides, your baby Nigel is at the age when he'd lift the skirts of the fat lady at the fair, if he thought he could fit between her thighs."

"Sir Arthur, my tender sensibilities!"

"Blister your sensibilities. This isn't the time for the vapors. Nigel knows what he's supposed to do. Annie is richer than he, more highly titled than he, and God knows is smarter than he. The only thing she's not is stronger than he. Nigel understands it's the only way."

"Fetch my laudanum. No, the big bottle. I intend to sleep until tomorrow afternoon."

The pins were all over the floor. Numbly, Lisanne gathered them into her hand and then tried to put them into her pocket, out of habit. The nightgown she wore didn't have a pocket, so the pins landed on the floor again.

Dear heavens, what was she supposed to do now? Lisanne knew she couldn't overpower Nigel, and it was too late to put a sleeping draught in *his* evening brew.

Servants were still moving around, thank goodness, making a great deal of noise. Nigel would never go beyond the line when a scream could bring a roomful of curious spectators—unless that was what Uncle Alfred wanted, enough people to witness her disgrace.

She couldn't stay up here because someone was sure to come looking. She couldn't go to her room, for Uncle held the key to her door from when he used to lock her in. The furniture was too heavy to make into a barricade,

96

and what was she supposed to do, hold off her cousin with the fireplace poker? For how long?

The pins were bundled into a beaded reticule from one of the trunks, the embroidered nightgown and undergarments carefully folded into the matching robe. In her dusty old gown and scuffed half boots, with cobwebs in her hair and the scent of camphor on her skin, Lisanne crept down the servants' stairway. She tiptoed past the family's bedroom level and then the public rooms, descending one level farther toward the kitchens without seeing anyone. The kitchens were blessedly empty, too. Lisanne unlatched the back door and let herself out into the night, whistling for Becka.

There was only one place she could go, one place she could be safe, and it wasn't Sevrin Woods.

Chapter Twelve

"*We* really have to stop meeting like this, sweetings." St. Sevrin was in that small back parlor again, the one with the working fireplace. He had been making inventories and estimates, lists of loans and mortgages, debts and past-due bills. He had no way of figuring how much it would cost to restore the estate to solvency or where to start. He was making great headway, however, with the new bottle of brandy on his desk.

Then he'd heard a dog barking and a tapping at the window. His fiancée, it seemed, did not care much for doors. Or propriety.

"Confound it, Baroness," he chided as he helped her over the windowsill, "what the devil are you doing prowling about the countryside in the middle of the night?"

Instead of answering, Lisanne turned to make sure the dog was inside, the window closed and latched. She was as messy as ever, but also seemed stiff and cold, which was no wonder, with the nights still chilly so early in the spring. Sloane drew her over to the fire, then pried her fingers away from the basket she carried. A cloth fell away to reveal a mound of raspberry tarts and a shank of ham.

"Well, at least you brought the wedding breakfast. Kelly will be thrilled. His culinary efforts don't extend to pastries, and we're growing tired of eggs and poultry. I daresay the chickens will be glad for the reprieve also."

"They're for Becka."

"What, all?" Sloane eyed the raspberry tarts with disappointment, but he eyed his bride-to-be with concern. She'd hardly said a word or moved an inch. He decided she needed a bit of internal warming, so he brought over his glass of brandy. "Here, sip this. You may as well be hung for a sheep as a lamb, alone in a bachelor's rooms, awash in Demon Rum. Dash it, don't you care anything about your reputation, my lady? My rep is bad enough for both of us."

"I care," she said in a toneless voice, staring at the fire. Sloane stared at the tarts. Becka stared at him, showing teeth that would have made a wolf envious. The duke forced his mind away from his stomach and onto his betrothed. She hadn't touched the brandy. She hadn't moved. "What if someone had seen you?" he prodded.

"I care," she repeated. "That's why I came. They . . . Uncle told Nigel to . . ."

"Findley and Nigel were going to do what?" His hands were on her arms. He didn't notice how tightly until she winced. "Sorry. But you were saying?"

"I was in the attics. I could hear his voice, telling my aunt. Nigel was going to . . . going to make certain I was ruined."

"Are you sure that's what he said? Maybe you misunderstood his meaning."

"You mean maybe my imagination ran away with me, and I invented the whole thing? Or maybe I was hearing voices? Maybe you don't believe me because you think I don't know the difference between truth and fantasy."

"No, no, I didn't mean anything of the kind. I was just

surprised. Your own relatives, by Jupiter." He was stroking her shoulders now. "I shouldn't have doubted you, sweetheart. I'm sorry."

She finally seemed to relax under his soothing caress. "You do believe me, that I wouldn't be safe there?"

"I believe you. It's the scurvy kind of trick that slimy bastard would try. I should have figured he'd pull something like this. You tried to tell me, didn't you? Thank goodness you had the sense to come to me."

"What shall we do?"

"Do? We shall get married, that's what." He strode to the hallway and shouted, "Kelly, on the double."

Kelly rushed into the room, then stopped short when he saw the disheveled female and the very large dog. He'd heard about the female, naturally, since he'd been the one trying to get this house in order for her while His Grace was chasing all over London after special licenses and such. No one had mentioned the dog. He bowed and uttered, "My lady," all the while eyeing the huge slobbering canine. Kelly didn't like dogs. The bigger they were, the more he didn't like them.

"My dear," said St. Sevrin, making the introductions, "this is the estimable Kelly. I couldn't manage without him. And Kelly, may I present your future mistress and duchess, Baroness Lisanne Neville. And her dog, Becka, who might be convinced to trade her raspberry tarts for some of your chicken stew."

Kelly's eyes lit up when he saw the tarts, all golden and dripping fruit. He took one step toward the basket, though, and Becka growled. The windows rattled with the force of it.

"Or perhaps not. We'll work on it later. For now I need you to take the curricle and go fetch us the vicar."

"But, Major, that is, Yer Grace, the vicar's due here in the morning."

Lisanne added her objection. "You can't just go awaken the poor man in the middle of the night."

St. Sevrin motioned Kelly to get going. "Tell him it's a matter of life and death." When the batman left, Sloane turned to Lisanne. "I wouldn't mind putting a bullet through your uncle, but I would mind having to flee the country at this point. The vicar is the only one who can eliminate the necessity."

"I don't see how. Uncle Alfred never listened to the vicar before."

"It's not a question of listening. Findley will be coming after you, I have no doubt of that. Until we are married, he is your legal guardian, so I have no rights but the power of my pistol to keep you from him. Therefore it's either shoot him or let him take you back with him, for whatever evil plan he has in mind."

"I wouldn't go."

He shrugged. "Then it's definitely pistols. Of course, if we were already married by the time he got here, he could just go shoot himself. Now *that* would be a fine wedding gift."

"You still want to marry me, even though there's bound to be an awful row?"

Even if he wasn't drowning in an ocean of bills, Sloane wouldn't send her back to that spawning ground of slugs. He was finding he had more of a sense of responsibility for Lisanne by the day. It wasn't an altogether uncomfortable discovery. "It's the only way, sweetings. How much time do you think we have? Kelly should be back within the hour with the vicar."

"The household was still awake when I left, so I doubt Nigel would come looking for me for yet a while."

"From what I saw of him, he'll spend half the night drinking his courage up. I've seen enough raw recruits to recognize a coward at first glance."

Lisanne couldn't deny Nigel's lack of bravery, and saw less reason to defend his honor. "They'll have to search through the house first. Maybe they'll just think I'm in the woods."

"No, Findley won't chance it. He has too much at stake, too little time. He knows the wedding is on for to-morrow."

"Well, they'll never come through the woods. Nigel is terrified of the place, even if Uncle could find the right path. If they ride around to the gate of the Hall, then down the road to the gate of the Priory and up the drive, the trip will add almost an hour in the dark, after they saddle the horses."

"That's cutting it close, but you do have a little time to rest. Kelly always has hot water on the boil. Perhaps you'd like to have some tea, or to wash up?"

Shyly, Lisanne pointed toward the basket. "I found a gown. It was my mother's."

And it was now under a ham. "Let's shake it out, shall we?" St. Sevrin took a step toward the basket. Becka growled, but Lisanne jumped to clutch the basket to her. "You mustn't see it. Not before the wedding. That would be bad luck."

Bad luck? Why not, this farce of a marriage had every-thing else going for it. Sloane shrugged. "You can change upstairs in my room—it's the only one uncovered yet— but the fire hasn't been started. The kitchen would be warmer, and there's a copper tub by the stove that we've been using for bathing. I can fill it for you."

"The kitchen will be lovely." She called the dog to fol-low them.

As he led his odd band down the corridor, St. Sevrin apologized. "I'm sorry this won't be any picture-perfect wedding. I was going to have Kelly scour the countryside for some flowers for you. Squire used to have a fine con-servatory."

"There are flowers on my gown."

He had to laugh at her practicality. "Well, that's all right, then. I'm sure it's lovely, and you'll be a beautiful bride. Your mother would be proud."

* * *

The duke must think she was going to wear her mother's wedding dress, not her nightgown, Lisanne thought as she nearly scrubbed her skin raw in the tub.

The bath was placed behind a screen for warmth, not modesty, and Lisanne stayed there as she dried herself and dressed, hoping that the heat from the water would steam out some of the gown's wrinkles. She sorely doubted that her mother would be proud. More likely Mama would be turning over in her grave to see her only daughter getting married in a creased nightgown that smelled of camphor and smoked ham, with its skirt pinned up. There was no time to sew the hem, and with every movement she made, the pins jabbed into Lisanne's legs and snagged her stockings. Besides, Lisanne refused to wear the heavy, muddy boots she'd run through the forest in, not with this gossamer flower-garden gown. So she was going to go barefoot at her wedding. No, she didn't think Mama would be proud.

Lisanne took baby steps toward the back door, where ivy was growing over the walls, and pulled down enough to make a wreath of sorts for her hair. As she was sitting at the table, trying to weave the vines with fingers that insisted on trembling, Kelly scratched on the kitchen entry.

"Vicar said we needed another witness, ma'am, so I brung his housekeeper's daughter Mary. His Grace said as how you might need help."

"Yes, please. Come in, Mary."

Mary was a sturdy country girl a few years older than Lisanne with work-roughened hands and a smile that showed overlapping front teeth. She had a little snub of a nose. "Oh, don't you look a treat, miss. My lady, I mean. Won't me mum be that sorry she missed seeing a real duchess get hitched."

Mary pulled a comb out of her pocket and got to work on Lisanne's hair. She didn't pull much more than she would plucking a chicken, but she chattered the while, so

Lisanne didn't have to think about what was waiting for her outside this room.

"Feeling poorly, she was," Mary explained. Lisanne knew very well that the vicar's housekeeper felt poorly about the Nevilles' attics-to-let orphan who ran around like a heathen savage. Mary's mother crossed to the other side of the street when she saw Lisanne coming, the hypocrite. There was no father to Mary that anyone had ever heard of, which was why Mary was still unwed and likely to remain so. Her mother was fierce in her piety now, though. Lisanne could just imagine what the housekeeper had said about being woken to attend Addled Annie's wedding—to a gazetted rake.

"I didn't bring no hairpins, Miss Annie. That is, my lady. That nice Mr. Kelly says as how we're to call you Lady Neville today, and Your Grace tomorrow."

"Lisanne is fine, Mary, and don't worry about the pins. At least you've taken out the snarls and debris. I'll just plait my hair as usual."

"Oh, that would be a sore shame, miss." Mary fluffed out the long blond locks till they fell halfway down Lisanne's back, with the slightest ripple left over from the braid. "And isn't a bride supposed to wed with her hair down? I heard that somewhere."

"In medieval times, I believe. But it will have to do. I've lost the ribbon, and could only tie the braid with this old piece of string from my pocket."

So they placed the ivy circlet atop Lisanne's head and declared her ready, which was a good thing, for His Grace was wearing a hole in the threadbare carpet in the little parlor and the vicar was developing mal de mer just watching.

While Lisanne bathed, St. Sevrin had gone upstairs and changed into formal dress. When he returned to the parlor, he was relieved to see that his bride's dog was still gone. Too bad the tarts were, too. He then primed and loaded his pistols and made sure his sword was ready to hand. He felt the same hum of excitement he used to feel on the eve of a battle. Too bad he was getting married instead.

Chapter Thirteen

"*My* God, you're beautiful." St. Sevrin didn't see the bare toes or the pins. That is, he saw them, but they didn't matter. He would have been surprised if his duchess—as he was already thinking of this Pocket Venus at Kelly's side—had appeared in normal garb. No wonder the rustics thought her fey. If ever there was a female who could pass for a fairy princess, it was Lisanne Neville in a gown of flowers with her sun-lightened gold hair trailing down her back.

Kelly escorted Lisanne farther into the room, Mary following behind. Becka had elected to remain in the kitchen with the ham. St. Sevrin approached Lisanne and took her small, trembling hand in his to lead her closer to where the vicar stood by the mantel.

"I count myself the most fortunate of men," he told her, softly pressing his lips to her palm. "But are you still sure you want to go through with this? Zeus, you could take London by storm and have any man you chose, even if you didn't have a shilling. I'd find a way to keep you out of Findley's clutches, I swear. You don't have to settle for a rackety old warhorse like me."

Lisanne looked up at him. In his black swallow-tailed

coat and white satin knee breeches, Sloane St. Sevrin had to be the most elegant gentleman she'd ever seen. His auburn hair was still damp from a recent combing, just now beginning to fall forward onto his forehead. He was willing to defend her, and every inch of his well-muscled frame bespoke the ability to do just that. More important, his brown eyes looked kind, and he held her hand gently. He needed her money and perhaps her understanding.

"I'm sure."

The duke was sure. Lisanne was sure. The vicar was not sure. All that time watching St. Sevrin pace had not convinced him that this was a suitable match. He was tired and irritable and couldn't see what all the fuss was about. "If you're both so determined to marry, I don't see why you cannot have the banns read." That would take three weeks, during which time cooler heads might prevail. "And you could hold the ceremony in the church, with a proper wedding." And he could go back to bed.

"Oh, this is much more romantic," cooed Mary, but no one listened.

"It's entirely legal, sir, so what's the difference if we wed tonight or tomorrow?" Lisanne asked.

"But without your guardian's approval, child, I cannot be comfortable."

Kelly muttered, "What, is that bounder such a big contributor to the church poor box?"

The vicar prepared to get even more annoyed that his honor was being impugned. "My judgment is not based on financial considerations, sirrah."

"Of course it is," St. Sevrin answered for Kelly, "else you would have written to Lady Lisanne's London solicitor ages ago about her treatment at Findley's hands."

When the vicar started to bluster about rendering unto Caesar what was Caesar's, and leaving him to God's work, the duke held up his hand. "I am sure the baroness—the duchess—and I shall be most generous to the community. For a start, we intend to rehire as many of the dismissed Neville Hall staff who are still in the neighborhood and might be convinced to work here at the Priory. If any of the old Priory retainers are still alive, they might apply, too."

"Now, that would be good for the village," the vicar had to admit.

Mary wanted to know if His Grace meant they wouldn't hire any new people. "All those maids and footmen is old folks by now. You need some younger hands to get this job done." She waved her arms around the decrepit surroundings.

"You can be my personal maid," Lisanne told her. "I shouldn't like strangers around."

"Coo, and won't those uppity servants choke on that! A'course, I never been a maid, my lady."

"That's fine. I've never had one."

It was St. Sevrin who called them back to order by clearing his throat. "The wedding? Nothing goes forward without the ceremony and the reverend's signature on the license."

The vicar still hesitated. Money was one thing, but the man's reputation . . .

The duke was out of patience. "My lady is spending the night here under my roof. Would you prefer she do so under the protection of my name, or under the cloud of other, even less reputable names? Make no mistake, I do intend to make this woman my wife, with or without benefit of clergy."

The vicar started reading, and faster when St. Sevrin started tapping his foot on the floor.

At last he was almost done. Out of breath, he was gasping, ". . . Let no man put asunder," when they heard a furious rapping on the front door.

"Go on," Lisanne urged. "Finish."

St. Sevrin nodded, so the vicar repeated, "What God

has joined together, let no man put asunder. I now pronounce—"

Footsteps were pounding down the hall.

Lisanne looked at the duke in disbelief. "Didn't you lock the door?"

"What, and deny Sir Alfred his grand entrance?"

"—You man and wife. You may kiss the bride."

"Like hell he can," roared the baronet from the doorway. He and Nigel came charging into the room along with the local sheriff, whose pistol was drawn.

Without thought, St. Sevrin stepped in front of Lisanne, protecting her. She peered around him to see a smile on his face. "Why, you're enjoying this!" she accused in a harsh whisper.

"Haven't had as much fun since Coruña," he admitted, pushing her back behind him, out of the line of fire in case he had to draw his own weapon. He was pleased he had Findley's measure: Like most bullies, the man was too cowardly to take him on by himself, so he'd brought an armed reinforcement. Of course, Findley hadn't counted on finding the matrimonial deed done, so was now having apoplexy.

"Unhand my niece, you scoundrel!" he was shouting. "This ceremony is a travesty. The marriage is illegal!"

The vicar was holding his pen above the papers, signing the license and the marriage certificate. "Oh, no, I made sure everything was in order. It's a proper marriage, Sir Alfred, all right and tight, so we can all go home and get a good night's sleep. There's no law I know of that says a bride and groom have to kiss at the end of the ceremony to make it legal."

"Oh, but I'm willing," St. Sevrin drawled for Findley's benefit.

"Don't you dare! Sheriff, shoot him if he tries! This marriage is illegal, I say! If you won't rip up those papers now, Vicar, I'll just have to go to the trouble of an annulment. Breach of promise. Foresworn vows. The jade was already promised to my son."

"Never!" Lisanne shouted, stepping out from St. Sevrin's shadow. She did allow him to keep her hand in his. "I wouldn't marry that toad if he were the last man on earth."

"Well, it ain't as though I'm in any great hurry to marry a great gaby like you, neither, Annie," Nigel was heard to respond before his father's elbow landed in his midsection, halting his disclaimer.

The vicar was shaking his balding head. "Oh, I don't approve of first cousins marrying. Too many children born with too little wit, don't you know."

"Like my niece, you mean," Sir Alfred said, but everyone was looking at Nigel, wondering at the proximity of his parents' relation. "I say she was promised to my son and that promise invalidates this farcical ceremony."

"It's a farce, all right," St. Sevrin muttered. "If Lady Lisanne was affianced to your son, Findley, why didn't her London trustee know anything about it? Here's his letter of permission. His name is on the license, too."

"They were too young," Sir Alfred blustered. "There was no reason to involve the solicitors yet. It was an understanding between my deceased brother-in-law and myself."

"An understanding that the baron didn't happen to mention in his will? Gammon. I saw his will, and he planned for every eventuality of his daughter's future. None mentioned your son. In fact, if you'll recall, he didn't even name you as full guardian. It won't wash, Findley. Give it up as a bad hand. The marriage is done. Fact. History."

"No! I'll have it annulled, I swear! I can do it, too. You won't like having your name spread through the mud."

St. Sevrin just laughed. It was not a pretty sound. "My name? You'd have to invent a new shade of black before you could darken my reputation any."

"Well, you won't like what I'll be forced to do to hers." Findley pointed at Lisanne and sneered. "Look at her, all decked out like a bird of paradise."

Not understanding, Lisanne thought it a rather nice compliment until she saw the darker frown on St. Sevrin's face. Mary came closer and whispered an explanation in her ear that made Lisanne gasp. "A trollop? Me?"

Sir Alfred hadn't paused. "I can have it annulled because the doxy's not in her right mind. Lunatics cannot enter legal contracts; everyone knows that. That London trustee had no business giving his permission. Only her guardian can."

"I am no doxy, Uncle, although you tried to make me one. And I am no lunatic."

He curled his lip. "I can have five doctors prove you are, and a houseful of servants, an army of witnesses, to swear to your freakish behavior."

The sheriff felt it was his duty to speak up. First he wiped his dripping nose on his sleeve. "I seen it myself, her going off in those woods, staring into space."

The vicar had to admit there had been a deal of talk that Miss Neville was short a sheet. Even his own housekeeper, this very evening, had called her by that old nickname, Addled Annie. "There may be some grounds here for deliberation, gentlemen."

"No," St. Sevrin thundered. "The lady has had an irregular upbringing, which can be laid at your doorstep, Findley. That's all. Ignorant country folk have always seen hobgoblins behind every turnip patch. They don't understand anyone different, and fear what they don't understand."

"Here now, who are you calling ignorant?" the sheriff demanded.

"Anyone stupid enough to mistake a lonely child for a moonling, that's who."

Sir Alfred returned to the fray. "The sheriff is right, St.

Sevrin, Annie is crackbrained. Everyone knows it but you. If you persist in this idiocy, we'll take it to a court of law and they'll overturn the marriage. Meantime the sheriff's duty is to see that you release the girl to her loving family."

"So loving that you'd have your son rape her?"

The vicar choked. Even the sheriff was taken aback. "Here, here, what's this, then?"

"You're as totty-headed as she is, Duke, to even suggest Nigel is capable of such a heinous act. No, I have my duty and the sheriff has his, to bring Annie away with us. I'm not leaving her here where you can force yourself upon her so that the marriage has to stand as consummated."

"Now, why does that have a familiar ring to it?" the duke wondered, crossing his arms.

Sir Alfred ignored St. Sevrin's facetious remark. "Take her, Sheriff."

"But what if he's already had her, Pa? She's been here for hours, and who knows when they met. And you said he's the devil with the females."

St. Sevrin didn't even bother taking aim. He just swung around and landed Nigel a facer. The clunch went down, blood spurting from his nose. "It's bad enough," the duke told Findley, "that you denied your niece the ladylike upbringing her birth deserved. It's worse that you didn't teach your son to be a gentleman."

Mary went over to the fallen youth and bent down to see if Nigel was still alive. When she saw his chest rise and fall, she kicked him in the ribs. "And that's for trying to get a feel of all the girls in town, you swine."

The sheriff sniffed. "I gots to take her." He took a step toward Lisanne, but now Becka was at her right side, the duke at her left, his own pistol drawn. The minion of the law wasn't sure which was the more formidable opponent. A distinctive click behind him said that Kelly had drawn the hammer on his gun, too. "I gots my duty."

"What you've got is a head cold, Sheriff. That's about all you can manage at one time." St. Sevrin was deadly serious now. "And no, you are not going to take Lady Lisanne—my wife—anywhere. We'll settle this tonight."

That sounded too much like a duel to Findley, and he was certain a rogue of St. Sevrin's caliber wouldn't challenge a runny-nosed bumpkin of a sheriff. He'd be the one looking down the barrel of that deadly pistol next. "It's not for you to settle anything, Duke. I demand a London tribunal to hear the case."

"Where you can hire a hundred so-called experts to tell any story you feed them? I've seen proceedings like that. The side with the most money and the most convincing quacks wins. No, Findley, you're trying a bluff because I wouldn't want *my wife* to have to face such an ordeal. Nor would anyone who truly cared for her welfare."

"I'll do it, I swear, to keep her out of your evil clutches. You rip up those papers or I'll challenge the marriage in every court in the land."

St. Sevrin turned to Lisanne. "Is Squire Pemberton still magistrate for the shire?" When she nodded yes, he asked, "And is he still regarded as an honest man? A fair man?"

"I think so," the vicar agreed. Mary bobbed her head when the duke looked at her questioningly.

"Then go get him, Sheriff. That's a job you ought to be able to accomplish. Kelly, you go with the officer to make sure he doesn't fill Pemberton's head with fustian before he even gets here. None of us is budging until this is settled."

The vicar groaned. So did Nigel. St. Sevrin ignored them both. He led Lisanne away from her fuming uncle to a chair at the other end of the room, and sent Mary to the kitchen for some tea.

Lisanne clutched his arm. "But what if he . . . ?"

Sloane patted her hand. "Don't worry, sweetings, you're not the one crazy enough to get between me and what I want. Your uncle is."

Chapter Fourteen

Squire Pemberton had his own system of justice: murderers were hanged, thieves were transported. That kept the criminal element out of his shire one way or the other. Any other miscreant coming before him, vandal, pickpocket, or public nuisance, was put to work. The poorhouse was kept in firewood, the church was repainted yearly, the roads were in good repair—and all at no expense to the worthy taxpayers. Everything neat, efficient, and equitable, that's how Pemberton liked to administer the law. He was good at it, he was fair at it, and he was fast at it.

This current mess of potage, however, fit into none of his guidelines. Getting up in the middle of the night to adjudicate an ugly situation didn't fit into any of his notions of justice, either. Pemberton was old, he was tired, and he'd earned every right to be cranky. Not even the glass of excellent brandy the duke offered was going to reconcile the squire to a night's disturbed slumber. Not even the sight of that jackanapes Nigel Findley with a wet cloth over his nose and claret down his shirtfront could make up for a cold, uncomfortable ride. The only high point that Pemberton could see was his old friend Neville's daughter finally turned out like a lady for once.

"All grown up, eh, missy?" he said, pinching her cheek on his way to the seat Kelly held out for him. "And pretty as a picture, besides."

"Here, here." Sir Alfred jumped up. "You can't go taking the chit's side without hearing all the evidence."

Pemberton settled his bulk in the chair and looked over his spectacles at the baronet. "Her side, is it? I thought we were here to decide what was best for the gel's future. I deuced well will take her side, with her welfare at the heart of any consideration. I'll just assume that's what *every* concerned party here wants, shall I?"

"Of course. I am only trying to make the best provision for my dear sister's only child." Findley could do nothing but take his seat again. At least he had one. He hadn't been offered any brandy, tea, or hospitality, not that he expected it in this den of infamy. He'd even had to tend to Nigel's nosebleed on his own, to his disgust.

Pemberton was going on: "And you can stop looking thunderclouds at me, St. Sevrin. I've known you since you were in short coats, and you were a resty lad then. Would have thought the army'd smooth out the rough edges. Guess not. But sit down anyway. There will be no more, ah, accidents like young Findley here suffered, or I'll charge you with contempt of court. That means three days' labor. The schoolhouse needs new steps. Don't suppose you'd be much good at it anyway, so don't aggravate me with any show of temper."

St. Sevrin sat down on the threadbare sofa next to Lisanne, sending a cloud of dust into the tea she was pouring for the vicar. She also offered the reverend gentleman on her other side a plate of raspberry tarts. Becka must be full of ham, St. Sevrin decided, for the big dog didn't even raise her head off Lisanne's feet when he helped himself to one of the pastries. Good, let the shaggy mongrel stay there so no one could see that his bride was barefoot.

The sofa smelled of mildew, but St. Sevrin also recognized the scent of musty old clothes coming from Lisanne and a whiff of the soap he used. She also had an inchworm climbing out of the ivy tiara she wore. Damn! That wasn't going to win any points with the magistrate. While Pemberton was greeting the vicar, St. Sevrin reached up and removed the offending wildlife, then had to look around for a place to put it. The sugar bowl seemed the likeliest until Pemberton changed his mind and wanted tea instead of the brandy. Gads, Squire would think they all had breezes in their cocklofts.

Lisanne had frown lines on her forehead he wished he could wipe away, so he tried a smile for her. Lud, what a damnable thing to put a sensitive female through. She looked like a wood nymph that could be blown away on a gentle breeze.

For himself, St. Sevrin wasn't worried. He was a gambler, after all. Of course this was the biggest gamble of his life—or Lisanne's. Usually when he wagered, Sloane knew the odds and could calculate his chances. He seldom put his precious blunt on the line for games of random chance or luck, only science and logic.

Tonight, though, Pemberton was the wild card, the joker in the deck. Sloane had no way of figuring which way the old man would lean. Of course he still had his hole cards, but the duke didn't want to use them unless necessary.

He lightly squeezed Lisanne's hand, between them, for what reassurance he could give. She squeezed his back. The girl had pluck, thank goodness. They'd get through this.

Squire was ordering the sheriff to put down his pistol in the name of civilization, if not out of fear the lobcock would sneeze and shoot the ceiling down on their heads. Kelly, too, had to lay his weapon aside before the magistrate would begin. St. Sevrin didn't mind; his was tucked into his waistcoat, ready to hand. He wasn't that much of a gambler.

First Pemberton listened to the vicar without letting Findley interrupt. He looked over all the papers: the special license, the marriage lines, the letter from the estate administrator. This last not only gave permission, but stated that the marriage settlements were extremely favorable to Mackensie's client.

"So you thought everything was in order?" Pemberton asked the vicar.

"I did question the need for such haste, although now I see why His Grace wished to get the wedding performed in a timely fashion."

"And to your thinking the marriage is legitimate?"

"In the eyes of the Church, certainly, with the archbishop's signature on the special license and two attendants to witness the vows. I truly thought I could go seek my bed."

"And do you still feel the marriage is lawful and binding?"

"Oh, there's no question of that. They're well and truly married. The question is whether they should stay so. Sir Alfred believes I have only to tear up the papers to have the marriage disappear, which is patently untrue. On the other hand, the gentleman did present some feasible grounds for having the proceedings annulled. He claimed that the bride's hand had been promised elsewhere, to his son Nigel, in fact, and that she was of such diminished mental capacity that her vows should not be binding."

Sir Alfred was smirking. "Not just feasible grounds for dissolution, but legal certainties. Do you want to hear me now?"

"I'd like to hear my wife snoring now, but I suppose I have to hear you out if the vicar is done. Vicar? Reverend?" The clergyman had nodded off, thinking his part in the proceedings was at an end. "Lucky devil."

So Pemberton listened to Sir Alfred spout about his beloved, befuddled niece, how she needed the care of her family, not some avaricious villain who chanced upon a pigeon for plucking, etc., etc. There was so much *cetera* that Pemberton was ready for a nap himself. He shut Findley up and listened to the sheriff swear how he thought he was protecting a loony, by trying to get her back home.

When St. Sevrin would have spoken, thinking it must be his turn, Pemberton bade him hold his horses. "I'll get to you next, Your Grace." He picked up his teacup, stared at the contents a moment, then set it aside. "I'll have that brandy after all."

Kelly started forward, as did Mary. Both should have left long ago, but since no one had ordered them out, they stayed. Even Sloane attempted to get to the bottle first, but Lisanne hopped up before he could rise. Unfortunately one of the pins in her hem stuck in the frayed fabric of the sofa's skirt. *"Merde,"* she cursed, and pulled at her entangled gown, revealing her bare toes. Nigel snickered through the cloth over his face, and St. Sevrin groaned. The vicar snored.

Pemberton wiped his spectacles, replaced them on the bridge of his nose, and took another look. "Thank you, my dear" was all he said when she put the glass in his hand. He waited until her back was turned on her way toward the sofa, to check the snifter for other life-forms. Then he addressed the baronet: "Sir Alfred, I am having a problem with your claims. If, as you say, your niece is of unsound mind, why should you wish to pursue her marriage to your son? You cannot want your grandchildren to be Bedlam-bred. No, you cannot have it both ways. If she is not competent to marry St. Sevrin, she is not fit to marry your son."

"So they won't marry."

Nigel was heard to mumble "Thank goodness" before

his father drowned him out with, "We'll just make sure Annie is kept safe at home."

"Her money, you mean," St. Sevrin put in, which drew the magistrate's attention his way.

"Findley's motives are suspect, Your Grace, but yours are transparent. Everyone knows you're badly dipped."

The duke just nodded, tight-lipped.

"And you have a devilish reputation as a womanizer. Who is to say you didn't seduce an innocent young girl away from her family?"

"I am," the duke replied. "I married Lady Neville in good faith."

"Yes, but you are a practiced rake who could find it all too easy to take advantage of a poor harebrained heiress."

St. Sevrin was on his feet. "I did not, and my *wife* is not a simpleton to be led astray by a facile tongue. My *wife* is an intelligent woman who knows her own mind."

"Intelligent enough to curse in French, although I'm sure her parents never intended her to learn such. Sit down, Your Grace, the lady's intelligence has never been in question. You're forgetting I've known her since she was born. I've even seen some of the translations she's done to continue her father's work. Very well received in learned journals, I assure you. What are you reading now, my dear?"

Lisanne searched for pockets to find her book. "I'm sorry, it's in my other gown. I am rereading Plato's *Phaedo*, sir. As extensive as Papa's library is, it hasn't been kept current and most of the volumes on agriculture do not bear a second reading."

"I'm sure, I'm sure. And in what language did you say you were reading Socrates, my dear?"

"Why, the Greek, of course. Oh, but I am also reading Herr Mittlebaum's book of natural medicines. His publisher has promised to make the necessary corrections."

Squire Pemberton turned to Nigel. "What was the last book you read, young man?"

"Book?" Nigel tried to think of one. "Well, a fellow doesn't want to fill his head with all that rumgumption."

"And your daughter?" the magistrate asked Sir Findley. "What books has she been reading?"

"How the devil should I know? And what's that got to—"

Lisanne knew. "Oh, Esmé is a prodigious reader, Squire. She reads Maria Edgeworth and Mrs. Radcliffe, all the Minerva Press novels she can find."

"Which put more nonsensical notions in a miss's head than any seven silver-tongued devils," Squire declared. "I know, my wife reads 'em and sighs when I can't make pretty speeches or ride *ventre à terre* to her rescue. Rescue her from what, I say, her lisping French coiffeur? Bah. Forty years, and she wants pretty speeches." He harrumphed again at the thought. "Anyway, I suppose we are all now in accord that Lady Neville's intelligence is not in question?"

Sir Alfred had to nod his agreement. "But—"

"And as to whether she can sew or paint or play a pretty tune, that has nothing to say to her competence to enter the married state. All that caterwauling and banging on the ivories always gives me the headache anyway. The only good thing about getting old is you don't hear it so well."

"But—" Sir Alfred was determined to be heard.

Squire Pemberton was growing deafer by the moment, it seemed. "Now, there is an important question to this annulment business that no one's mentioned yet. The likeliest cause for dissolving a marriage is when the bride cannot or will not perform her marital duties. Is that a problem, my dear?"

Without so much as blinking, Lisanne answered that it was no problem whatsoever. "His Grace requires a son for the dukedom and another for the barony."

"I see you've your work cut out for you, lad," the

squire chuckled, bringing the first blush to St. Sevrin's cheeks in more years than he could remember.

Pemberton sighed. "So we're left with the issue of mental competency. There's no doubt that there's an odd kick to missy's gallop." He pointedly stared at her bare feet. "The villagers talk, the country folk whisper. I ignore most of it, but I've heard tales even before yours, Sir Alfred, and the sheriff's tonight. Now, I don't claim to be any physician, but I am the one you asked to decide this argle-bargle."

"Ask her about the fairies," Nigel prompted, and his father took it up. "Yes, ask her if she speaks to the Little People in the woods, Squire, so we can all go home."

Lisanne looked at the duke, trying to judge his reaction. Sloane merely raised one eyebrow. "It's your call, sweetings."

She studied her hands a moment, when the only sounds were the vicar's snores and the sheriff's snivels. "Yes," she finally answered. "I did think I spoke to the Wood Folk, when I was a child."

"And now?"

Sadly she shook her head no. "Now I am grown up."

"She's lying!" her uncle insisted, shouting so loudly he woke up the vicar. "Make her say whether she believes in fairies or not."

"Fairs?" the vicar asked. "Are we discussing the village fairs?"

"Go back to sleep, Reverend," Squire Pemberton directed, waiting for Lisanne's answer.

Instead she asked him a question: "Is your wife insane? She's said time and again that she refuses to step foot on Priory land because it's haunted. But has she ever seen a ghost? Spoken to one? Has anyone who claims to believe in ghosts seen one? And you, sir," she inquired of the yawning vicar, "do you believe in angels?"

"Why, of course I do, child."

"Yet you've never seen one or spoken to one, have you?"

The vicar laughed. "You have to be a saint to speak to an angel, or in heaven among them."

"Yes, but you believe anyway. And without meaning any blasphemy, there is the belief in God Himself. How many people do you know who have ever seen Him, or spoken to Him—and gotten a reply?"

"But we see His works, child. That is enough. It is for the prophets and the martyrs to converse with the Almighty."

Squire nodded. "I get your point, missy. 'There are more things in heaven and earth, Horatio, than are dreamt of in your philosophy.' "

"And belief is an act of faith, not an act of lunacy."

"Is this place really haunted, Pa?" Nigel wanted to know, looking over his shoulder.

Findley hadn't quite followed the discussion, either. "Didn't she just admit she believes in pixies?"

"I believe anything is possible."

"Well then, missy," Squire asked, "do you think it's possible to make a go of this marriage?"

Chapter Fifteen

"*Y*ou mean you're going to let her marry this wastrel?" Findley squawked, as if the hand of doom were closing around his throat.

St. Sevrin's patience was seconds away from doing just that, but it was the magistrate who answered: "I'm not going to *let* her do anything. She's already done it."

"But, but he's a ne'er-do-well, just marrying her for the money. He'll gamble it all away in a sennight and leave her destitute."

"I doubt even St. Sevrin could go through Neville's fortune in a sennight." Pemberton glanced at the papers again. "According to this, Her Grace will have a handsome jointure of her own that the duke can't touch."

Findley threw his hands in the air. "Fine, then she'll waste it herself. Most likely give it all to beggars and orphans, the way she does with whatever money I give her. Can't even trust her with an allowance, like my Esmé."

"Tut, tut," the vicar put in. "There's nothing wrong with charity, Sir Alfred."

Pemberton agreed. "She might even manage to do some good with her fortune, Findley, amazing as it might seem to you."

"Then let her give *your* blunt away!" Findley yelled, tripping over his own greed.

Squire coughed. That was all.

"Well, she don't know what she's getting into, then. Her aunt and I kept her insulated from the evils"—a sidelong sneer in the duke's direction—"of men such as St. Sevrin. Wild to a fault, profligate with money they never earn, careless of their own lives or others', and as immoral as a band of baboons."

"Actually, baboons have close-knit families," Lisanne began, to be shushed by St. Sevrin with a laugh.

"I've heard better defenses from a pickpocket caught red-handed."

Squire wasn't laughing. "I regret that Sir Alfred does have a point, my dear. I've never seen you at the assemblies or tea parties in the neighborhood. You've had no London come-out, no exposure whatsoever to young men that I know of." He ignored Nigel completely. "Are you certain you know what you are doing, marrying a man with His Grace's lamentable reputation?"

Lisanne looked at her new husband, the lines on his face, the puffiness near his eyes, the brandy glass never far from his hand. She also saw the strong jaw and straight nose. More important, she saw the damp spot near his knee where he'd let Becka rest her drooling chin while he scratched her ears.

"Major Lord Shearingham was a hero," she said. "General Wellesley trusted him with his plans and his platoons. I can trust the Duke of St. Sevrin no less."

Kelly, from the back of the room, called out, "Here, here."

Sloane lifted her hand to his lips and spoke for her ears only: "Thank you, Duchess. I shall do my damnedest to live up to your confidence."

Squire wasn't quite satisfied that Lisanne knew what she was in for, taking on a here-and-therein. "Some women get the deuced romantical notion that a reformed

125

rake makes the best husband. Most likely from that drivel they read. I say the tiger doesn't change its stripes until it's a fur rug. You aren't thinking of trying to reform St. Sevrin, are you, my dear?"

She smiled and softly answered: "I thought we had determined that I am not crazy, sir."

The magistrate and the vicar laughed. Even St. Sevrin's mouth turned up.

"You'll do, lass," Squire Pemberton pronounced. "You'll do fine. Congratulations, Your Grace, you've won a fine wife for yourself. See that you deserve her." He started to lift his bulk out of the chair. The vicar was already heading for the door.

"No!" Sir Alfred screamed. "No, I am not satisfied. Justice has not been served! This travesty of a wedding has to be annulled. I'll go to the lord high magistrate in London. I'll go to the archbishop himself!"

"Why not the prince?" St. Sevrin taunted. "Our Regent would do anything to get out of his own marriage. Perhaps he'd look more kindly on your petition." He stood slowly and flexed his fingers before forming them into fists. "Damn weak left," he muttered, then warned the baronet, "Of course, if you approach Prinny or the courts or the Church, if you so much as breathe the word annulment ever again, I'll tear you limb from limb."

Findley stepped closer to the sheriff. "You . . . you can't do that! This is England, you devil, not some army outpost or battlefield." He turned to Pemberton. "Tell him he can't do that!"

"Oh, but I can," St. Sevrin breathed while Squire looked on, "and I would derive great pleasure out of it, too, after what you've done to my lady; but I don't need to." He paced closer to the baronet, who seemed to shrink with every step the duke took. "No, I do not need to, because you aren't going to make any more trouble. I let you play the game out your way, Findley, so you would be satisfied, so there would be no question of the legality of this marriage. I let you embarrass my wife with this inquest, and I let you abuse the hospitality of my house. But you still aren't content, are you?"

"I'll never rest, I tell you, until I have Annie back where she belongs! I'm not afraid of your threats." Everyone could see his spindly knees knocking together.

"Very well, then, it's time I laid the rest of my cards on the table. First, my wife's name is Lisanne, not Annie. That's 'Her Grace' to you. Second, if you don't shut up, don't get out of my sight with your spineless sprig of a son, I'll be the one to go to court. I'll have you charged with embezzlement so fast your head will spin. You'll have to answer to the magistrates and Mr. Mackensie for every shilling you've spent on your wife and children, not on your niece. I'll bring in the local merchants to discuss your so-called contracts, and the Neville tenants to discuss improvements that were never done to their farms."

"A bunch of country yokels? You can't prove anything!"

"Mr. Mackensie never throws anything away. Every inflated bill you sent, every bogus expenditure, they are all there, just waiting for you to make a peep about the state of my marriage or my wife's mind."

"No one will believe you. Everyone knows you're a drunk and a debaucher."

St. Sevrin studied his fingernails. "You really are getting on my nerves, Findley. Do you actually believe anyone in London will take the word of a jumped-up bartholemew babe over a duke's? Over that of a wealthy duchess and her eminently respected solicitor? Think for once, Findley. You would have to make reparation of all that money. Do you have that much squirreled away? I doubt it. You'd be ruined. You could even land in gaol or the penal colonies."

Squire nodded. "Thieves get transported. That's the way of it."

"Wouldn't do much for Esmé's Season, neither, Pa," Nigel volunteered.

"The nodcock is right for once. Your entire family will be ostracized, Findley. Think, man. One word from you about my wife means one word from me to Prinny. You won't be accepted anywhere except Botany Bay. I am willing to let it rest, Findley—I won't even sue for reparations—if you are willing to let us alone."

"Let's go, Pa," Nigel urged. "Before he sets the dog on us. He's done everything else."

Defeated, deflated, Sir Alfred turned to leave.

"I'll have your word, Findley," St. Sevrin called after him. "Your word as a gentleman, for what it's worth, in front of witnesses, that you accept this marriage."

The bitter flavor of failure was too strong in Findley's mouth for him to answer. He jerked his head in acquiescence and left. Kelly slammed the door behind him and his little entourage.

Champagne would have been a nice touch, had there been any. Instead Squire lifted his glass of brandy and toasted the newlyweds. The vicar raised his cup of tea to their health, and Kelly gave Mary a sip from his flask to put their seal on the marriage.

"Good health, long life, strong sons . . . Did I forget anything, Reverend?"

The vicar had to think a moment, so sleepy was his brain. It was gone after two in the morning, and his tea was cold. "Uh, happiness and understanding, joy in each other, that's what I always wish for the young people I wed." Right now he wished them all to the devil, the good Lord forgive him.

Kelly had one more toast to make: "And no more plaguey relatives."

Then they were gone. Squire Pemberton had his own rig, but Kelly had to drive the others back to the vicarage. Mary would gather her belongings, tell her mum the good news, and return in the morning to take up her new employment. Kelly allowed as how he may as well sleep with the horses in the little stable behind the manse, for otherwise he'd no more get home than he'd have to turn around to fetch Mary back.

Mostly they were all giving the Duke and Duchess of St. Sevrin privacy, which was the last thing their graces wanted, unless it was another visit from Uncle Alfred.

Sloane helped Lisanne carry the tea things and the glasses back to the kitchen, neither knowing what to say or what to do. Becka padded after them and the remaining pastries.

"I could brew a fresh pot of tea, if you'd like," she offered, and "Are you warm enough? You could wrap yourself twice around in my greatcoat on the peg there," he suggested. They both declined. The dog started gnawing on the ham bone.

When the sound started grating on his nerves, Sloane cleared his throat. "I don't think we'll have any more problems with your relations."

"No, I don't suppose so. You gave Uncle Alfred no choice. Thank you for what you did. And for what you didn't do."

"What I didn't do?"

"You didn't shoot him or strangle him or knock him down. I shouldn't have liked to see that, even if he deserved it. Reasoning is always better than brute force. Nigel doesn't count because he has no reason."

"I daresay we've seen the last of them either way. Findley has a small holding in Richmond, doesn't he?"

Lisanne licked her dry lips. "Yes, outside of London. I, ah, did tell Esmé that she could still make her come-out from Neville House. It's right in Town and has a huge ballroom."

"And a much more prestigious address to boot. But don't you think we should have discussed it first?"

Her chin came up. "You said Neville House was to be mine, to do with as I would."

"Yes, and I also thought you would be more comfortable there while St. Sevrin House undergoes repairs."

"Don't you think we should have discussed *that* first?"

Sloane ran his hand through his already disarranged hair. "I see we both have a great deal to learn about being married. The vicar did wish us understanding."

"And I thought you understood I had no wish to go to London, to either house. I told you I didn't intend to live in your pocket, and I am more comfortable in the country."

"Yes, you did tell me all that, but I thought that going to Town as a married lady, as a duchess, would be different. You wouldn't be on the marriage mart or dependent on the goodwill of those high-in-the-instep hypocrites who rule Almack's." And he wouldn't have to worry about leaving her here alone.

"No, it makes no difference. I prefer to stay in the country. I have my work with the botanical medicines, and the tenants will need some direction until you find a competent bailiff. The steward from Neville Hall is a good man and can begin improvements, but there is too much work on the two estates for one man."

"And you would help?" No other female of his acquaintance would turn down a London Season for the farmyard. No other female of his acquaintance would be a ha'penny's bit of good there, either. In her pretty gown and neatly combed hair, she'd let him forget for a moment how very different his bride was from women of her class. Hell, she was different from women of *any* class. He didn't want to think about that right now.

"I can help," she was saying, without artifice or boasting. "I know the land." Not "I have studied the land," or "I have read agricultural journals," but "I know the land." Lisanne was trying to tell him, trying to make him understand, as the vicar said they should. "In the woods—"

"No." He didn't want to hear about that right now, either. "It's late, Duchess, and your eyelids are drooping. Go to bed. We'll talk another time. I'm afraid my room is the only one made up for now. I'll show you the way."

Her eyelids weren't drooping at all now. Lisanne's blue eyes were wide-open as they flew to his. She didn't even have to put the question into words. "No, I am not going to join you tonight, Duchess. We're both too tired and upset. I'll take Kelly's pallet here by the stove. It's no hardship after the army."

Instead of arguing as he thought she might, Lisanne merely gathered up her old dress and her boots and followed him down the hall. As he lit her way up the stairs and down the echoing corridor, Sloane felt he had to reassure his barefoot bride that she was safe. "The Priory ghosts only appear when there's a death or disaster in the family, or so the story goes. There's nothing to be frightened of."

"Oh, I'm not afraid of ghosts, Your Grace. Besides, Becka will be with me."

Fine, St. Sevrin thought on his way back down the stairs, he got to sleep on a thin mattress on the floor while a great hulking dog shared his bed upstairs. And he'd never even got to kiss the bride.

Chapter Sixteen

*N*othing to be frightened of? Lisanne was alone in this great ramshackle mansion with a complete and total stranger who now had her life in his keeping. She very well knew that all the signed settlements and legal documents in the world wouldn't change the fact that a woman was her husband's property. The duke could force her to go to London. He could force her to share his bed.

He said he wouldn't come to her tonight. But that's what he was saying now. In a few hours, after a few more bottles of spirits, what then? She'd seen Nigel in his cups too often to trust a man's promises. Even her uncle's meanness was magnified tenfold by a night at the bottle. And this man, her husband, was already a creature of violence and strength, used to getting his own way, reveling in the challenge. What could be more challenging than a woman—no, a wife—who refused her favors?

And what of tomorrow or next week if he couldn't find some village girl to satisfy his needs? How long would Sloane be willing to wait? Lisanne wasn't ready. Nothing to be frightened of? Perhaps St. Sevrin had taken too many hits to the head at Gentleman Jackson's Boxing Parlor.

Lisanne looked around the bedroom for hints of the man's character, even knowing he'd only been here a matter of days. The room had his mark already, or his man Kelly's. The massive canopied bed was neatly made, albeit with a bedstead that appeared moth-eaten. The comb, brush, and mirror on the dresser were aligned with military precision. The book on the nightstand was a history of the Mahratta Wars. Lisanne was not surprised, nor at the wine bottle and glass next to it. He'd been a good soldier. Lately he'd been drinking a good deal of his life away. Perhaps he was in pain from that wound he'd mentioned. She'd have to ask about it when she knew him better.

The pitcher and basin were chipped, the towel slightly damp, the mirror tarnished, but those told nothing of the man. There was no other sign that anyone had stayed here. Lisanne unfolded her old dress and emptied the pockets. Books, bottles, stones, an iris root, various bits of bark and greenery wrapped in scraps of cloth came forth, with paper and pencil, sewing kit, a handful of pins and half of a roll gone hard. She fed the last to Becka and scattered the rest on the night table, the dresser, the washstand. Now the dark-paneled room had life, her life.

Despite its original purpose, Lisanne didn't want to sleep in her lovely wedding gown, nor in the dusty, creased muslin she'd worn all day and would likely wear on the morrow. Even less did she want to sleep in her shift and slip, in case St. Sevrin came into the room for his book or his bottle—or his bride.

Feeling like a trespasser but having no choice, Lisanne opened the clothespress. The neatly hung coats and breeches were not many, but even her untutored eye could tell they were of the finest quality. Among them Lisanne found a white lawn nightshirt. She put it on instead of her mama's gown, which she tenderly hung between the rows of waistcoats.

Lisanne was comforted by the nightshirt's softness, the lingering scent of her husband's lemon and spice cologne, and the fact that it trailed down past her feet.

She put another log on the fire and sank down in front of it, her arms around Becka. As she was wrapped in his nightshirt, she knew she could be wrapped in the security of knowing Sloane would look out for her interests. He terrified her, but he could make her feel protected. He wouldn't let anything happen to her.

In a way, that was even more frightening. Lisanne had just given up her name and her fortune. She was liable to lose her self to him next.

She could get used to having someone to lean on. She could learn to depend on his strength and his honor. And then she'd have nothing when he left.

He'd take care of her, she had no doubt, maybe even come to care *for* her, but he'd go his own way. Lisanne knew she couldn't hold a man like St. Sevrin. She'd never thought she could, so wouldn't let herself hope for the impossible. She wouldn't let herself grow fonder of his daring, his infrequent half smile, or that lock of auburn hair that fell into his eyes.

Nothing to be frightened of? Giving her heart into the keeping of a man like St. Sevrin was scarier than facing a hundred moaning medieval monks.

Lisanne couldn't fall asleep, not in his bed with his scent on his pillow. She was being suffocated. Her books and notes couldn't interest her tonight, nor his volume on the India campaign. She was too anxious to sleep, too anxious to concentrate on anything else. What had she done? And what could she do now?

She could put the robe that matched her mother's nightgown on over his nightshirt. She could carry her boots in one hand, a candle in the other, and leave.

She and Becka did not head for Neville House—

Lisanne would never give her uncle the satisfaction of seeing that she was worried over her choice. Instead she set out for where she would find peace, where she could be the Lisanne Neville she knew, nobody's wife, nobody's fool.

Sloane didn't believe in ghosts. He didn't need them to disturb his rest; he had specters of his own. Not ready for sleep, he took the brandy bottle back to the parlor. He wasn't castaway, not even slightly above par, not nearly foxed enough to dull his mind to what he'd done.

The Duke of St. Sevrin had taken a child-bride, for her money. The devil could worry about what the world might say; Sloane was outraged enough himself. Lisanne Neville was too innocent to touch, too unworldly to understand his corruption. She hadn't known what a vile deed he was committing by binding her clear light to his murky shadows. He knew. He'd done it anyway.

In a way he was worse than that bastard uncle of hers who let Lisanne stay a child for his own gain. Sloane was forcing her to be a woman for *his* own gain. Findley had kept her from meeting the decent young men she could choose from; Sloane was keeping her from marrying the man she deserved. A beautiful, intelligent, and wealthy female making a marriage of convenience without ever knowing an infatuation, calf-love, or grand passion was bad enough. The bargain Lisanne was getting was horrid.

Sloane had taken the baroness from the elegant comfort of her home to this crumbling heap of his. Not even Findley, with his lax guidance and grasping, conniving ways, kept her in such deplorable conditions: a dented copper bathtub in the kitchen, a tea set with no two cups matching and half of those chipped, and worse meals than her dog usually ate. Zeus, Sloane hoped Becka liked chicken. The dog and the duchess were in the one passable bedroom the vast pile boasted, passable if you kept your eyes closed to the warped paneling and your nose closed to the mildewed hangings. The wind whistled through the cracks in the windowpanes and under the rotted sash, and something nibbled noisily behind the wainscoting. He couldn't even offer her a decent night's rest. This place wasn't going to be liveable for ages, if he could find anyone willing to work where ghosts supposedly roamed the halls.

The souls of the dead monks were said to stir at the death of a Shearingham or a disaster befalling the household. Most likely the old shades were celebrating the misfortune of their nemesis, for it had been a Shearingham who razed their monastery and claimed the surrounding fertile lands. Presumably the steady decline in the St. Sevrin fortunes gave the ghosts many an opportunity to rejoice in the halls and attics of the rebuilt manor, and gave the local Devonshire population many a cold shiver. Sloane remembered his father tossing in a losing hand and calling it another merry monk. He wondered now if Lisanne would hear the wind howling through the cracks and crannies, and think the monks were abroad, proving this day another disaster.

No, she'd said she didn't believe in ghosts. She believed in—St. Sevrin would not think about that now. He poured himself another glass of brandy and contemplated the number of panes of glass the Priory would be needing. He finally had the money to fix the windows and seal all the drafts, to put on a new roof to stop the leaks. He would have the blunt as soon as he got to London and completed the arrangements with Mr. Mackensie.

The expense was going to be enormous, Sloane knew, and the effort even greater. There were priorities to be set, adjustments to be made. The land had to come first, but he was a soldier and a gambler, not a farmer. How the hell was he to make the right decisions? St. Sevrin did not intend to go through the Neville treasury without making sure he'd get a return on his investment, enough to repay Lisanne. It might take forever, but he'd die trying to give back her riches rather than go to his grave a fortune hunter. What the deuce was he giving her right now?

Those blasted woods, that's what. St. Sevrin carried his glass over to the window where he'd first seen Lisanne appear like a mist from the woods. Her woods now, where she could study nature's secret remedies to her heart's content. It was an odd interest for a young woman, extraordinary actually, but a rationale his mind could accept.

He stared out, almost knowing what he would see if he waited long enough. Yes, there she was, looking like a ghost indeed in flowing white robes with her pale hair streaming behind, crossing the lawn. She was going to the woods in the middle of the night rather than sleep in his house, in his bed. A dark shadow at her side meant that Becka was with her, keeping Lisanne safer than he could. Hell, Sloane had missed the path back from Neville House this afternoon and wandered for an hour before he found himself back at his starting point, having to ride all the way around by way of the road.

No, Sloane wouldn't go chasing after his wife or make a cake of himself by getting lost in his own home woods. If she'd wanted company, she knew where he was.

But the duke didn't know where she was, not really. No scientific investigations took place at night in a dark forest. Was Lisanne in the woods or in a world of her own creating, as her uncle had implied? What was she, this wife, this duchess, this fairy child?

She'd wanted the woods, and he'd given them to her. Had he done the right thing, right for her? Lud, he didn't know. Lisanne didn't want parties and gowns, jewels or foreign travel, nothing he could buy for her with her own money. If there was anything she did crave, she could purchase it herself now that he'd granted her control of her own funds. There was, however, one other thing he could give to make her happy: his absence. St. Sevrin had seen the fear in his wife's eyes, fear of him. No female should fear the man sworn to protect her. He could save Lisanne that, at least.

He was afraid, too, afraid of what could happen to her away from the woods, out in his world. Sloane thought he now understood how a father must feel giving his beloved daughter away in marriage. But no girl could stay a child forever, and this lady was his wife, not his daughter. She was almost nineteen, St. Sevrin reminded himself, old enough to bear children.

Children. Two sons at least. His Grace rather thought he'd like a little golden-haired daughter also. But what if his children were born . . . odd? No, he might as well say the word to himself, here in the solitude of his empty house, where only the dead monks could laugh at another Shearingham's comeuppance. What if his heirs, his successors, his bid for immortality, were crazy, like their mother?

No, this duchess wasn't ready for children. Let her grow up, he thought, get used to being mistress of a household of her own. Let her find her way out of the woods.

St. Sevrin had all those papers to sign, business to transact, and bankers to meet in London anyway. He had to put a wedding notice in the newspapers. After he settled his own accounts, then he had to see about finding agricultural advisers and architects, workmen and wise investments. Mackensie would help—and Mackensie was in Town.

Kelly would stay on here, starting to organize things and looking after the duchess. St. Sevrin went over to the desk and pulled out a sheet of paper to begin a list of instructions. He felt better immediately, getting something done. This was more like it, rather than sitting around fretting. He wouldn't be gone all that long anyway, the duke rationalized to himself; and they both, he and Lisanne, needed time to come to terms with this marriage. It was going to be one hell of a honeymoon. The devil take it, it had been one hell of a wedding.

There was no sense going to bed, Sloane decided, especially not on Kelly's hard pallet. This wouldn't be the first time he'd stayed up all night, not by half. And he could fetch his things from the bedroom now while Lisanne was out, without having her panic at his presence in her chamber.

It was better this way, he told himself. He'd be gone before she returned to the house, unless the fairies decided to keep her this time.

Chapter Seventeen

Either his London business was more complicated than he thought, or St. Sevrin was more cowardly. Either way, he did not return in the sennight or so he promised Kelly, who got left in Devon.

"What, now that you're a duke, you figure an old batman ain't hoity-toity enough for your new consequence? I'll be handing in my resignation, then. Save you the bother of dismissing me."

"Stubble it, Kelly. I always was a duke, since selling out, anyway. Now I can finally afford to pay you what you're worth, if I get to Town and get the finances squared away." His Grace was still in the small parlor making lists when Kelly returned in the morning with Mary. The duke was packed and ready to go. "But I need to leave you in charge here now." He indicated the pages of directions and instructions, the foremost of which was to look after the duchess.

Whatever Kelly hadn't heard at the wedding and the magistrate's hearing, he'd gotten an earful of from Mary on the way back this morning. Kelly didn't truck with gossip, but his new mistress was a puzzle and a problem, that was for sure. And that dog of hers was a hound from hell. "I ain't no nanny," he complained.

"No, you're the only man I would trust with my life, or my wife."

"Why don't you take her with you, then, if you're so worried about the missus?"

"Because she doesn't wish to go, and she is not ready to be presented to the ton. You might have noticed my lady is not exactly rigged out in the height of fashion."

"Don't seem much of a duchess to me." Kelly remembered the bare feet.

"She was a baroness long before I was a duke. And she's bright. She'll figure it out. You just need to help her along with hiring servants and such to get a start on cleaning this place and the grounds. I wager there will be lines applying for positions as soon as the vicar eats breakfast. Your job is to make sure no one shows Her Grace any disrespect and that those slimy relatives of hers don't come around. I'll be returned before you know it, with your back pay and a bonus, old man, so quit your grousing. Furthermore, I'll lay you odds that you and Becka will be firm friends by then."

Kelly hoped His Grace didn't put any of his new cash on the bet, but he didn't say anything, just took up the pages of instructions again.

"Oh, and Kelly, that girl Mary who is to work here . . ."

"Yer Grace?"

"She's young and innocent. Hands off."

"Could say the same for yer lady, Yer Grace."

"And I married her, by George. I won't have you carrying on under my wife's roof."

"What, married one night and turning Reformer, are you? You never frowned at a little slap and tickle before."

"I wasn't head of a respectable household before, either. Mary's a comely lass, but it just won't do. Vicar's connections and all."

"Next you'll be telling me you won't be enjoying a

quick tumble or two whilst you're in London and I'm stuck here like one of the blasted monks."

"I'm telling you I mean to be more discreet." The duke tossed some coins in Kelly's direction. "Here's just about the last of my pocket money till I get to the bankers. Find yourself a wench who works on her back, not one who works in my house."

St. Sevrin had no trouble with the bankers or Mr. Mackensie. He was quick to send a draft for Kelly to open a household account in Devon to pay the new servants and keep Lisanne in comfort. Next the mortgages got paid, so he wasn't laying out interest on top of interest on his father's loans. Then he settled long-outstanding bills with various delighted tradesmen who'd written him off as a bad debt ages ago. It was an unusual and pleasant experience to be warmly welcomed by the merchants he visited to start the refurbishment of St. Sevrin House. Yes, being beforehand with the world had its definite advantages. Better vintages of wine, for one.

Sloane might awaken these mornings with his usual hangover, but he didn't suffer from the load of worry and guilt that had been weighing heavily on his shoulders—except when he thought of his duchess, that is. So he sent more money to Kelly, new books from Hatchard's he thought Lisanne might enjoy, trinkets, fabrics, and the most expensive French modiste he could convince to leave her own establishment and travel to Devon to outfit a duchess. Then he didn't feel so like her money-grubbing uncle when he thought of Lisanne. And he was pleased with the refurbished suite he was having decorated for her at the town house. The duchess's apartment was going to resemble a garden bower, no matter how many consultants he had to hire and fire.

That's what St. Sevrin told everyone to explain why his bride wasn't in Town with him, that he was preparing the house for her. The wedding notice had been in the papers the day after he arrived in London and questions were rife. She'd be coming once the Season was in full swing, the duke told his cousin Humbert, taking great satisfaction from the prig's deflated ambitions.

Aunt Hattie, his mother's half sister and the only blood relation he cared for, was not as easy to put off. Harriet, Lady Comstock, was a walking repository of genealogy and gossip. She wasn't happy with the match.

"The breeding's sound, even if Neville did marry beneath him, and the fortune is certainly welcome," Hattie acknowledged, "but the mother was delicate. No getting around it, she was sickly, and there are some deuced odd rumors going around about the chit. You'd do best to puff her off soon, let the tabbies see she's not got two heads or anything."

When Sloane explained how St. Sevrin House wasn't ready to receive its mistress, Lady Comstock snorted. "Then put her up at the Clarendon, boy. It doesn't look right, keeping her hidden away in Devon. What, is she platter-faced? You wouldn't be the first connoisseur to lower his sights to the pocketbook."

"Not at all. In fact, she's quite stunningly beautiful in a unique way." St. Sevrin found himself at a loss to explain what made Lisanne so different from other pretty chits. "She's a tiny bit of fluff, looks like she could fly away. And she's young. There's plenty of time to introduce her around."

"She's what? Eighteen, almost nineteen? I was married three years by my nineteenth birthday."

"Lisanne is a young eighteen," St. Sevrin admitted uncomfortably. "She has no Town bronze, no sophistication. No mother, don't you know."

"Hoydenish, eh?"

"Not precisely." He didn't elucidate, feeling disloyal to be discussing Lisanne this way.

Aunt Hattie had no such scruples. "Then what? Shy? Stupid? No, I cannot imagine you shackled to a mutton-head, no matter the purse. So what's wrong with the gel that you don't want to show her off? You need her on your arm if you hope to be received in polite Society again, you know."

The devil take polite Society. "She's neither tongue-tied nor bacon-brained. She just wouldn't know how to go on."

"That flibbertigibbet Findley woman couldn't teach a dog how to bark. And you're no better, you cawker, leaving the gel in the country. How do you expect the chit to take her place in the world if you don't show her?" She batted at him with her lorgnette. "Bah! I'll just have to go take her in hand myself. 'Twould be better done in the country, away from the wagging tongues. Time enough for the harpies to get their claws into your diamond after we've polished her up a bit."

Since this was precisely the result the duke had hoped for with this morning call, he left his aunt's house satisfied, promising to join her in Devon as soon as his business was concluded.

Some of his business was taking a bit longer than expected. With members of the Quality just now trickling back to Town for the Season, St. Sevrin was hard-pressed to find all the gentlemen who held his personal vouchers. When he did, he had to suffer their congratulations, ribald comments, and sly references to his well-filled pockets. It was only polite to accept their toasts and their invitations for a hand of whist or a round of piquet. Now that he didn't need the money, the duke's luck was in, but his patience was quickly wearing out. Members of White's could be stared down with a frosty St. Sevrin sneer; the denizens of the lesser haunts of the gambling set soon learned that the Duchess of St. Sevrin was not a topic for conversation, not if they wanted to finish the night with all their teeth.

* * *

The duke had left a sheaf of directions for his man Kelly, and a one-page note for his wife: *Enjoy yourself, Duchess.* How was she supposed to do that, when she was so busy?

He was right: maids and footmen and gardeners and stable hands started parading onto Priory grounds the same morning St. Sevrin had left. Some were Neville Hall retainers dismissed when the Findleys brought in their own staff. Lisanne recalled many of them and made them welcome. Others declared themselves to be previous employees of the Priory, let go without their back pay. A third group had no claim on the available positions except that they were poor and needed the work. Lisanne hired them all.

When Kelly protested, she insisted that there was certainly enough work for all of them. "But some is too old to do a day's labor, Yer Grace."

"Then they shall do half a day's labor. Or, if the older maids cannot help with the scrubbing, perhaps they can sew. And footmen who cannot repair shingles can polish the banisters. I am sure you can find jobs for everybody."

Kelly was sure they didn't need seven grooms, not when His Grace owned three horses, and one of them was in London with him. For that matter, the ex-soldier saw no need for a kennel master when the only canine on the premises slept in the master bedroom. But his instructions were clear: he was to make sure the duchess was happy. If she was happy filling the stables with a crippled goat and an ancient, abandoned peddler's pony, the kennels with baby birds fallen out of nests and sick rabbits, and the Priory itself with servants older than the dirt they were cleaning, he wasn't about to argue. It was her money.

And the money started coming in from London. Kelly opened a household account for Lisanne at the bank in Honiton, and a separate, personal one for the duchess's generous allowance plus her income from the Neville holdings.

With which the duchess hired more derelict dependents to trip over each other. She had them working on the servants' quarters first so they'd have somewhere decent to sleep, and the kitchens so they could have nourishing meals. The people from her parents' household remembered a sweet, sunny child. They were proud their lady was thinking just as she ought. The Priory workers had never known an employer to care a whit about the hired help. There was a lot of head-shaking. Those rumors must be true, that the new duchess was dicked in the nob. Her disappearing for hours into that patch of trees didn't sit easy, either, not once someone resurrected those old stories about haunted woods.

Then Neville Hall's previous housekeeper arrived from her daughter's overcrowded cottage and took over the chatelaine duties, to Kelly's temporary relief. She had the crews working in shifts, getting the walls, rugs, and furniture spotless until repairs and replacements could be ordered. Kelly had the gardeners and grounds people in military formations, stripping overgrown ivy off the stone walls, scything the lawns, reclaiming what was left of formal plantings.

Now Lisanne could turn her efforts to the Priory farmland, with Kelly trailing behind arguing that His Grace had left definite instructions concerning the hiring of a bailiff.

"Oh, the man arrived this morning while you were at the bank. He wanted to evict what tenant farmers still remain and turn the entire property into sheep pasturage. I dismissed him."

"You dismissed the duke's man?"

"He thought the home woods would offer good hunting."

"So you sacked him the same day he got here?" No one had ever disobeyed Kelly's master, not when he was a fresh lieutenant, not when he was a major, and absolutely not when he was a duke. "Oh, lud, His Grace'll have my head for sure."

"Nonsense. He'll see how much progress we've made." With the help of Neville Hall's steward, Lisanne found families willing to move into the abandoned farmsteads, and men to help make repairs so they'd be comfortable. She had Kelly order new seed drills from Taunton and plowshares from Manchester. She was knee-deep in mangel-wurzels and manure, when she wasn't writing away for the latest strain of wheat or inspecting farms for breeding stocks of sheep, cattle, and pigs. And there was a new crop of orphaned lambs and cows with swollen udders for her to tend.

Kelly had to admit Her Grace had an eye for livestock, but he didn't think farming was any more suitable an occupation for the duke's lady than captaining the mop brigade. Of course, it was better than the hours she spent trudging around in the woods with her dog and coming back to brew Zeus only knew what. With all the oldsters in the house, the duchess was constantly concocting remedies for chilblains and shingles, sore gums and inflamed joints. She even interrogated Kelly about the duke's troublesome war wounds and packed a bottle of salve for him to send on to London. No, it wasn't fitting at all, but what Kelly was supposed to do about it he couldn't begin to guess. From what he heard, no one had ever changed Lady Lisanne's mind about anything, though Findley had almost died trying.

The old retainers and the new tenants were all grateful to the duchess, and were all afraid of her. The Priory ghosts were as nothing to Lady St. Sevrin. The people didn't dare talk when Kelly might hear, but he knew. The hushed voices and the sideways looks told the tale. There was no disrespect, but there was a distance.

The only one Kelly could trust with his worries was Mary, who was as devoted to the duchess as the dog was.

Mary was waging her own campaign to get Lisanne to behave more in keeping with her—and Mary's—high estate. She started by burning the dresses sent over from Neville Hall.

"Spotted and stained every one, I tell you, Mr. Kelly. Why, I wouldn't wear such a thing to clean the vicar's cellars. It's no wonder these ninnies whisper about our lady when we ain't looking. So I fixed them. Set some of the old maids, them as can still see good enough, to altering some gowns we found in one of the closets. His Grace's mother's, maybe."

Kelly sighed over the tea the two were enjoying in the butler's pantry. Since Kelly was doing that job, he felt entitled to that privacy. There was a bit of the bottle in his tea, none in Mary's. Kelly sighed again over lost opportunities. "No matter, Her Grace'll just get them new gowns soiled. I never seen such a one for mucking about."

Mary took offense at the slur to her mistress. "Lots of high-born ladies garden. Don't they have them fancy rose societies?"

"When ladies of Quality grow their own flowers, they have three gardeners to do the dirty work. And they wear gloves to keep their hands smooth and hats to keep the sun off their faces and smocks to protect their gowns."

So Mary set the old maids to making smocks out of old bed ticking and sheets. And she made sure her lady was wearing gloves when she left the house. The duchess usually came back with the gloves in her pocket, along with sundry other items Mary was reluctant to handle, but at least the altered gowns stayed fairly neat. No afternoon caller, tenant farmer, or tradesman was going to mistake the duchess for one of her own scullery maids.

"I'll work on hats next week."

Kelly poured some of his brandy into Mary's teacup. "You'll need this."

Then parcels and packages started arriving daily from His Grace in London. He was detained on business, he wrote, but meantime he sent bonnets and shawls and slippers that had Mary in alt, and books—Miss Austen's novels, Scott's romantic tales, Wordsworth's poetry—that had Lisanne staying up half the night in the library after she was finished with the day's accounts.

Next to arrive was a French dressmaker with enough yard goods to guarantee the aged seamstresses sinecures for life. Lisanne couldn't have cared less about her new wardrobe. She refused to be fitted, in fact, or make decisions about colors, styles, or trims, but the modiste had her orders and her deposit. The Duchess of St. Sevrin was going to be dressed like a lady, even if she persisted in rambling around the countryside like a Gypsy.

And then the duke sent his aunt. Lisanne wanted a new mule for the plows. Lady Comstock came close.

Chapter Eighteen

"*A*nd what time do we take dinner, my dear?" Aunt Hattie, as she told Lisanne to call her, was standing in the Priory hall amid bags and boxes and an army of servants.

"Dinner?" Lisanne blinked. She was used to asking for a tray at whatever hour she came in from the fields or the woods, or wandering to the kitchen and helping herself and Becka to whatever she found. The habit would have wreaked havoc in any respectable kitchen, with the staff never knowing when or what the mistress would be wanting, but the duchess hardly ate enough to keep a bird alive. In fact, had Cook known it, most of her breads and rolls and cakes did just that—go to keep the birds alive. If a particular cut of beef or a slab of mutton went missing from the servants' own meal, no one was going to argue with the big dog over it. There was enough to go around, thank heaven and marriages of convenience.

Such slipshod scheduling was not at all *convenable* for a duke's household. Or a duke's aunt. "Yes, my dear, dinner. I prefer Town hours, of course, but I would understand if you'd like to dine earlier, shall we say seven? That way we have a lovely evening to become better acquainted and catch up on our needlework. Perhaps play a hand of cards or read aloud. Then there's music. So soothing to the digestion, I find. You do play, don't you, my dear? That's when we don't have company, of course. I haven't seen Mrs. Squire Pemberton in ages, I swear."

Lisanne was inching toward the door. She and Becka could live in the woods, or in that derelict cottage no one wanted. Then two of the footmen carried in a large portrait in a heavy gilt frame. The painted gentleman was in wig and satin breeches, and held a bust of Homer. The footmen set the picture down, awaiting instructions.

"Ah, Lionel, there you are."

"I'm sorry, Lady Comstock, ah, Aunt Hattie, but that's James, and this is Harry."

"No, not the footmen, dear, the portrait." Lady Comstock whipped a scrap of lace out of her black crepe sleeve and dabbed at her eyes. "I keep dear Lord Comstock's portrait with me so that I don't feel so alone. Dear Lionel was lofted above ten years ago."

He'd gone in a hot air balloon? Lisanne didn't have time to ask the question, for Lady Comstock was making the introductions. "Lionel, dear, this is our new niece, St. Sevrin's duchess."

Gracious, Lisanne thought, the lady was as balmy as . . . as she herself was supposed to be. No wonder Sloane had sent the poor unfortunate widow to Devon for a repairing lease. Lady Comstock was the duke's aunt, and this was the duke's house. His wife could do no less than show proper courtesy. The poor thing likely had no one to talk to except a picture of her deceased husband. Besides, perhaps she was as below hatches as the rest of the duke's connections and had nowhere else to go. "Did you say you preferred to dine at seven, my—Aunt Hattie? I'll just go notify Cook. There is much for me to be doing about the estate, but I shall be pleased to keep you company in the evenings."

Lady Comstock went upstairs behind the housekeeper, satisfied for now. The girl was as beautiful as St. Sevrin had claimed. Those big blue eyes alone could have made her fortune if she didn't already possess one, but Hattie couldn't decide if they were full of innocence or wisdom. The chit was decidedly not the standard milk-and-water miss. And that hair was impossible, of course, and the browned skin. The pastel gown was all wrong, too, over-fussy for such a little dab of a thing. No, the gel wasn't ready for London, aside from the fact that she had the social graces of a newborn chick.

Luckily Hattie had planned on spending a month or so with the girl, getting her in shape before her jackanapes of a nephew arrived to take over. Meantime Lady Comstock could have a lovely time with St. Sevrin's carte blanche at Ackerman's Repository, helping the duchess order new furnishings for the Priory. There was nothing Hattie liked so much as spending other people's money, unless it was ordering other people's lives.

She had the footmen put Lionel's portrait over the mantel in a clean but shabby bedchamber, right where she could see him every day, and rejoice that the dastard was dead and she was alive to enjoy his wealth. "And no," she told him, not for the first time, "that bust of Homer doesn't make you look one groat smarter, you old nincompoop."

The campaign began. Lisanne knew she was being manipulated, but didn't have the heart to disappoint the duke's unfortunate relict. If Lady Comstock was content to play with fabric swatches and furniture patterns all day while the duchess accomplished something worthwhile, Lisanne couldn't mind approving the choices or giving an opinion when she had one. "I like light colors better than dark," she offered. "And florals rather than stripes."

She knew Aunt Hattie was also busy with the French dressmaker, for the gowns Mary now laid out for her in the evenings were of brighter, prettier colors and simpler styles. Mary was learning from Lady Comstock's fancy dresser, too, for she begged to try new hairdos on her mistress. "Just for the practice, like." Some of them even stayed up through dinner.

And bonnets. With Lady Comstock trimming the chip straw herself after dinner—a favorite hobby of hers, she declared—Lisanne could not refuse to wear them. The silk flowers sewn to the brims were rather pretty, and they did keep the sun out of her eyes now that the weather was getting nicer and nicer. Best of all, the hats were the perfect size for transporting the nests of field mice disturbed by the plows.

Even company dinners were not so terrible. Squire Pemberton was always ready to debate the classics, while his wife enjoyed Aunt Hattie's Town gossip. Mrs. Squire Pemberton finally even stopped looking over her shoulder for the Priory ghosts. Lisanne didn't mention Lord Comstock upstairs in his wife's bedchamber, and her guests never mentioned Sevrin Woods. The vicar was eager to discuss Lisanne's plans for a new school, now that she had the poorhouse almost empty, and he didn't mind taking up a hand of whist, either. Everyone learned to ignore what Lisanne ate, or didn't, after the time Aunt Hattie asked why she wasn't eating the superb beef Bourguignonne Cook had prepared for the guests. Lisanne's reply, that it was Spotted George on the platter, cost everyone their appetites. No one asked again.

There weren't many return invitations, which aggravated the normally active Lady Comstock to no end. Not even Devon could be this dull. Hattie was giving up the London Season, for heaven's sake; she didn't mean to

153

give up all social entertainments. And how was the chit going to learn how to go on if she never got out? It was Mary who heard through her mum at the vicarage, who heard everything, that there were no big parties, period. None of the better families were throwing lawn picnics or country balls, because no one wanted to have the duke's relatives under the same roof as the duchess's relatives, not after hearing how St. Sevrin had threatened Sir Alfred.

So Lady Comstock decided to get rid of the Findleys. They were sponging on Lisanne's generosity, after all. She called on Cherise Findley while the duchess was overseeing a ditch-draining or something equally as disgusting—but in a hat.

Lady Comstock's mission didn't take the twenty minutes assigned for a morning call. Lady Findley wasn't half done complaining about her ills when Aunt Hattie suggested a sojourn to Brighton. Sea bathing was relaxing for the nerves, she advised, and might even clear up Esmé's complexion. Personally she would have taken the bonbons away from that plump little peagoose, but that was none of Lady Comstock's concern. Getting these mushrooms out of Devon was.

The prince might be in Brighton soon, she emphasized, and all the truly fashionable members of the ton would summer there. Just the place to begin introducing a young deb. Lady Comstock even offered to write some letters of introduction, smoothing the chit's way. Or the Findleys could stay on here at Neville Hall, Hattie allowed, inspecting her manicure. Of course they expected the duke back anyday now. . . .

The Findleys were gone by the end of the week, their servants with them since Sir Alfred wasn't about to pay the staff for a summer vacation. Aunt Hattie sent a box of bonbons to enliven their journey. Then she sent to Neville Hall all the superannuated servants Lisanne insisted on keeping on her payroll. The place needed a caretaking staff, she explained, and Lisanne was satisfied the people were given healthy, productive lives. Lady Comstock was satisfied that the Priory was at last beginning to look like a gentleman's residence, not a retirement home for domestic help.

Things were going so swimmingly, in fact, that Kelly decided to travel up to London and see what was keeping His Grace. With that battle-ax aunt of the duke's in charge, Kelly hadn't had a bout of dyspepsia in weeks. He also hadn't had a night on the Town. The senior footman was promoted to butler.

Kelly left and he didn't come back, either, to Lady Comstock's consternation. Lisanne didn't seem to notice as spring changed to summer, and there were plants to tend and crops to watch, but Aunt Hattie fretted over her nephew's long stay in Town, away from his bride. Letters availed Hattie nothing, for the dratted boy sent money, not answers. And Lisanne never mentioned his name.

Hattie was beginning to get a bad feeling about this marriage. She loved the girl as a daughter by now . . . no, as a niece. No daughter of hers would be caught dead at a sheepshearing. Lisanne stood by with a salve, in case the sheep got nicked. His Grace wasn't to know, but it was the same salve she'd sent for his wound. Then again, she wasn't to know that he'd used it on his new stallion's scraped leg. Communication between the two, now that Kelly was gone, was nil, which pleased Lady Comstock even less. Lisanne could be the redemption of her wild nephew, and Sloane could keep the girl from getting lost in her books and botanicals—if they ever spoke to each other.

Lisanne was as ready for London as she'd ever be, Aunt Hattie felt. Whether London was ready for such an original remained to be seen, but with her contacts and connections Hattie would see the little duchess creditably established. The job would be easier with the Season winding down and everyone leaving Town for country house parties and seaside resorts. St. Sevrin's bride would be a nine days' wonder this year, and be just another eccentric aristocrat by next fall's Little Season. The problem was, of course, that Lisanne refused to leave Devon.

By now Lisanne knew Lady Comstock was no grieving widow. She also knew that Hattie kept Lord Comstock's portrait nearby just to aggravate the man if he was listening, as much as Lionel's nip-farthing ways had aggravated Hattie during their marriage. The duke's aunt kept to her widow's weeds because they were a perfect foil to her silver hair and the Comstock diamonds, not because she was in perpetual mourning. Her blacks were elegant, expensive, and fashionable silks and lace. No dreary black bombazine for this widow.

Lisanne quickly realized that St. Sevrin's aunt wasn't in Devon on any repairing lease, either. She was ruralizing because it suited her managing ways to refurbish a huge manor house and rearrange Lisanne's life. By the vast correspondence Lady Comstock sent and received, she was no humble relict of some minor lord; Mathilda Comstock was a force to be reckoned with among the *belle monde*, knowing everyone and everything that went on among the Upper Ten Thousand.

Lisanne had been well and truly diddled, but she didn't mind. In fact, she respected the older woman's family loyalty. Lady Comstock was only doing her best to make Lisanne an acceptable member of the duke's world. It was an impossible task, of course, but most likely Aunt Hattie had a long list of instructions from the duke, too.

Because of her fondness for the lady, Lisanne did not take offense when Aunt Hattie complained yet again that St. Sevrin hadn't returned from London, and that Lisanne refused to accompany her to go find him.

"If you have some place else to go, ma'am, please

don't feel you have to stay on my account. I know you're missing the opera and theater and all the balls. I have my work here."

"You have no proper companion here if I leave. And your place is at your husband's side."

"Why, no, ma'am. The duke and I agreed that we wouldn't hang on each other's sleeves."

"Well, I do not approve of these modern marriages when the husband and wife go their separate ways as soon as the heir is born."

"Neither do I. We need two heirs."

"Don't be pert, girl. And if you and my nephew are so agreed that you require two sons, the wretch should be here seeing about the successions, unless you're already breeding." She ended this last on a hopeful note, which Lisanne had to disappoint.

"Then, by all that's holy, what is keeping that clunch in London?"

"Why, I suppose all the entertainments you've been so eager to tell me about, to lure me there. St. Sevrin loves London, ma'am. It's his way of life. He wouldn't be happy in the country. I do not look for him anytime soon."

"Fustian. He hates London and all the shallow posturing that goes on. He's chided me often enough for being a vain, silly creature who only cares for gowns and gossip. He couldn't wait to buy his colors and be gone off soldiering."

"That was in his younger days. He seems to have adapted recently."

"What, by cutting a swathe through the *demi monde*? What else was he to do, with no future, no occupation? That's why he drinks and gambles to excess, just for something to do."

"Well, there's plenty for him to do here. Do you think St. Sevrin is any good at baling hay? Painting the barn? Darning the tapestries?" Lisanne held up her corner of the hanging currently under repair, trying to keep the hurt from her voice. If he disliked London so much, but stayed there anyway, it could only mean he disliked his wife in Devon even more. "No, he won't come."

Chapter Nineteen

St. Sevrin was ready to go home. He'd paid his debts and worked out his investments so they were already returning a profit. He wouldn't have to dip so deeply into the Neville capital for the rest of the major improvements needed at the Priory.

And after a month or two—almost three, he admitted to himself—of Aunt Hattie's company, even his ugly phiz should look good to his bride. If he knew his aunt, Lisanne had the benefits of the best finishing school in the country without ever leaving Devon. The old Tartar's wily ways, sharp tongue, and encyclopedic knowledge of the upper class would have the young duchess up to snuff by now. He wouldn't be returning to that odd, appealing little waif.

In a way St. Sevrin was sorry. Such a child of nature shouldn't be forced into a prunes-and-prisms world. He shrugged and sipped his wine. No one said life was fair.

Aunt Hattie hadn't said the girl was mad. Different, an original, refreshing, yes. Mad, no. Of course the breeze blowing through Hattie's upper story was so strong she mightn't recognize windmills in anyone else's attics.

Trying to disturb Uncle Lionel's eternal rest by toting his portrait around was barmy enough.

No matter, if there was a hint of lunacy, Hattie's frequent letters wouldn't be urging Sloane to return to the Priory to start setting up his nursery. She cared too much about the *haut monde*'s opinion to try to foist moonlings into their midst.

So Sloane was ready to go do his duty for God, King, and country. The marriage would be consummated.

Then Kelly came to Town. On vacation, he said, not supplanting the man St. Sevrin had valeting him, nor the butler who almost slammed the door in the grizzled veteran's face. He needed a holiday, Kelly declared, after chasing after the duchess for all those weeks. " 'Twere like trying to catch a butterfly on horseback, without a net or a saddle." He was ready to rejoin the regiment, Kelly told his employer reproachfully, unless His Grace was relieving him of guard duty.

"What, that little thing running you ragged? Maybe you better think of retiring altogether, Kelly. Lady Comstock writes she's got the chit in hand, so you couldn't have much to do."

Kelly helped himself to a glass of wine. "That's as may be, but Lady Comstock only sees Her Grace for a few hours at night. I'm trailing after her all day, when I can keep up. This farm, that field, a sickly calf here, a mildewed row there. It's more'n a body can bear, never sitting still less'n she's at the accounts or in the library."

"But she has no business doing anything but her embroidery and flower gardening. That's why I hired a new bailiff."

"I wrote you, Her Grace didn't like the man."

"So she didn't like him. I—" St. Sevrin tossed back the contents of his glass. "My God, she fired him, didn't she? Who the hell is running the place and making the improvements I requested? Did spring crops even get planted?" There went his hopes of keeping the Priory self-sufficient and solvent. Another chunk of investment money would have to be withdrawn to meet expenses.

"Now, I told you everything is aces, Yer Grace. I wouldn't of left, otherwise. Her Grace has everything in hand. Them cottages are all repaired, with good families moving in to work the farms, that stream's been rerouted so the bottom land don't flood, new breeding herds are getting fat, and the school is half finished." Kelly scratched his head. "Did I write you about the school? Not much for letters, don't you know."

"I'd never have guessed," the duke answered dryly. "But Lady Lisanne can't be running the estate. Those old tenant farmers won't accept a woman in charge, especially not one who's—"

"They don't like it, but they listen. When she picks up a handful of dirt and tells them how much manure to put in the field, how much lime and how much ashes, they listen. And if she says they should plant wheat here and corn there and turnips in the lower acre, they do it. They know your man wanted to throw them all off the land and turn it over to sheepherding."

"What, get rid of the farms? They've been there since the monks had the Priory. And what about the dairy cows? The Priory used to make a profit on the milk."

"That's what Her Grace said, before giving the new bailiff his walking papers."

"And you say she's doing all right?"

"Better'n all right, I'd guess. Everyone's saying it'll be the best harvest in memory if the weather holds."

St. Sevrin poured out another glass of wine for himself and one for Kelly. Here he'd been spending hours poring over the agricultural journals, trying to learn a lifetime of responsible landlording in a month. He'd been corresponding with Coke about new methods and visiting the patent office for new tools. He was cluttering up his mind with boring claptrap, stuff his lady wife knew by instinct, or whatever.

The Priory didn't need his sad lack of expertise. It had the baroness. The baroness's money. The baroness's skills. He may as well stay in London.

The Priory mightn't need St. Sevrin's help, but he found someone who did. A roistering night at Horse Guards with old Army comrades ended with a sobering message from the Peninsula. The sketchy information reported a devastating battle near Formieva, with many British deaths and casualties. Hardest hit was St. Sevrin's old regiment, which had valiantly held the line under Lieutenant Trevor Roe after the commanding officers had fallen. Lieutenant Roe was not expected to survive the loss of his leg.

If he was being treated in the field hospital, he didn't stand a chance. Sloane had enough experience to know the surgeons killed more soldiers than they saved. And any who did manage to recover from the savage amputations and bullet extractions were prey to blood poisoning from the filthy conditions and fevers from the infections. Then they had to face the weather-wracked hospital ships, when the generals chose to dispatch them, and the epidemic influenzas and dysentery. Major Lord Shearingham had gone through it all.

Trevor Roe wasn't going to. They'd been friends since school days and had signed up together. Trev had been the one to pull Sloane out from under his horse after he'd gone down from the saber slash that opened his chest and side. Trev had dragged him off the field, dodging bullets and flying hooves, stuffing his own uniform jacket into the wound to stop the bleeding.

No, St. Sevrin wasn't going to let his friend die in some stinking, fly-infested field hospital. He went to the docks to hire a yacht while Kelly purchased bandages, medicines, sheets, and blankets. None of the suitable craft were for lease, so the duke bought one, crew and all. This he could do. He went home to gather his own bags—and that jar of Lisanne's salve he'd been using on his stallion's cut leg. It worked for the horse.

It worked for Lieutenant Roe, and the three other wounded officers St. Sevrin managed to cram aboard his new vessel. Being warm and dry and tended around the clock with cooling drinks and nourishing broths had to speed their recovery also. Just being away from the contagion-ridden wards saved them from exposure to all manner of pestilences.

Lieutenant Roe's family was renting a place near Brighton for the summer, so St. Sevrin had his crew sail straight there. The Viscount Roehampton was so grateful to Sloane for bringing his son home that he insisted St. Sevrin stay on. He even invited the other wounded lads to recuperate in Brighton's healthful atmosphere, too, while Trevor finished his convalescence under his mother's loving care. Unfortunately the Viscountess Roehampton cried every time she looked at her son's crutches. Nor was she quite comfortable having five grown bachelors roistering under her roof, with the worst-reputed of them, St. Sevrin, being hale and hearty and a social pariah.

The other officers quickly removed to their own families or to the barracks in London. St. Sevrin was itching to leave, but Lord Roehampton, at his wife's urging, decided to put a flea in Prinny's ear about the duke's noble generosity. And his abysmal reputation.

As a result, St. Sevrin was to be awarded a medal for service to the Crown at one of the prince's extravagant, interminable dinners at his Oriental pavilion. Sloane couldn't insult the monarchy by leaving beforetimes, and he couldn't insult Trevor's father by expressing his wish that the Regent had seen fit to spend the nation's wealth on its loyal troops rather than on its overfed aristocrats. Bloody hell, he thought, a medal.

A medal wasn't enough for the prince. He wanted St. Sevrin to take his rightful place in decent Society. It was time the duke gave up his wicked ways, demanded one of the most debauched rulers in British history. The drinking, gambling, whoring—all of which the Regent practiced daily—had to stop, at least until St. Sevrin was respectable enough for the queen's drawing room. To attain such respectability, Prinny declared, St. Sevrin needed a wife. And not just any man's wife, he tittered in his latest mistress's married ear, but the Duchess of St. Sevrin herself. Prinny expected to meet the duke's bride at the fall Season. Country girl or not, she was a baron's daughter and could thus redeem the duke's reputation.

"If she doesn't pull a toad out of her pocket," Sloane muttered between clenched jaws as he bowed himself out of the royal presence.

"Well, what have you got against bringing her to London, anyway?" Trevor wanted to know when St. Sevrin arrived home in an ugly mood that hadn't been improved by enough bottles of ale to float an armada of grievances. Kelly's grin wasn't helping much, either, as he brushed off His Grace's formal attire.

"She doesn't want to come, that's why."

"So what? Hell, she's your wife. She has to."

Kelly laughed.

"You haven't met Lisanne."

"No, but I'd like to. Want to thank her for that stuff she sent with you. It helped a lot. Doctor here said it was one of the cleanest wounds he'd seen, fastest healing, too. Now all I have is pain in the leg I don't have. It's phantom pain, he says. Only imaginary."

"Then you'll really like my wife."

This time Kelly cleared his throat.

"Oh, hell, it doesn't matter. Prinny was three sheets to the wind himself. He won't remember."

But St. Sevrin's cousin Humbert remembered. He'd also been in Brighton, hanging on the prince's coattails. By chance or by design, he'd managed to meet Esmé and

164

Nigel Findley, who usually traveled in very different social circles. Lisanne's relatives were delighted to meet one of the prince's cronies; Humbert was delighted to hear about his new cousin by marriage. He was even more pleased to pass on what his groom heard from Esmé's maid.

The fall Season started with rumors flying about how Prinny was insisting St. Sevrin produce his bride, and how the duke was refusing because she was freakish. The prince wasn't happy, and the duke wasn't happy.

"Bloody hell. I should have run that bastard through ages ago."

"Which bastard?"

"Findley. Nigel. Humbert. Prinny. All of them."

Trevor looked over his shoulder to make sure no one in this alehouse heard his friend call the Prince of Wales a bastard or threaten his life. Then again, the tavern was such a low dive that half of its patrons were illegitimate. The other half would have killed their own mothers for the price of a bottle of Blue Ruin, much less the frivolous prince.

Sloane and Trevor were in London because Lieutenant Roe had been miserable in the bosom of his family. Their pity was smothering him, and his father's offer of an allowance was demeaning. He was a grown man, not a boy. He wasn't even the heir, just a second-rate second son. Trevor was depressed about his lost leg, his shattered career, and his bleak future. Even Whitehall, his last hope, had turned him down for a desk job. There were already too many crippled officers on the payroll.

That's why the two ex-soldiers were in an alehouse: so Trevor could drink himself into oblivion.

They were in *this* rat hole of a pub because St. Sevrin couldn't let his friend drink alone and the duke was playing least in sight. He and Trevor were staying at St. Sevrin House, which was looking more elegant every day under Kelly's supervision. The two friends were looking more seedy and degenerate every night. At least in this part of town St. Sevrin wouldn't be forced to defend his lady's name with his fists.

Thunderation, her name was mentioned in the betting books. St. Sevrin had never cared what anyone said about him, but Lisanne was his wife, by Jupiter! There were too many wagging tongues for Sloane to challenge, so he just let fly at the first man he saw smirking or simpering about the duke's fairy-tale match. His temper had seen him thrown out of White's and Watier's and Brooks's. The prince's disfavor, encouraged by Humbert, would keep him out. On the plus side, his left punch was getting stronger.

On the negative side, Trevor had started issuing challenges right and left in defense of the duchess. "Can't fence, but I can still shoot straight." He couldn't even see straight, but that hadn't stopped Lieutenant Roe. "M'best friend's wife, don't you know," he slurred. "M'hostess. M'benefactress, 'cause it was her blunt that brought me home so cozily."

So St. Sevrin landed Trevor a hard right to the jaw and carried him unconscious out of the Cocoa Tree to a hackney carriage, and to this gin mill the jarvey recommended.

Sloane pounded his bottle on the sticky, stained table. "It's a damnable situation."

"Right, when a man can't leave his wife in the country when he wants."

"No, not that situation. This one." St. Sevrin waved his hand around the dingy, smoke-filled room. "Here I am, a rich man finally, and I can't even drink in a decent club where the customers bathe occasionally."

"Uh, Sherry, I don't think it was a good idea to mention you were well-heeled. Not in a place like this."

Luckily Trevor was handy with his crutches, and St. Sevrin had his pistol.

Confound it, this couldn't go on. Sloane could turn

tail and drag himself and Trevor off to Devon, but he wouldn't give Humbert and the Findleys the satisfaction. He hadn't backed down from a challenge yet. Furthermore, if he left he'd never be able to return, not while Prinny was Regent . . . or King. There was nothing for it but to send for the infuriating chit and hope for the best: hope she came, and hope she was wearing shoes.

Besides, they were all out of that salve.

Chapter Twenty

*T*he duchess didn't answer St. Sevrin's summons to present herself in London. His aunt did, in person.

Lady Comstock marched right past the new butler, right past the new valet, and into her nephew's new bedchamber, where he was nursing a hangover, which was nothing new.

"You look like you've been run over by a hay wagon," she began, pulling back the drapes to flood the room with morning light.

"Several, thank you, Aunt Hattie," Sloane corrected, wincing at the glare but dutifully reaching for his dressing gown. There would be no going back to sleep this morning. He opened the door and bellowed for coffee. And tea for the lady, he shouted as an afterthought. He came back and sat in the chair across from his aunt. "Where's my wife?"

"Oh, so you remember you have a wife, do you?"

Sloane got up, went back to the door, and shouted for a bottle of brandy. He didn't reply until after the servants had left. "Now, Aunt Hattie, you know very well that I recall my wife. Didn't I send her that fan from Brighton? And what about the fancy lace headpiece from Portugal?

I wrote and told you I was going to the Peninsula to fetch Trev, I know I did."

Hattie raised her lorgnette at how much brandy was in his cup, how little coffee. "You think that's enough? A trinket? A footnote to your letters? How did you get to be such a fool?"

"I believe I was born that way, Aunt. You know, male. So where is my bride, at your house? She's in a pet over my lack of attention, is that it? Very well, I'll go beg her pardon."

"You don't know the girl at all, do you?" His aunt shook her head. "More's the pity." She made him wait while she buttered a scone, the sight of which did nothing for St. Sevrin's roiling stomach. "No, she's not at my house. She's not even at your house in Devon. She's gone home to Neville Hall to live in her own house, alone except for a parcel of old servants. She left one of the tenants' sons as overseer at the Priory and disappeared with her dog and her maid. She won't receive visitors or answer letters."

"Why the devil did she do a thing like that?"

"Not because the place held happy memories, from what I've gathered. No, somehow the child has got it in her head that you won't come home while she is at the Priory. Since you haven't yet—"

"Dash it, I've been busy. Bankers, solicitors, then helping Trevor get around."

"—Lisanne is convinced that she is keeping you here in London with her presence in Devon. If you don't have to deal with her in Devon, she's decided, then you'll leave this sinkhole of depravity. She feels responsible for your absence and even more responsible for your further slide into degradation." Lady Comstock fixed the duke with a gimlet stare, taking note of the bloodshot eyes and the bruises.

"That's absurd." It wasn't, of course. It was damn near the truth, that Sloane was running from his bride and running amok defending her name, but that was none of Aunt Hattie's business. Or Lisanne's. "I'd like to know how in tarnation she heard anything about my 'further slide.' You wouldn't know anything about that, would you?" She knew everything else, with her network of letter-writing spies.

"What, do you think I would tell that sweet child that her husband is throwing drunken tantrums in the men's clubs because some chowderhead teases him over his wife's idiosyncrasies?"

"Tantrums? Teases? Idiosyncrasies? Madame, you certainly have a way with words. So what did you tell her?"

"I didn't have to tell her anything, you clunch. Your name is in every scandal sheet and gossip column. She can read, you jackass. And what tidbits Lisanne might have missed that harebrained cousin of hers makes sure to write. The little Findley twit thinks she's doing the duchess a favor, in exchange for having her Season at Neville House. So, yes, your wife knows all about your brawls and your binges. She is as well informed of Prinny's edicts as she is of the betting books at White's. And she knows every rumor making the rounds."

"Then why the deuce doesn't she come to London and disprove them all? That's why I sent for her, you know."

"Because she believes you wouldn't have done so unless your hand was forced. Lisanne thinks you don't want her here, that you're afraid she'll shame you worse. I think *she's* afraid of that, too."

"And will she? Will she make me an even bigger fool than I am now?"

"How could you ask that? You have to know she's intelligent and caring. You said yourself she was beautiful. Good heavens, boy, if you truly dislike her, by all that's holy, why did you marry her in the first place?"

Because of her eyes. Because she needed him to keep her safe. Because she wanted something so badly she was willing to bargain with the devil to get it. Sloane wiped his mouth with the napkin. "For the money, of course. That's what everyone is saying, isn't it?"

"Gammon. Everyone knows you were dished, but you could have found some cit's daughter to trade for your title ages ago if that's what you wanted."

"Ah, but I didn't . . . until things got so bad I had no choice. By then, of course, my reputation was so black no merchant banker would let me through the door. Lisanne Neville was the only heiress crazy enough to marry me."

Lady Comstock stood up and slapped him.

St. Sevrin wasn't in the mood for a long, boring carriage ride with its tolls and grooms and changes to inferior cattle. So he rode the roan stallion into Devon. The horse was the meanest brute St. Sevrin had ever owned, but had the strength to go forever on little rest. Sloane called him Diablo, Devil. The roan's previous owner hadn't called him anything intelligible, not with his jaw broken from a flying hoof. Not surprisingly, the duke had gotten a good price. He hoped to use the beast for breeding someday, if Diablo didn't kill him first.

The stallion took a bite out of the arm of an ostler in Reading, and kicked in his stall in Wincanton. There were two more places St. Sevrin wouldn't be welcomed to visit again, two more drafts on his bank.

At least Diablo wasn't boring, not by half. The manhater tried to unseat St. Sevrin every time the duke's thoughts wandered and his hands relaxed on the reins, which was often, with everything on St. Sevrin's mind. Most times Sloane stayed aboard, sometimes he didn't, but he always managed to hang onto the reins and not get trampled. By the time they reached Devon, the duke was bent and bruised. He was not defeated, however, which he considered good practice for the coming battle with his wife.

Lisanne *was* coming with him to London. He'd had

enough of this nonsense. So she had doubts. Everyone did. It made no never mind. They were married, by George, and by her own wishes.

St. Sevrin reached the Priory in late afternoon, in time to be awed at the difference in the old place. The drive was smooth and rut-free, and the grounds finally resembled lawns, not fields of grass and weeds. An army of gardeners was pruning hedges and trimming flower beds that were bouquets of vibrant colors.

A groom ran out to take his horse, then whistled up three more stable hands after St. Sevrin's warning and Diablo's flattened ears. They'd do. The duke turned his attention to the Priory itself. Every windowpane on the four-story building was in place and gleaming in the late-day sun. No ivy grew over the scrubbed brick facing, and fresh slates appeared on the roof. The ancient pile had never looked this good, not in Sloane's lifetime, not in his father's or grandfather's, either, he'd wager.

The front door opened before he could reach it, and a dignified, deferential butler bowed him inside. A nearby footman stepped forward to take his saddlebags. Another went to notify Cook, a third to order his bath.

My word, the duke wondered, was this the same place? The wood paneling shone, almost reflecting the patterns of the brilliant rugs on the floor. There were exquisite antique furnishings wherever he looked, even paintings on the walls. Good taste had failed in this one instance, for someone had managed to unearth or buy back the Shearingham ancestors' portraits. It was a waste of blunt, Sloane considered, for there was not an admirable one in the bunch, but it was a nice thought. The vases of flowers everywhere added a delightful touch of home—just not his home. Sloane could smell the late summer blooms, chrysanthemums, asters, and others he didn't recognize, instead of the mildew and mustiness of his last visit.

Upstairs, his bedchamber had been similarly transformed, complete with flowers on the nightstand. In minutes, more courteous help was bringing a hot bath and taking his clothes away to be pressed. Then the butler and a footman carried in an excellent meal, considering the kitchens had no warning of his arrival, and an excellent vintage of wine.

The servants weren't familiar like Kelly, but then they hadn't been through a war with him. For the first time, Sloane actually felt like a duke. He knew he had done nothing to earn these people's respect, but they gave it to the title anyway, or to the person who paid the bills. He sent compliments to the cook and thanked the house-keeper for a fine job.

This was how Neville Hall was always kept, the elderly woman informed him. Of course it was easier when the master and mistress were in residence, she added with a faint hint of censure. The staff did like to have their work appreciated.

Sloane was so appreciative and so comfortable and so loathe to get back on that bone-rattler, he decided to wait until the morning to visit his wife. Besides, he didn't want to frighten her, marching in at night as though he meant to claim his conjugal rights then and there.

He went to bed early and left word that he was to be awakened early, knowing from his aunt and Kelly how Lisanne could disappear for hours. Unfortunately Diablo also had a good night's sleep. He didn't want to be saddled. He didn't want to be ridden. And he definitely didn't want to take that shortcut through the woods. Since the duke didn't fancy having his head laid open by low branches or his neck broken against a tree trunk, he wisely decided to ride the long way around.

The carriage drive and grounds of Neville Hall were in the same flawless condition as the Priory's, and the house, a more modern stone edifice, was equally as well maintained. The groom who came to take Sloane's horse, however, was bent over, leaning on his stick. The fellow was never going to be able to hold the stallion, much less get him to the stable and rubbed down.

"Is there anyone else around to help?"

"Aye, Old Bill. I'm Young Bill."

If this was Young Bill, St. Sevrin marveled that Old Bill could still wield a pitchfork. He didn't much have to, the duke saw when he took Diablo around to the stable himself. Inside the vast structure were a decrepit pony nodding in its stall, two donkeys, a goat with a bandaged leg, and Old Bill, asleep on a stool in a patch of sunlight.

Diablo seemed interested in the goat, so he let Sloane get him settled in the stall next door with only one half-hearted attempt to bite the duke's hand off, and one kick that missed by feet instead of the stallion's usual inches. Sloane walked back to the house.

No one answered the front door, so he knocked again. This time the door creaked open. No, the creak was from the joints of the bewigged butler who bowed and asked his business.

"I'm St. Sevrin. I've come to see my wife."

The butler squinted at him. "No, you're not the duke. He has gray hair and a red nose."

"That was my father. I am the new duke."

The footman in the hallway had taken his hat and gloves, but didn't leave the marble entry. "What'd he say?"

"He says he's the new duke. Wants the duchess."

"Who's nude? Not Her Grace. Maybe no hat and no gloves, but she ain't never gone nude, has she, Weldon?"

Weldon had been butler at the Priory when Sloane was a boy. He should have been pensioned off then, except there was no money for a pension. He should have been dead by now. When Aunt Hattie said some of the old servants had been moved to Neville Hall, he'd thought she meant previous servants, not *old* servants.

He raised his voice: "Could you tell Her Grace that her husband is here?"

The footman pulled an antique blunderbuss from behind the door. "Her Grace ain't no hussy, neither."

Weldon took Sloane's hat and gloves from the table and tried to hand them back to the duke, missing him by as wide a mark as Diablo had. "Her Grace isn't receiving."

"Like hell she isn't." He took the stairs two at a time, barely noticing the silk wall hangings or the gleaming wood. He did manage to register that a Turner landscape hung in the landing, and a small Vermeer at the top of the stairs. Fine, he got his rackety ancestors; she got the masterpieces. Then again, he got the antique furniture; she got the antique servants. Sloane thought he had the better deal.

He started opening doors and shouting until a mob-capped head stuck out of a room down the hall. It was that girl from the vicarage, done up in a gray maid's uniform with a frilly starched apron. She bobbed him a curtsy. "Your Grace."

"Ah, Mary, is it? I was beginning to think everyone in the place was either deaf, dumb, or blind. Could you tell Her Grace that I wish to speak to her."

"I'm that sorry, Your Grace, but my lady isn't here."

She didn't sound a bit sorry to Sloane. In fact, she sounded downright hostile. It was a big house, and he didn't want to wander around for hours until he found Lisanne, so he smiled and held out a coin. "Could you tell me where I might find her?"

The maid looked at him as if he were a cat offering her a dead snake. Or a live snake. "My lady pays me fine. And, no, I can't."

Sloane put the coin back in his pocket and the steel back in his voice. Loyalty to an employer was one thing, standing in his way was another. "I am not leaving until I speak to her."

Mary crossed her arms over an ample bosom that made Sloane wonder if Kelly had obeyed any of his instructions. Then the brazen chit had the nerve to glare at him when she noticed where his eyes had strayed. "I can't tell Your Grace where my lady is because I don't know. She doesn't tell me anymore. She doesn't visit the tenants, she doesn't work in her stillroom, and she doesn't sit in the library. She never goes near the kitchen nor the dining room, neither, that's for sure. Most of the time she lays on her bed in here." Mary jerked her head to the room behind her. "Or she's gone without telling anyone where."

St. Sevrin knew where she was. They all knew where she was. The Duchess of St. Sevrin was in those blasted, bloody woods.

Chapter Twenty-one

Sevrin Woods covered over two hundred acres. That was two hundred acres of thick old growth trees, lakes, meadows, and deer tracks without one recognizable footpath or guidepost. Lisanne could be anywhere.

Before setting out, Sloane stopped in the kitchen to get some bread and cheese to carry along with him. The crone at the stove was so palsied, it was no wonder that the duchess didn't eat her cooking. Shaking hands didn't make for accurate measurements, if the ingredients got in the pot at all. The bread was fine, though, hot and crusty; and he had his choice of cheese, cold chicken, or sliced ham. He had his own flask for liquid refreshment, and there would be clear water in the streams. He didn't dare ask Methuselah's uncle at the front door to fetch something up from the wine cellar.

Sloane headed for what he thought was the clearing where he'd found Lisanne crying last spring, crying because she had to marry him or lose everything. She wasn't there, if it was even the same place, but he stayed and called her name. Then he whistled, hoping the dog could hear him and bark. Instead a flock of sparrows started chirping at him from the trees until he threw out some of the bread.

He began to see what she loved about this place. Aside from its natural beauty, the forest had absolutely nothing to do with the woes and worries of the world beyond its borders. The old oak trees were changing their colors, and a bed of orange and yellow leaves already blanketed the ground, leaving no sound but the birdsong and the scurrying of little creatures darting back and forth after his crumbs. He could be anywhere in time, anywhere in place. If there'd been an apple tree, St. Sevrin wouldn't have been surprised to see Eve peeking from behind its leaves. Druids could have chanted here, or Roman fauns presided at the Bacchanalia. The woods were ageless, unaware, and uncaring about man's petty concerns.

Although St. Sevrin felt small and young, dwarfed in size by the massive boles and soaring branches, a heartbeat in the life span of this ancient place, he also felt protected and sheltered. He couldn't understand why the locals had such fear of this expanse, but he was glad they did, for Lisanne's sake.

He wandered all morning and into the afternoon, watching the direction of the sun when he could spot it through the leaves. He never found his wife and, oddly enough, he never found the route to the Priory. He did find streams to hurdle, huge fallen logs to clamber over, and endless prickly vines to catch on his clothing. By three o'clock, according to his pocket watch, he was filthy, sweaty, and hungry, having shared his snack with squirrels, deer, and even a curious badger. He was also hoarse, having spent most of the time calling for Lisanne.

He gave it up. Even if he found her, he was in no condition or frame of mind to address his lady wife. It took Sloane two hours to find his way back to Neville Hall.

There was no need to bother the relics in the house, he decided. They'd most likely already forgotten he'd called. He headed directly for the stable to collect Diablo. Becka came charging out of the stable, growling.

"Stubble it, fleabag, I'm in no mood for your nonsense." The dog—and his wife—had likely been hiding out in the stable all day, laughing at him. St. Sevrin strode into the building. He needed a few moments for his eyes to adjust from the bright daylight before he saw her, but there she was, as heart-stoppingly beautiful as ever. She was wearing a pretty sprigged muslin gown and a silly hat on her head—and she was in Diablo's stall.

The duke reached for the pistol that should have been at his side. Hell and thunderation, of course he hadn't thought he needed a weapon to call on his own wife. No matter, he'd kill the stallion with his bare hands if the devil harmed her. Guilt washed over him that he hadn't destroyed the vicious animal weeks ago, but had brought him here, of all places.

Sloane knew not to make any sudden moves and doubted if his feet could have done so anyway, having been glued with panic to the packed dirt floor. He tried to speak, but nothing came out of his dry mouth. He swallowed stable dust and enough saliva to be able to croak out, "Come away, Duchess."

Lisanne looked up—yes, her blue eyes could still pierce him to the core with their disappointment and distrust—but she didn't move.

"Please, sweetings, please get out of there. Slowly. I should have told the grooms, but I never thought anyone would even try to get near the stallion. He's mean, Lisanne, mean and dangerous." He took a slow, desperate step closer. "Please come to me now."

"He's not mean, just lonely. I was introducing him to Nana."

St. Sevrin took another snail-step nearer to the stall, where he could see the lame goat in there with Diablo and Lisanne. Sloane didn't care if the goat ended up in the stallion's water trough or his stomach, he wanted his wife away from those metal-shod hooves and bone-crushing teeth. He held his arms open, willing her just once to do what any reasonable person would. He'd never ask anything of her again. If she wanted to stay in Devon, he'd drag the damned prince here to meet her. "Please, Duchess."

Lisanne fed Diablo the last sugar cube from her pocket and kissed the velvet patch on his nose. St. Sevrin groaned. Then she bent and kissed the goat. "Lisanne, now!"

Telling the animals that she'd be back soon, Lisanne finally turned and opened the stall door. St. Sevrin rushed over, snatched her up, and slammed the gate behind her. He ran outside with Lisanne in his arms to Old Billy's— or Young Billy's—vacant stool, where he just sat, clutching her to him, his eyes closed on the nightmare he'd see for the rest of his days. They stayed like that while his heart pounded so loudly and rapidly he thought it must be using up two years of his life. At last he managed to gasp, "Don't ever . . . do that . . . to me again."

Lisanne didn't try to struggle in his arms. She felt the hard muscle, the solid chest, and knew it would be useless, but she felt no need to break loose. Actually she was amazed. St. Sevrin might be suffocating her, he might even be breaking every bone in her body, but he really seemed to care. She freed one arm and reached up to touch his cheek. "There was no danger, truly. Animals like me."

His eyes snapped open. "Confound it, girl, I wonder you haven't been eaten alive by the wolves in Sevrin Woods with that attitude."

She flashed a quicksilver smile. "There are no wolves in England. But if there were . . ."

He shook her gently, still not letting her off his lap. "Don't tell me. I haven't recovered yet." Then he held her away a bit. "Here, let's have a look at the fearless Amazon I married." The uncertain look on her face made him add, "Perhaps not altogether fearless, then. I won't bite, you know."

Lisanne trusted animals, not men. She stared down at her gloves, soiled now with the stallion's licking. She turned her hands over, so he wouldn't see.

The duke didn't notice. He was taking inventory elsewhere. Lisanne's blond hair was bundled in some kind of net at the back of her neck, and her healthy golden glow had almost faded to insipid ivory. "You're much too pale."

"Lady Comstock said tanned skin was to be avoided at every cost. She told me to wear a hat at all times."

He untied the strings and tossed the bonnet aside. "The hell with hats. You need the sunshine. And your clothes still don't fit. What the deuce was that Frenchwoman doing anyway?"

Fingering the neckline of her gown, which did have excess material, Lisanne defended the modiste. "I've lost a bit of weight recently, that's all. The gowns Madame Delacroix made were lovely. And this one was clean this morning." She wrinkled her nose at the smudges coming from proximity to him. The earthy scent of him, all horse and sweat and soap, was fascinating, disturbing, and not to be mentioned aloud, she was sure. "I usually wear a smock when I am gardening or with the animals."

He didn't care about her clean clothes. "How could you lose anything? You never weighed more than a handful of feathers." He was undoing the net holding her hair and spreading it out with his fingers so that long golden curls fell across her shoulders. "There, that's more like it. I hardly recognized the stylish lady." Sloane pulled her skirts up an inch or two. "Too bad, shoes. They've made you into one of those uppity debutante creatures, haven't they?"

Lisanne had to smile. Truly he was outrageous. "Your aunt worked so hard at it, too."

The duke turned serious. "Not hard enough, it seems,

if you're hiding out here, not eating, not visiting your friends. Did someone insult you? Threaten you?"

She looked away. "There is nothing wrong, no problem."

"Even a dolt like me can see that something is desperately wrong. Otherwise you would have come to London with Aunt Hattie or stayed at the Priory, which has never looked better, incidentally. I thank you for your efforts there."

"Your aunt did most of it, along with the staff. They take great pride in it, you know."

"So why did you run away?"

He was going to persist until she told him, Lisanne could tell. She got up and walked away from him. It might be easier to explain if she didn't see the pity in his eyes. "I have made mice feet of everything. I made you so unhappy you wouldn't come home."

"I was giving you time to get used to the idea of marriage," he lied. "And then I had to go help my friend Trevor home from the Peninsula."

She didn't bother turning to face his excuses. "You didn't come and that made me unhappy, thinking I had stolen your comfort, your choices. You couldn't come home, and you couldn't find a wife to please you more because we were already married. And then I realized I would never know love, either. To spend the rest of my life among strangers and servants . . ."

He rose and started massaging the back of her neck. "I didn't know love was part of our bargain, sweetings. You were such a pragmatic little negotiator, I never suspected you harbored dreams of romance. As I recall, you wanted the woods and financial security. The forest is intact, every confounded inch of it, I made sure today. You're not lacking for funds, are you?"

She shook her head, no.

"We did agree on children, I remember. We'll get to that in time. And you did offer me a long tether if I didn't embarrass you. You've read the *on dits* columns. I guess I've failed you there, Duchess, but not in the way you meant."

Lisanne turned to face him again, her eyes wet with unshed tears. "No, I failed you, with all that gossip. I knew you wouldn't want your wife's name a byword. I should have known that they would—"

Sloane put a finger over her lips. "Sh. There was another stipulation that I didn't fully understand at the time. You didn't want to be locked up. But what have you done here, Duchess, except make your own prison? Do you like this life you've chosen?"

"No. Do you like yours?"

"No, and I am even more responsible for my own bars and shackles. Both of us can do better."

"We can't do much worse, can we?"

He smiled, but only for a second. "I am more sorry than you can imagine that I've made you so miserable, Duchess. My only excuse is that I am not in the habit of thinking of anyone's feelings but my own. I cannot promise love, for I doubt that I am capable of the poet's emotion, but I will try to be a better friend if you'll let me. And as for no one else loving you, Aunt Hattie will have my liver and lights if I don't restore you to happiness, and Kelly will resign. Your Mary almost carved me for Christmas dinner, and my friend Trevor already swears he adores you like a sister. He tells all and sundry that you saved his life with your medicine."

"Nonsense, Lady Roehampton wrote a very pretty letter to Aunt Hattie about how you snatched her darling son from the jaws of death with your rescue ship. They were schoolgirls together, did you know?"

"Aunt Hattie went to school with every female in creation. Nevertheless, Trev has declared himself your knight-errant. We better hope Lady Roehampton doesn't get wind of his challenging anyone who sullies your name. Luckily most chaps won't accept a challenge from a one-legged man."

"And you? What kind of challenges do you accept?"

"Oh, I don't bother with duels anymore. You must have heard that by now, how I'm an uncivilized lowlife, using my fists instead of my manners. I did enough killing in the war. Now I just bounce the insulting bastards on their heads once or twice. Shuts them up quickly enough."

"I've caused you such trouble."

"And I've caused you pain. We're even. Now we have to stop hurting each other. Do you think we can?"

"You aren't just being nice so I'll go to London with you, are you?"

"I have to admit that I came here with every intention of carrying you off, willy-nilly, just to stop the damnable gossip. I won't. If you don't want to go to London, you don't have to. But I won't go without you, Duchess. Then, of course, you'll be worrying that I'm in Prinny's black books or that I'm missing the gaming hells and horse races, the clubs and balls. I won't, of course, but you won't be sure, will you?"

Lisanne scuffed her shoe in the stable-yard dirt. He was being so reasonable, so understanding. "What if I make the gossip worse by going? I could shame you even more, you know."

"Sweetheart, you are a beautiful, beautiful woman. You'll have the male half of London at your feet. The women will adore you because you are gentle and intelligent and no threat to their husband-hunting daughters, since you are already taken. Besides that, you are a duchess, a wealthy, wellborn lady in your own right, with a better pedigree than half the patronesses at Almack's. Aunt Hattie will be there to help, and Trevor, and myself. Just think of the members of the ton as yipping lapdogs and scrappy barn cats. If you can tame Diablo, you'll have those mongrels and mousers eating out of your hand."

Lisanne wondered how he saw himself, as a pampered pug or a well-fed feline. Most likely as the big bad wolf that ate unsuspecting little girls, couldn't be domesticated, and wasn't around anymore. Wolves mated for life.

She had to take the chance. "I will go."

"Good girl!" He swung her up and onto the stool so their eyes met at the same level. Lisanne was about to protest that she wasn't a girl, wasn't to be treated like a child, when he pressed a cool, soft kiss on her lips that deepened to a warm, hard embrace. He knew.

"About those sons . . ."

"I have to start packing." Lisanne jumped off the stool and ran toward the house, leaving her hat, her hair net, and her bemused husband. Her cheeks were burning with embarrassment, but her lips were burning with something else altogether.

Chapter Twenty-two

$\mathscr{I}$t wasn't the packing that slowed them down, or the second carriage necessary to carry the vast amount of trunks Mary insisted Her Grace needed to make the proper splash in London. The third carriage wasn't a problem, either, once Lisanne saw to the careful packing of her bottles and boxes and buckets of plant cuttings. St. Sevrin simply hired extra horses and drivers and outriders.

It wasn't even the dog who caused all the delays. Becka liked to ride up with the driver of her mistress's traveling carriage, her ears and jowls blowing in the breeze, when she wasn't running alongside or off on her own errands. They didn't have to wait all that long on lonely stretches of highway for Becka to return.

No, it was the goat that kept them so many extra days on the road, the lame goat that had to come in a slower wagon of her own, with ample straw and sweet rolls. The Duchess of St. Sevrin wasn't going to make a splash, the duke thought. She was going to create a tidal wave, riding into town with this particular entourage, not the least of which was his own huge roan stallion making sheep eyes at a nanny goat. It was downright humiliating, but made for an easier mount.

When he was done riding, when Diablo had been tied behind the goat's wagon to play Romeo to Nana's Juliet, St. Sevrin rode in the carriage with his wife. At first he suggested Mary exchange places outside with Becka for a while so he and Lisanne could get to know each other. That dog in the carriage, however, was not a good idea, even with the windows opened. It was easier to let Mary stay and speak of impersonal matters: the estates, his investments, what sights Lisanne might like to see, his friend Trevor Roe.

"I confess, I'm worried about Trev. It's not good for a man to have no future and nothing to do. I know. His family will support him, but I know he'd rather earn his own keep than be handed it like a remittance man." St. Sevrin was chafing enough under the yoke of his wife's fortune.

"Is he honest? Intelligent? No, I take that back. He must be if he's your friend."

"Thank you, Duchess, for thinking all my friends are paragons. May you never meet the scum I play with at cards."

"Those are not your friends." She was positive. "You wouldn't have gone to all the trouble of fetching one of them home, would you? Lieutenant Roe was obviously worth the effort, worth your worrying over him now."

"Trev is a good man and a good friend. He was a deuced good officer, with a head for details and strategy that even Old Hokey recognized. He was one of Wellesley's aides when he went down. Trev's no scholar, but he's certainly more intelligent than most of the gossoons they have working at the War Office now."

"Then why don't you make him your man of business? Mr. Mackensie won't be around forever, and you admitted yourself he doesn't keep up with the shipping ventures you're interested in." She hesitated a moment. "And if you're not to be in London all the time, you'll need someone responsible to look after your banking interests and such. Perhaps you could make him a loan so he'd be a partner instead of a mere employee. That way he'd have a share in the profits and could pay you back when he makes his own fortune."

"And I'd have an excuse for keeping him at St. Sevrin House rather than letting him go to his parents' stuffy mausoleum of a place or cheap bachelor digs with no one to watch out for him. He can have an office of his own and his own apartment. It's a brilliant idea, sweetings, thank you!" He kissed her gloved hand right there in front of Mary, who giggled.

After luncheon, the duke again rode in the carriage. "Now that you've settled Trevor so happily, my sweet, what about Kelly? He's too good a man to waste opening doors or ironing cravats."

Lisanne had it all worked out. "Oh, he's to be your estate manager when I—we—return to Devon." Lisanne wasn't sure how long before St. Sevrin's interest in the country, or his interest in her, waned. He might want her to go to London to make things more comfortable for him now, but he might forget about his promise to come home later to take up the reins of his holdings. She couldn't trust the duke yet, but she could trust Kelly. "The people like him and respect him for being a veteran, but more for being farm-bred himself. He knows a great deal and can learn more from working with the bailiff at Neville Hall. There is too much work for one man, or even two, to do it all. Even if . . . if you are there, you'll need help. And Mary will be happy."

The maid was blushing scarlet. St. Sevrin laughed. "Ah, so the wind sits in that corner, does it? I'm not surprised. It's a fine man you'd be getting, Mary, if you can bring him up to scratch."

"Oh, I aim to, Your Grace. He's already hooked. I just have to reel him in."

"Poor Kelly, he never had a chance, did he?" No more than he had, Sloane supposed. He wasn't exactly complaining. His duchess was looking charming in an apple green merino traveling costume, and another of those silly bonnets with a posy of silk roses tucked under the brim. She looked like a sprite peeking out from a garden. She was a good traveler, too, when she wasn't worried about her dog, her plants, the goat, or the drivers out in the rain. Lisanne would have ridden farther without breaks, but Sloane made sure they stopped long enough at every change of horses for her to eat something. He wasn't bringing any undernourished nymph to Town.

Sloane also stopped early enough every evening for a leisurely dinner and a good night's rest—in separate rooms. The duchess had enough in her dish now, he decided, being out in the world for the first time in her life. Hell, she'd never been out of Devon. And she was too frail. And shouldn't be breeding during the Season he meant for her to enjoy. St. Sevrin did make sure that they shared a good night kiss, though, for her to think about in her solitary chamber. He stayed down in the taproom, so he *wouldn't* think about it.

Back in the carriage, Sloane was pleased to find his wife didn't jabber on like some females he knew, but asked reasonable questions about everything she saw. St. Sevrin was looking forward to showing her the sights of London, the Opera House, Astley's Amphitheater, Hyde Park with its swans and Serpentine and Society on the strut. He was sure she'd adore the stuff he'd disdained for ages. As the cortege moved closer to Town and traffic got heavier, Sloane grew more eager, more assured of the welcome she'd receive there. Lisanne, however, grew less and less confident with every mile. She was twisting her gloves and biting her lip and not asking about the passing scenes. She wasn't doing more than crumbling her toast, either, and feeding it to whatever creature was handy.

To keep her from dwelling on tomorrow, from retreating into that quiet shell she erected, Sloane teased: "Now that you've got Trevor's future mapped out, and Kelly's, what have you planned for me, Duchess? You haven't left me much to do but sign the checks. Surely you don't intend me to become just another useless pet of Society, do you?"

"I doubt if Society would relish a bored timber wolf in its midst," she answered without thinking, and blushed when he laughed.

"They haven't in the past, sweetings. What am I to do, then, besides escort the newest comet about Town?"

"You have to make the decisions. You can't expect Kelly or Lieutenant Roe to know your mind. You can't do everything, of course. I know, for I tried. There's always a leaking roof or a blocked drain just when you're thinking about next year's crop rotations. Or there's an account that doesn't balance when you're needed to choose a new doctor for the village. Kelly and Trevor can handle the details. Besides, you'll be starting the horse-breeding farm you've always wanted. A racing stud, is it?"

"My word, woman, are you a mind reader besides? I've never mentioned that to anyone. How did you know?"

"Why else would you have bought a difficult animal like Diablo? And then, when you saw what he was, why would you keep him a stallion? I'm not a fool, Your Grace."

He kissed her hand again. "No, but you married one, Your Grace."

He wasn't such a fool, for he'd designed a room Lisanne couldn't help but adore. The walls were painted a pale yellow, but then he'd had an artist come in to paint trellises and flowers from floor to ceiling, with painted vines climbing the gauze-covered windows. Painted clusters of wildflowers adorned the white lacquered furniture, with matching live bouquets on every surface. The bed hangings and upholstered lounge and chairs were deep forest green, with make-believe birds in brilliant colors woven into the fabric.

Lisanne just kept turning in circles, trying to take it all in, together with the fact that St. Sevrin had done it for her. "It's the most beautiful room I've ever seen."

The duke was standing by the doorway, frowning. "Then why are you crying?"

"Because it's the most beautiful room I've ever seen."

The duke shrugged and went downstairs while Lisanne refreshed herself after the long journey. Mary was already bossing the line of footmen over the placement of Her Grace's trunks.

St. Sevrin waited in the library, which he'd also furnished with Lisanne in mind. Not that he'd made another garden in this wood-and-leather domain, but when Sloane had restocked the shelves of books his father had sold off, he'd considered her tastes as well as his own. The walls held all the classics, plus whole sections devoted to modern works on botany, agriculture, and medicine. He'd bought whatever he thought she might enjoy, encyclopedias and foreign dictionaries, along with current works of poetry and fiction that mightn't have come her way. Considering that he'd never seen her without a book in her pocket or nearby, even in the carriage, he thought she might like the library. He found a measure of peace there himself usually, studying the farming journals or investment guides.

His Grace would find no peace today, for Trevor found him there and demanded to know what had kept them so long. Bets were on at the clubs that St. Sevrin had decamped for parts unknown rather than presenting his wife in Town.

Instead of discussing his stallion's affection for a goat,

Sloane mentioned Lisanne's proposal to his friend. Trevor was thrilled. "Told them at Whitehall I had a head for figures. This'll be much better. Mother will have kitten fits, of course, that I'll be going into trade, but the pater will be so relieved, he'll come down heavy with my share for investing."

Trevor was still excited when Lisanne came down. "I'd get down on one knee to thank you, Your Grace, but since I only have one knee and Sherry would have to haul me up off your carpet, I'll just declare myself your devoted slave. And now I'll leave you to start my packing, so you might have your privacy."

"No," they both shouted.

"It's part of the package," Sloane told him. "You've got to be nearby to be of sufficient help. This place is surely big enough for all of us to rattle around in."

"And I'll feel better about being in London if I have familiar faces around me. Please stay."

"My lady, you are as gracious as you are beautiful. I accept, if only to have more time to convince you to leave this cad and run off with me."

"What, are you trying to give her a disgust of London already?"

Then Aunt Hattie arrived, to St. Sevrin's relief. He wasn't worried about Trev turning Lisanne's head; he was worried about getting her launched properly. He didn't know the first thing about introducing a proper female around. Sloane hardly knew any proper females, in fact, and Trev wasn't much better, having been with the army even longer. For certain they couldn't take Lisanne to their usual haunts, and neither was currently high on the invitation lists of polite hostesses. Sloane vowed to himself to keep out of low company while his wife was in Town, since it would be easier to establish her respectably if he could salvage his own reputation.

Aunt Hattie was also convinced to stay in Berkeley Square to preside over Lisanne's presentation, and Trevor was quick to enlist his mother on her behalf, too. Viscountess Roehampton was as starchy a matron as any of Almack's patronesses, but she felt a debt to the duke and his little duchess.

While the duke and his new *chargé d'affaires* got busy over their investment schemes, the two pillars of Society got busy over Lisanne's introduction to the ton. They decided not to pitchfork her into the Season, where a green girl could flounder so easily, but to ease her into the stream. In a well-orchestrated campaign, Lady St. Sevrin was carefully escorted to the theater to sit in the Roehampton box, and to the park in Lady Comstock's barouche. She was taken along on morning calls to the dowager's friends, who just happened to be the most influential women in the *belle monde*. She was introduced to small groups at select dinner parties, and slightly larger ones at musicales and card parties. The duke, meanwhile, was permitted to take his wife sightseeing when nothing more important was planned, if he swore not to let her appear blue, collect interesting weeds in her pockets, or try to rescue every overworked cart horse in London. He was expressly forbidden to take her to the Tower with its filthy, flea-ridden menagerie.

Finally Lisanne's mentors deemed her ready for her presentation to royalty. With their connections, Ladies Comstock and Roehampton managed to get their protégée a private audience with the queen and her son, instead of one of the chockablock drawing rooms. After all, Lisanne was a duchess, not a debutante, and it was the prince himself who had asked to meet her, in her mandatory hooped skirt and feathered headdress.

Prinny seemed very pleased about it, too. "Now we see why you wanted to keep this beautiful creature in the hinterlands, St. Sevrin. Glad we convinced you otherwise, what? Beauty is to be shared, St. Sevrin, that's our credo. And we hear you are back at the clubs again, too.

Good man. Next we'll be looking for you to take your rightful place in Parliament. We are well satisfied."

St. Sevrin was, too. Lisanne wasn't Prinny's type, thank goodness. He mopped his brow in relief when they were in their carriage. The meeting had gone remarkably well considering what could have happened if his bride had pulled a baby rabbit from her pocket. Sloane marveled that Lisanne hadn't seemed nervous about meeting the monarchs in the least. She only regretted that the poor king wasn't well enough to join them, which had the queen declaring her a very sweet child.

That very sweet child lit into her husband on the way home. She pulled out the ridiculous ostrich plumes that had taken an hour to place correctly in her hair and frowned across at him. "Do you mean to tell me that you don't sit in the Lords? Even my papa made sure he came for important sessions. I have been in London a sennight now, and I have seen more disease, hunger, filth, and crime than in my entire life in Devon. And you have the power to do something for the climbing boys, the child prostitutes, the unemployed veterans—and you don't?"

The duke wished he could take her in his arms and shut her mouth with a kiss, but those damnable hooped skirts were in the way. "Hold, Duchess. I've been to the stodgiest of tea parties, the most boring of musical evenings, and even a lecture on the healing properties of fungus. You and your watchdogs have dragged me to church on Sundays, by Jupiter, and to every historic cathedral betweentimes. Must I suffer another sermon after facing Prinny's? Have a heart, sweetings."

"I do. For the people you could be helping."

"Do you see your goodness in everyone? Even me?"

"I see that you aren't nearly as evil as you play at being."

If she could see what he was thinking about doing under her hooped skirts, she might reconsider. He smiled. "What makes you think I'm not all bad, Duchess?"

She smiled back. "I saw you pet the goat."

Chapter Twenty-three

*H*er Grace was officially out. His Grace was unofficially back in the prince's favor. Both their graces were in good graces with the ton. For now. Invitations came pouring in, but more from curiosity, Lisanne knew, than any sense of friendliness.

In her own quiet way, Lisanne saw much and said little. With the two voluble *grande dames* by her side, she was not required to add much to the conversation. When the dowagers weren't around, St. Sevrin and Trevor kept her entertained with their dissections of the war news, the international influences on commerce, and the state of the government—or outrageous compliments so she'd be used to having the butter boat poured over her head, they insisted.

Lisanne was hardly ever alone. A female wasn't supposed to be, it seemed. She couldn't take Becka to the locked park across the street without a footman at her heels. Heaven forfend she go to the bookstore by herself, or walk the short distance.

For now Lisanne was willing to listen to all the strictures and heed the warnings. She was here for one purpose only, and that was to see her husband's honor polished. If St. Sevrin required her to be a pattern card of conformity in order to be invited to the highest sticklers' boring parties, she would toe the mark—in shoes. If she had to be dressed to the nines to cast a good reflection on his image, she'd stand for being poked and prodded and dragged from shop to shop. She was going to make him proud of her and satisfied with this marriage, even if it killed her.

At night, alone in her bed, Lisanne had time to reflect on her situation, both the good and the bad. London was filthy, blanketed in soot, choking in poverty. It was also exciting, amusing, and informative. Just so, many of the people she was meeting were vain and empty pleasure-seekers. Why would anyone wish to be acceptable to such people? She'd be happier in the company of the carriage horses. But others, especially among the dowager's circles of wealthy, powerful women, were able to accomplish untold good with their fund-raising and endowments, pushing their husbands toward legislated reform. Lisanne arranged for Mr. Mackensie to set aside a percentage of her income for just such charitable gifts, in addition to what she handed out to every unfortunate on the streets. When St. Sevrin took his seat, she'd be able to plead her causes with him.

Meanwhile she was becoming accepted. Even the servants at St. Sevrin House were starting to turn to her for orders, not to Aunt Hattie or Kelly or His Grace. She knew they weren't comfortable with her, the aloof, polite footmen in burgundy livery and the skittery maids in their crisp aprons, but they obeyed her and catered to her wishes. Only the cook seemed actually to welcome her presence, though, especially after Lisanne provided a soothing footbath for her bunions. Mrs. Reilly also put sweetened milk out each night for the Brownies who brought the kitchen luck, so the bread would keep rising and rodents would stay out of her larder. With so many milk-mustached cats in the yard, how could the mice do else? Mrs. Reilly was happy enough to let Lisanne fill her sacks and pockets with rolls, apples, and sugar when she left for the park or the stables. The others, from the pastry cook to the potboy, looked away.

Lisanne saw those same averted glances whenever she arrived at the theater on her husband's arm or at a milliner's shop with Aunt Hattie. At formal gatherings ladies stared at her over their fans, as if she couldn't see their assessing eyes. A few gentlemen ogled her through their absurd quizzing glasses, to be chilled by St. Sevrin's frown or Lady Comstock's cut direct. Still, conversations broke off when she arrived, none of the younger females approached her on their own, and practiced hostesses tended to fumble over handing her a teacup.

She was accepted because she had to be—with the queen's nod, her illustrious sponsors, her title, and her fortune. But she wasn't approved. Gossip followed and flowed around her like a chiffon overskirt. The Findleys had brought their servants with them to Town, the same servants who had seen Addled Annie reviled all her life. Even if Uncle Alfred never spoke a bitter word, even if that rattlepate Esmé never chattered to her twenty-three bosom bows, rumors flew. St. Sevrin's cousin Humbert decided country air might be more salubrious to his health after the duke overheard him at White's, but still the scandalmongers were working overtime. Lisanne had Trevor's promise not to challenge anyone and her husband's word not to engage in fisticuffs, not if he wanted to redeem his own reputation. Therefore she wasn't upset by the gabblegrinders. Her husband was.

Everyone was waiting for her to do something outrageous. Her husband included. Lisanne was used to relatives and strangers looking at her as if she had horns growing out of her head. She wasn't used to seeing the question in her husband's dark eyes. That hurt.

While Sloane was being kind, keeping her away from the crushes, walking with Becka and Lisanne in the park, taking her to Horticultural Society lectures, he still needed a drink to face his wife. He still went out again after seeing her to the door after their evening entertainment, giving her a quick kiss for the servants' benefit. He still came home in the early hours of the morning, loud, unsteady, reeking of spirits and smoke. He still wasn't a real husband.

They'd have children sooner or later, Lisanne was confident of that. She'd seen the desire in St. Sevrin's eyes after their all too brief embraces. But how could she share such intimacy with a man who was afraid of her, afraid she'd start banging her head against the wall or start rolling her eyes and speaking in tongues? Sloane trusted her to run his households. He didn't trust her to give him normal, healthy sons, not even now when she was trying so hard to fit into the mold of propriety. Lisanne never even whistled the sparrows to her hand anymore, except here, at her own bedchamber's windowsill. Sloane didn't trust her, so she couldn't trust him not to walk out of her life the moment she displeased him.

Lisanne felt she was treading on eggshells. St. Sevrin was charming, amusing, respectful of her opinions and appreciative of her womanly charms now that her gowns fit better. She wanted his love.

If her life was going to have any meaning beyond acts of charity and the performance of her duties, Lisanne needed him to love her the way she was coming to love him. He wasn't perfect, heaven knew, and she wasn't about to accept his faults without trying her hardest to change them. Still, she could see past those shortcomings to the man underneath, and love him. Why couldn't he accept her for what she was? Why couldn't he try to love her, just a little.

Dash it, Sloane thought, why couldn't he protect her the way he'd sworn? Lisanne was being so good, so brave, enduring what no sensitive, intelligent female should have to. Confound it, his duchess could manage a huge estate. She was worth ten of Almack's simpering debs, so why did she have to suffer being inspected by every bitch and biddy on their committee? And why couldn't he scotch those blasted rumors? Blister it, Sloane couldn't fight what he couldn't see.

Findley *et fils* swore they'd kept their mummers dubbed, and Humbert was forcibly encouraged to seek greener pastures to spread his manure. Damn, the lady was stuck with St. Sevrin; she shouldn't have to be stuck with a reputation for peculiarity also. Besides, Lisanne's peculiarities were a deal more endearing than the average miss's airs and affectations. And she brewed the most effective morning-after remedy he'd ever tried.

Sloane was ready to take his wife home to Devon. She'd been seen, had been declared a diamond of the first water, and had been given the stamp of approval on an Almack's voucher. What more did anyone want? St. Sevrin wanted her happy, and he wanted her to himself. He wanted her, period. Possessive, protective, physically attracted—but it wasn't love he felt, the duke told himself. He couldn't love, couldn't be faithful to one woman. He never had been, never would be. Then again, he'd never gone so long without any woman at all, a sacrifice in his effort not to disgrace Lisanne. He'd shown her the delights of London; now he wanted to show her the delights of the marriage bed, without his best friend and his aunt looking on.

Aunt Hattie wouldn't hear of them leaving Town yet. Lisanne hadn't attended Almack's or a single rout party, to confront and confound the ton en masse. As a matter of fact, Lady Comstock declared, Lisanne ought to stay until they could throw a grand ball in her honor. Lisanne couldn't think of many things she'd like less—the plague, perhaps—and St. Sevrin knew the preparations for one of his aunt's extravaganzas could take months.

"Why can't she just share the Findley chit's come-out in two weeks?" he asked at dinner that night. "It's being held in Lisanne's own house, after all."

"Or you could move the cousin's presentation over to here," Trevor suggested. "The ballroom is larger, and you'd put out a more lavish spread than that nip-cheese Findley."

St. Sevrin put down his fork. "No, that won't do. I've forbidden the dastard my house. I don't intend to go back on my word now and have that leech trying to bleed Lisanne dry."

"If the ball is at Neville House," Aunt Hattie mused over her turbot in oyster sauce, "then by rights the two of you ought to be on the receiving line."

Lisanne was used to letting the others make such decisions. Someone was always telling her where to go or what to wear, and she really didn't mind, since they knew London ways better than she did. This time, though, she cleared her throat. Three pairs of eyes turned in her direction. The leaves were all removed from the mahogany table, so there was no vast distance between St. Sevrin at the head and Lisanne at the foot. Tonight it seemed like a mile. Lisanne felt that Sloane just wanted to see the job of introducing her around over and done, so he could pack her off to Devon and get on with his life. "I will not share Esmé's come-out."

As far as St. Sevrin was concerned, that was that. They were already asking a lot of Lisanne. If she didn't want to stand next to that gormless family, so be it. "Fine, we'll give out that the Findleys are merely renting Neville House. You wouldn't be expected to be hostess or honoree at a tenant's affair. We don't even have to attend."

Aunt Hattie almost choked on her asparagus. "What, do you want to undo all our work? The Findleys are encroaching mushrooms, but they are Lisanne's encroaching mushrooms and everyone knows that. Do you want them to think that she is not welcomed by her own family? Or"—another choke—"that she charged them for the use of her house?"

Lisanne cleared her throat again. When she had their attention, she quietly explained, "I did not say I wouldn't go, just that I wouldn't stand on the receiving line or share Esmé's limelight when she has planned for this night her entire life. I'll have many other opportunities; my cousin will not, if I know my uncle."

Trevor nodded, impressed. "Deuced generous of you, Duchess, considering."

Aunt Harriet knew better than to waste her breath arguing with her niece-by-marriage when Lisanne made one of her soft, even-toned declarations. The chit was nigh immovable when she got on her uppers. "But you'll attend?"

"Yes, I'll attend, Aunt Hattie, and hope that you will accompany me to lend your countenance to Esmé's presentation. And you, Your Grace, will please dance at least one dance with Esmé to raise her status among the other debs."

"Thank you, my sweet. That's the first time anyone has considered my dancing with a young miss to be anything less than scandalous."

"Hell," Trevor muttered into his napkin, "it's the first time I've been glad of my wooden leg."

Aunt Hattie had plans of her own for that ball at Neville House. A hint here, a reminder there, and she and Viscountess Roehampton would have every notable in Town at that party. At long last they'd all make the acquaintance of the newest reigning Toast and her reformed rake. That spotted chit's come-out would be successful beyond her mother's fondest dreams. Feckless Findley and his featherheaded wife might even get the chit fired off in one Season, when all the bucks and beaux came to ogle St. Sevrin's duchess.

Yes, they'd attend the ball at Neville House and kill off those unpleasant rumors once and for all. So content was

Aunt Hattie with her plan that she thought she might even warn the Findleys to expect a few more guests. A few hundred more. Aunt Hattie helped herself to another serving of syllabub as a reward. Yes, Sir Alfred would just love laying out his blunt for all those extra lobster patties and bottles of champagne.

Chapter Twenty-four

Aunt Harriet's excellent plan was sure to succeed except for one thing: the ball was going to be cancelled. Esmé was sick. With less than two weeks before the party, Sir Alfred was ailing, too, since he had already ordered the extra supplies. With such elevated company now expected, his wife had insisted on more flowers, a finer orchestra, and additional servants. Findley immediately dismissed the new help—and a few of the old.

When he was told the news, St. Sevrin decided the Findley chit must be suffering the green sickness because her beautiful, wealthy cousin would be making her first formal appearance at the ball. People were coming to see Lisanne, not some brash baronet's bran-faced daughter, and everyone knew it. If the brat had any honor, she'd be mortified that the ball was being held in Lisanne's house, without Lisanne's name on the invitations. Then again, if the brat had any honor, Lady Findley must have played her husband false.

He marched over to Neville House to demand the ball proceed as planned, sulky debutante or not. No one, least of all that flat, Findley, who'd caused all the difficulties in the first place, was going to steal Lisanne's chance to shine. If they weren't going to hold the party, Sloane would give the Findleys two days to pack and vacate his wife's house. Then he'd hire an army to remake the party for Lisanne. She wouldn't like it, but if they couldn't leave London until she had a ball, then a ball she would have. And it would be the finest one money—her money—could provide. If that's what it took to put to rest any notion that the Duchess of St. Sevrin was some harum-scarum hare-brain, that's what the duke would do.

Unfortunately Esmeralda truly was sick. Sloane met two doctors leaving as he entered Neville House. He knew both by reputation and couldn't discount their claims that the chit was seriously ill with blinding headaches, nausea, and fever. One of the doctors even suggested the girl might succumb to the mysterious ailment. The eminent physicians were arguing as St. Sevrin handed his hat and gloves to the butler. "I say she should be bled to relieve pressure on the brain."

"No, no, a purge is what she needs, to cleanse the system of its poisons."

"Cold baths, of course."

"Hot compresses, I insist."

When they were gone, the butler regretted that Sir Alfred was not receiving visitors. Prostrate with grief, he was, Pomfrey reported. It was more likely that Findley was in a stupor, St. Sevrin decided, knowing his only hope of maintaining this lifestyle was upstairs sick in bed. If Sir Alfred couldn't get Esmé buckled to a wealthy peer, he was up River Tick.

Nigel was not at home, not that St. Sevrin wanted to speak to that chinless clunch. From the odd word or two he'd heard about Town, Sloane concluded the sprig had most likely taken himself off to some low-rent brothel rather than be exposed to his sister's contagion. He'd rather have the pox, it seemed.

And Lady Alfred? She was suffering spasms and swoons.

Well, St. Sevrin couldn't throw them out, and he'd be damned if he'd pray for the chit's recovery, but he saw nothing else to do.

Lisanne did, of course. She told Aunt Hattie not to cancel her friend's invitations, not quite yet. She was going to Neville House to see for herself how matters stood.

St. Sevrin was adamant. "No. I forbid it. You are not putting one foot under that man's roof. A ball is one thing. Not even Findley would dare insult you in front of three hundred guests. I don't care if that coxcomb Nigel is away from home, I don't want you breathing his filthy air. Besides, we are supposed to attend Almack's tonight. Aunt worked hard enough to get you those vouchers, and the old harpies' noses get out of joint when someone refuses the invite."

He was still adamant three hours later, after he'd made the third trip back to Berkeley Square fetching books, bottles, and bundles of dried twigs and weeds from the stillroom she'd somehow found time to set up at St. Sevrin House. The Findleys' servants would never find what Lisanne needed, and she had to have Mary with her to help.

The duke didn't know what his wife was doing in Esmé's bedchamber, and he didn't want to know. He also didn't want any of Sir Alfred's staff to know. Bad enough Lisanne had tossed the two surgeons out; St. Sevrin didn't need a bunch of underpaid ignoramuses carrying tales of witchcraft and sorcery to the pubs. So he sat in a chair outside the room, or installed Kelly there when he was on an errand. Sloane even slept in the damned chair and got a crick in his neck. Heaven knew where Lisanne slept, for she refused to come away and leave Mary in charge, or the girl's mother, by George.

No, the girl's mother was less than useless with her weeping and wailing. If Lisanne hadn't dosed her with

206

laudanum and sent the skitter-wit off to bed, Sloane would have ordered Kelly to take Lady Cherise for a soothing ride in the country. One way.

Even the food was terrible. How the devil did they think to feed the most demanding palates in London with this tripe the sulky servants fetched up? Sloane had meals brought over from St. Sevrin House to make sure Lisanne ate properly. If the Findley chit survived, they were holding that ball, and Sloane wasn't having his wife disappearing through the cracks in the floor.

The only good thing was that Sir Alfred and Nigel stayed away. Actually Sloane wished one of them would arrive and make some snide comment about Lisanne's untoward knowledge of herbs and healing. By the second day, the duke was itching for a fight. By the third, he would have strangled the Findley chit himself, to put them all out of their misery.

Then Lisanne came out of the room, looking exhausted but happy. Esmé would recover. She was out of danger and should recuperate in time for the ball. Of course Esmé had lost a deal of weight, which St. Sevrin thought might improve her figure, and she would be interestingly pale, but Esmé would be ready to dance in ten more days of careful nursing. Lisanne was willing to take turns with Mary now, so they both could get some rest. She didn't trust the Findleys' servants, and neither did the duke.

There were ten days before the ball, and nothing was being done that he could see. The chandeliers weren't being taken down for cleaning, the rugs weren't being lifted for beating. A few questions revealed that the guest rooms hadn't been aired and the silver hadn't been polished. Damn, that silver would have Sloane's wife's crest on it! The devil take it if he'd let her come to such a shabby affair.

So the duke planned the ball, with Trevor and Aunt Hattie assisting while Kelly watchdogged Lisanne and

Mary. St. Sevrin's own housekeeper came to oversee the cleaning while his own kitchens were busy preparing the menu. Trevor handled the guest lists, and Aunt Hattie selected flowers and ribbon decorations—more lavish than Sir Alfred would ever have permitted. The baronet slunk around, keeping out of the way of his nephew-by-marriage and that dangerous glint in St. Sevrin's eye.

Lady Findley dithered around, clutching a vinaigrette. She might be useless, but she was grateful.

"And I am so sorry I let those dreadful rumors make the rounds," she confessed.

"You? You were the one who tried to ruin your own niece?" St. Sevrin couldn't believe his ears, or that he was pulling this shrew's chestnuts out of the fire.

Cherise clutched her smelling salts. "Oh, dear, it wasn't that I was trying to ruin Annie, exactly."

"Her name is Lisanne, and what were you trying to do, exactly?"

"I didn't have any goal in mind, Your Grace. I . . . I was just upset. I knew what the servants were saying, of course, and then, when people started asking me about the new duchess, I simply told them what they wanted to hear."

"Do you dislike your own niece so much, then?"

"Oh, gracious no, I like her very well. But she wasn't an easy child to deal with, you know."

St. Sevrin could imagine. She wasn't an easy woman to deal with, either. He nodded for Lady Findley to go on. Guilt and gratitude made her want to explain.

"I never expected to take the place of her mother, you must understand. But Annie—Lisanne—hardly let me into her thoughts, much less her heart. And then she *would* go her own way. Sir Alfred really only wanted her to be like other children, but then he couldn't bear to be bested by a little girl. I suffered greatly from my nerves when they brangled."

What about how Lisanne suffered? St. Sevrin wanted to ask, but didn't.

"Then she grew up all of a sudden and married you. And she was beautiful and titled, smarter than both of my children combined, and wealthier than Golden Ball. Meanwhile she had left us on the brink of ruin, according to Sir Alfred. How could I not resent her good fortune?" Cherise mopped a tear from her eye. "It was so easy not to rebuke the servants for their gossip, or to recall one of Annie's odd starts for an interested ear. But I'll make it up to her, I swear. Everyone at the ball will know how good she is, how kind and wise, how hard she worked at her studies. If she hadn't spent all that time with her plants and such, and wasn't so sweet a girl to come help us, my Esmé might have perished."

The thought alone sent Lady Findley to rest on her couch, a hanky soaked in rosewater upon her furrowed brow, until she remembered that frowning caused lines.

Lady Cherise was as good as her word on the night of the ball. She replied to every guest passing through the receiving line that, yes, Esmé had made a remarkable recovery and, yes, she was in looks tonight, with all credit to her cousin. To hear her aunt, Lady St. Sevrin had snatched Esmé back from the jaws of death. An angel, she was, a saint.

Esmé added her bit about her kind and gentle cousin, who knew everything there was to know about herbal teas and tisanes. If anyone complimented Esmé on the decorations or the refreshments for the party, she was quick to heap accolades on the duke, too. Without her cousins, Esmé told everyone who would listen, there would be no ball at all. Instead the party was a success beyond everyone's expectations, except Aunt Hattie's.

Whereas the guests arrived at most of the humdrum debutante balls, greeted the hosts, sampled the refreshments, and had a drink or a dance or a hand or two of cards before moving on to the next, livelier entertainment, tonight everyone stayed at Neville House, waiting for its mistress.

Aunt Hattie had their entrance timed to the last second. The receiving line had been disbanded, the dancing had begun. Not many of the gentlemen had retired to the card rooms yet; not many of the chaperones along the walls had dozed off. Lady Comstock fussed with her turban a moment outside the ballroom until she heard the current dance set draw to a close. Then she had the butler announce them. She kicked the man halfway through, and hissed, "Louder."

Pomfrey started again. "My Lady Harriet Comstock, the Honorable Lieutenant Trevor Roe." Aunt Hattie and Trev moved off to the side to watch, Trevor using just one cane now. Hattie whispered, "Louder still," to the butler. She needn't have, for there wasn't a sound in the room as all eyes turned to the door.

"Her Grace, the Duchess of St. Sevrin and Baroness Neville, His Grace, the Duke of St. Sevrin."

Lisanne looked up at her husband inquiringly. He patted the hand resting on his arm. "You were a lady before I met you."

Pomfrey the butler nodded. He'd been one of those quick to spread tales about the odd little hoyden running wild in Devon. Tonight there was a lady, beyond the shadow of a doubt.

Lisanne was wearing a gown of azure tissue-silk, almost the color of her eyes, with a silver gauze overskirt that was strewn with star-shaped brilliants. The neckline was cut low enough that St. Sevrin wanted to take her home to bed, but high enough that Aunt Hattie wouldn't let her insert a lace filler. With the most beautiful gown she'd ever owned, Lisanne wore the fabled St. Sevrin sapphires. Instead of wearing the pendant as a necklace, however, Lisanne wore it as a headpiece woven through her pinned-up golden hair, with the magnificent central stone hanging onto her forehead. No milk-and-water miss, no ordinary young female here. Everything about her, the soft smile, the straight back, the outrageous display of gems, bespoke wealth, breeding, and confidence in her own unique character. If a flock of butterflies had taken up residence in her stomach, only St. Sevrin knew, by the trembling of her fingers. He squeezed her hand.

Esmé skipped up to them and kissed Lisanne's cheek as Lady Findley made her way to them. On cue, waiters circulated with glasses of champagne and Sir Alfred, by arrangement and under extreme duress, proposed a belated toast to the newly married pair. Every word Findley spoke might have been a drop of hemlock on his lips, but not a soul in the room could suspect that the exquisite young duchess was anything but a beloved member of the family.

As the orchestra struck a waltz, St. Sevrin took his wife's hand, but she wanted to introduce Trevor to her cousin first.

"You must be sure to rest, Esmé. I recommend Lieutenant Roe as an admirable companion to sit out the next dance."

Esmé was agreeable. She hadn't been given approval to waltz anyway, and Lieutenant Roe was tall, dark, and heroic. Besides, he was the son of a viscount. She led him to a row of gilt chairs.

"Well done, Duchess," St. Sevrin congratulated. "And now I believe it is our dance." They came together as if the room were empty, with no one else for either of them. The gliding movement, the closeness, the way their thighs touched occasionally, or their chests—oh, how St. Sevrin wished they were not in a ballroom. Lisanne could only marvel that waltzing with her dance instructor was never like this.

All too soon the set was over and the duke had to lead

Lisanne back toward his aunt and hers. The cream of Society was waiting to meet his duchess. He smiled and kissed her hand. "It's your night, sweetheart."

Chapter Twenty-five

*B*efore she was home in Devon Lisanne had a lot of miles to travel, and one more hurdle, Almack's. Aunt Hattie insisted they attend, despite Lisanne's success at Esmé's ball. Everyone near enough to get an introduction had come away from Neville House declaring the new duchess an absolute delight. The very next day some of Lisanne's admirers started coming to her with odd complaints and illnesses, until the doctors set up a cry that she was practicing medicine without a license. Now debutantes and dandies brought her their bilious bulldogs and felines with fur balls. They all stayed to tea, of course. St. Sevrin House was suddenly the place to be seen, with the most eligible *partis* hoping for a smile from the newest Toast, with the Season's debs hoping for a chance to imitate Lisanne's style.

Kelly had to find the duchess space in the stable mews for treating her upper-crust patients, in addition to the injured birds, broken-down carriage horses, and stray mongrels she seemed to acquire the way other ladies acquired new hats.

Trevor was a help and, not so coincidentally, Esmé, who had never touched a four-legged beast except with a fork before this. Lisanne was pleased at their growing friendship, but not counting her chickens until they hatched egg-shaped betrothal rings.

St. Sevrin had taken himself off to consult a ship-builder in Folkestone. It was either that or cause chaos in Lisanne's parlor by bodily ejecting all those young pups drooling at her skirts. Skirts which he, incidentally, had not been able to get near.

The night of Esmé's ball, when they were all buoyed with success and champagne, he'd decided to visit his wife's bedchamber. That poise, that gown, left no doubt of Lisanne's womanhood; Sloane was ready to prove his manhood. He was more than ready. He was eager, aching, and panting as badly as those adoring moon-calves at the very thought of making Lisanne his.

Unfortunately she was already asleep when he pushed open the connecting door to their rooms. After nursing Esmé and preparing for her first major ball, Lisanne looked exhausted in the light of his candle. Sloane could see the shadows under her eyes and didn't have the heart to waken her. The next day his house was filled with callers, his desk was hidden under stacks of invitations, and the place was turning into an infirmary for asthmatic lapdogs. Let her enjoy her success, St. Sevrin decided, as long as he didn't have to watch. He'd be back for Wednesday's crucible at Almack's. Then they were leaving, no matter what Aunt Hattie said.

According to that venerable lady, a female wasn't entirely *comme il faut* until she'd been approved by the patronesses at that bastion of propriety. A lady might be popular, acclaimed in the newspapers and journals, but she wasn't past ridicule if she didn't pass through those hallowed doors. If Lisanne didn't do it now, they'd have the whole thing to go through again next Season, or whenever the duchess came back to Town.

Lisanne would go through one more senseless ordeal then, one more humiliating rite of passage into her husband's world. She'd do it, but only for him. If St. Sevrin were ever to take his proper place in the governing of the country, he'd need a wife above reproach. For that matter, Aunt Hattie felt that Sloane needed to be seen at Almack's, satin knee breeches and all, to bolster his own reputation.

As for the duchess, she'd seen enough sights and met enough people to be convinced that she wouldn't miss this frantic bustle once she was back in Devon. Only Lisanne knew how hard it was for her to face such crowds in her own drawing room when she was used to hours—no, days—of solitude.

It might have been easier if she had her husband's support, especially since she was making herself miserable on his behalf. Sloane had been attentive at Esmé's ball, hovering nearby to make introductions and accept congratulations. He'd left her side only for the one dance with Esmé, crowning that miss's triumphal come-out. And Lisanne knew he was attracted to her: she could feel the tingling heat pass between their gloved hands during that waltz. He might have been counting the freckles on her cheeks, so intently did he stare at her. She'd hoped that night that he would . . . but he hadn't. Now he was gone, leaving her to deal with this gathering of peageese in her parlor.

Sometimes a single grain of sand can make a pearl, a thing of great beauty. In other situations, that same grain of sand can make a blister on somebody's foot. Which is to say that, over time, the smallest irritations can grow larger with constant rubbing.

Lisanne's nerves were being rubbed raw. She was dressed to the teeth again, in a gown whose cost would have fed a hundred beggars. She was wearing a tiara besides, adding the weight of guilt, at how many children could be educated with one of its diamonds, to the weight of the foolish bauble. She already had a headache.

The Almack's hostesses were adding to the pain with their subtle interrogations and sly innuendos. Sloane had said they were like sleek house cats. To Lisanne they seemed more like hunting jaguars, sniffing out new prey.

She'd been separated from her party almost instantly by Sally Jersey, who wanted her to meet Lord Alvanley, who may have been a cousin to her mother. Did Her Grace know? Her Grace knew that Lord Alvanley's eye looked grotesque through the quizzing glass he so rudely used to inspect her.

Lady Drummond-Burrell was interested in orchids, and in finding out how well-studied Lady Lisanne was on the exotic plants. Lisanne was well-studied enough to know that she could have been talking Hindustani, for all the other lady understood.

Speaking the formal French of the Russian court, Princess Lieven obviously hoped to trip the newcomer up on her schoolgirl grammar. The princess was wearing a taffeta gown with ermine borders, at least fifteen dead ermines, Lisanne calculated. She responded in Russian and moved on.

Maria Sefton might have measured the depth of Lisanne's curtsy to an inch, gauging if this interloper knew the proper degree of deference. Lisanne held her head high. She was a duchess by marriage, a baroness by birth. She would not kowtow to anyone so impolite as to make guests—paying guests at that—run this gauntlet of sharpened claws.

Lisanne caught her husband's eye across the room. St. Sevrin shrugged as if to say she was on her own now, before he returned to his conversation with the dashing redhead at his side.

Aunt Hattie had warned Lisanne how it would be, that they couldn't shield her from the tabbies tonight, not unless they wished to give rise to more questions about her competence. Aunt Hattie hadn't warned her that St. Sevrin would take the opportunity to get up a flirtation with one of the most notoriously willing widows still invited to Almack's.

Sloane was even sharing the contents of the flask in his pocket with the dazzling female, while Lisanne sipped tepid orgeat brought by some lordling produced by Sally Jersey as a suitable partner. Suitable, hah! With greasy hair and eyes that never rose above her bosom, the man wasn't suitable to walk her dog.

Well, Lisanne fumed, she was quite competent to handle this on her own if her husband chose to abandon her. She didn't like being passed around as if she were a new shipment of yard goods to be inspected or a new mix of snuff to be sampled. She didn't like not being permitted to sit with Trevor and Esmé, not being permitted to choose her own dance partners. She absolutely despised the fact that while she was suffering through Lord Higgenbotham's lumbago and Sir Sheldon's sweaty palms and fetid breath, St. Sevrin was having a high old time peering down the widow's low neckline. Any lower and the collar would be a belt around her waist.

My, how that grain of resentment rankled.

Lisanne was walking through this genteel fire for St. Sevrin, damn his roving eyes, to establish him as a gentleman of stature and honor. He, meanwhile, was taking the first opportunity to confirm his reputation as a rake. He even looked the part in his elegant black and white formal wear with a single ruby in his cravat highlighting the reddish glints to his hair. No other gentleman present had such broad shoulders or well-muscled legs. No other gentleman present interested Lisanne in the least. In fact, she was sick and tired of the whole business of being presented, being approved, being accepted. St. Sevrin hadn't even accepted her as his wife, by Jupiter. Her chin rose. She'd been accepted down paths where these fools couldn't hope to tread. How dare they sit in judgment of her. How dare he dally with that deep-chested demirep.

Lisanne wanted to go home, not to Berkeley Square,

but to Devon. Now. Lisanne had proved she was a lady, now she'd prove she was what they had all believed anyway, St. Sevrin most of all. He kept waiting for her to do something outlandish, didn't he? She wasn't going to disappoint him again, the way she'd done in their marriage.

She watched as Sloane escorted his new friend out of the ballroom proper. They'd already had two dances. One more and the widow may as well be standing on the corner of Covent Garden, so they must be headed for the card room. At least Almack's did not tend toward secluded corners and private chambers. St. Sevrin never played for the chicken stakes permitted here, though, so likely there was a higher ante, such as the woman's favors. The redhead would win when pigs flew.

Lisanne sent her latest partner, a clumsy dancer and a clumsier conversationalist, off to the refreshment room for another tasteless drink while she took up a position next to a potted plant at the edge of the dance floor. The palm tree looked as parched and brittle as Lisanne felt.

"How do you do, sir?" she asked. Getting no response except a startled look from the two chaperones nearby, Lisanne went on: "It's a terrible crush here, isn't it? I'm finding it hard to breathe myself, with all these perfumed bodies, so it's no wonder your fronds are drooping." One of the chaperones had scurried away to whisper in a different ear. The other stayed, fascinated, her mouth open, as Lisanne continued her one-sided chat. "I suppose we should be happy they use perfume, my dear, for I understand some of the guests see water as rarely as you appear to."

Out of the corner of her eye she could see a wave of motion travel across the room like a breeze blowing through a field of wheat. Not quite every eye in the room was turned in her direction, but almost. Sticking her gloved fingers into the pot, Lisanne scrabbled around until she had a sample of the dirt in her previously immaculate hand. Then she sniffed at the dirt and went so far as to stick her tongue out near it, pretending to taste the soil. That may have been too far, for the thud she heard could only be Aunt Cherise's limp body hitting the floor.

Aunt Hattie was across the room, trying desperately to extricate herself from an old court card in a bagwig who kept shouting, "What's that they're saying? They're awarding a palm?"

Esmé and Trevor were arguing over what to do. Trevor won and limped off to get the duke.

Lisanne had a moment before all of them, plus a few of Almack's outraged hostesses, converged on her. So she recommended that her friend ask for some ground fish bones, or tea made from well-rotted manure. "Perhaps that's what they are serving here. The stuff tastes like—"

Esmé got to her first. "My, what a sense of humor my cousin has," she commented to the room at large. "So witty, so amusing. Why, she kept us all in stitches back in Devon."

Aunt Hattie was out of breath, but she managed to wheeze, "My dear duchess, I am the one in the family who is supposed to be eccentric. You're much too young to affect quirks to be interesting, isn't that so, Lionel? I mean Sloane, of course."

St. Sevrin's mouth was smiling. His eyes were shooting daggers. "I believe my bride was trying to get my attention, ladies, that's all. I admit to being derelict in my attentions this evening. I'm still not used to leg-shackles, don't you know."

A few nearby gentlemen laughed in commiseration. A new bride was a deuced nuisance, and that flame-haired widow could make any man forget his own wife, even if the wife was a tiny golden-haired beauty. More than one of the men wished he'd been quick enough to console St. Sevrin's bride.

"You see me a chastened man, Duchess," the duke was

claiming for the spectators' benefit. "I swear not to leave your side again tonight."

With that he bowed to their audience and led Lisanne onto the dancing area. Actually the grip on her forearm was more like a vice clamp, cutting off circulation. "Smile, damn you," he whispered.

Lisanne pasted a smile on her face that matched his for insincerity, and they got through the set. Without stopping to speak to anyone, St. Sevrin led her off the dance floor and out the door to the entry hall, where Aunt Hattie and Trevor were already waiting with their wraps. The carriage was at the curb.

Trevor looked from the duke to the duchess and suggested that he and Lady Comstock take a hackney home.

St. Sevrin was already helping his aunt into the coach. "No, for if you're not along, I might strangle her."

Ordinarily the carriage was spacious enough for the four of them. Not tonight. Ordinarily they'd have been chatting about the evening's entertainment. Not tonight.

"Hell and damnation," the duke finally ground out. "Why the deuce did you have to pull this stunt tonight?"

"Those women were being hateful, and I am tired of being scrutinized like an insect under a microscope. I decided that since you never cared what anyone said about you, I wouldn't care, either."

His voice was as sharp as a knife. "I may have been careless with my own reputation, Duchess, but I do believe that you knew how very much I cared about yours. That's what this whole time in London has been about. All of Aunt Hattie's efforts, all those boring teas and dinner parties, were to make your peers respect you. Now it's all wasted, damn it."

"I just gave them what they expected."

"You gave me a kick in the—The devil take it, you don't even talk to your own potted plants."

"Yes, I do."

"You do not."

"I do."

"You don't."

"Children!" Aunt Hattie had her hands over her ears. "Stop this instant, or I'll faint like that ninnyhammer Findley woman, I swear."

Lisanne folded her hands in her lap and with utmost reserve stated, "I always sing while I am working in the garden. Or I hum. The plants like it."

The duke snorted. "Then I suppose we should consider ourselves lucky this one didn't request an operatic aria."

Trevor chuckled, which rewarded him with a kick from Aunt Hattie. Since it was his wooden leg she kicked, Trev didn't notice, but Aunt Hattie gasped.

"You see, now you've given my aunt a spasm with your idiotic behavior."

"My behavior? My behavior? I wasn't the one ogling some female's bosom all night!"

"Aha! I was right all along. You were jealous, that's what. You were bitten by the green-eyed monster and tried to bite me back." The idea didn't seem to bother Sloane as much as he thought it should.

"Why should I be jealous? We had an agreement and . . . and I don't care what you do."

"You were jealous, admit it."

"I was not!"

He folded his arms over his chest and winked at Trevor, who was grinning by now. "She likes me, you know."

"I do not."

Sloane smiled. "Then give me another explanation for this night's debacle."

First there was silence. Then a low murmur: "I want to go home."

Chapter Twenty-six

Spun sugar and steel were an unlikely mixture, but that was St. Sevrin's duchess. They couldn't stay in London—who knew what she'd do next to get her way?—and Sloane wouldn't cave in and take her home. A man had to have some pride left, some sense of mastery. Besides, in Devon Lisanne would disappear into the estate books or the library or those blasted woods. St. Sevrin had a better idea. He gave her one day to pack, one day to make whatever arrangements she needed. They were going on their honeymoon.

The yacht was waiting in Bristol, back from another trip to pick up injured officers from the Peninsula. They'd sail to Ireland, to Liam McCardle's horse farm. If there was one thing St. Sevrin knew, it was gambling. He had some of his own money put by, winnings and earnings on his investments, and now he was going to start that racing stud. He had to do it soon, before winter set in and they couldn't travel to Ireland, where Liam, another retired army officer, was breeding the finest Thoroughbred mares. Somewhere in Portugal they had discovered that Liam was a distant relative of Sloane's own Irish mother Fiona, although Lady Comstock repudiated the connection. McCardle had written back to Sloane's request with an invitation to come at any time. The house was not up to ducal standards, but it was always open to Sherry, especially if his pocketbook was open for horse-trading.

That was the first part of Sloane's plan. The second was to carry his impossible wife on board the yacht and not let her out of their cabin until she was breeding. If she were enceinte, that nonsense at Almack's would be chalked up to the well-known vagaries of incipient motherhood and forgiven in a minute.

His third intention was to make her enjoy it. With no maid, no dog, no duties, no one to care about her behavior or his, Sloane meant to show Lisanne how much he cared, how little other women appealed to him. The gist of the strategy was that he wanted his wife, and was deuced tired of waiting.

While Lisanne was leaving instructions with an appalled Kelly about the dog and the other invalids now placed in his care—made bearable only because Mary was being left behind to help him transport the menagerie back to Devon—the duke was stocking the yacht's master cabin. Loaded aboard were champagne and oysters, wine and cheese, baskets of flowers.

Lisanne was charmed by his preparations despite herself and Sloane's high-handed ways. Maybe they could have a real marriage after all, and maybe she'd learn to be satisfied with whatever he could give. For now she was eager and anxious, excited and aquiver about their long-delayed wedding night and her first boat ride.

It might be her last ride anywhere, Lisanne was so sick. All of St. Sevrin's grand schemes were going overboard, along with the champagne and oysters, the wine and cheese. He never thought for an instant that his intrepid wife might get seasick! He never thought to bring peppermint, ginger, or any of the usual remedies. He never thought he'd be spending his honeymoon holding a basin and a damp face cloth. At least he'd proven his devotion, although Lisanne was too miserable to care. Somewhere between Swansea and the Irish Sea, St. Sevrin vowed to stop drinking if only she'd recover.

By the time they docked in Ireland, Lisanne had to be carried off the boat, begging Sloane to promise that they'd walk home.

Liam was delighted to welcome Sherry and his new wife, although privately he considered the duchess too wan and weak for a man of St. Sevrin's iron. With apologies for his bachelor quarters, Liam placed Lisanne in his housekeeper's care and took Sherry off for a taste of home-brewed Irish whiskey. When the duke stuck to one glass of ale and hurried back to make sure his lady was sleeping peacefully, Liam reassessed his opinion. Perhaps there was more to Her Grace than met the eye.

By the next morning, Lisanne was recovered enough to join the men at the paddock, having already visited the barns, made friends with the head groom's children, and helped cook breakfast.

"I see you are feeling much better, Your Grace," Liam offered, while Sherry helped her to a seat on the fence railing.

Lisanne threw off her bonnet, letting her unpinned hair fall to her shoulders. She laughed out loud, the happiest sound Sloane had ever heard from her. She opened her arms to include the rolling green hills, the clear, clean air, the beautiful horses in the field. "How could I not feel wonderful in this enchanted land? It's just too bad that it's an island."

Soon it was time to get to the serious business of selecting a mare to breed St. Sevrin's future champions. Stable boys led the horses past them while Liam recounted their ancestry and racing history. Every one of the mares was a winner.

Lisanne pointed to a pretty bay with a star on her forehead. "That's the one you should buy."

"What, on a look?" Sloane scoffed. "I'll need to see

them run, study the stud books, check them for soundness. It's not as easy as picking a bonnet, sweetings."

Lisanne just laughed. She pulled her carved flute out of the pocket of her red wool cape, along with some string, papers, a handful of clover wrapped in a handkerchief, and an apple. She played a few notes and, sure enough, the bay mare trotted right over to the fence and daintily accepted the apple from her hand.

"Can you play some more, Your Grace?" Liam asked, thinking, like Sloane, that it was pure coincidence. "Maybe the other mares will like your music, too."

So Lisanne played a tune, like nothing St. Sevrin had ever heard. He thought he recognized birdcalls and the running notes of rippling streams and the song butterflies might sing, if they could. The other horses pricked their ears, but the bay mare stayed by the fence near Lisanne's boot, swaying to the music.

There were tears in the eyes of the old grooms, and clapping from the young ones. Liam was stunned. "No wonder you like it here, lassie. There must be a bit of the old country in you." He slapped his friend's back as a blushing Lisanne climbed down and ran off. "Your wife is magnificent, Sherry."

St. Sevrin turned to watch as Lisanne skipped away with the groom's children laughing behind her, like some Pied Piper. The oldest boy yelled back that they were going to show the duchess where a dragon lay buried, and a real true fairy ring. "You don't think she is . . . different?"

"Different? I'll say she is. She's one in a million, you lucky dog. If every woman was like your duchess, there'd never be a bachelor left in the world." With that Liam left St. Sevrin at the gate, most likely to follow Lisanne, too.

Damn, Sloane thought while pretending to study the field of horses, Lisanne just wasn't like other women. "I'll never understand her," he muttered to himself.

"Seems to me, boyo, ye don't have to understand the lassie to love her."

There was no one nearby. St. Sevrin shook himself. He'd known that giving up drinking was going to wreak havoc with his system. He'd expected shaking hands and sweaty skin—not hearing voices. He tried to get his attention back on the mares, ignoring Lisanne's bay, for what did his wife know of race horses? "Now, which one of you is going to bring me the luck of the Irish?"

The same voice, with a shade more impatience, spoke again: "Seems to me ye've already got all the luck ye need, ye blitherer, and the good advice."

St. Sevrin looked around, then down. Far down. At about ankle height, he spotted a tiny gentleman in a green suit. St. Sevrin reached for the flask that had always been in his pocket until today when he needed it. Since giving up demon drink was obviously too hard, Sloane switched his vow to giving up wenches. That was easy; his wife was the only woman he desired. Seeing Lisanne in his dreams was one thing, seeing leprechauns in broad daylight was another. "What am I supposed to do now?" Sloane asked his hallucination, "catch you and make you tell me where you've hidden your gold?"

The little man wagged his finger at the duke. "Ye've already found the pot o'gold, spalpeen, ye're just too clottish to recognize it."

That touched a sensitive nerve. "I didn't marry her just for the money."

"I know that, ye noddy Englishman. Does she?"

Either he was suffering from the lack of drink, or else he was going crazy. As crazy as his wife.

St. Sevrin decided to buy two mares, the one with the best record and breeding, and the one Lisanne picked. Liam was willing to take the yacht as payment for one of them. The duke hustled his wife through quick good-byes and onto a blessedly short, smooth ferry crossing. He hired a carriage to take them the rest of the way home to Devon.

At the first inn, St. Sevrin waited until after dinner and tea, and then fifteen minutes, no more, before he knocked on his wife's door. She was sitting at a dressing table braiding her hair for the night, wearing a lacy nightgown that made the breath catch in his throat.

"You're not sick?" he asked. "Not tired? You have no injured bird to tend or the innkeeper's children to read a story?"

She shook her head, smiling, hoping. She knew he wasn't drinking, for her, just as she knew he'd bought the bay mare for her.

Encouraged, Sloane went on with the speech he'd prepared over the last two days. "Lisanne, I want to be the best husband I can, the husband you deserve. But I need you to show me how."

"In London?" she asked, troubled.

He stood behind her and unbraided her hair, then reached for the brush on the dresser and started feathering the blond curls down her back. "I don't want to go back to London, not without you. But I don't want to be in your way if you don't wish me in Devon, either. I never want to see you hidden away like a hermit. I think we can have a good life together. Will you let me try?"

"I think I would like that very much." She already liked how her toes were tingling at his touch, but it wasn't enough. "I know it wasn't in our agreement, but do you think you could come to love me?"

"I don't know." He stopped brushing and Lisanne lowered her chin so he wouldn't see the tears forming in her eyes in the mirror's reflection. She'd taken his crumbs, like the birds in her hand. Maybe she could love enough for the both of them.

Sloane moved to stand in front of her, then crouched so their eyes met. He cupped her chin in his hand, one finger brushing at a crystal teardrop. "I don't know what love is, sweetings. You're the one with the wisdom of the ages, it seems. You tell me. If you are on my mind every minute,

227

waking or sleeping, if I would gladly lay down my life to make you happy, and if I want you with me for the next century at least—what do you call that?"

"I'd call that love." Now tears of joy fell unashamed. "But . . . but are you sure you're not afraid I'm insane?"

"Precious, I'm only afraid you're too sane to love me back."

Later, deep in his embrace, with nothing between them but satisfied desire, Lisanne whispered, "Now that is something you never have to worry about."

"Are you sure the children are safe playing in the woods by themselves, Lisanne? I know you trust Buck to look after them, but shouldn't they have someone besides a dog, even if he is Becka's son?"

"Stop worrying, darling. They don't need the dog. They'll be fine."

St. Sevrin wasn't satisfied. "The boys are one thing, but even little Fiona? Are you sure?"

"I am certain, my love, as certain as I am that I love you."

"Well, in that case, let's go upstairs. We might as well take advantage of the peace and quiet for once."

Please read on for a sneak peek
of Barbara Metzger's

Ace of Hearts

Available from Signet Eclipse

$\mathcal{T}$he Earl of Carde was dying. Part of him had already died when he lost his beloved young wife and baby daughter in the coaching accident. Dearest Lizbeth had taken little Lottie north to her family's home on the coast, near Hull, but the carriage had toppled over a cliff. Lizbeth had died instantly, they told him later, along with her maid, the driver, a groom, and the horses. Missing from the carnage, though, were the newly hired replacement guard—and Lottie.

Lord Carde had rushed north through the rain and snow and icy winter weather, but too late, of course. He searched for Lottie anyway, leading the shepherds and drovers, the shopkeepers and the sheriff, the entire community, through the cold. No trace was found of either the child or the guard, only a child's bonnet and some bloodstains, quickly washed away by the freezing rain. The locals said the man must have run off, fearing he'd be blamed. The child would have been carried away by wild dogs, they whispered, or found by Gypsies, or else the three-year-old had wandered toward the chill waters. She would never be seen again.

Broken in body and spirit, the earl returned home to Cardington to bury his beautiful young second wife in his family crypt at Carde Hall on another sleet-shrouded day. The congestion in his lungs turned putrid, and the fevers stole what strength he had left. He called for his sons.

The earl was proud of his boys, products of his first marriage. His heir, Alexander Chalfont Endicott, was fourteen, a serious, bespectacled lad, tall and wiry. Nicknamed Ace by his school friends because of his initials and the Carde connection, Viscount Endicott would make a good earl. Lord Carde was not worried about the succession.

His second son, the Honorable Jonathan Endicott, was eleven, but still boyishly rounded. He was no scholar, the masters at Eton reported, but the earl knew Jack, as they called him, was pluck to the backbone, horse-mad, and athletic. He'd do.

Both boys were dark-haired like their mother, but with the earl's own aquiline nose. They were the fulfillment of his duty to king and country, his legacy to the world, the future of his house and name and family honor. Yes, they made him proud.

But they never made him laugh with dimpled smiles, high-pitched giggles, and pleas for one more horsey ride on Papa's back. They never climbed next to him in his library chair for tickling, or curled on his lap like a sleeping blond angel. Sons were all well and good, the earl thought, looking at the two somber boys at the foot of his bed, manfully trying to hide their fears. But they weren't his precious baby girl.

He raised one trembling hand to wipe a tear from his eyes and beckoned the boys closer so he could whisper to them with all the voice left to him.

"You will take my place, Alexander, and do a fine job of it. Your uncle will help."

Viscount Endicott nodded, a lock of black hair falling into his eyes. He brushed it away, or a tear of his own. "Yes, Father. I shall do my best."

"I know you will, lad. And you, Jack. Help your brother. Being earl is no easy task."

"But Ace is only a schoolboy," the younger boy complained, not ready for the truth he saw in the doctors' and servants' eyes. "And you are the earl!"

Lord Carde tried to take a deep breath, and they could all hear the rasping sound of it in his throat. "So I am, and so Alexander will be. You will be his right hand."

"But—" Jack began, but Alexander kicked him. "Yes, Father."

The earl took another breath. "Good. Now I want another promise from you, lads."

"Anything, Father," Alexander said and Jack nodded.

"Find your sister."

Jack was sniffling, and his brother handed him a handkerchief, frowning. "But you looked everywhere, Father."

"And hired men to keep looking. But none of them will care as much as you. I know she is alive somewhere, needing you." The earl took Alexander's hand and placed it on his own steadily weakening heart. "I know it, here."

"But we are only boys, sir, like Jack said."

"You are my boys, though. Endicotts. 'Ever true.' Don't forget that, our motto, and do not let anyone else forget to keep looking. Promise me."

"I swear, Father, to keep searching for Lottie until she is home with us."

"Me, too."

The earl sighed and closed his eyes, his elder son's hand still in his. Alexander reached his other hand out to his brother, who grasped it firmly.

"Father," Jack whispered, despite the doctors' frowns.

The earl's eyelids fluttered half open.

"Will you see Lottie's mother in Heaven?"

The earl's dry lips twitched to a smile. "I . . . I hope so, lad."

"Tell her we'll try. But, Father . . ."

Moments went by while they waited for the earl to find another breath. "Yes?"

"Will you see our mother, too?"

Lord Carde reached out his other hand to his younger son, who climbed onto the high bed, at his brother's nod, to take it. "I'll see your mother, too . . . and thank her . . . for the fine . . . young men she . . ."

The Earl of Carde was engaged. Affianced. Promised. He was thrice betrothed, thrice accursed. Bad enough he was parson-pledged—but to three different women? He was regally, royally, ridiculously damned, done in, and ditched. How, by all that was holy and a great deal that was not, had such a nightmare befallen him?

Alexander Chalfont Endicott, Carde to most, Alex to a few, Ace to his closest intimates and the gleeful London gossip columnists, took off his glasses and poured himself another glass of brandy, despite the early-morning hour. He deserved the fog of his poor eyesight and the fog of inebriation. If he drank enough, perhaps he could forget this past week. If he smashed his spectacles to smithereens, perhaps he could ignore the scandal sheets.

Ace of Hearts, they were calling him, with cartoons depicting the winning hand, a stacked deck, three of a kind. Every blasted joke about his title and rumors of his situation were spread out on his desk, and on breakfast tables and in boudoirs throughout London, if not all of England, he supposed. Alex cursed, shoved the newspapers and his glasses to the floor, and tried to let the brandy bring him solace.

An hour later, he still had three hopeful brides, but now he had a headache, too. He rubbed the bridge of his somewhat beakish nose, yet another legacy from his father, along with the title and fortune that made him a prize on the marriage market.

He cursed his nose, his headache, the avaricious, ambitious, velvet-draped vultures of the *ton* and Fate. Mostly, he cursed himself for being a fool. How had this mess happened? He'd shown three women respect and admiration—that was how. He'd forgotten that the so-called frail sex had no sense of fair play. Honor was not in their vocabularies, nor in their blood. Hell, any man who turned his back on a female deserved a knife stuck in it. But three times? Alex groaned at the injustice, and the headache.

After all, he was not a rake. He'd sown his wild oats as a young buck, of course. What man worth his salt didn't? Later, when he first came into his majority and control of his own fortune, perhaps he had cut too wide a swath through the demimonde, the gambling dens and the opera dancers. He outgrew that nonsense soon enough, when he realized the full weight of the earldom and the extent of his responsibilities. Between his estates and investments, his seat in Parliament, his reform committees, and social commitments, the young lord barely had time for reading a book, much less carousing all night.

Whatever his personal inclinations, Alex never forgot what was due his name and his legions of dependents. He took his responsibilities to heart. No half measures for the Earl of Carde.

He laughed now, but without humor. Half measures, indeed. Who else found three fiancées when he set out to fill his nursery?

Again setting his personal desires aside, Alex had decided it was time for him to take a bride and beget heirs for the earldom. After all, he was twenty-seven and his only brother was in the army. Who knew what dangers that daredevil was riding into on the Peninsula, if he would return a hero, or not at all? Alex sorely missed Jack, his best friend and confidant, and worried over him constantly, but Jack was a man now, too, and had made his own choices. So Alex had set out to find a suitable countess. His first mistake was mentioning his intentions to a few of his acquaintances at White's Club. As soon as rumors started circulating that the Earl of Carde was contemplating wedlock, Alex was a dead man. His second mistake was not shooting himself and being done with the misery.

First, his mistress decided that they were engaged. His mistress, by Harry! A man didn't marry his mistress, not even if she was wellborn and beautiful, a wealthy old baron's widow. He was not even keeping Mona, Lady Monroe, under his protection, for heaven's sake, and for a modicum of propriety. The richly—and lushly—endowed widow had her own house and horses and servants. He merely bought the occasional expensive bauble to show his appreciation.

Alex couldn't imagine where Mona got the notion in

her gorgeous red head that he'd take another man's wife as his countess, and a lustful, licentious woman at that. Somehow she must have plucked the idea from the morass of her social-climbing mind.

"Darling," she'd said when he was drifting off in satiated slumber one recent night, "we really should talk about the wedding."

"Hm? Were we invited to someone's wedding, then?" He'd rolled over, pulling the blankets around her. "Remind me in the morning."

"Our wedding, silly."

That had him wide awake, in a hurry. The blankets and sheets were on the floor, as was the earl, barefoot and bare-assed, scrambling for his spectacles. "Our wedding?" He practically leaped into his inexpressibles. "We have no wedding plans that I am aware of," he said out loud. "Or ever shall," he muttered under his breath, pulling his shirt over his head.

"Oh, but you asked me," Mona said with a purr and a pout that she must have thought adorable. He thought it predatory. "Last week, after Lady Carrisbrooke's birthday party."

He remembered the dinner party, and all the champagne served afterward. He might have lost count of how many glasses he'd swallowed, but surely he would recall losing his mind? He vowed never to go near the stuff again. "Refresh my memory."

"We came home, here, afterward. And we were, ah, making love."

What they did was *not* making love. It was fornicating, plain and simple. What else was their relationship about? "Go on. We were in bed." Or so he assumed. Mona had a fondness for the fur rug in front of the fireplace. "And . . . ?"

"And you said, 'I wish this could last forever.' I said it could, and you said yes. In fact you shouted yes so loudly that I feared my maid might come running."

Now he remembered. He remembered where her luscious red lips were at the time, what she was doing with her tongue and her hands, and precisely what he wished to last forever. "Great gods, you could not have taken that for a proposal of marriage! Why, a man would promise you the moon, if he was soaring toward the stars. He'd offer you his heart on a silver platter if he thought you might stop otherwise."

"You promised me a ring."

"And I bought you that emerald, didn't I?" He looked at the huge stone on her finger, flashing in the candlelight. He draped his neck cloth over his collar and said, "That was not the Carde engagement diamond." Which was here, in town, in case he found the lady of his choice. Mona, Lady Monroe, was not and never would be his choice for the Countess of Carde. "The emerald was a gift, nothing more. Consider it a parting gift, in fact."

"I think not. You nearly begged for forever. Then you bought me a ring. What else was a woman to think but that you were offering marriage?"

"That I was grateful for a good f—" Alex couldn't say it, not even in his anger. Whatever else she was, Mona was a female, and he was a gentleman—a gentleman on his way out the door as soon as he located his shoes.

"I have to be thinking of my future, you know," she said, raising one knee in a suggestive pose.

To hell with his shoes. Alex would walk barefoot, through hot coals, to get out of here. He did, however, need his coat, with his keys and purse, to hire a hackney. "You can't have gone through Monroe's fortune so fast. Hire yourself a good man of business."

He was searching under the dressing table when she said, "But I want respectability."

Alex looked around the room with its flickering candles, the scent of sex mixed with her heavy perfume, the pink satin bedcovers in a heap on the floor next to her filmy red robe. "You should have thought of that sooner, then."

Mona brushed that aside with a flick of her long nails. "I want a title."

Ah, there was his coat, under the bed. "Well, this one is not for hire, madam. The Earls of Carde have always married for love, nothing else. And I never, ever said I loved you."

"Ah, but you will come to, after the wedding."

His hand was on the doorknob. "There will be no wedding, Mona. Not soon, not later."

"But they say you are looking for a bride."

A pure, innocent bride, not a harlot who knew a hundred ways to pleasure a man—and might have a hundred men before the wedding lines were dry. A man might dream of a wife with the skills of a seductress, the lustiness of a light skirt, but he wanted to be the one to teach her. Alex's Lady Carde was going to be just that, a lady, through and through. "I am still looking."

"Oh, I think you will stop your search when my solicitor threatens you with breach of promise."

Now Alex had to smile. A man in the extremes of ecstasy could not be held accountable for any promises, pledges, or pleas. If there wasn't already a law to that effect, he'd bring one up at the next sessions of Parliament. "Any barrister with balls under his robe will laugh at any such lawsuit."

"Not my former brother-in-law, the new baron, who craves respectability as much as I do. He would not like the scandal. Nor would you, I think."

Mona was right. Alex did not like the scandal—and there were only rumors so far, fanned by Lady Lucinda, his next lapse in judgment.

Lady Lucinda Applegate was a leading light of London. She might have been considered an old maid at the advanced age of twenty-five, firmly on the shelf, except that she was a duke's daughter. Instead of being called a spinster, she was called particular. Lud knew she'd had offers aplenty, and turned them all down. Despite the fact that her father was a gamester and had wagered away most of his fortune and her dowry, the lady was still much sought after in the beau monde. Lady Lucinda was a tall, stunning, raven-haired incomparable whose beauty was marred only by a nose matching Alex's own in aristocratic dimension. So elevated was her beak, so haughty her attitude, that Lady Lucinda Applegate was labeled Close-the-Gate by the same would-be wits who called him Ace.

She could have looked as high as she wished for a husband. Perhaps she was tired of looking, or perhaps an earl was high enough. . . .